Praise for
Robert Asprin's *New York Times* bestselling
***Phule's Company* series**

"Plenty of odd characters . . . fun!"   —*Locus*

"A winning story . . . part science fiction, part spoof, part heart-warmer."   —*Publishers Weekly*

"Light without being frivolous, and displays Asprin's considerable expertise about fencing and things military, especially leadership."   —*Chicago Sun-Times*

"Reminiscent of 'M.A.S.H.' "   —*Analog*

"A grand mix of common sense, outrageous and hilarious foolishness stirred with a dash of wisdom into a delectable mess to be served with tongue in cheek."   —*KLIATT*

"Reliably entertaining . . . a fun read, light without being vapid and clever without being heavy-handed. This series is Asprin's strongest to date, and it's off to a good start."   —*Amazing*

"Asprin knows how to make me laugh . . . I suggest you sign up for this particular grand tour of duty."   —*Fear*

Robert Asprin Myth Series Omnibuses

ANOTHER FINE MYTH/MYTH CONCEPTIONS
MYTH DIRECTIONS/HIT OR MYTH
MYTH-ING PERSONS/LITTLE MYTH MARKER
M.Y.T.H. INC. LINK/MYTH-NOMERS AND IM-PERVECTIONS

M.Y.T.H. INC. LINK

MYTH-NOMERS AND IM-PERVECTIONS

ROBERT ASPRIN

ACE BOOKS, NEW YORK

M.Y.T.H. INC. LINK/MYTH-NOMERS AND IM-PERVECTIONS

An Ace Book / published by arrangement with
Starblaze Editions of the Donning Company/Publishers

PRINTING HISTORY
Ace mass-market edition / September 2002

M.Y.T.H. Inc. Link/Myth-nomers and Im-pervections copyright © 2002
by Donning Company.
M.Y.T.H. Inc. Link copyright © 1986 by Robert L. Asprin.
Myth-nomers and Im-pervections copyright © 1987 by Robert L. Asprin.
Cover art by Walter Velez.
Cover design by Judy Murello.
Text design by Julie Rogers.

Visit our website at
www.penguinputnam.com
Check out the ACE Science Fiction & Fantasy newsletter!

ISBN: 0-441-00969-7

ACE®
Ace Books are published by The Berkley Publishing Group,
a division of Penguin Putnam Inc.,
375 Hudson Street, New York, New York 10014.
ACE and the "A" design
are trademarks belonging to Penguin Putnam Inc.

PRINTED IN THE UNITED STATES OF AMERICA

10 9 8 7 6 5 4 3 2 1

M.Y.T.H. INC. LIN

AUTHOR'S INTRODUCTION TO
M.Y.T.H. INC. LINK
(1986)

The series of books loosely referred to throughout the known dimensions as **The Myth Adventures of Aahz and Skeeve** has been growing steadily in popularity since they premiered back in 1978. (Actually, you probably don't have to be told this, as you are already holding a volume in your hands. The ones who need to be informed are those who would never *dream* of picking up a fantasy book . . . like that guy in the next aisle browsing through mysteries, or your roommate. So what you want to do is tap them on the shoulder or over the head, and . . .)

Excuse me! I tend to get excited and digress when there's the smell of money in the air . . . especially if it's moving away. Where was I?

Books . . . growing in popularity . . . oh, yes!

The question I am asked most often as a writer is not "Where do you get your ideas?", but rather, "Is there going to be another Myth book?" The answer, for a while anyway, is a definite "Yes!" After completing **Little**

Myth Marker (#6 in the series . . . collect 'em all!) I signed a contract with Donning/Starblaze for an additional six books, of which this is the first. While we're still "discussing" if they will be written at the rate of one or two a year, it *is* sure at this point that the series will be around for a while.

I realized after completing the manuscript for this volume that the title might be unclear to the casual reader. This is a terrible thing to realize so close to publication, particularly since the book has already been promoted under that title, so it's too late to change it. In desperation, I'm resorting to the cheap device of an author's intro to attempt to clarify things.

#7 is titled **M.Y.T.H. Inc. Link** because it marks a definite change in the series from the first six and therefore "links" the beginning of the series to what comes after. (Cute, eh? Confusing, but cute.) Unfortunately, most of the changes involve the writer, and, as such, may not be readily apparent to the reader. In a vain attempt to alleviate that situation, I thought I would take advantage of this breaking point in the series to give the reader a little insight into the mind of a writer and how a series, specifically this one, comes to exist. If you couldn't care less, feel free to skip directly into the main body of the book (as the rest of this introduction contains nothing you need to read) and (hopefully) enjoy it.

Writers not only "live" what they write, they occasionally use that fact to regulate their actual lives. That is, if they are feeling "down," sometimes writing something "up" can improve their mood. This was how the first Myth book came into existence.

At the time (1976) I was writing my first novel, **Cold Cash War**, for St. Martin's Press. That particular book is a grim little number about corporate wars, and contains occasional scenes that can only be described as grisly. Wounded mercenaries burying themselves while still alive to rob the other side of the body count and executives arranging to have their rivals shot down in the streets were the norm in that universe. It was an interesting project, and, as it was my first, I could really get wrapped up in it. Unfortunately, I was still working full time at a nine-to-five job and had a wife and two kids. It was unfortunate in that I discovered that if I wrote **Cold Cash** for too many nights at a stretch, I'd start looking at my fellow office workers, not to mention passersby on the sidewalk and my own family, as targets or attackers. This is not the best condition to ensure one's continued mental health.

I decided I needed another writing project to use as a break for **Cold Cash** (if you just stop writing, you never get back to it!), preferably something a bit lighter. To that end, I started building the idea for my next book.

Being a fan of Conan and Kane and that crowd, I had always wanted to try my hand at Heroic Fantasy, and this seemed like as good a time as any. The field had been getting increasingly solemn and grandiose, and to my eye was long overdue for a good lampooning. (Anything or anyone who falls into the trap of taking themselves too seriously is fair game for this, and, fortunately for writers such as myself, there is no shortage of targets these days.)

First, I needed a main character. Since Heroic Fantasy was already loaded with brawny barbarian swordsmen hunting wizards, I decided to go to the opposite extreme and do my story from the point of view of a magician. To keep it interesting, he had to be fairly incompetent . . . say, maybe an apprentice. It's always helpful to give your lead character an associate or sidekick. This allows you to use dialogue to impart information to the reader without resorting to lengthy introspection. For a confidant to a magician . . . why not a demon? To contrast personalities, I'd have to make him as snorky and unpleasant as my lead is nice.

Right about here, fate took a hand. I have always been a fan of the Bob Hope/Bing Crosby "Road" movies, and it turned out that at the same time I was tinkering with these new characters, there was a weeklong festival of the entire set of those films on television. Of course, as a dedicated writer working on a book with a deadline, I was immune to such temptation, right? If you believe that, you have a lot to learn about writers . . . or at least *this* writer. Each evening found me camped in front of the idiot tube to catch one more round of the particular brand of insanity those movies abound in. To combat the guilts of feeling *totally* irresponsible, I kept a notepad on my lap so I could "work on character development" during the commercials. Trying to switch moods back and forth between the "Road" movies and **Cold Cash** was impossible, so it made more sense to be futzing around with *my* comedy while watching theirs. In the process, the bantering swindlers whose plans always land them in inordinate amounts of trouble wandered off the screen and onto my notepad . . . and the characters of Aahz and Skeeve started to take shape.

By the time **Cold Cash** was done, I was ready to present Aahz and Skeeve as a proposal for my next book. When I mentioned this to my agent, however, I discovered there was a minor detail I had overlooked. "Humor doesn't sell!" I was told. "We're trying to get your career launched right now, and you need a really strong book to follow **Cold Cash!** Got anything else?" This attitude startled me, but it was easily confirmed. A brief glance at a year's worth of *Publishers Weekly* showed that indeed, unless you were Erma Bombeck with a national following via a syndicated column, humor simply did not show on the best-seller lists. Consequently, I went with another project, **The Bug Wars**, and relegated the Aahz and Skeeve proposal to a bottom drawer.

There it remained while I spent roughly a year working on **The Bug Wars**. Then one evening in late 1977 my phone rang. It was Kelly Freas, the artist who had done the cover painting for the issue of *Analog* in which an excerpt of **Cold Cash** had been published, and a longtime friend from the convention circuit. He explained that he was starting a new line of books (Starblaze) with a

Virginia-based publishing house (Donning) and was currently soliciting submissions. Did I have any unpublished manuscripts lying around? Needless to say, I was flattered, but I had to admit the only thing I had ready for submission was a humor presentation . . . and he wouldn't want that, would he? There was a noticeable hesitation; then he suggested I send it in so he could take a look at it.

In an impressively short time, he got back to me with his reaction: He liked the characters and the setting, but felt the story was weak. If I thought I could come up with another story line, he'd cut me a contract. Being as greedy and prone to flattery as the next person, I agreed. When I discovered he needed it "just as soon as possible so that it can be one of our premiere titles," I was a bit less confident, but said I would give it my best shot. What the heck, I was on a roll.

To give you an idea of how much I had gotten caught up in the momentum of the deal, it wasn't until then that I realized none of this had been cleared with my agent. With a certain degree of abashed trepidation, I phoned my agent and explained the situation. There was a weighty pause, then he agreed. "I can see where you'd want to do a favor for an old buddy," he said, "and you might as well give him something that isn't going to go anywhere." I always thrive on encouragement.

So, I had characters, a setting, a contract, but no story. Facing an ASAP deadline and pressured by my agent to "finish it off quick and get back to serious writing," I resorted to a time-honored resource for writers under pressure . . . I stole a story line! Actually, I rationalized it rather neatly. This book is a parody, right? Why not take a "done to death" story line and do it one more time with the tongue-in-cheek respect it deserves? (This was the start of a pattern, but more about that later. . . .)

With a sort of preordained story line and characters I already knew like they were family, the writing went fairly quickly. To be precise, I wrote the thing front to back in five weeks while working full-time days. As an added bonus, I tossed in chapter quotes. After all, the books I was parodying usually had chapter quotes for songs or characters invented by the author for just that purpose, so why not do the same for mine? (When the book became a series, I found out "why not!" If you do it in the first volume, the readers expect it in subsequent volumes. It's a lot harder to come up with 120 cute quotes than it is to invent 20! I often spend more time on the *##!! quotes than I do writing the book!)

The manuscript went in and was accepted without a hitch. (There are certain advantages to dealing with artists who are editors. They tend to leave your writing alone!) The problem which arose was, of all things, on the title. I had always had problems titling books, and this one had been no exception. What I had finally come up with was **The Demon And I**. Doesn't make it, Kelly said. I promised to try to think of an alternative. Three weeks later, press time for the catalog was upon us, and I was still trying to think of a better title. On the day of the noon deadline, I was sitting on the phone with Kelly at 11:45, still trying to come up with a title. **Demon on Square One?** How about **Demon at Large**? Better, but not funny.

Funny . . . funny . . . My mind started darting over lines and movie titles from classic comedy. What do you think of **Another Fine Mess**? Hmmm . . . Kelly put down the phone and bounced the title off his wife, Polly, whose taste exceeds the sum of ours combined. He was back in a moment. Did I say **Another Fine Mess**, or **Another Fine *Myth?*** I confirmed the former. Another conference. Well, it wasn't red-hot, but it seemed to be the best we had to come up with. They'd go with that.

Three hours later (and that much closer to sundown, when I normally start thinking,) my brain started to turn over like a car engine on a cold morning. **Another Fine Myth . . . Hit or Myth. . . . Myth Conceptions!** I hurriedly grabbed the phone and called Kelly back.

On the off chance he wanted to buy another book with these characters, I explained, and definitely if there was a possibility of turning it into a series, the "Myth" bit could come in handy to tie the titles together! In fact, it was a natural to use **Myth Conceptions** as a title for the first book, and hold **Another Fine Myth** for the sequel! How solid was that noon deadline?

It turned out the noon deadline had been real. (A sure sign of an inexperienced editor. The real pros *never* tell you the truth about when they need a manuscript or title, just to allow time for the wayward creative minds to miss the supposed deadline and still hit the real deadline!) He did, however, like the idea. While we couldn't change the title from **Another Fine Mess** to **Myth Conceptions**, we could change it to **Another Fine Myth** and claim a typo in the catalog! We'd just hold the **Myth Conceptions** title for the second one . . . we *were* talking about doing a second one, weren't we? Whoops!

So the series was launched. Over the years, Donning kept contracting them from me, usually one at a time, and I kept swiping plots to parody. The mad magician out to take over the world, the select force against an army, the master heist, the big game, the war against organized crime . . . all the old familiar chestnuts (which I follow avidly myself) were dragged out and run over one more time. Some strange things happened along the way, however.

I had promised myself from the beginning that Skeeve would grow and develop as the series continued. This would theoretically keep me from falling into the trap of telling the same story and using the same gags over and over again. Rereading the manuscripts as they piled up, however, I began to realize how much of my own growth and development was easing onto the pages. Since I started writing the Myth series, I have been raising (or, more accurately, assisting in raising between books) two children of my own, and experiencing all the trials and doubts that go with parenthood. I went from being a full-time cost accountant with a regular paycheck to a full-time writer with a spastic cash flow, and hence became

even more concerned with money than I had been when
it was plentiful. I tried to start a corporation of my own,
only to have it fold within the first six months. With the
success of the books, I even experienced the heady sen-
sation of being a minor celebrity and having total strangers recognize my name. All these experiences and more
became a part of Skeeve's development and the evolution
of his relationship with his rat-pack of friends. Because
of this, the friends themselves began to take on new life
and dimensions until they began crowding in on the central story of Skeeve.

This brings us to **M.Y.T.H. Inc. Link.** (Remember? I
started out tell you you about that? It's the book you're
holding right now.) In this volume the readers get a
chance to see the Myth universe and, more importantly,
Skeeve through eyes other than those belonging to the
central character. Lest the diehard Skeeve fans panic, let
me hasten to assure them I haven't finished with Skeeve's
viewpoint . . . not by a long shot! In the upcoming volumes, however, the Skeeve-narrated volumes will have
the regular "Myth" titles, and those from other viewpoints
will be designated by the "M.Y.T.H. Inc." label. This particular volume has sections of both, hence the "Link" between old and new formats. Get it? Oh well, maybe it will
become clearer after you read this one.

The other major change which is occurring is that with
the contractual assurance that there will be future volumes, I can work a larger canvas as a storyteller (yes, that
is a mixed metaphor) than I was able to when planning
one book at a time. Not every story element has to be
resolved within a single book, and setups for future stories
and situations can be seeded in. Among other things, this
means that I will probably be moving away from the pre-
dictable "old plot parodies" I have been indulging in in
the past, and creating situations and tales unique to the
Myth universe and its inhabitants.

(If that sounds like you'll have to buy every volume

to stay abreast of what's happening, it's not entirely ac-
cidental. I've learned a lot from co-editing **Thieves'
World**™, too!)

The new path I have chosen for *Myth* and myself is
extremely challenging to an author, but one I feel is a
necessary option to either shutting the series down or
"cranking out one more of the same." There are those in
both the book and comic industries who insist that series
readers rapidly become addicted to the status quo, and will
protest or rebel against any attempt to change it. I can
only hope the loyal *Myth* readers find the new directions
as enjoyable and intriguing as I do. If not, tough! This is
the way it's going to be for at least five more books.

While I can occasionally sound very uncaring and set
in my ways, like any author I am always curious about
reader reactions . . . particularly when instituting a major
pattern change. In case you weren't aware of it, you can
always write me (or any author, assuming they're alive)
in care of the publisher. If you'd like a larger forum in
which to air your feelings, there's always the Myth-
Adventures Fan Club, P.O. Box 95, Sutter, CA 95982
(blatant plug!) with their quarterly publication. Please include a stamped, self-addressed envelope.

In closing, I would like to sincerely thank all the *Myth*
readers for their loyalty and interest over the years. All
your letters are read (even if I don't get a chance to answer them all) and deeply appreciated. After all the earlier
warnings from my (ex-) agent and the lack of interest
from other publishers, the appearance of the *Myth* books
on genre and chain-store best-seller lists has not only increased my stature in the field to where I am now offered
the six-book contracts that allow me to experiment with
new concepts, but combined with the popularity of Piers
Anthony's **Xanth** books has forced publishers to review
their attitudes toward humorous fantasy. The door has
been opened for a new wave of talented writers, whose
efforts are even now available on the stands. For these

hitherto unrecognized humorists as well as for myself and the *Myth* gang, again, I thank you.

—Robert Lynn Asprin
Ann Arbor, 1986

I:

"Petty crime is the scourge of business today."

—D. LOREAN

I actually liked our new office facilities better than the old. Even though Aahz had argued hard to keep the Even Odds as a bar (read "money-making venture"), the rest of us ganged up on him and insisted that since we had an extra building it would make more sense to remodel it into offices than to keep trying to do business out of our home. I mean, who really needs a lot of strangers traipsing in and out of your private life all the time? That practice had already landed us in trouble once, and the memory of that escapade was what finally convinced my old mentor to go along with the plan.

Of course, remodeling was more of a hassle than I had expected, even after getting one of the local religious temples to do the carpentry. Even working cheap they were more expensive than I had imagined, and the hours they kept . . . but I digress.

I had a large office now, with a desk, "in" basket, Day-Timers Scheduler, visitor chairs, the whole nine yards. As

I said, I liked it a lot. What I didn't like was the title that went with it . . . to wit, President.

That's right. Everybody insisted that since incorporating our merry band of misfits was my idea, I was the logical choice for titular head of the organization. Even Aahz betrayed me, proclaiming it was a great idea, though to my eye he was hiding a snicker when he said it. If I had known my suggestion would lead to this, believe me I would have kept my mouth shut.

Don't get me wrong, the crew is great! If I were going to lead a group, I couldn't ask for a nicer, more loyal bunch than the one currently at my disposal. Of course, there might be those who would argue the point with me. A trollop, a troll, two gangsters, a moll, and a Pervert . . . excuse me, Pervect . . . an overweight vamp, and a baby dragon might not seem like the ideal team to the average person. They didn't to me when I first met them. Still, they've been unswerving in their support of me over the years, and together we've piled up an impressive track record. No, I'd rather stick with the rat-pack I know, however strange, than trust my fate to anyone else, no matter how qualified they might seem. If anything, from time to time I wonder what they think of me and wish I could peek inside their heads to learn their opinions. Whatever they think, they stick around . . . and that's what counts.

It isn't the crew that makes me edgy . . . it's the title. You see, as long as I can remember, I've always thought that being a leader was the equivalent of walking around with a large bulls-eye painted on your back. Basically the job involves holding the bag for a lot of people instead of just for yourself. If anything goes wrong, you end up being to blame. Even if someone else perpetrated the foul-up, as the leader you're responsible. On the off chance things go right, all you really feel is guilty for taking the credit for someone else's work. All in all, it seems to me to be a no-win, thankless position, one that I would much rather delegate to someone else while I had fun in the field. Unfortunately, everyone else seemed to have the same basic opinion, and as the least experienced member of the crew I was less adept at coming up with reasons to dodge the slot than the others. Consequently, I became the President of M.Y.T.H. Inc. (That's Magical Young Trouble-shooting Heroes. Don't blame me. I didn't come up with the name), an association of magicians and trouble-shooters dedicated to simultaneously helping others and making money.

Our base of operations was the Bazaar at Deva, a well-known rendezvous for magic dealing that was the crossroads of the dimensions. As might be imagined, in an environment like that, there was never a shortage of work.

I had barely gotten settled for the morning when there was a light rap on the door of my office and Bunny stuck her head in.

"Busy, Boss?"

"Well . . ."

She was gone before I could finish formulating a vague answer. This wasn't unusual. Bunny acted as my secretary and always knew more about what I had on the docket than I did. Her inquiries as to my schedule were usually made out of politeness or to check to be sure I wasn't doing something undignified before ushering a client into the office.

"The Great Skeeve will see you now," she said, gesturing grandly to her charge. "In the future, I'd suggest you make an appointment so you won't be kept waiting."

The Deveel Bunny was introducing seemed a bit slimy, even for a Deveel. His bright red complexion was covered with unhealthy-looking pink blotches, and his face was contorted into a permanent leer, which he directed at Bunny's back as she left the room.

Now, there's no denying that Bunny's one of the more attractive females I've ever met, but there was something unwholesome about the attention this dude was giving her. With an effort, I tried to quell the growing dislike I was feeling toward the Deveel. A client was a client, and we were in business to help people in trouble, not make moral judgments on them.

"Can I help you?" I said, keeping my voice polite.

That brought the Deveel's attention back to me, and he extended a hand across the desk.

"So you're the Great Skeeve, eh? Pleased to meet you. Been hearing some good things about your work. Say, you really got a great setup. I especially like that little number you got working as a receptionist. Might even try to hire her away from you. The girl's obviously loaded with talent."

Looking at his leer and wink, I somehow couldn't bring myself to shake his hand.

"Bunny is my administrative assistant," I said carefully. "She is also a stockholder in the company. She earns her position with her skills, not with her looks."

"I bet she does," the Deveel winked again. "I'd love to get a sample of those skills someday."

That did it.

"How about right now?" I smiled, then raised my voice slightly. "Bunny? Could you come in here for a moment?"

She appeared almost at once, ignoring the Deveel's leer as she moved to my desk.

"Yes, sir?"

"Bunny, you forgot to brief me on this client. Who is he?"

She arched one eyebrow and shot a sideways glance at the Deveel. We rarely did our briefings in front of clients. Our eyes met again and I gave her a small nod to confirm my request.

"His name is Bane," she said with a shrug. "He's known to run a small shop here at the Bazaar selling small novelty magic items. His annual take from that operation is in the low six figures."

"Hey! That's pretty good," the Deveel grinned.

Bunny continued as if she hadn't heard.

"He also has secret ownership of three other busi-

nesses, and partial ownership of a dozen more. Most notable is a magic factory which supplies shops in this and
other dimensions. It's located in a sub-dimension acces-
sible through the office of his shop, and employs several
hundred workers. The estimated take from that factory
alone is in the mid seven figure range annually."

The Deveel had stopped leering.

"How did you know all that?" he demanded. "That's
supposed to be secret!"

"He also fancies himself to be a lady-killer, but there is
little evidence to support his claim. The female companions
he is seen in public with are paid for their company, and
none have lasted more than a week. It seems they feel the
money is insufficient for enduring his revolting personality.
Foodwise, he has a weakness for broccoli."

I turned a neutral smile on the deflated Deveel.

". . . And *that*, sir, is the talent that earns Bunny her
job. Did you enjoy your sample?"

"She's wrong about the broccoli," Bane said weakly.
"I hate broccoli."

I raised an eyebrow at Bunny, who winked back at me.

"Noted," she said. "Will there be anything else, Boss?"

"Stick around, Bunny. I'll probably need your help
quoting Mr. Bane a price for our services . . . that is, if he
ever gets around to telling us what his problem is."

That brought the Deveel out of his shocked trance.

"I'll tell you what the problem is! Miss Bunny here
was dead right when she said my magic factory is my
prize holding. The trouble is that someone's robbing me
blind! I'm losing a fortune to pilferage!"

"What percentage loss?" Bunny said, suddenly attentive.

"Pushing fourteen percent . . . up from six last year."

"Are we talking retail or cost value?"

"Cost."

"What's your actual volume loss?"

"Less than eight percent. They know exactly what
items to go after . . . small, but expensive."

I sat back and tried to look wise. They had lost me completely about two laps into the conversation, but Bunny seemed to know what she was doing, so I gave her her head.

"Everybody I've sent in to investigate gets tagged as a company spy before they even sit down," Bane was saying. "Now, the word I get is that your crew has some contacts in organized crime, and I was figuring . . ."

He let his voice trail off, then shrugged as if he was embarrassed to complete the thought.

Bunny looked over at me, and I could tell she was trying to hide a smile. She was the niece of Don Bruce, the Mob's Fairy Godfather, and it always amused her to encounter the near-superstitious awe outsiders felt toward her uncle's organization.

"I think we can help you," I said carefully. "Of course, it will cost."

"How much?" Bane countered, settling back for what was acknowledged throughout the dimensions as a Deveel's specialty . . . haggling.

In response, Bunny scribbled something quickly on her notepad, then tore the sheet off and handed it to Bane.

The Deveel glanced at it and blanched a light pink.

"WHAT!! That's robbery and you know it!"

"Not when you consider what the losses are costing you," Bunny said sweetly. "Tell you what. If you'd rather, we'll take a few points in your factory . . . say, half the percentage reduction in pilferage once we take the case?"

Bane went from pink to a volcanic red in the space of a few heartbeats.

"All right! It's a deal . . . at the original offer!"

I nodded slightly.

"Fine. I'll assign a couple of agents to it immediately."

"Wait a minute! I'm paying prices like these and I'm not even getting the services of the head honcho? What are you trying to pull here? I want . . ."

"The Great Skeeve stands behind every M.Y.T.H. Inc. contract," Bunny interrupted. "If you wish to contract his personal services, the price would be substantially higher . . . like, say, controlling interest?"

"All right, all right! I get the message!" the Deveel said. "Send in your agents. They just better be good, that's all. At these rates, I expect results!"

With that, he slammed out of the office, leaving Bunny and me alone.

"How much *did* you charge him?"

"Just our usual fees."

"Really?"

"Well . . . I did add in a small premium 'cause I didn't like him. Any objections?"

"No. Just curious is all."

"Say, Boss. Would you mind including me in this assignment? It shouldn't take too long, and this one's got me a little curious."

"Okay . . . but not as lead operative. I want to be able to pull you back here if things get hairy in the office. Let your partner run the show."

"No problem. Who are you teaming me with?"

I leaned back in my chair and smiled.

"Can't you guess? The client wants organized crime, he *gets* organized crime!"

Guido's Tale

"Guido, are you sure you've got your instructions right?"

That is Bunny talkin'. For some reason the Boss has deemed it wise to delegate to me her company for this job. Now this is okay with me, as Bunny is more than enjoyable to look at and a swell head to boot, which is to say she is smarter than me, which is a thing I do not say about many people, guys or dolls.

The only trepidation with which I view this pairin' is that as swell as she is, Bunny also has a marked tendency to nag whenever a job is on. This is because she is handicapped with a problem, which is that she has her cap set

for the Boss. Now we are all aware of this, for it was
apparent as the nose on your face from the day they first
encountered. Even the Boss could see this, which is sayin'
sumpin', for while I admire the Boss as an organizer, he
is a little thick between the ears when it comes to skirts.
To show you what I mean, once he was aware that Bunny
did indeed entertain notions on his bod, his response was
to half faint from the nervousness. This is from a guy I've
watched take on vampires and werewolf types, not to
mention Don Bruce himself, without so much as battin'
an eye. Like I say, dolls is not his strong suit.

Anyway, I was talkin' about Bunny and her problem.
She finally managed to convince the Boss that she wasn't
really tryin' to pair up with him, but was just interested
in furtherin' her career as a business type. Now this was
a blatant lie, and we all knew it . . . even though it seems
to have fooled the Boss. Even that green bum, Aahz,
could see what Bunny was up to. (This surprised me a
bit, for I always thought his main talent was makin' loud
noises.) All that Bunny was doin' was switchin' from one
come-on to another. Her overall motivational goal has
never changed.

The unfortunate circumstances of this is that instead of
wooin' the Boss with her bod, which as I have said is
outstandin', she is now tryin' to win his admiration with
what a sharp cookie she is. This should not be overly
difficult, as Bunny is one shrewd operator, but like all
dolls she feels she has limited time in which to accomplish
her objective before her looks run out, so she is tryin'
extra hard to make sure the Boss notices her.

This unfortunately can make her a real headache in the
posterior regions to work with. She is so afraid that someone else will mess up her performance record that she can
drive a skilled worker such as myself up a proverbial tree
with her nervous double-check chatter. Still, she is a swell
doll and we are all pullin' for her, so we put up with it.

"Yes, Bunny," I sez.

" 'Yes, Bunny' what?"

"Yes, Bunny, I'm sure I got my instructions right."

"Then repeat them back to me."

"Why?"

"Guido!"

When Bunny gets that tone in her voice, there is little else to do but to humor her. This is in part because part of my job is to be supportive to my teammate when on an assignment, but also because Bunny has a mean left hook when she feels you are givin' her grief. My cousin Nunzio chanced to discover this fact one time before he was informed that she was Don Bruce's niece, and as he had a jaw like an anvil against which I have had occasion to injure my fist with noticeable results, I have no desire to confirm for myself the strength of the blow with which she decked him. Consequently I decided to comply with her rather annoying request.

"The Boss wants us to find out how the goods of a particular establishment is successfully wanderin' off the premises without detection," I sez. "To that end I am to intermingle with the workers as one of them to see if I can determine how this is bein' accomplished."

"And . . ." she sez, givin' me the hairy eyeball.

". . . And you are to do the same, only with the office types. At the end of a week we are to regroup in order that we may compare observations and see if we are perhaps barkin' up the wrong tree."

"And . . ." she sez again, lookin' a trifle agitated.

At this point I commence to grow a trifle nervous, for while she is obviously expectin' me to continue in my oration, I have run out of instructions to reiterate.

". . . And . . . ummm . . ." I sez, tryin' to think of what I have overlooked.

". . . And not to start any trouble!" she finishes, lookin' at me hard-like. "Right?"

"Yeah. Sure, Bunny."

"Say it!"

". . . And not to start any trouble."

* * *

Now I am more than a little hurt that Bunny feels it is necessary to bring this point to my attention so forceful like, as in my opinion it is not in my nature to start trouble under any circumstances. Both Nunzio and me go out of our way to avoid any unnecessary disputes of a violent nature, and only bestir ourselves to bring such difficulties to a halt once they are thrust upon us. I do not, however, bring my injured feelings to Bunny's attention as I know she is a swell person who would not deliberately inflict such wounds upon the self-image of a delicate person such as myself. She is merely nervous as to the successful completion of the pending job, as I have previously orated, and would only feel bad if I were to let on how callous and heartless she was behavin'. There are many in my line of work who display similar signs of nervousness when preparin' for a major assignment. I once worked with a guy what had a tendency to fidget with a sharp knife when waitin' for a job to commence, usually on the bods of his fellow caperers. One can only be understandin' of the motivationals of such types and not take offense at their personal foibles when the heat is on. This is one of the secrets of success learned early on by us executive types. Be that as it may, I am forced to admit I am more than a little relieved when it is time for the job to begin, allowin' me to part company with Bunny for a while.

As a worker type, I report to work much earlier than is required for office types like Bunny. Why this is I am not sure, but it is one of those inescapable inequities with which life is fraught . . . like your line always bein' the longest when they are broken down by alphabet.

To prepare for my undercover maneuverin's, I have abandoned my normally spiffy threads in order to dress more appropriate for the worker types with which I am to intermingle. This is the only part of the assignment which causes me any discomfort. You see, the more successful

a worker type is, the more he dresses like a skid-row bum
or a rag heap, so that he looks like he is either ready to
roll in the mud or has just been rolled himself, which is
in direct contradiction to what I learned in business college.

For those of you to whom this last tidbit of knowledge
comes as a surprise, I would hasten to point out that I
have indeed attended higher learnin' institutes, as that is
the only way to obtain the master's type degree that I
possess. If perchance you wonder, as some do, why a
person with such credentials should choose the line of
work that I have to pursue, my reasons are twofold: Fir-
stus, I am a social type who perfers workin' with people;
and second, I find my sensitive nature is repelled by the
ruthlessness necessitated by bein' an upper management
type. I simply do not have it in me to mess up people's
lives with layoffs and plant shut-downs and the like.
Rather, I find it far more sociable to break an occasional
leg or two or perhaps rearrange a face a little than to live
with the more long-term damage inflicted by upper management for the good of their respective companies.
Therefore, as I am indeed presented with the enviable position of havin' a choice in career paths, I have traditionally opted to be an order taker rather than an order giver.
It's a cleaner way to make a livin'.

So anyway, I reports for work bright and early and am
shown around the plant before commencin' my actual duties. Let me tell you I am impressed by this set-up like I
have seldom been impressed by nothin' before. It is like
Santa's North Pole elf sweatshop done up proper.

When I was in grad school, I used to read a lot of
comics. Most particularly I was taken by the ads they used
to carry therein for X-Ray Glasses and Whoopie Cushions
and such, which I was unfortunately never able to afford
as I was not an untypical student and therefore had less
money than your average eight-year-old. Walkin' into the
plant, however, I suddenly realized that this particular set
of indulgences had not truly passed me by as I had feared.

The place was gargantuous, by which I mean it was really big, and jammed from wall to wall to ceilin' with conveyor belts and vats and stacks of materials and boxes labeled in languages I am not privileged to recognize, as well as large numbers of worker types strollin' around checkin' gauges and pushin' carts and otherwise engaged in the sorts of activities one does when the doors are open and there's a chance that the management types might come by on their way to the coffee machine and look in to see what they're doin'. What was even more impressive was the goods in production. At a glance I could see that as an admirer of cheap junk gimmicks, I had indeed died and gone to pig heaven. It was my guess, however uneducated, that what I had found was the major supplier for those ads which I earlier referenced, as well as most of the peddlers in the Bazaar who cater to the tourist trade.

Now right away I can see what the problem is, as most of the goods bein' produced are a small and portable nature, and who could resist waltzin' off with a few samples in their pockets? Merchandise of this nature would be enough to tempt a saint, of which I seriously doubt the majority of the work force is made up of.

At the time I think that this will make my job substantially easier than anticipated. It is my reasonin' that all I need do is figure out how I myself would liberate a few choice items, then watch to see who is doin' the same. Of course, I figure it will behoove me to test my proposed system myself so as to see if it really can be done in such a manner, and at the same time acquire a little bonus or two I can gloat about in front of Nunzio.

First, however, I had to concentrate on establishin' myself as a good worker so that no one would suspect that I was there for anythin' else other than makin' an honest wage.

The job I was assigned to first was simple enough for a person of my skills and dexterity. All I had to do was sprinkle a dab of Pixie Dust on each Magic Floating Coaster as it came down the line. The major challenge seemed to be to be sure to apply as little as possible, as Pixie Dust is expensive even at bulk rates and one definitely does not want to give the customer more than they paid for.

With this in mind, I set to work ... only to discover that the job was actually far more complex than I had originally perceived. You see, the Pixie Dust is kept in a large bag, which floats because that is what the Pixie Dust within does. The first trick is to keep the bag from floatin' away while one is workin' with it, which is actually harder than it sounds because the Pixie Dust is almost strong enough to float the bag *and* whoever is attemptin' to hold it down. There is a safety line attached to the bag as an anchor, but it holds the bag too high to work with. Consequently one must wrestle with the bag while applyin' the Pixie Dust, a feat which is not unlike tryin' to hold a large beach ball under water while doin' needlepoint, and only rely on the safety line to haul the bag down into position again should it get away, which it often does. One might ask whyfor the line is not made shorter to hold the bag in the proper position and thereby make the job simpler. I suppose it is the same reason that working-type mothers will drown their children at birth if they feel there is the slightest chance they will grow up to be production engineers.

The other problem I encountered was one which I am surprised no one saw to fit to warn me about. That is that when one works with Pixie Dust, it must be remembered that it floats, and therefore pours up instead of down.

When first I attempted to sprinkle a little Pixie Dust on a Magic Floating Coaster, I was puzzled as to why the coaster would not subsequently float. On the chance that I had not applied a sufficient quantity of the substance in question, I added some more ... and then a little more, not realizin' that it was floatin' up toward the ceilin' instead of down onto the coaster. Unfortunately, I was bent over the coaster at the time, as I was tryin' to keep the bag from floatin' away, and unbeknownst to me the dust was sprinklin' onto me rather than the coaster in question. The first admissible evidence I had that things was goin' awry was when I noticed that my feet were no longer in contact with the floor and that indeed I had become as buoyant as the bag which I was tryin' to hold down. Fortuitously, my grip is firm enough to crumble bricks so I managed to maintain my hold on the bag and eventually pull myself down the safety line instead of floatin' to the ceilin' in independent flight. Further, I was able to brush the Pixie Dust off my clothes so as to maintain my groundward orientation as well as my dignity.

The only thing which was not understandable about this passing incident was the uninvolvement of the other worker types. Not only had they not come over to assist me in my moment of misfortune, they had also refrained from making rude and uproarious noises at my predicament. This second point in particular I concerned myself with as bein' unusual, as worker types are notorious jokesters and unlikely to pass up such an obvious opportunity for low amusement.

The reason for this did indeed beome crystalline when we finally broke for lunch.

I was just settlin' in to enjoy my midday repast, and chanced to ask the worker type seated next to me to pass me a napkin from the receptice by him as it was not within my reach. Instead of goin' along with this request as one would expect any civilized person to do, this joker mouths off to the effect that he won't give the time of day to any company spy, much less a napkin. Now if there is one thing I will not tolerate it is bein' called a fink, especially when I happen to be workin' as one. I therefore deem it necessary to show this individual the error of his assumptions by bendin' him a little in my most calm, friendly manner. Just when I think we are startin' to communicate, I notice that someone is beatin' me across the back with a chair. This does nothin' to improve my mood, as I am already annoyed to begin with, so I prop the Mouth against a nearby wall with one hand, thereby freein' the other which I then use to snag the other cretin as he winds up for another swing. I am just beginnin' to warm up to my work when I hear a low whistle of warnin' from the crowd which has naturally gathered to watch our discussion, and I look around to see one of the foremen ambling over to see what the commotion's about.

Now foremen are perhaps the lowest form of management, as they are usually turncoat worker types, and this one proves to be no exception to the norm. Without so much as a how-do-you-do, he commences to demand to know what's goin' on and who started it anyway. As has been noted, I already had my wind up and was seriously considerin' whether or not to simply expand our discussion group to include the foreman when I remember how nervous Bunny was and consider the difficulty I would have explainin' the situation to her if I were to suffer termination the first day on the job for roughin' up a management type. Consequently I shift my grip from my two dance partners to my temper and proceed to explain to the foreman that no one has started anythin' as indeed nothin' is happenin' . . . that my colleagues chanced to fall down and I was simply helpin' them to their feet is all.

My explanations can be very convincing, as any jury can tell you, and the foreman decides to accept this one without question, somehow overlookin' the fact that I had helped the Mouth to his feet with such enthusiasm that his feet were not touchin' the floor when the proceedin's were halted. Perhaps he attributed this phenomenon to the Pixie Dust which was so fond of levitatin' anything in the plant that wasn't tied down. Whatever the reason, he buys the story and wanders off, leavin' me to share my lunch with my two colleagues whose lunch has somehow gotten tromped on during playtime.

Apparently, my display of masculine-type prowess has convinced everyone that I am indeed not a company spy, for the two guys which jumped me in such an unprofessional manner is now very eager to chat on the friendliest of terms. The one I have been referrin' to as the Mouth

turns out to be named Roxie, and his chairswingin' buddy
is Sion. Right away we hit it off as they seem to be
regular-type guys, even if they can't throw a punch to
save their own skins, and it seems we share a lot of common interests . . . like skirts and an occasional bet on the
ponies. Of course, they are immediately advanced to the
top of my list of suspects, as anyone who thinks like me
is also likely to have little regard for respectin' the privacy
rights of other people's property.

The other thing they tell me before we return to our
respective tasks is that the Pixie Dust job I am doin' is
really a chump chore reserved for new worker types what
don't know enough to argue with their assignments. It is
suggested that I have a few words with the foreman, as
he has obviously been impressed with my demeanor, and
see if I can't get some work more in keepin' with my
obvious talents. I am naturally grateful for this advice, and
pursue their suggestion without further delay.

The foreman does indeed listen to my words, and sends
me off to a new station for the balance of the day. Upon
arrivin' at the scene of my reassignment, however, it occurs to me that perhaps I would have been wiser to keep
my big yap in a closed position.

My new job really stinks . . . and I mean to tell you
this is meant as literal as possible. All I had to do, see,
was stand at the end of a conveyor belt and inspect the
end product as it came off the line. Now, when I say "end
product," this is also meant to be interpreted very literal-
like. The quicker of you have doubtlessly perceived by
now the product to which I am referrin', but for the benefit
of the slower readers and sober editors, I will clarify my
allusions.

What I am inspectin' is rubber Doggie Doodle, which
comes in three sizes: Embarrassing, Disgusting, and Un-
believable. This is not, of course, how they are labeled,
but rather how I choose to refer to them after a mere few
moments' exposure. Now since, as I have mentioned before, this is a class operation, it is to be expected that our

product has to be noticeably different than similar offerin's on the market. It is unfortunate that as the Final Inspector, I must deal with the finished product, which means before it goes into the boxes, but after the "Realistic, Life-like Aroma that Actually Sticks to Your Hands" is added.

It is also unfortunate that I am unable to locate either the foreman or the two jokers who had advised me for the rest of the afternoon. Of course, I am not permitted the luxury of a prolonged search, as the conveyor belt continues to move whether the inspector is inspectin' or not, and in no time at all the work begins to pile up. As I am not particularly handy with a shovel, I deem it wisest to continue workin' and save our discussion for a later, more private time.

Now mind you, the work doesn't really bother me all that much. One of the chores me and Nunzio toss coins over back home is cleanin' up after the Boss's dragon, and after that, Doggie Doodle really looks like a bit of an understatement, if you know what I mean. If anything, this causes me to chuckle a bit as I work, for while I am on assignment Nunzio must do the honors all by himself, so by comparison my end of the stick looks pretty clean. Then too, the fact that Roxie and Sion is now playin' tricks on me is a sign that I am indeed bein' accepted as one of the worker types, which will make my job considerably easier.

The only real problem I have with my assignment is that, considerin' the product with which I am workin', I feel it would be unwise to test the security-type precautions when I leave work that night. Even if I wished to liberate a few samples, which I was not particularly desirous of doin' since as I have noted we already have lots at home of a far superior quality, the "Realistic, Life-like Aroma that Really Sticks to Your Hands," would negate its passin' unnoticed by even the densest security-type guard.

As it turns out, this was a blessin' incognito. When

closin' time finally rolls around, I discover that it would
not be as easy to sneak stuff out of this plant as I had
originally perceived. Everything the worker types took out
of the plant with 'em was given the once and twice over
by hard-eyed types who definitely knew what they were
doin', and while we didn't have to go through a strip
search, we did have to walk one at a time through a series
of alarm systems that used a variety of rays to frisk us for
objects and substances belongin' to the company. As it
was, I almost got into trouble because there were still
lingerin' specks of Pixie Dust on me from my morning
duties, but Roxie stepped forward and explained things to
the guards that was rapidly gatherin' and they settled for
reclaimin' the Pixie Dust without things gettin' too personal.

This settled things between me and Roxie for the Doggie Doodle joke, and after I bounced Sion against the wall
a few times to show my appreciation for his part in the
prank, we all went off in search of some unprintable di-
versions.

Now if this last bit seems, perchance, a little shallow
to you, you must first consider the whole situational before renderin' your verdict. I think it's been referenced
before that the factory under investigation is located in
one of those unlisted dimensions the Deveels specialize
in. As the only way into this dimension from the Bazaar
is through the owner's front-type operation, and as he is
not wild about the notion of hundreds of worker types
traipsin' through his office each shift, part of the contract
for workin' in said factory is that one has to agree to stay
in this unlisted dimension for a week at a time. To this
end, the owner has provided rooms for the worker types,
but as he is cheap even for a Deveel, each room is shared
by bein's workin' different shifts. That is to say, you only
have your room for one shift, and the rest of the time
you're either workin' or hangin' out. Just so's we don't
get bored between workin' and sleepin', the owner has
also provided a variety of bars, restaurants, movies, and

video joints for our amusement, all of which cost but can
be charged back against our paychecks. If this seems like
a bit of a closed economy to you, I would hasten to remind you that no one has ever accused the Deveels of
bein' dumb when it comes to turnin' a profit. Anyway,
all of this is to explain why it is that I am forced to go
carousin' with Roxie and Sion instead of retirin' to my
room to re-read the classics as would be my normal bent.

Now to be truthful with you, this carryin' on is not
nearly so bad as I am lettin' on. It is simply that it is
embarrassin' to my carefully maintained image to admit
how really dull these evenings was, so's I reflexively sort
of try to build them up more than I should. I mean, you'd
think that off hours with a bunch of guys what work at a
magic joke and novelty factory would be a barrel of
laughs. You know, more fun than callin' in phony heist
tips to the cops. Well, they surprised me by contentin'
themselves to drinkin' and gamblin' and maybe a fistfight
or two for their amusements . . . like I say, the same old
borin' stuff any good-natured bunch of guys does. Mostly
what they do is sit around and gripe about the work at
the plant and how underpaid they are . . . which I do not
pay much attention to as there is not a worker type alive
that does not indulge in this particular pastime. In no time
flat I determines that nobody in the work force is well
enough versed in the finer points of non-backer entrepre-
neurmanship, which is to say crime, to converse with me
on my own level. This is not surprisin' in the age of specialization, but it does mean I don't get nobody to talk to.

What I am gettin', though, is depressed . . . a feelin'
which continues to grow as the week rolls on. It is not
the work or the company of the worker types which is
erodin' at my morale, but rather the diminishin' possibility of puttin' a wrap on this job.

It seems the more I observe in my undercover-type
investigation, the more puzzled I become as to how the
pilferage is bein' accomplished. The better I get to know
my fellow worker types, the more I am convinced that

they are not involved in any such goin's on, even in a
marginal manner. This is not to say that they are lackin'
in the smarts department, as they are easily as quick on
the uptake as anyone I ever worked with in school or the
business. Rather, I am makin' a tribute to the tightness of
the plant security which must necessarily be penetrated in
order to perpetrate such an activity.

As I have earlier said, this is an age of specialization,
and none of the worker types I meet have adequately applied themselves to be able to hold a candle to me in my
particular field of endeavor. Now realizin' that after a
week of intense schemin', I have not yet come up with a
plan for samplin' the merchandise that I feel has enough
of a chance of succeedin' as to make it worthwhile to try,
I cannot convince myself that the security can be cracked
by any amateur, however talented.

Considerin' this, I am edgin' closer to the unpleasant
conclusion that not only is it long odds against us findin'
a fast answer, there is a chance we might not be able to
crack this case at all. Such thoughts cause me great anx-
ieties, which lead to depression as I am as success-
oriented as the next person.

My mood truly bottoms out at the end of the week,
specifically when I am presented with my paycheck.
Now, I am not countin' on the money I earn as a worker
type, as I am already bein' well subsidized by the Boss.
Nonetheless I am surprised to see the amount my week's
worth of toil has actually brought me. To be truthful, I
have again yielded to the temptation of understatement. I
was not surprised, I was shocked . . . which is not a good
thing for, as anyone in the Mob can tell you, when I am
shocked I tend to express the unsettlement of my nerves
physically.

The fact that I am not needin' the money in question
means that I was only a little shocked, so it only took
three of my fellow worker types to pull me off the payroll
type what slipped me the bad news. Of course, by that
time I had also been hit by a couple of tranquilizer darts
which I am told is standard issue for most companies in

the Bazaar to ease personnel relations. If, perchance, your company does not already follow this policy, I heartily give it my recommend, as it certainly saves depreciation on your payroll types and therefore minimizes the expense of trainin' new ones.

Anyway, once I am calmed down to a point where I am merely tossin' furniture and the payroll type has re-composed himself, which is to say he has received suffi-cient first aid to talk, he explains the realities of life to me. Not only has the cost of the aforementioned carousin' been deducted from my earnin's, but also charges for my room which, realizin' the figure quoted only represents a third of the take on that facility, puts it several notches above the poshest resort it has ever been my decadent pleasure to patronize. Also there is an itemized bill for every bit or scrap of waste that has occurred at my duty station durin' the week, down to the last speck of Pixie Dust. Normally I would be curious as to how this ac-countin' was done, as it indicates a work force in the plant even more efficient than the security types which have been keepin' me at bay, but at the time I was too busy bein' outraged at bein' charged retail instead of cost for the materials lost.

All that keeps me from truly expressin' my opinion of the situation is that Roxie explains that I am not bein' singled out for special treatment, but that this is indeed a plant-wide policy which all the worker types must suffer. He also points out that the cost of the first aid for the payroll type is gonna be charged against my paycheck, and that what I have left will not be sufficient for me to indulge myself in another go 'round.

Thus it is that I am doubly disheartened when I hook up with Bunny for our weekly meetin' and debriefin', bein' as how I am not only a failure but a poor failure which is the worst kind to be.

"Guido, what's wrong?" she sez when we meet. "You look terrible!"

As I have said, Bunny is a swell head, but she is still

a skirt, which means she has an unerring instinct for what to say to pick a guy up when he's under the weather.

"I am depressed," I sez, since she wasn't around when I explained it to you. "The workin' conditions at the plant are terrible, especially considerin' the pay we aren't gettin'."

At this, Bunny rolls her eyes and groans to express her sympathy.

"Oh, Guido! You're talking just like a . . . what is it that you call them? Oh, yes. Just like a worker type."

"That's 'cause I *am* a worker type!"

This earns me the hairy eyeball.

"No, you're not," she sez real hard-like. "You're an executive for M.Y.T.H. Inc. here on an investigation. Now quit being negative and let's talk about the job."

It occurs to me that she has a truly unusual concept of how to avoid negative thinkin'.

"Suit yourself," I sez, givin' her my best careless shrug like I usually save for court performances. "As far as the job goes, I am truly at a dead end. After a week I have discovered nothin' and don't have the foggiest where to look next."

"Good!" she sez, breakin' into a smile which could melt an iceberg, of which there are very few at the Bazaar with which I could test my hyperbole. Naturally I am surprised.

"Perhaps my small-but-normally-accurate ears are deceivin' me, Bunny. Did I understand you to say that it's a good thing that I am gettin' nowhere in my investigations?"

"That's right. You see, I think I'm on to something at my end, and if you're coming up empty in the plant, maybe you can help me with my theories! Now here's what I want you to do."

Followin' Bunny's suggestion, I start out the next week by bracin' the foreman to reassign me to work in the warehouse on inventory. At first he is reluctant as he does not like worker types tellin' him his job, but after I point out to him how small the hospitalization benefits provided by the owner really are, he becomes far more reasonable.

All I have to do to give Bunny the support she requests is to double-check the materials comin' into the plant, and send her an extra copy of each day's tally in the inter-office mail. This pleases me immensely, as it is not only easy work, it also gives me substantial amounts of free time with which I can pursue a project of my own.

You see, I am still more than a little steamed over the hatchet job which was performed upon my paycheck. I therefore take it upon myself to commence conductin' my own unofficial survey as to workin' conditions around the plant, and since my eye has the benefit of business school trainin', which most of the workin' types have not bothered with, it becomes rapidly apparent that the situational stinks worse than the Doggie Doodle did.

Just as an example, the plant has made a practice of hirin' all sorts of bein's, many of which is extremely difficult to describe without gettin' vulgar. Now this is not surprisin' considerin' the Bazaar is the main source for their recruitin', but it makes for some teeth-grindin' inequalities in the pay scales.

Before the wrong idea is given, let me elucidate for a moment on the point of view I am comin' from. I personally don't care much who or what is workin' next to me as long as they can carry their share of the job. You will notice I have not even mentioned that Roxie is bright orange and Sion is mauve, as I feel this has nothin' to do with my assessment of their personalities or their abilities. I will admit to bein' a little uneasy around bein's what got more arms or legs than I do, but this is more a professional reaction, since should the occasion arise that we might have a difference of opinion, my fightin' style is intended for opposition what can throw the same number of punches and kicks per side as I can, and a few extra fists can make a big difference. But, as I say, this is more a professional wariness than any judgment on their overall worth as bein's. I only mention this on the off chance that some of my remarks about strange bein's might be taken as bein' pergerdous, a rap of which I have never been convicted. I am not that sort of person.

As I was sayin', though, the plant has lots of strange bein's workin' the line. The indignity of the situation, however, is that even though they got these extra arms and in some cases is doin' the work of several worker types, they is gettin' paid the same as anyone else. While to some this might seem unfair to the ones bein' so exploited, I see it as a threat to the worker types with the usual count of arms and legs, as it will obviously save the company significant cost if they can hire as many of the former as possible, whilst layin' off a disproportionate number of the latter.

Another inequality I observe concerns the security types which I have been unable to circumvent. Now this has been a source of curiosity to me since I first arrived at the plant, since it doesn't take an accountin' whiz to figure out that if the plant is payin' the security types what they're worth, their cost should be substantially more than would seem economically wise. I chance across the answer one time when I happen to eavesdrop on a couple off-duty lunchin' security types who are gripin' about their jobs. It seems that they are underpaid as much as us workin' types, despite the fact that they are safeguardin' stuff worth millions! While this is doubtlessly unfair, I do not include it in my notes because I have found that it is not only not unusual, but is actually customary for plants or societies to underpay their guardian types. I suppose that as bonkers as it seems, this is in actuality the way things should be. If guardian types made a decent wage, then criminal types like me would go into that line of work as it has better hours and better retirement benefits than the career path I am currently pursuin', and if there was no crime there would be no need for guardian types and we would all end up unemployed. Viewin' it that way, the status quo is probably for the best.

Anyway, I continues to keep my eyes and ears open until I feel I have gathered sufficient injustices to make my point, then I wait for the right moment to present my findin's. This proves to be no great test of my patience, since, as I have noted, the worker types love to gripe about their jobs and tonight proves to be no exception to this rule.

"What do you think, Guido?" Roxie sez, turnin' to me. "Do the guys workin' the Dribble Toilets have it worse than the ones workin' the Battery-Operated Whoopie Cushions?"

I make a big show of thinkin' hard before I give my answer.

"I think," I sez carefully, "that if brains was dynamite, the whole plant wouldn't have the powder to blow its nose."

It takes him a minute to get my drift, but when he does, his eyes go real mean.

"What's that supposed to mean?"

"I mean I've been sittin' here listenin' to you guys bellyache for nearly two weeks now, and ain't none of youse heard a thing that's goin' on."

"All right, Mr. Doggie Doodle, if you're so smart why don't you tell all of us who have been workin' here for years what it is you've learned in a whole two weeks."

I choose to ignore the Doggie Doodle crack, as there are now several tables of worker types listenin' to our conversation and I'm afraid I'll lose their attention if I take the time to bust Roxie's head.

"Youse guys spend all your time arguin' about who's gettin' honked the worst, and in the meantime you're missin' the point. The point is that you're *all* gettin' the Purple Shaft."

With that I commences to itemize a dozen or so of the more reprehensible examples of the exploitation of worker types I have noted in my investigation. By the time I am done, the whole bar is listenin', and there is an ugly murmur goin' around.

"All right, Guido. You've made your point," Roxie sez, tryin' to take another swallow of his drink before he realizes that it's empty. "So what are we supposed to do about it? We don't set company policy."

I shows him the smile that makes witnesses lose their memories.

"We don't set company policy, but we *do* decide whether or not we're gonna work for the wages offered in the conditions provided."

At this, Roxie lights up like he just won the lottery.

"That's right!" he sez. "They control the plant, but without us workers there won't be no Doggie Doodle to ship!"

The crowd is gettin' pretty worked up now, and there's a lot of drink buyin' and back slappin' goin' on when someone just has to raise a discouragin' word.

"So what's to stop 'em from just hiring a new work force if we hold out?"

That is Sion talkin'. As you may have noticed, he don't mouth off near as much as Roxie does, but when he opens up, the other worker types are inclined to listen. This time is no exception, and the room starts to quiet down as the worker types try to focus on this new problem.

"C'mon, Sion," Roxie sez, tryin' to laugh it off. "What idiots would work for these wages under these conditions?"

"Roxie, *we've* been doing just that for years! I don't think they'll have any more trouble finding a new work force than they had finding the old one."

I decided it was time I took a hand in the proceedin's.

"There are a few things you are overlookin', Sion," I sez. "First off, it will take time to hire and train a new work force, and durin' that time the plant ain't producin' Doggie Doodle to sell, which means the owner is losin' money which he does not like to do."

Sion just shrugged at that one.

"True enough, but he'd probably rather take the short-term loss of a shutdown than the long-term expense of giving us higher wages."

"Which brings up the other thing you're overlookin'."

"Which is?"

"There is one intolerable workin' condition a new work force would have to endure that we haven't . . . to wit, us! We don't have to get past us to come to work each mornin', and whilst the security types are aces at guardin' a plant, it is my best appraisal that they would not be able to provide bodyguard service for an entire new work force."

This seemed to satisfy the objection in question, and we then got down to workin' out the details, for while from the outside it may seem simple to organize a labor movement, there is much to be planned before anythin' can actually be set into motion. The other two shifts had to be brought on board and a list of demands agreed upon, not to mention the buildin' of a contingency fund in case the other side wanted to try starvin' us out.

A lot of the guys wanted me to run the thing, but I felt I could not accept in clear consciousness and successfully proposed Roxie for the position. The alibi I gave is that the worker types should be represented by someone who has more than two weeks' experience on the job, but in reality I wasn't sure how much longer I had before the Boss pulled me back to my normal duties and I did not want the movement to flounder from havin' its leader disappear sudden like. The chore I did volunteer for was givin' lessons in how to handle any outsiders the plant tried to hire, as most of the current worker types did not know a sawed-off pool cue from a tire iron when it came to labor negotiations.

Between workin' in the warehouse and helpin' with the movement, I was so busy I almost missed my weekly meetin' with Bunny. Fortuitously I remembered, which is a good thing as Bunny is a doll and no doll likes to be forgotten.

"Hi, Babe!" I sez, givin' her one of my seediest winks. "How's it goin'?"

"Well, you're sure in a chipper mood," she sez, grinnin' back at me. "I thought I'd have good news for you, but I guess you already heard."

"Heard? Heard what?"

"The assignment's over. I've cracked the case."

Now this causes me a little guilt and embarrassment, as I have not thought about our assignment for days, but I cover for it by actin' enthusiastic instead.

"No foolin'? You found out how the stuff is bein' liberated?"

"Well, actually it turns out to be a case of embezzlement, not pilferage. One of the Deveels in Accounting was tinkering with the receiving records and paying for more than was coming in at the shipping dock."

"Bunny," I sez, "try to remember that my degree is not in accounting. Could you perhaps try to enlighten me in baby talk so's I can understand the nature of the heist?"

"Okay. When we buy the raw materials, each shipment is counted and a tally sent to Accounting. That tally determines how much we pay our supplier, as well as alerting us as to how much raw material there is in inventory. Now our embezzler had a deal going with the suppliers to bill us for more material than we actually received. He would rig the receiving tallies to tie out to the overage, pay the supplier for goods they never shipped, then split the extra money with them. The trouble was that since the same numbers were used for the inventories, the records showed that there were more goods in inventory than were actually there, so when the plant came up short, the owner thought the employees were stealing from him. The missing goods weren't being pilfered, they were never in the plant at all!"

I gave a low whistle of appreciation.

"That's great, Bunny! The Boss'll be real proud of you when he hears."

That actually made her blush a little.

"I didn't do it all by myself, you know. I wouldn't have been able to prove anything if you hadn't been feeding me duplicate records on the side."

"A mere trifling," I sez expansively. "I for one am goin' to make sure the Boss knows just what a gem he has workin' for him so's you get your just esteem in his eyes."

"Thanks, Guido," she sez, layin' a hand on my arm. "I try to impress him, but sometimes I think . . ."

She breaks off and looks away, and it occurs to me that she is about to commence leakin' at the eyes. In an effort to avert this occurrence which will undoubtedly embarrass us both, I wrench the conversation back to our original topic.

"So what are they goin' to do with this bum now that you caught him?"

"Nothing."

"Say what?"

"No, that's not right. He's going to get a promotion."

"Get outta here!"

She turns back, and I can see she's now got an impish grin on, which is a welcome change.

"Really. It turns out he's the owner's brother-in-law. The owner is so impressed with the smarts it took to set up this scam that he's giving the little creep a higher position in the organization. I guess he wants him stealing for the company instead of from it."

It takes me several moments to realize that my normally agile mouth is stuck in the open position.

"So where does that leave us?" I manage at last.

"With a successful investigation under our belts along with a fat bonus for resolving the thing so fast. I've got a hunch, though, that part of that bonus is gag money to ensure we don't spread it around that the owner was being flimflammed by his own brother-in-law."

Now I am indeed glad that we have resolved the pilferage assignment without implicatin' any of the worker types I have been buddies with, but at the same time I am realizin' that with the job over, I will not be around to help them out when the Doggie Doodle hits the fan.

"Well, that's that, I guess. We'd better report in to the Boss and see what's been happenin' while we've been gone."

"Is something wrong, Guido? You seem a little down."

"Aaah! It's nothin', Bunny. Just thinkin' that I'll miss some of the guys back at the plant, is all."

"Maybe not," she sez, real mysterious like.

Now it's my turn to give her the hairy eyeball.

"Now, Bunny," I sez, "if you've got sumpin' up your sleeve other than lint, I would suggest you share it with me. You know I am not good when it comes to surprises."

"Well, I was going to wait until we got back home, but I suppose it won't hurt to give you a preview."

She looks around like there might be someone listenin' in, then hunches forward so I can hear her whisper.

"I picked up a rumor back at the plant office that there may be a union forming at the magic factory. I'm going to suggest to Skeeve that we do a little prospecting . . . you know, put in a bid. Can you imagine what we could charge for breaking up a union?"

I develop a sudden interest in the ceiling.

"Uh, Bunny?" I sez. "I know you want to impress the Boss with how good you are at findin' work for us, but I think in the longer run that it would be in the best interests of M.Y.T.H. Inc. to pass on this particular caper."

"But why? The owner stands to lose ten times as much if a union forms than he was dropping to embezzlement. We could make a real killing here. He already knows our work."

In response, I lean back and give her a slow smile.

"When it comes to makin' a killin', Bunny, I would advise you not to try to teach your grandmother, which in this case is me, how to steal sheep. Furthermore, there are times when it is wisest not to let the client know too much about your work . . . and trust me, Bunny, this is one such time!"

II:

"It all hinges on your definition of 'a good time'!"

—L. BORGIA

An outside agitator and a union organizer! And to
... think I was paying him to slit my throat!!"

I somehow managed to keep a straight face, which was
harder than it sounds.

"Actually, Mr. Bane, I was paying him to help uncover
the source of your inventory leak, which he did, and you
were paying him to work in your factory, which he also
did. I'm not sure exactly what it is that you're complaining about."

For a moment I thought the Deveel was going to come
across the desk at my throat.

"What I'm complaining about is that your so-called
agent organized a union in my factory that's costing me
a bundle!"

"There's no proof he was involved. . . ."

"So how come his name comes up every time. . . ."

". . . And even if he was, I'm not sure what concern it
is of mine. I run a business, Mr. Bane, with employees,

not slaves. What they do on their off hours is their affair, not mine."

"But he was acting as your agent!!!"

". . . To investigate the pilferage problem, which, I'm told, has been settled."

As we were speaking, Chumley poked his head into my office, saw what was going on, and came in all the way, shifting to his big bad troll persona as he did. In case you are wondering, I was working without a receptionist at the time, having deemed it wise to have both Bunny and Guido lie low for a while after finding out what had *really* happened on their last assignment. As an additional precaution, I had insisted that they hide out separately, since I was afraid that Bunny would kill Guido if they were alone within an arm's reach of each other. For some reason my secretary seemed to take Guido's labor activities very personally.

". . . Now, if you'll excuse me, Mr. Bane, I'm rather busy at the moment. If you wish to pursue the matter further, I suggest you take it up with Big Crunch here. He usually handles the complaints for our company."

The Deveel started to speak angrily as he glanced behind him, then did a double-take and swallowed whatever it was he was about to say as his gaze went up . . . and up! As I can testify from firsthand experience, trolls can look very large when viewed from up close.

"Little Deveel want to fight with Big Crunch? Crunch likes to fight!"

Bane pinked slightly, then turned back to me.

"Now look, Sk . . . Mr. Skeeve. All that's in the past, right? What say we talk about what your outfit can do to help me with this labor thing?"

I leaned back in my chair and put my hand behind my head.

"Not interested, Mr. Bane. Labor disputes are not our forte. If you'd like a little free advice, though, I'd advise you to settle. Prolonged strikes can be very costly."

The Deveel started to bare his teeth, then glanced at

Chumley again and twisted it into a smile. In fact, he didn't say another word until he reached the door, and even then he spoke with careful respect.

"Um . . . if it ain't asking too much, could you send this Guido around, just to say hi to the workers? What with him disappearing the way he did, there are some who are saying that I had him terminated. It might make things a little easier for me in the negotiations."

"I'll ask him . . . next time I see him."

The Deveel nodded his thanks and left.

"Bit of a sticky wicket, eh, Skeeve?" Chumley said, relaxing back into his normal self.

"Just another satisfied customer of M.Y.T.H. Inc. stopping by to express his gratitude," I sighed. "Remind me not to send Guido out on assignment again without *very* explicit instructions. Hmmmm?"

"How about a muzzle and leash?"

I shook my head and sat forward in my chair again, glancing over the paperwork that seemed to breed on my desk whenever Bunny was away.

"Enough of that. What can I do for you, Chumley?"

"Hmm? Oh, nothing, really. I was just looking for little sister to see if she wanted to join me for lunch. Has she been about?"

"Tananda? As a matter of fact, I just sent her out on an assignment. Sorry."

"No matter. What kind of work are you giving the old girl, anyway?"

"Oh, nothing big," I said, rummaging through the paper for the letter I had been reading when Bane burst in. "Just a little collection job a few dimensions over."

"ARE YOU OUT OF YOUR BLOODY MIND??!!!"

Chumley was suddenly leaning over my desk, his two moon eyes of different sizes scant inches from my own. It occurred to me that I had never seen the troll really angry. Upon viewing it, I sincerely hoped I would never see it again. That is, of course, assuming I could survive the first time.

"Whoa! Chumley! Calm! What's wrong?"

"YOU SENT HER OUT ON A COLLECTION JOB ALONE?"

"She should be all right," I said hastily. "It sounded like a pretty calm mission. In fact, that's why I sent her instead of one of our heavy hitters . . . I thought the job called for finesse, not muscle. Besides, Tananda can take care of herself pretty well."

The troll groaned and let his head fall forward until it thudded on my desk. He stayed that way for a few moments, breathing deeply, before he spoke.

"Skeeve . . . Skeeve . . . Skeeve. I keep forgetting how new you are to our little family."

This was starting to get me worried.

"C'mon, Chumley, what's wrong? Tananda will be okay, won't she?"

The troll raised his head to look at me.

"Skeeve, you don't realize . . . we all relax around you, but you never see us when you aren't around."

Terrific.

"Look, Chumley. Your logic is as enviable as ever, but can't you just say what the problem is? If you think Tananda's in danger . . ."

"SHE'S NOT THE ONE I'M WORRIED ABOUT!"

With visible effort, Chumley composed himself.

"Skeeve . . . let me try to explain. Little sister is a wonderful person, and I truly love and admire her, but she has a tendency to . . . overreact under pressure. Mum always said it was her competitive reaction to having an older brother who could tear things apart without trying, but some of the people she's worked with tend to simply describe it as a mean streak. In a nutshell, though, Tananda has a bigger flair for wanton destruction than I do . . . or anyone else I've ever met. Now, if this job you're describing calls for finesse . . ."

He broke off and shook his head.

"No," he said with a ring of finality to his voice.

"There's no other way to handle it. I'll just have to catch up with her and try to keep her from getting too out of hand. Which dimension did you say she was headed for again?"

The direct question finally snapped me out of the mind-freeze his explanation had put me in.

"Really, Chumley. Aren't you exaggerating just a little? I mean, how much trouble could she cause?"

The troll sighed.

"Ever hear of a dimension called Rinasp?"

"Can't say that I have."

"That's because there's no one there anymore. That's the last place little sister went on a collection job."

"I've got the name of the dimension here somewhere!" I said, diving into my paperwork with newfound desperation.

Chumley's Tale

Dash it all to blazes anyway! You'd think by now that Skeeve would have the sense to look a bit before he leaped . . . especially when his leaping tends to involve others as it does! If he thinks that Tananda can't . . . If he can't figure out that even I don't . . . Well, he has no idea of the way our Mum raised us, is all I've got to say.

Of course, one cannot expect wonders from a Klahd raised by a Pervert, can one . . . hmmm?? Well, Chumley old boy, time to muddle through one more time, what?

I must admit this latest collection assignment for Tananda had me worried. At her best little sister tends to lack tact, and lately . . .

As near as I can tell, there was bad blood building between her and Bunny. They had never really hit it off well, but things had gotten noticeably sticky since Don Bruce's niece set her cap for Skeeve. Not that little sister had any designs on the lad herself, mind you. If anything, her feelings toward him are more sisterly than anything else . . . Lord help him. Rather it seems that it's Bunny's tactics that are setting Tananda's teeth on edge.

You see, what with Bunny trying to be so spit-spot efficient on the job to impress Skeeve, little sister has gotten it into her head that it's making *her* look bad professionally. Tananda has always been exceedingly proud of her looks and her work, and what with Bunny strutting around the office going on about how well the last assignment went, she feels a wee bit threatened on both counts. As near as I could tell, she was bound and determined to prove that what she had picked up in the Guttersnipe Survival School was more than a match for the education Bunny had acquired at whatever finishing school the Mob had sent her to. Combined with her normal tendency for over-exuberance, it boded ill for whoever it was she was out to collect from.

I was also underwhelmed by the setting for this pending disaster. I mean, really, what kind of name is Arcadia for a dimension? It sounds like one of those confounded video parlors. I probably would have been hard-pressed to even find it if I hadn't gotten directions along with the name. The coordinates dropped me at the edge of a town, and since they were the same ones little sister had used, I could only assume I wasn't far behind her.

At first viewing, Arcadia seemed pleasant enough; one might almost be tempted to call it quaint—the kind of quiet, sleepy place where one could relax and feel at home. For some reason, I found myself fervently hoping it would be the same when we left.

My casual inspection of the surroundings was cut short by a hail from nearby.

"Welcome to Arcadia, Stranger. Can I offer you a cool glass of juice?"

The source of this greeting was a rather gnomish old man who was perched on the seat of a tricycle vending cart. He seemed to take my appearance, both my physical makeup and my presence at this time and place, so casually I almost replied before remembering that I had a front to maintain. It's a bit of a bother, but I've found no one will hire a well-mannered troll.

"Good! Good! Crunch thirsty!"

With my best guttural growl, I grabbed two of the offered glasses and popped them in my mouth, rolling my eyes as I chewed happily. It's a good bit . . . one that seldom fails to take folks aback. The gnome, however, never batted an eye.

"Don't think I've seen you before, Stranger. What brings you to Arcadia?"

I decided to abandon any further efforts at intimidating him and instead got right to the point.

"Crunch looking for friend. Seen little woman . . . so high . . . with green hair?"

"As a matter of fact, she was just by a little bit ago. She a friend of yours?"

I nodded my head vigorously and showed my fangs.

"Crunch likes little woman. Pulled thorn from Crunch's foot once. Where little woman go?"

"Well, she asked me where the police station was, then took off in that direction . . . that way."

An awfully nice chap, really. I decided I could afford to unbend a little.

"Crunch thanks nice man. If nice man needs strong friend, call Crunch, okay?"

"Sure thing. And if I can help you any more, just give a holler."

I left then before we got too chummy. I mean, there are precious few people who will be civil, much less nice, to a troll, and I was afraid of getting more interested in continuing my conversation with him than with finding Tananda. For the good of Arcadia, that would never do.

As it was, I guess my little chat had taken longer than I had realized, for when I found Tananda she was sitting dejectedly on the steps of the police station, her business inside apparently already concluded. Things must have gone better than I had dared hope, as she was not incarcerated, and the building was still standing.

"What ho, little sister," I called, as cheerily as I could manage. "You look a little down at the mouth. Problems?"

"Oh. Hi . . . Chumley? What are you doing here?"

Fortunately, I had anticipated this question and had my answer well rehearsed.

"Just taking a bit of a holiday. I promised Aahz I would stop by this dimension and check out a few potential investments, and when Skeeve said you were here as well, I thought I would stop by and see how you were doing."

"That can be summarized in one word," she said, resting her chin in her hands once more. "Lousy."

"Run into a spot of trouble? Come, come. Tell big brother all about it."

She gave a little shrug.

"There's not all that much to tell. I'm here on a collection assignment, so I thought I'd check with the local gendarmes to see if this guy had a record or if they knew where he was."

"And . . ." I prompted.

"Well, they know who he is all right. It seems he's a wealthy philanthropist . . . has given millions for civic improvements, helps the poor, that kind of stuff."

I scratched my head and frowned.

"Doesn't sound like the sort of chap to leave a bill unpaid, does he?"

"The real problem is going to be how to check it out. It seems he's also a bit of a recluse. No one's seen him for years."

I could see why she was depressed. It didn't sound like the kind of chore that could be finished in record time, which is, of course, what she wanted to do to make a good showing.

"Could be a bit of a sticky wicket. Who is this chap, anyway?"

"The name is Hoos. Sounds like something out of Dr. Seuss, doesn't it?"

"Actually, it sounds like a bank."

"How's that again?"

Instead of repeating myself, I simply pointed. Across the street and three doors down was a building prominently labeled Hoos National Bank.

Tananda was on her feet and moving in a flash.

"Thanks, Chumley. This may not be so bad after all."

"Don't forget. We're terribly close to the police station," I cautioned, hurrying to keep up.

"What do you mean, 'we'?" she said, stopping abruptly. "This is *my* assignment, big brother, so don't interfere or get underfoot. Capish?"

Realizing I was here to try to keep her out of trouble, I thought it ill-advised to start a brawl with Tananda in the middle of a public street, much less in front of a police station.

"Perish the thought. I just thought I'd tag along . . . as an observer. You know I love watching you work. Besides, as Mums always said, 'You can never tell when a friendly witness can come in handy.'"

I'm not sure if my words assured her, or if she simply accepted that a confirming report wouldn't hurt, but she grunted silently and headed into the bank.

The place was pretty standard for a bank: tellers' cages, tables for filling out deposit or withdrawal slips, etc. The only thing that was at all noteworthy was a special window for Inter-Dimensional Currency Exchange, which to me indicated that they did more demon business than might be expected for such an out-of-the-way dimension. I was going to point this out to Tananda, but she apparently had plans of her own. Without so much as a glance at the windows, she marched up to the manager's office.

"May I help you, Miss?" the twitty-looking fellow seated there said with a notable lack of sincerity.

"Yes. I'd like to see Mr. Hoos."

That got us a long, slow once-over with the weak eyes, his gaze lingering on me for several extra beats. I did my best to look innocent . . . which is not that easy to do for a troll.

"I'm afraid that's quite impossible," he said at last,

returning his attention to the work on his desk.

I could sense Tananda fighting with her temper and mentally crossed my fingers.

"It's extremely urgent."

The eyes flicked our way again, and he set his pencil down with a visible sigh.

"Then perhaps you'd better deal with me."

"I have some information for Mr. Hoos, but I think he'd want to hear it personally."

"That's your opinion. If, after hearing it, I agree, then you might be allowed to repeat it to Mr. Hoos."

Stalemate.

Tananda seemed to recognize this as well.

"Well, I don't want to start a panic, but I have it on good authority that this bank is going to be robbed."

I was a little surprised by this, though I did my best not to show it. The bank manager, however, seemed to take it in stride.

"I'm afraid you're mistaken, young lady," he said with a tight smile.

"My sources are seldom wrong," she insisted.

"You're new to Arcadia, aren't you?"

"Well . . ."

"Once you've learned your way around, you'll realize that there isn't a criminal in the dimension who would steal from Mr. Hoos, much less try to rob his bank."

This Hoos chap was starting to sound like quite a fellow. Little sister, however, was not so easily deterred.

"What about a criminal from another dimension? Someone who isn't so impressed with Mr. Hoos?"

The manager raised an eyebrow.

"Like who, for example?"

"Well . . . what if I and my friend here decided to . . ."

That was as far as she got.

For all his stuffiness, I had to admit the manager was good. I didn't see him move or signal, but suddenly the bank was filled with armed guards. For some reason, their attention seemed to be centered on us.

I nudged Tananda, but she waved me off irritably.

". . . Of course, that was simply a 'what if.' "

"Of course," the manager smiled, without humor. "I believe our business is concluded. Good day."

"But . . ."

"I said 'Good day.' "

With that he returned to his work, ignoring us completely.

It would have been bordering on lunacy to try to take on the whole room full of guards. I was therefore startled to realize little sister was starting to contemplate that very action. As casually as I could, I started whistling Gilbert and Sullivan's "A Policeman's Lot Is Not a Happy One" as a gentle reminder of the police station not half a block away. Tananda gave me a look that would curdle cream, but she got the message and we left without further ado.

"Now what, little sister?" I said, as tactfully as I could manage.

"Isn't it obvious?"

I thought about that for a few moments.

"No," I admitted frankly. "Seems to me you've come up against a dead end."

"Then you weren't listening in there," she said, giving me one of her smug grins. "The manager gave me a big clue for where to try next."

". . . And that was?"

"Don't you remember he said no criminal would rob this Hoos guy?"

"Quite. So?"

". . . So if there's a criminal connection here, I should be able to get some information out of the underworld."

That sounded a tad ominous to me, but I have long since learned not to argue with Tananda when she gets her mind set on something. Instead, I decided to try a different approach.

"Not to be a noodge," I noodged, "but how do you propose to find said underworld? They don't exactly list in the yellow pages, you know."

Her pace slowed noticeably.

"That's a problem," she admitted. "Still, there must be a way to get information around . . ."

"Can I offer you a glass of cold juice, Miss?"

It was my friend from the morning with his vending cart. A part of me wanted to wave him off, as interrupting little sister in mid-scheme is not the healthiest of pastimes, but I couldn't think of a way to do it without breaking character. Tananda surprised me, however. Instead of removing his head at the waist for breaking into her thought process, she turned her most dazzling smile on him.

"Well, hi there!" she purred. "Say, I never did get a chance to thank you for giving me directions to the police station this morning."

Now, little sister's smiles can be devastating to the nervous system of anyone of the male gender, and this individual was no exception.

"Don't mention it," he flushed. "If there's anything else I can do to be of assistance . . ."

"Oh, there is one teensy-tiny favor you could do for me."

Her eyelashes fluttered like mad, and the vendor melted visibly.

"Name it."

"Wellll . . . could you tell me where I could find a hardened criminal or five? You see, I'm new here and don't know a soul I could ask."

I thought this was a little tacky and fully expected the vendor to refuse the information in a misdirected attempt to shelter the pretty girl from evil influences. The old boy seemed to take it in stride, however.

"Criminals, eh?" he said, rubbing his chin. "Haven't had much dealings with that sort for a while. When I did, though, they could usually be found down at the Suspended Sentence."

"The what?"

"The Suspended Sentence. It's a combination tavern/inn. The owner opened it after getting off a pretty sticky trial. It seems the judge wasn't wrong in letting him go, since he's gone straight, as far as I can tell, but there's a bad element that hangs out there. I think they figure some of the good luck might rub off on them."

Tananda punched me lightly in the ribs and winked.

"Well, that sounds like my next stop. Where'd you say this place was, old timer?"

"Just a couple of blocks down the street there, then turn left up the alley. You can't miss it."

"Hey, thanks. You've been a big help, really."

"Don't mention it. Sure you wouldn't like some juice?"

"Maybe later. Right now I'm in a hurry."

The old man shook his head at her retreating back.

"That's the trouble with folks today. Everybody's in such a hurry. Don't you agree, big fella?"

Again I found myself torn between entering a conversation with this likable chap and watching over little sister. As always, family loyalty won out.

"Ahh . . . Big Crunch in hurry too. Will talk with little man later."

"Sure. Anytime. I'm usually around."

He waved goodbye, and I waved back as I hurried after Tananda.

Little sister seemed quite preoccupied when I caught up with her, so I deemed it wisest to keep silent as I fell in beside her. I assumed she was planning out her next move . . . at least, until she spoke.

"Tell me, big brother," she said, without looking at me. "What do you think of Bunny?"

Now Mums didn't raise any stupid children. Just Tananda and me. It didn't take any great mental gymnastics to figure out that perhaps this was not the best time to sing great praises of little sister's rival. Still, I would feel less than truthful, not to mention a little disloyal, if I gave false testimony when queried directly.

"Um . . . well, there's no denying she's attractive."

Tananda nodded her agreement.

". . . In a cheap, shallow sort of way, I suppose," she acknowledged.

"Of course," I said carefully, "she does have a little problem with overachievement."

"A *little* problem! Chumley, you have a positive talent for understatement. Bunny's one of the pushiest bitches I know."

I was suddenly quite glad I had not verbalized my thought comparing Bunny's overachievement problem with little sister's. I somehow doubted Tananda was including herself in her inventory of pushy bitches. Still, there was one more point I wanted to test the ice with.

"Then again, her performance may be influenced by her infatuation with Skeeve."

At this, Tananda lashed out with her hand at a signpost we were passing, which took on a noticeable tilt. Though she isn't as strong as yours truly, little sister still packs a wallop . . . especially when she's mad.

"That's the part that really grinds me," she snarled. "If she thinks she can just waltz in out of left field and take over Skeeve . . . I was about to say she'd have to do it over my dead body, but it might give her ideas. I don't really want to have tasters munching on my food before I enjoy it. She's got another think coming, is all I've got to say!"

I gave her my longest innocent stare.

"Why, little sister!" I said. "You sound positively jealous. I had no idea you entertained any romantic designs on Skeeve yourself."

That slowed her pace a tad.

"Well, I don't, really. It's just that . . . blast it, Chumley, we helped raise Skeeve and make him what he is today. You'd think he could do better than some primping gold digger from Mobdom."

"And just what is he? Hmmm?"

Tananda shot me a look.

"I'm not sure I follow you there, big brother."

"Take a good look at what it is we've raised. Right

now Skeeve is one of the hottest, most successful magician/businessmen in the Bazaar. Who exactly do you expect him to take up with for female companionship? Massha? A scullery maid? Maybe one of the vendors or come-on girls?"

"Well, no."

I had a full head of steam now. Tananda and I rarely talk seriously, and when we do it usually involves her dressing me down for some indiscretion or other. I wasn't about to let her slip away on this one.

"Of course Skeeve is going to start drawing attention from some pretty high-powered husband hunters. Whether we like it or not, the lad's growing up . . . and others are bound to notice, even if you haven't. In all honesty, little sister, if you met him today for the first time instead of having known him for years, wouldn't you find him a tempting morsel?"

"He's still a little young for me, but I see your point . . . and I don't tumble for just anybody."

"Since when?" I said, but I said it very quietly.

Tananda gave me a hard look, and for a moment I thought she had heard me.

"To hear you talk," she frowned, "I'd almost think you were in favor of a Bunny/Skeeve match-up."

"Her or somebody like her. Face it, little sister, the lad isn't likely to tie onto some nice, polite, 'girl-next-door' sort with his current life-style . . . and if he managed to, the rest of us would eat her alive in crackerjack time."

Tananda's pace slowed to almost a standstill.

"You mean that hanging around with us is ruining Skeeve's social life? Is that what you're trying to say?"

I wanted to take her by her shoulders and shake her, but even my gentlest shakes can be rather violent and I didn't want to get arrested for an attempted mugging. Instead, I settled for facing her with my sternest expression.

"Now, don't go all maudlin on me. What I'm trying to say is that Skeeve is used to associating with heavy hitters, so it's going to take a tougher-than-average lady fair to be comfortable around him, and vice versa. He'd be miserable with someone like that Luanna person."

"What's wrong with Luanna?"

I shrugged and resumed our stroll, forcing Tananda to keep up.

"Oh, she's pretty enough, I suppose. But she's a small-time swindler who's so shortsighted she'd sell him out at the first hint of trouble. In short, she'd be an anchor around his neck who would keep him from climbing and potentially drag him down. If we're going to fix the lad up with a swindler, she should at least be a big-league swindler . . . like, say, a certain someone we know who has the Mob for a dowry."

That at least got a laugh out of Tananda, and I knew we had weathered the storm.

"Chumley, you're incredible! And I thought women were manipulative matchmakers. I never realized it before, but you're a bit of a snob, big brother."

"Think yew," I said in my best clipped accent. "I accept that observation with pride . . . when I consider the alternatives. I feel everyone would prefer to be snobs if they ever really had the choice."

"Why are we stopping?"

"Well, if we're done deciding Master Skeeve's future for the moment, I believe we have a spot of business to attend to."

She looked where I was pointing and found we were indeed standing in front of a dubious-looking establishment, embellished with a faded sign which proclaimed it to be the Suspended Sentence. The windows that weren't painted over were broken or gone completely, revealing a darkened interior. It might have been an abandoned building if it weren't for the definite sounds of conversation and laughter issuing forth from within.

Tananda started forward, then halted in her tracks.

"Wait a minute, big brother. What did you mean, 'we'?"

"Well, I thought that since I was here, I'd just . . ."

"Wrong," she said firmly. "This is still my assignment, Chumley, and I'm quite capable of handling it by myself."

"Oh, I wouldn't breathe a word."

"No, you'd just loom over everybody with that snaggletoothed grin of yours and intimidate them into cooperating with me. Well, you can just wait out here while I go in alone. I'll do my own intimidating, if you don't mind."

This was exactly the sort of thing I was afraid of.

"It would be less brutal if I were along," I argued weakly.

"Why, big brother," she said with a wink. "A little brutality never bothered me. I thought you knew that."

Outflanked and outmaneuvered, I had no choice but to lean against the wall and watch as she marched into the tavern.

"Oh, I know, little sister," I sighed. "Believe me, I know."

Though forbidden to take active part in the proceedings, I was understandably curious and kept one ear cocked to try to ascertain what was happening from the sound effects. I didn't have long to wait.

The undercurrent of conversation we had noted earlier ceased abruptly as Tananda made her entrance. A pregnant pause followed, then there was a murmured comment prompting a sharp bark of laughter.

I closed my eyes.

What happened next was so preordained as to be choreographed. I recognized little sister's voice raised in query, answered by another laugh. Then came the unmistakable sound of furniture breaking. No, that's not quite right. Actually, the noise indicated the furniture was being smashed, as in swung quickly and forcefully until an immovable object was encountered . . . like a head, for example.

The outcries were louder now, ranging from indignation to anger, punctuated by breaking glass and other such cacophonies. Years of hanging around with Tananda had

trained my ear, so I amused myself by trying to catalogue
the damage by its sound.

That was a table going over . . .

. . . Another chair. . . .

. . . A mirror (wonder how she missed the
glasses?). . . .

. . . That was definitely a bone breaking. . . .

. . . Someone's head hitting the bar, the side, I
think. . . .

. . . *There* go the glasses. . . .

A body hurtled through the plate-glass window next to
me and bounced once on the sidewalk before coming to
a halt in a limp heap . . . a fairly good-sized one, too.

Unless I was mistaken, little sister was resorting to
magic in this brawl or else she wouldn't have gotten that
extra bounce on a horizontal throw. Either that or she was
really annoyed! I debated whether or not to chide her for
breaking our unwritten rules regarding no magic in bar-
room brawls, but decided to let it slide. On the off chance
that she was simply overly perturbed, such comment
would only invite retaliation, and Tananda can be quite a
handful even when she isn't steaming.

By this time, the din inside had ceased and an ominous
stillness prevailed. I figured it was jolly well time I
checked things out, so I edged my way along the wall and
peeked through the door.

With the exception of one lonely chair which seemed
to have escaped unscathed, the place was a wreck with
everything in splinters or tatters. Bodies, limp or moaning,
were strewn casually about the wreckage, giving the overall effect of a battlefield after a hard fight . . . which, of
course, it was.

The only surprising element in the scene was Tananda.
Instead of proudly surveying the carnage, as was her normal habit, she was leaning against the bar chatting quietly
with the bartender. This puzzle was rapidly solved, as the
individual in question glanced up and saw my rather dis-
tinctive features in the doorway.

"Hey, Chumley! Come join us in a drink to my long-overdue remodeling."

Tananda glanced my way sharply, then nodded her approval.

"Come on in, big brother. You'll never guess who owns this dive."

"I think I just figured it out, actually," I said, helping myself to a drink from a broken bottle that was perched on the bar. "Hello, Weasel. Bit of a ways from your normal prowl grounds, aren't you?"

"Not anymore," he shrugged. "This is home sweet home these days. Can't think of anyplace else I've been that would let me operate as a respectable businessman."

Tananda gagged slightly on her drink.

"A respectable businessman? C'mon, Weasel. This is Tananda and Chumley you're talking to. How long have we known you? I don't believe you've had an honest thought that whole time."

Weasel shook his head sadly.

"Look around you, sweetheart. This is my place . . . or at least it used to be. Been running it fair and square for some time now. It may not be as exciting as my old lifestyle, but it's easily as profitable since I never lose any time in the slammer."

Little sister was opening her mouth to make another snide remark when I elbowed her in the ribs. While I'm not above a bit of larceny myself from time to time, I figured that if Weasel genuinely wanted to go straight, the least we could do is not give him a hard time about it.

"So tell me, old chap," I said. "What brought about this amazing reform? A good woman or a bad caper?"

"Neither, actually. The way it was, see, was that I was framed . . . no, really, this time. I hadn't done a thing, but all the evidence had me pegged for being guilty as sin. I thought I had really had it, but this guy pops up and backs me hard. I mean, he springs for a really good mouthpiece, and when the jury finds me guilty anyway, he talks to the judge and gets me a suspended sentence. As if that weren't enough, after I'm loose again, he spots me the cash I need to start this place . . . a nice no-interest loan. 'Pay it back when you can,' he sez. I'll tell you, I ain't never had anybody believe in me like that before. Kinda made me think things over about how I was always saying that I had to be a crook 'cause no one would give me a fair shake. Well, sir, I decided to give the honest life a try . . . and haven't regretted it yet."

"This mysterious benefactor you mentioned . . . his name wouldn't happen to be Hoos, would it?"

"That's right, Chumley. Easily the finest man I've ever met. You see, I'm not the only one he's helped out. Most of the people in this dimension have had some kind of hand up from him at one time or another. I'm not surprised you've heard of him."

Tananda trotted out her best smile.

"That brings us to why I'm here, Weasel. I'm trying to find this Hoos character, and so far the locals haven't been very helpful. Can you give me an introduction, or at least point me in a direction?"

The smile that had been on Weasel's face disappeared as if he had just been told he was left out of a rich uncle's will. His eyes lost their focus, and he licked his lips nervously.

"Sorry, Tananda," he said. "Can't help you there."

"Wait a minute, old buddy." Tananda's smile was a little forced now. "You must know where to find him. Where do you make your payments on this place?"

"Made the last payment half a year ago. Now if you'll excuse me . . ."

Tananda had him by the sleeve before he could take a step.

"You're holding out on me, Weasel," she snarled, abandoning any attempt at sweetness. "Now either you tell me where I can find this Hoos character or I'll . . ."

"You'll what? Wreck the place? You're a little late there, sweetheart. You want the last chair, be my guest. It doesn't match the rest of the decor now, anyway."

From little sister's expression, I was pretty sure what she was thinking of destroying wasn't the chair, so I thought I'd better get my oar in before things got completely out of hand.

"If you don't mind my asking, old chap, is there any particular reason you're being so obstinate over a simple request?"

Tananda gave me one of her "stay out of this" looks, but Weasel didn't seem to mind the interruption.

"Are you kidding?" he said. "Maybe you weren't listening, but I owe this guy . . . a lot more than just paying back a loan. He gave me a chance to start over when everybody else had written me off. I'm supposed to show my appreciation by setting a couple of goons on his trail?"

"Goons?"

She said it very softly, but I don't think anyone in the room mistook Tananda's meaning. In fact, a few of her earlier playmates who were still conscious started crawling toward the door in an effort to put more distance between themselves and the pending explosion.

Weasel, however, remained uncowed.

"Yeah, goons. What happened in here a few minutes ago? An ice-cream social?"

"He's got you there, little sister."

That brought her head around with a snap.

"Shut up, Chumley!" she snarled. "This is my assignment. Remember?"

"Wouldn't have it any other way. I do think Weasel has a point, though. You really don't give the impression of someone who wants a peaceful chat."

At first I thought she was going to go for my throat. Then she took a deep breath and blew it out slowly.

"Point taken," she said, releasing her grip. "Weasel, I really just want to talk to this guy Hoos. No rough stuff, I promise."

The bartender pursed his lips.

"I don't know, Tananda. I'd like to believe you. I suppose if Chumley says it's on the up-and-up . . ."

That did it. Tananda spun on her heel and headed for the door.

"If it takes Chumley's say-so, then forget it. Okay? I'll do this my way, without help, even if it kills someone."

"Hey, don't go away mad," Weasel called after her. "Tell you what I'll do. When the police ask what happened here, I'll keep your name out of it, okay? I'll just play dumb and collect from the insurance. It'll kill my rates, but . . ."

"Don't ruin your new record on my account. Total up the damages and I'll cover the cost personally."

With that she slammed out into the street, cutting off any further conversation.

"Is she kidding?" Weasel said. "It's gonna cost a bundle to fix this place up again."

"I really don't know, old boy. She's really mad, but by the same token, she's mad enough that I wouldn't cross her. If I were you, I'd start totaling up the damages. Eh, what?"

"I hear that," he nodded. "Well, you'd better get after her before she gets into trouble. Sorry to be such a hard case, but . . ."

"Tut, tut," I waved. "You've been more than generous, all things considered. Well, cheerio."

I had expected to have to repeat my earlier performance of catching up with little sister, but instead I found her sitting on the curb just outside the bar. Now, she's not one to cry, either from anger or frustration, but seeing her there with her shoulders hunched and her chin in her hands, I realized that this might be one of those rare times.

"I say, you're really taking this quite hard, aren't you?" I said, as gently as I could.

She didn't look around.

"It's just that . . . oh, pook! Weasel's right, and so are you. I've been charging around like a bull in a china shop, and all that's been accomplished is that even my friends won't help me out. Bunny'll never let me forget it if I can't even pull off a simple collection assignment."

Squatting beside her, I put a reassuring arm around her shoulders.

"I think that may be your problem, little sister. You're trying so hard to set a speed record to impress Bunny that you're rushing things . . . even for you. Now, I suggest that we retire someplace and think things through a bit, hmmm? Forget about getting the job done fast and just concentrate on getting it done."

That perked her up a bit, and she even managed a weak smile.

"Okay," she said. "Even though I still want to handle this on my own, I suppose there's nothing wrong with using you for a consultant since you're here. What I really feel like right now is a stiff drink to settle me down. I don't suppose you've spotted anyplace besides the Suspended Sentence where we could . . ."

"Care for a glass of juice?"

We looked up to find the old boy with his vending cart smiling down on us. For a moment I was afraid that Tananda would snap at him, but she gave him a grin that was far more sincere than her earlier smile.

"Thanks, but I had something stronger in mind. And while we're on the subject of thanks, I appreciate the information you gave me earlier . . . the second time, that is. I guess I was in too much of a hurry before to remember my manners."

"Don't mention it. It seems like most folks are in a hurry these days. Me, I always felt you should take your time and enjoy things. We've all got so little time, the least we should do is savor what time we have."

Tananda smiled at him with genuine warmth instead of her usual manipulative heat.

"That's good advice," she said. "I'll try to remember it. Come on, Chumley. We've got some planning to do . . . slow and careful planning, that is."

"Well, just holler if I can be of any help."

"Thanks, but what we really need is someone who can

put us in touch with Mr. Hoos. I don't suppose you'd happen to know where I could find him?"

"Oh, that's easy."

"It is?"

I think we said it simultaneously. It was that kind of a surprise.

"Sure. Just stand up, blink three times, and he'll be right here."

That sounded a bit balmy to me, and for the first time I started doubting the old boy's sanity. Little sister, however, seemed to take him seriously. She was on her feet in the blink of an eye, blinking furiously.

"Well?" she said, peering around.

"Pleased to meet you, Missy. My name's Hoos. What's yours?"

We gaped at him . . . it seemed to be the logical thing to do at the time.

"You!?" Tananda managed at last. "Why didn't you say something before?"

"Didn't know until now it was me you were looking for."

It was really none of my business, but I had to ask.

"Just out of curiosity, why was it necessary for little sister to blink three times?"

As I spoke, I realized I had forgotten to use my Big Crunch speech patterns. Hoos didn't seem to notice.

"Wasn't, really. It's just you've been working so hard to find me, I thought I should throw in a little something to keep the meeting from being too anti-climactic. So, what can I do for you?"

There was a gleam of mischievousness in the old boy's eye that led me to believe he wasn't as daft as he would like people to believe. Tananda missed it, though, as she fumbled a battered sheet of paper out of her tunic.

"Mr. Hoos," she said briskly. "I'm here representing a client who claims you owe him money on this old account. I was wondering when he could expect payment, or if you would like to set up a schedule for regular submissions?"

Hoos took the paper from her and studied it casually.

"Well, I'll be . . . I could have sworn I wrote him a check on this the next day."

"He did say something about a check being returned," Tananda conceded.

"Must of held onto it until I closed out. Darn! I thought I had covered everything."

"You closed out the account with the bank?"

Hoos winked at her.

"No, I closed out the bank. That was back when I was consolidating my holdings."

"Oh. Well, as I was saying, if you'd like to set up a payment schedule . . ."

He waved a hand at her and opened the top of his vending cart. From my height advantage, I could see that the bottom of it was filled with gold coins.

"Why don't we just settle up now?" he said. "I've got a little cold cash with me . . . get it? Cold cash? Let's see, you'll be wanting some interest on that . . ."

"MR. HOOS!"

We turned to find the bank manager striding rapidly toward us.

"I thought we agreed that you'd handle all your transactions through the bank! Carrying cash is an open invitation to the criminal element, remember?"

"What kind of a shakedown is going on here?" Weasel demanded, emerging from the door behind us. "This sure doesn't look like a friendly chat to me!"

A crowd was starting to form around us as people on the street drifted over and shopkeepers emerged from their stores. None of them looked particularly happy . . . or friendly.

"I know you want to handle this yourself, little sister," I murmured. "Would you mind if I at least showed my fangs to back some of this rabble off a ways? I want to get out of here alive, too."

"NOW JUST HOLD ON, *EVERYBODY*!"

Hoos was standing on the seat of his vending cart holding up restraining hands to the mob.

"This little lady has a legitimate bill she's collecting for. That's all. Now just ease off and go back to whatever you were doing. Can't a man do a little business in private any more?"

That seemed to placate most of the onlookers, and they began to disperse slowly. Weasel and the bank manager didn't budge.

"Let me see that bill," the manager demanded. "Do you recall incurring this debt, Mr. Hoos?"

"Yes, I recall incurring this debt, Mr. Hoos," Hoos said, mimicking the manager's voice. "Now, if you don't mind, I'll just pay it and the matter will be settled."

"Well, this is most irregular. I don't know why they didn't simply follow regular channels and present their claim at the bank."

"We *did* stop by the bank," Tananda snapped. "All we got was a runaround."

The manager peered at her.

"Oh, yes. I remember," he drawled. "What I don't recall is your saying anything about submitting a claim for payment. There was some mention made of a bank robbery, though. Wasn't there?"

"You *were* moving a bit fast there, little sister," I chided gently.

"You mean to say you were working legit, Tananda?" Weasel chimed in. "Why didn't you say so in the first place?"

"I did! What's going on here, anyway, Weasel?"

"Mr. Hoos is a very rich man," the bank manager said. "He is also quite generous . . . sometimes too generous for his own good."

"It's my money, ain't it?" Hoos retorted. "Now, where were we? Oh, yes."

He started shoveling handfuls of coins into a paper bag.

". . . We were talking about interest on this bill. What

do you think would cover the trouble I've caused missing payment the way I did?"

"See what we mean?" Weasel said. "Mr. Hoos, any interest due should have been set at the time of the debt. Paying any more would be just giving your money away."

The bank manager gave us a weak excuse for an understanding smile.

"As you can see, many of us in this dimension who owe our good fortune to Mr. Hoos have taken it upon ourselves to protect him from unnecessary expense . . . not to mention from those who would seek to take advantage of his generosity."

". . . After you've benefited from that generosity yourself," I added innocently.

That got a cackle of laughter out of Hoos.

"That's right, Big Fella," he said. "Don't think too harshly of the boys, though. There's nothing quite as honest as a reformed criminal. Would you like me to tell you what the manager here was doing before I bailed him out?"

"I'd rather you didn't," the manager huffed, but there was a pleading note in his voice.

I saw that mischievous glint in the old boy's eyes again and found myself wondering for the first time who had *really* framed Weasel just before he decided to reform. I think little sister caught it too.

"I don't think any interest will be necessary, Mr. Hoos," she said, taking the bag from him. "I'm sure my client will be happy with the payment as is."

"Are you sure? Can't I give you a little something for your trouble?"

"Sorry. Company policy doesn't allow its agents to take tips. Weasel, you'll send me a bill for the damages to your place?"

"You got it, sweetheart," the bartender waved.

"There, now," Hoos said, reaching into his cart. "I can cover that expense for you, at least."

Tananda shook her head.

"It's baked into our operating budget. Really, Mr. Hoos, I'm already working legit. I really don't need any extra boosts. C'mon, Chumley. It's time we were going."

Waving goodbye to the others, I took my place beside her as she started the gyrations to blip us through to our home base on Deva.

"Perhaps I shouldn't mention it, little sister," I said softly, "but unless my eye for damage has deserted me completely, isn't that bill going to come to more than our company's share of the collection?"

"I said I'd cover it personally, and I will," she murmured back. "The important thing is that I've completed this assignment in record time . . . and if you say anything to Bunny about the damages, I'll make you wish you had never been born. Do we understand each other, big brother?"

III:

"It's all a matter of taste."

—B. MIDLER

I really have to compliment you, dear. It never ceases to amaze me how much you do with so little."

That was Bunny's comment following Tananda's report on her last assignment. I had asked her to sit in to take notes, and I had to admit she had been extremely attentive while Tananda was speaking . . . which was more than I managed to do. From the report, the assignment was so routine as to be dull, though I personally wanted to hear Chumley's side of it before I made any final judgments on that score. That particular troll, however, was nowhere to be found . . . a fact which made me more than a little suspicious. Bunny was as efficient as ever, though, covering for my wandering thoughts by providing compliments of her own.

"Why, thank you, Bunny," Tananda purred back. "It really means a lot to me to hear you say that, realizing how much you know about operating with minimal resources."

It occurred to me that it was nice that these two were getting along as well as they did. Our operation could be a real mess if the two of them took to feuding.

It also occurred to me that there were an awful lot of teeth showing for what was supposed to be a friendly meeting. I decided it was time to move on to other subjects before things got *too* friendly.

"Things have been pretty quiet around here while you've been gone, Tananda," I said. "Not much new at all. How about it, Bunny? Any new prospects we should know about?"

Bunny made a big show of consulting her note pad. Right away, this alerted me. You see, I know that Bunny keeps flawless notes in her head, and the only time she consults her pad is when she's stalling for time trying to decide whether or not to bring something to my attention. I may be slow, but I *do* learn.

"Welll . . ." she said slowly. "The only thing I show at all is an appointment with somebody named Hysterium."

"Hysterium? Why does that name sound familiar? Wait a minute. Didn't I see a letter from him about a week back?"

"That's right. He's a land speculator and developer who's been trying to get in to see you for some time now."

"That shouldn't be a problem. What time is the appointment for?"

Bunny was staring at her notes again.

"Actually, I was thinking of postponing the meeting, if not canceling it altogether," she said.

"Why would we want to do that?"

I was annoyed, but curious. I really wasn't wild about Bunny trying to make my decisions for me. Still, she had a good head for business, and if this guy made her hesitate, I wanted to know why.

"It's like I was trying to tell you before, Skeeve. Your time is valuable. You can't just give it away to any fruitcake who wants an appointment."

". . . And you figure this guy's a fruitcake?"

"He must be," she shrugged. "What he wants to talk about simply isn't our kind of work. As near as I've been able to make out, he wants us to serve as interior decorators."

That brought Tananda into the conversation.

"You're kidding. Interior decorators?"

Bunny actually giggled and turned to Tananda conspiratorially.

·"That's right. It seems he started building a motel complex counting on the fact that his would be the only lodging available in the area. Since he's started construction, though, four others have either announced their intentions to build or have started construction themselves . . . right on his doorstep. Of course, since his original plan didn't include any competition, the design is more utilitarian than decorative. It's going to make his place look real shabby by comparison, and he's afraid of losing his shirt."

"That's bad," Tananda winced. "So what does he want us to do about it?"

"Well, apparently our outfit is getting a bit of a rep for being miracle workers . . . you know, 'If you're really up against a wall, call THEM!'? Anyway, he wants us to come up with an alternate design or a gimmick or something to catch people's attention so that his place will fill up before the competition rents out room one."

"Us? The man must be crazy."

"Crazy or desperate," Bunny nodded. "I know we'd have to be crazy to take the job."

I waited until they were done laughing before I ventured my opinion.

"I think we should take it," I said at last.

I suddenly had their undivided attention.

"Really? Why should we do that?"

I steepled my fingers and tried to look wise.

"First off, there's the fee . . . which, if I remember the letter correctly, was substantial even by our standards. Then again, there's the very point you were raising: we've

never done anything like this before. It'll give us a chance
to try something new . . . diversify instead of staying in a
rut doing the same types of jobs over and over again.
Finally . . ."

I gave them both a lazy smile.

". . . As you said, it's an impossible job, so we won't
guarantee results. That means if we fail, it's what's expected, but if we succeed, we're heroes. The beauty of it
is that either way we collect our fee."

The women exchanged quick glances, and for a moment I thought they were going to suggest that I take an
extended vacation . . . like, say, at a rest home.

"Actually," Bunny said slowly, "I did have a course in
interior decorating once in college. I suppose I could give
it a shot. It might be fun designing a place on someone
else's money."

"But, dear," Tananda put in, "you're so valuable here
at the office. Since there's no guaranteed success on this
one, it might be better if I took it on and left you free for
more important assignments."

Bunny started to say something in return, then glanced
at me and seemed to change her mind.

"I suppose if your heart's set on it, there's no reason
we couldn't *both* work on it together. Right, Skeeve?"

Now *that* had to be the dumbest idea I had heard all
day. Even if the two of them were getting along fine now,
I was sure that if they started butting heads over design
ideas, any hope of friendship would go right out the window.

Fortunately, I had a solution.

"Sorry," I said carefully, "I actually hadn't planned on
using either one of you on this assignment."

That hung in the air for a few moments. Then Tananda
cleared her throat.

"If you don't mind my asking, if you aren't going to
use either of us, who are you giving the assignment to?"

I came around my desk and perched on the edge so I
could speak more personally.

"The way I see it, the new design will have to be attention-getting, a real showstopper. Now when it comes to eye-catching displays, I think we've got just the person on our staff."

Massha's Tale

"Are you sure the great Skeeve sent you?"

Now I'll tell ya, folks, I'm used to people overreactin' to me, but this guy Hysterium seemed to be gettin' a little out a hand. I mean, Deveels are supposed to be used to dealin' with all sorts of folks without battin' an eye. Still, he was the client, and business is business.

"What ya sees is what ya gets, Cute, Rich, and Desperate."

It never hurts to spread a little sugar around, but this time the customer just wasn't buyin'.

"*The* Great Skeeve? The one who runs M.Y.T.H. Inc.?"

This was startin' ta get redundant, so I decided it was time ta put a stop to it once and for all. I heaved a big sigh . . . which, I'll tell you, on me is really something.

"Tell ya what . . . Hysterium, is it? Never was much good with *names*. If you want I'll go back and tell the Prez that you decided not to avail yourself of our services. Hmmm?"

All of a sudden, he got a lot more appreciative of what he was gettin'.

"No! I mean, that won't be necessary. You . . . weren't quite what I was expecting, is all. So you're agents of M.Y.T.H. Inc., eh? What did you say your names were again?"

I don't know what he was expecting, but I was willin' ta believe we weren't it . . . at least, I wasn't. Even when I'm just lazin' around I can be quite an eyeful, and today I decked myself out to the nines just ta be sure to make an impression. Of course, in my case it's more like out to the nineties.

No one has ever called me petite . . . not even when I was born. In fact, the nurses took ta calling my mom the "Oooh-Ahh Bird," even though I didn't get the joke until I was older. The fact of the matter is, folks, that I'm larger than large . . . somewhere between huge and "Oh, my God," leaning just a teensy bit toward the latter. Now I figure when you're my size there's no way to hide it, so you might as well flaunt it . . . and, believe me, I've become an expert on flauntin' it.

Take for example my chosen attire for the day. Now a lot of girls moan that unless you got a perfect figure, you can't wear a bare midriff outfit. Well, I've proven over and over again that that just isn't so, and today was no exception. The top was a bright lime green with purple piping, which was a nice contrast to the orange-and-red-striped bottoms. While I feel there's nothing wrong with going barefoot, I found these darling turquoise harem slippers and couldn't resist addin' them to the ensemble. Of course, with that much color on the bod, a girl can't neglect her makeup. I was usin' violet lipstick accented by mauve eye shadow and screaming yellow nail polish, with just a touch of rouge to hide the fact that I'm not gettin' any younger. I'd thought of dyein' my hair electric blue instead of its normal orange, but decided I'd stick with the natural look.

Now, some folks ask where I find outfits like that. Well, if ya can keep a secret, I have a lot of 'em made especially for me. Face it, ya don't find clothes like these on the rack . . . or if ya do, they never fit right. Be sure ta keep that a secret, though. The designers I patronize *insist* that no one ever find out . . . probably afraid they'll get swamped with orders. They never put their labels in my clothes for the same reason. Even though I've promised not to breathe a word to anybody, they're afraid someone might find out by accident . . . or was that *in* an accident? Whatever.

Oh, yes. I was also wearin' more than my normal allocation of jewelry, which, for anyone who knows me, means quite a lot. Ta save time, I won't try to list the whole inventory here. Just realize I was wearin' multiples of everything: necklaces, dangle bracelets, ankle bangles, earrings, nose rings . . . I went especially heavy on rings, seein' as how this was for work. You see, not only are my rings a substantial part of my magical arsenal, Mom always said it wasn't ladylike to wear brass knuckles, and my rings give me the same edge in a fight, with style thrown in for good measure.

Anyway, I really didn't blame the client for bein' a little overwhelmed when we walked in. Even though he bounced back pretty well, all things considered, I think it took the two of us ta prove ta him just how desperate he really was.

"Well, I'm Massha," I said, "and my partner over there is Vic."

Hysterium nearly fell over his desk in his eagerness to shake Vic's hand. My partner was dressed stylishly if sedately by my standards, in a leisure suit with a turtleneck and ankle-high boots. His whole outfit was in soft earth tones, and it was clear the Deveel had him pegged as the normal member of the twosome. Call it a mischievous streak, but I just couldn't let it stand at that.

"Actually, Vic isn't one of our regular staff. He's a free-lancer we bring in occasionally as a specialist."

"A specialist?" Hysterium noted, still shakin' Vic's hand. "Are you an interior decorator?"

My partner gave him a tight smile.

"No, I'm more of a night-life specialist. That's why I'm wearing these sunglasses. I'm very sensitive to the light."

"Night life? I'm not sure I understand."

I hid a little smile and looked at the ceiling.

"What Vic here is tryin' to say," I told the Deveel as casually as I could, "is that he's a vampire."

Hysterium let go of the hand he had been pumpin' like it had bitten him.

"A vampire?!"

Vic smiled at him again, this time lettin' his outsized canines show.

"That's right. Why? Have you got something against vampires?"

The client started edgin' away across the office.

"No! It's just that I never . . . No. It's fine by me. Really."

"Well, now that that's settled," I said, takin' command of the situation again, "let's get down to business. If I understand it right, you've got a white elephant on your hands here and we're supposed to turn it into a gold mine by the first of the month."

Hysterium was gingerly seatin' himself behind his desk again.

"I . . . Yes. I guess you could summarize the situation that way. We're scheduled to be ready to open in three weeks."

". . . And what kind of budget have we got to pull this miracle off with?" Vic said, abandoning his "looming vampire" bit to lean casually against the wall.

"Budget?"

"You know, Big Plunger. As in 'money'?" I urged. "We know what our fees are. How much are you willin' to sink into decorations and advertisin' to launch this place properly?"

"Oh, that. I think I've got the figures here someplace. Of course, I'll be working with you on this."

He started rummagin' through the papers on his desk.

"Wrong again, High Roller," I said firmly. "You're going to turn everything over to us and take a three-week vacation."

The Deveel's rummagin' became a nervous fidget. I was startin' ta see how he got his name.

"But . . . I thought I'd be overseeing things. It *is* my project, after all."

"You thought wrong, Mister," Vic said. "For the next three weeks it's *our* project."

"Don't you want my input and ideas?"

Fortunately, Vic and I had talked this out on the way over, so I knew just what to say.

"Let me put it to you this way, Hysterium," I said. "If you had any ideas you thought would work, you'd be tryin' them yourself instead of hirin' us. Now, three weeks isn't a heck of a lot of time, and we can't waste any of it arguin' with you over every little point. The only way to be sure you don't yield to the temptation of kibitzin' and stay out from underfoot is for you not ta be here. Understand? Now make up your mind. Either you let us do the job without interference, or you do it yourself and we call it quits right now."

The Deveel deflated slightly. It's always a pleasure doin' business with desperate people.

"Don't you at least need me to sign the checks?" he asked weakly.

"Not if you contact the bank and tell 'em we're cleared to handle the funds," I smiled.

"While you're at it," Vic suggested, "let the contractor know we'll be making a few changes in the finishing work his crew will be doing. Say that we'll meet him here first thing in the morning to go over the changes. Of course, we'll need to see the blueprints right away."

Hysterium straightened up a little at that, glancin' quickly from one of us to the other.

"Can you at least let me in on your plans? It sounds like you have something specific in mind."

"Not really, Sugar," I winked. "We're just clearin' the decks so we can work. The marchin' orders are to turn a third-rate overnight hotel into the biggest tourist trap Deva has ever seen. Now will you get movin' so we can get started?"

It took us quite a while to go over the blueprints. You see, buildin' things had never been a big interest of mine, so it took a while to understand what all the lines and notes meant. Fortunately, Vic had studied a bit of

architecture at one point when he was thinkin' of givin'
up magic, so he could explain a lot of it to me . . . or at
least enough so I could follow what he was talkin' about.

"Let's face it, Massha," he said at last, leanin' back in
his chair. "No matter how long we stare at the drawings,
they aren't going to change. What he's built here is a box
full of rooms. The place has about as much personality
as an actuary . . . which is to say, a little less than an accountant."

"You gotta admit, though," I observed, "the setup has
a lot of space."

I could see why our client was nervous. The place was
plain, but it was five floors of plain spread over a considerable hunk of land. There was a lot of extra land for
expansion, which at the moment seemed unlikely. Hysterium had obviously sunk a bundle into puttin' this deal
together, money he would never see again if nobody
rented a room here.

"Tell me, Vic. Your home dimension is entertainment-
oriented enough so that the competition for crowds has to
be pretty heavy. What's packin' 'em in these days, anyway?"

The vampire frowned for a few moments as he thought
over my question.

"Well, it depends on what kind of clientele you're after. You can go after the family groups or folks who have
already retired. My favorite is the young professionals.
They usually haven't started their families yet or are passing on them completely, which means they've got both
money and time. For that set, clubs are always big. If I
really wanted to pull crowds into a new place, I'd probably open a good disco."

"Now we're talkin'. Do you think you could put one
together in three weeks?"

My partner shook his head and laughed.

"Hold on a second, Massha. I was just thinking out
loud. Even if I could come up with a plan for a club,
there's no room for it."

Now it was my turn ta laugh.

"Vic, honey, if there's one thing we've got it's room. Look here . . ."

I flipped the blueprints to the drawin's of the first floor.

". . . What if we knocked out the inside walls here on the ground level? That'd give us all the space we'd ever need for your disco."

"Too much space," the vampire said, studyin' the plans. "The key to one of these clubs is to keep it fairly small so people have to wait to get in. Besides, I'm afraid if we knocked out *all* the internal walls, there wouldn't be enough support for the rest of the structure."

An idea was startin' ta form in my head.

"So try this. We keep the whole outer perimeter of rooms . . . turn 'em into shops or somethin'. That'll give extra support and cut back on your club space. And if that's still too big . . ."

"About four times too big."

"Uh huh. What would you say ta a casino? I haven't seen one yet that didn't draw tourists by the droves."

Vic expressed his admiration with a low whistle.

"You don't think small, do you? I'm surprised you aren't thinking of a way to make money off the grounds as well."

"I can't make up my mind between a golf course and an amusement park," I said. "That can wait for a while until we see how the rest of this works out."

Right about then, I noticed Vic babes had his cheaters off and was studyin' me. Now, I'm used to bein' stared at, but there was somethin' kinda unsettlin' about his expression that was outside the norm, if ya know what I mean. I waited for him ta speak his mind, but after a while the silence started gettin' to me.

"What're you lookin' at me that way for, Young and Bloodthirsty? Did I grow another head sudden-like when I wasn't lookin'?"

Instead of answerin' right away, he just kept starin'

until I was thinkin' a bustin' him one just ta break the
suspense.

"You know, Massha," he said finally, "for a so-called
apprentice, you're pretty savvy. With the way you dress
and talk it's easy to overlook, but there's quite a mind
lurking behind all that mascara, isn't there?"

Now if there's one thing I have trouble handlin' it's
praise . . . maybe 'cause I don't hear that much of it. To
keep my embarrassment from bein' too noticeable, I did
what I always do and ducked behind a laugh.

"Don't let the wrappin' fool ya, Fangs. Remember, I
used ta be an independent before I signed on with
Skeeve's gang. Magician for the city-state of Ta-hoe and
then Vey-gus over on Jahk, that was me."

"Really? I didn't know that."

Just goes to show how rattled I was. I couldn't even
remember how little Vic knew about our operation and
the people in it.

"That was when I first ran into the Boy Wonder. He
was in trouble then, too . . . in fact, Skeeve seems to have
a knack for trouble. Remind me sometime to tell you
about the spot he was in when I *did* join up."

"Why not now?" he said, leanin' back in his chair.
"I'm not going anywhere, and there's no time like the
present for learning more about one's business associates."

As you've probably noticed, I was eager to get off the
spot, and talkin' about Skeeve seemed to be just the ticket
I was lookin' for.

"Well, at the time his big green mentor had taken off
for Perv, see . . . some kinda family problem. Anyway, the
king puts the touch on Skeeve to stand in for him, supposedly so's his royalness could take a bit of a vacation
. . . say, for a day or so. What the Man neglected to mention to our colleague was that his bride-to-be, a certain
Queen Hemlock, was due ta show up expectin' ta tie the
knot with whoever was warmin' the throne just then."

"Queen Hemlock?"

"Let me tell you, she was a real sweetheart. Probably would have ended up on the gallows at an early age if she hadn't been the daughter of a king. As it was, she ended up runnin' the richest kingdom in that dimension and was out to merge with the best military force around . . . which turned out to be the kingdom that Skeeve was babysittin'."

Vic frowned.

"If she was already in a position to buy anything she wanted; what did she need an army for?"

"For those doodads that *weren't* for sale. You see, we all have our little dreams. Hers was to rule the world. That was Queen Hemlock for you. The morals of a mink in heat and the humble aspirations of Genghis Khan."

"And the two of you stopped her?"

"To be truthful with you, Skeeve did. All I did was round up the king so we could put him back on the throne where he was supposed to be. Skeeve set 'em up with a pair of wedding rings that never come off which also link their lives. That meant if Queenie wanted to off Kingie and clear the path for a little world-conquering, she'd be slitting her own throat at the same time."

"Where'd he find those? I never heard of such a thing."

I gave him a chuckle and a wink.

"Neither has anyone else. What they got was some junk jewelry from a street vendor here at the Bazaar along with a fancy story concocted by one Skeeve the Great. What I'm sayin' is that he sold 'em a line of hooey, but it was enough to cool Hemlock's jets. Smooth move, wasn't it?"

Instead of joinin' in with my laughter, the vampire thought for a few moments, then shook his head.

"I don't get it," he said. "Now, don't mistake me . . . I think Skeeve's a swell guy and all that. It's just that from all I can find out, he doesn't use all that much magik, and what he does use is pretty weak stuff. So how has he built up an organization of top-flight talent around him like you and the others?"

"I'll tell ya, Vic, there's magik and there's magik. Skeeve has . . . how can I explain it? He may not be strong in the bibbity-bobbity-boo department, and he hasn't got the woman sense of a Quasimodo, but he's got enough heart for three normal folks."

I punched him lightly on the arm.

"Remember when I said he has a knack for gettin' into trouble? Well, the truth is that more often than not he's bailin' someone else out who really deserves to get what's comin' to 'em. In that Hemlock caper I was just tellin' you about, he could have headed for the horizon once he figured out that he'd been had . . . but that would have left a whole kingdom without a leader, so he stuck it out. When I met him, he was workin' at gettin' Tananda loose after she got pinched tryin' ta steal a birthday present for Aahz. Heck, as I recall, the first time we crossed paths with you we were settin' up a jailbreak for his old mentor. That's Skeeve, if ya see what I mean. He's always gettin' in over his head tryin' ta do what he thinks is right, and a body gets the feelin' . . . I don't know, that if you stand beside him he just might be able to pull it off. Even if it don't work out, you feel you've been doin' somethin' good with your life instead of just hangin' in there for the old number one. Am I makin' any sense at all?"

"More than you know," Vic said. "If I'm understanding you properly, he sets a high personal standard, and consequently draws people to him who are impressed by the sincerity of his actions . . . who in turn try to match the proportionate output they perceive in him. It's an interesting theory. I'll have to think about it."

I couldn't help but notice that once old Fangs got wrapped up in somethin', he started soundin' more like a college prof than a night-lovin' partygoer. It made me a little curious, but since I don't like people tryin' to peek at more of me than I'm willin' to show, I decided to let it go.

"Speakin' a theories," I said, "we got one that isn't goin' to work itself out without a lotta pushin' from us."

The vampire stretched his arms and yawned.

"All right. I'll take care of the disco and the architect if you can start checking into the casino and the shops. Okay?"

I had to admit I was a little taken aback by his enthusiasm.

"You mean right now? It's pretty late."

He showed me his fangs in a little grin.

"For you, maybe. Us night people are just starting to wake up, which means it's just the right time for me to start scouting around for a band and bar staff. Since we're on different missions anyway, though, I've got no problem if you want to catch a few Z's before you do your rounds. What say we meet here same time tomorrow for an update?"

Now, folks, I may strut a bit and loud-talk even more, but I'll also be the first to admit that little Massha doesn't know everythin'. One of the many things I know next ta nothin' about is how ta run a casino. Considerin' this, it was easy ta see I was goin' ta require the services of an expert . . . in casinos, that is.

It took me a while to locate him, but I finally ran my mark to ground. He was slouched at a back table in a dingy bar, and from the look of him things hadn't been goin' real good. I was glad ta see that . . . not that I wished him ill, mind you; it just made my sales pitch a little easier.

"Hiya, Geek," I said, easin' up to his table. "Mind if I join ya?"

He blinked his eyes a couple times tryin' ta focus 'em before he realized that the person talkin' to him really was that big.

"Well, well, well. If it isn't one of the M.Y.T.H. Inc. hotshots. What brings you to this neck of the woods, Massha? Slumming?"

I pulled up a chair so's I could sit close to him. I mean,

he hadn't said no, and that's about as close to an invitation as I usually get.

"I know you're busy, Geek, so I'll give it to ya straight. We're cookin' up a little deal and I'd like you to be a part of it. Interested?"

"Well, whaddaya know. After making me sell my club and putting me out on the street, the Great Skeeve has a deal for me. Isn't that just ducky!"

Now I may not know casinos, but I know drunk when I see it. Seein' as how it was just sunset, which for the Geek is like early morning, he was in pretty bad shape. The trouble was, I needed him sober. Normally I'd a taken him off someplace and let him sleep it off, but I was in a hurry. This called for drastic action.

Glancin' around the place to be sure there were no witnesses, I leaned forward, wrapped my arms around his neck, and gave him the biggest, juiciest kiss I knew. One of the other things I know more than a little about is kissin', and this particular sample lasted a fairly long time. When I felt him startin' ta struggle for air, I let go and leaned back.

"Wha . . . Who . . . Massha!" he said, gaspin' like a fish out of water. "What happened?"

I batted my eyelashes at him.

"I don't think I catch your drift, Big Red."

The Geek just sat there blinkin' for a few seconds, one hand on the top of his head like he was afraid it was goin' ta come off.

"I . . . I don't know," he managed at last. "I've been drunk for . . . what day is it? Never mind! . . . for a long time. Now all of a sudden I'm wide awake and stone cold sober. What happened? How long have you been here?"

I smiled ta myself and mentally accepted a pat on the back. My record was still intact. I've been told more times than you can count that nothin' sobers a body up as completely or as fast as a little hug and a kiss from Massha.

"Just long enough to catch the curtain goin' up," I said. "Now that we're all present and accounted for, though, I want ya ta listen close to a little proposition."

The Geek used ta be one of the biggest bookies at the Bazaar. At one point, he had his own club, called the Even Odds. Of course, that was before Skeeve caught him usin' marked cards and suggested strongly that he sell us his club. I wasn't sure how the Prez would react to my cuttin' the Geek in on this new project, but he was the only one I could think of who had the necessary knowledge to set up a casino and was currently unemployed.

"I don't know, Massha," he said after I had explained the situation. "I mean, it sounds good . . . but a casino's a big operation. I'm not exactly rolling in investment capital right now."

"So start small and build. Look, Geek, the house is going ta be providin' the space and decor rent free. All you have to do is set up security and round up some dealers to work the tables."

"Did you say 'rent free'?"

It occurred ta me that maybe I shouldn't have sobered him up quite so much. Now he was back ta thinkin' like a Deveel bookie.

"Well . . . practically. The way I figure it, the house will take a piece of the action, which means you'll only have ta pay rent if you lose money."

"That's no problem," the Geek said with a smile. "With the dealers I'm thinking of, there's no way we'll end up in the red."

Somehow, I didn't like the sound of that.

"I hope it goes without sayin' that we expect you ta run a clean operation, Geek," I warned. "I don't think the Great Skeeve would like ta be part of settin' up a crooked casino. Content yourself with the normal winnings the odds throw the house. Okay?"

"Massha! You wound me! Have I ever run anything but a clean game?"

I gave him a hard stare, and he had the decency to flush slightly.

"Only once that I know of," I said, "and if I recall

correctly it was Skeeve who caught you at it that time. If
I were you, I'd keep my nose clean . . . unless you want
ta wake up some morning on a scratchy lily pad."

The Geek sat up a little straighter and lost his smug
grin.

"Can he really do that?"

"It was just a figure of speech, but I think you catch
my meanin'. Just remember, the only times you've lost
money on your crew is when you got suckered into bettin'
against us."

"That's true," the Deveel said with a thoughtful nod.
"Speaking of Skeeve, are you sure there won't be a problem there? The last time I saw him we weren't on the best
of terms."

"You worry about the casino and leave Skeeve ta me,"
I smiled confidently, hopin' I knew what I was talkin'
about. "Anyway, Skeeve's not one ta hold a grudge. If
memory serves me correctly, Aahz was all set ta tear your
throat out that last meeting, and it was Skeeve who came
up with the suggestion that let you off the hook with your
skin intact."

"True enough," the Geek nodded. "The Kid's got
class."

"Right. Oh! Say, speakin' a class, you might try to run
down the Sen-Sen Ante Kid and offer him a permanent
table of his own."

The Deveel cocked his head at me.

"No problem, but do you mind my asking why?"

"Well, the last time he was in the vicinity for that
match-up with Skeeve, I got stuck baby-sitting that character assassin you fobbed off on us. That means I'm the
only one on our team who didn't get a chance ta meet
him . . . and, from what I hear, he's my kinda guy. Besides, he might appreciate settlin' down instead of hoppin'
from game to game all the time. Aren't any of us gettin'
any younger, ya know."

"Ain't that the truth," the Geek said with a grimace.
"Say, that might not be such a bad idea. Having the best

Dragon Poker player at the Bazaar as a permanent player at the casino would be a pretty good draw."

We talked a while more, but it was all detail stuff. The Geek was on board, and the casino was startin' ta take shape.

Casinos may not be my forte, but nobody knows retail stores like yours truly. Bunny may be aces when it comes ta findin' class outfits at decent prices, and Tananda sure knows her weapons, but when it comes ta straight-at-ya, no-holds-barred shoppin', they both take a back seat ta Massha.

I had noticed this place long before the assignment came up, but it stuck in my mind so I thought I'd check it out. There were big "Going Out Of Business" and "Everything Must Go" sale signs all over the window, but they had been there for over a year, so I didn't pay 'em much heed.

For a storefront shop, the place was a disaster. Their stock could only be described as "stuff" . . . and that's bein' generous. There were T-shirts and ash trays and little dolls all mixed in with medications and magazines in no particular order. The shelves were crammed with a small selection of the cheap end of everything. They didn't have as many clothing items as a clothing store, as many hardware items as a hardware store . . . I could go on, but you get the point. If you wanted selection or quality in anything, you'd have ta go somewhere else. In short, it was just the sort of place I was lookin' for.

"Can I help you, lady?"

The proprietor was perched behind the counter on a stool readin' a newspaper. He didn't get up when he talked ta me, so I decided ta shake him up a little.

"Well, yes. I was thinkin' a buyin' a lot of . . . stuff. Can you give me some better prices if I buy in volume?"

That brought him out from behind the counter with a pad and pencil which had materialized out of thin air.

"Why, sure, lady. Always ready to deal. What was it you were thinking of?"

I took my time and looked around the place again.

"Actually, I was wonderin' if you could quote me a price on everything in the store."

"Everything? Did you say everything?"

"Everything . . . including your sweet adorable self."

"I don't understand, lady. Are you saying you want to buy my store?"

"Not the store, just what's in it. I'm thinkin' this place could do better in a new location. Truthfully now, how has business been going for you lately?"

The owner tossed his pad and pencil back onto the counter.

"Honestly? Not so hot. My main supplier for this junk just raised his prices . . . something about a new union in his factory. I either gotta raise my prices, which won't help, since this stuff is hard enough to move as it is, or go out of business, which I've seriously been consider-ing."

I thought it would be best not to comment on the union he'd mentioned.

"You don't think a new location would help?"

"New location . . . big deal! This is the Bazaar at Deva, lady. One row of shops is like any other for pedestrian traffic. On any one of those rows you can find better stuff than I got to sell."

This was turnin' out ta be even better than I had hoped.

"Just suppose," I said, "just suppose the new location was in a hotel, and suppose that hotel had a casino and disco. That would give you a captive clientele, since no-body wants ta leave the building and wander around to find somethin' they can buy right where they are."

"A hotel and casino, eh? I dunno, though. Junk is still junk."

"Not if you had an exclusive to print the name of the place on everythin' you sell. Junk with a name on it is souvenirs, and folks expect ta pay more for them. Right?"

The proprietor was startin' ta get excited.

"That's right! You got a place like this, lady? How much ya asking for rent?"

"Minimal, with a piece of the action goin' ta the house. How does that sound?"

"How much floor space do you have available? If I can expand, I can get a volume discount from my supplier and *still* raise my prices. Say, do you have a printer lined up yet?"

"Hadn't really thought about it."

"Good. I got a brother-in-law who does good work cheap . . . fast, too. How about a restaurant? All those folks gotta eat."

Now that was one that had slipped by both Vic and me.

"A restaurant?"

". . . 'Cause if you don't, I know a guy who's been looking to move his deli since they raised the rent on the place he's got."

I had a feelin' my problems with the storefronts was solved.

"Tell ya what, Well Connected. You pass the word ta the folks you think would fit into this deal, and I'll be back tomorrow with the floor plans. We can fight out who gets which space then."

All in all, things went fairly smoothly carryin' out our plans for the revised hotel. It turned out, though, that for all our figurin' there was one detail we overlooked.

"We need a name!" Vic moaned for the hundredth time as he paced the office.

I looked up from where I was doodlin' on Hysterium's desk pad.

"What was he going to call it again?"

"The Hysterium Inn."

"Really, is it all that bad for a name?"

We looked at each other.

"Yes," we said at the same time.

"We could come up with a better name in our sleep."

"Terrific, Vic. What have you got?"

"Beg pardon?"

"The name. You said you could come up with a better one in your sleep."

"I said *we* could come up with a better name in our sleep. This is supposed to be a team, you know."

I shrugged helplessly.

"I'm not asleep."

"We need a name!" my teammate moaned for the hundred and first time.

"Look on the bright side, Fangs. At least we don't have ta overcome an established advertisin' campaign."

The vampire plopped into a chair.

"You can say that again," he growled. "I don't believe how cheap that Deveel is. He was going to open without any advertising at all!"

"Zero competition, remember? If you're figurin' on bein' the only game in town, you don't have ta advertise."

"Well, I think we can kiss the idea of bringing this job in under budget goodbye," Vic said grimly. "Sorry, Massha. I know how hard you've worked cutting corners expense-wise."

"Forget it," I waved. "How do you figure we should promote this place, anyway?"

"The usual newspaper ads aren't going to be enough . . . even though we'll have to do them anyway. This close to opening, we're going to have to come up with something extra to get the word out."

"How about billboards?"

Vic scrunched up his face.

"I don't know, Massha. I don't think a couple of billboards will do it."

"I was thinkin' more like lotsa billboards . . . more like fifty of them blanketin' the area for a ten-mile radius."

". . . Widely spaced further out, and closer together the

nearer you get," he added thoughtfully. "I like it! Of course, it'll cost."

"So I shave a little here and there on the decorations. We'd better get on those right away. Nothin' too classy, mind you. We don't want to scare anybody away. What we need is someone who does the signs for the Reptile Farms. That kinda excitement."

"I know just the guy," Vic said, scribblin' down a note. "That brings us back to our original problem."

"Right. We need a name."

The vampire's head came up with a snap.

"Hey! That's my line."

"Sorry."

"This is the pits, you know?"

"How about that? The Pitts?"

"No. How about the Funny Farm?"

"Uh-uh. The Snake Pit?"

"Will you get off pits?"

"Well, then, how about . . ."

What we finally settled on was The Fun House. Our judgment was influenced a bit by the fact that I managed to locate a down-at-the-heels carnival. We let 'em set up on our grounds, and they gave us our pick of their displays for decorations.

The best of the lot was the outsized figures they had on top of their rides . . . and particularly The Fun House. These figures were of bein's from all over the dimensions and were animated to move their arms and heads while hidden speakers went "Ho Ho Ho" at passersby. I thought they were terrific and had them installed all over the outside of the hotel . . . except for the Fat Lady. Her I had installed in the men's john off the lobby.

Once we had that, the rest of the decorations fell into place. There wasn't much we could do to make the shape of the building excitin', so I had it painted with wide stripes . . . like a circus tent, only with more colors.

Vic did the disco, and it was a beaut. He did the whole place in black: floors, walls, ceiling, furniture, everything. He also attached chairs and tables to the walls and ceiling at different angles with life-sized dummies in evening attire. The overall effect was one of disorientation, so that when the band was goin' and the lights flashin', you weren't really sure which way was up. To add to the effect, the dance floor was slanted a bit and rotated slowly. It was like bein' suspended in space and bein' buffeted by cosmic winds and gravity at the same time. He even named the club "The Pit" in appreciation of me and to apologize for comin' down so hard on the name when I suggested it for the hotel.

The casino was all mine, and I decided ta go for broke. I found a painter with a sense of humor, and we did the place in camouflage . . . except instead of usin' greens and browns, we leaned heavy on the basic colors in day-glo shades. For a crownin' touch, we spaced mirrors all around the place, but we used the distortion mirrors from the carnival Fun House. This not only gave the place the illusion of bein' larger, but when the customers glanced at themselves in the mirrors, they had the same kind of meltin' lines as the decor. It definitely raised questions in the mind as to exactly which reality we were operatin' in.

Vic was afraid the impact of the whole operation was a bit bright, but I argued that the whole idea was ta stand out from the crowd and let people know we were there. I did, however, unbend enough to agree that we should have Skeeve on hand for our meetin' with Hysterium the night before our opening. I mean, negotiatin' never was my strong suit, and I had no idea how the client was going to react to our rather innovative ideas.

"You've ruined me! That's what you've done! Ruined me!"

That was our client speakin'. You may guess from the sound of it that he was less than pleased with our work.

When you realize that that was how he was soundin' after we had spent an hour calmin' him down, you've got an idea of exactly how unhappy he was.

"I'm not sure I understand what your problem is, Mr. Hysterium," Vic said. "If you have a complaint . . ."

"A complaint?" the Deveel shrieked. "I wouldn't know where to start! What did you people think you were doing, anyway?"

"We were turnin' your dump into a profit-makin' hotel. That's what we were supposed to do."

I was tryin' to stay out of this 'cause a my temper, but I had to get a word or two in here somewhere.

"A hotel? A hotel? This isn't a hotel! What I left you with was a hotel! What I came back to is a sideshow! And what do *you* mean by profitable? All the rooms on the first floor are gone! That cuts my rental earnings by twenty percent!"

"Twenty percent of an empty hotel is still nothing!" I shot back.

"Massha's right," Vic said, stepping between us. "We needed that space for attractions to draw in some customers. Besides, everything we put in there generates revenues for the hotel."

"Not if they don't sell anything!" Hysterium argued. "Have you been in any of those places? Have you seen the junk they're selling? And the prices . . . they're charging more for a cup of coffee in that club you put in than I'm used to paying for a whole meal!"

"Not everybody eats as cheap as you do," I muttered under my breath.

"What?"

"I said you stand ta clear a heap when they do . . . sell stuff to the customers, that is."

"But there aren't going to be any . . . Ohhh! I'm ruined!"

The Deveel sank into a chair and hid his face in his hands.

"Of course, if you had wanted design approval, you

should have stayed around. As it was, Massha and Vic had no recourse but to use their own judgment."

That was Skeeve speakin' from his chair in the corner. So far, he hadn't done much more than listen to the rantings.

"Stayed around?" Hysterium's head came up with a snap. "They made me go! They said I'd have to trust them if I wanted to use your outfit's services."

"Precisely," Skeeve nodded, changin' tactics without batting an eye. "You wanted our services, you trusted us, and we serviced you. I don't see what the complaint is."

"What the complaint is, is that you charged me an arm and a leg . . . in advance . . . to put me out of business! If I had lost money on a regular hotel it would have been bad enough, but to lose money *and* be made a laughingstock to boot. . . ." There were tears formin' in the developer's eyes. "That was my wife's family money I invested. I could turn a profit if I only had the capital, I told them. Now . . ."

His voice broke and his head sank again.

"If that's the only problem, maybe we can work something out."

"Forget it! Cutting your fee wouldn't help. I need to make money, not lose less."

"Actually, I was thinking more of taking the hotel off your hands. Buying it outright."

I shot a glance at Skeeve. He was leanin' back in his chair studyin' the ceiling.

"Are you serious?" the Deveel said hopefully.

"Why not? That way you turn a profit of . . . say, fifteen percent over cost? . . . for the building and land, and making the place work, much less dealing with its reputation, will be our problem. That's what we agreed to do in the first place . . . sort of."

Hysterium was on his feet pumpin' Skeeve's hand almost before the Prez had stopped talkin'.

"I'll tell you, Skeeve . . . Mr. Skeeve . . . you're a real

gent. This is terrific! Just when I thought . . . I can't tell you how much I appreciate . . ."

"Don't mention it," Skeeve said, retrievin' his hand. "Why don't you go on over to my office right now? My secretary is still there. Just explain everything to her, and she'll start drawing up the papers. I want to have a few words with my agents, then I'll be along to sign off on the deal."

"On my way," the Deveel waved. "Gee. I can't get over . . ."

"Now, you realize, of course, we don't have that kind of cash on hand. We'll have to give a down payment and arrange some kind of payment schedule."

"Fine. Fine. As long we get a contract guaranteeing my profit."

Then he was gone, leavin' us ta stare at each other in silence. Finally, Skeeve gathered us up with his eyes.

"The placed is booked solid?" he said, confirmin' what we had told him in our debriefing.

". . . For three weeks, with a waiting list for cancellations," Vic confirmed. "We're taking reservations for as much as a year and a half in advance."

". . . And Hysterium doesn't know?"

"He never asked, and we never got the chance to tell him," I shrugged. "You saw how he was."

Skeeve nodded thoughtfully.

"That means, if my calculations are correct, we'll be able to pay him off in full in less than three months . . . not including the take from the casino and the shops."

He rose and stretched, then gave us a wink.

"C'mon, you two," he said. "I think I'll invest an arm and a leg and buy you both a drink!"

IV:

*"If you're too busy to help your friends,
you're too busy!"*

—L. IACOCCA

Actually, I wasn't all that wild over The Fun House.
I mean, it was making us money hand over fist, but
I somehow never figured on owning a hotel/casino. In
particular, I didn't think it was a good idea to set the
precedent of buying out dissatisfied customers, no matter
how profitable the deal turned out to be. As it was, Hysterium's relatives (on his wife's side) were trying to get
the deal invalidated on the basis that he must have been
out of his mind, or at least not in his right mind, to sell
such a lucrative business at the price he did. I wasn't
particularly worried, as this was still the Bazaar at Deva,
and if everyone who signed off on a bad deal here was
declared insane, the economy would collapse.

The part that really bothered me about the deal was
that it meant associating with the Geek again. In past dealings with him, he had consistently proven to be primarily
concerned with lining his own pockets without much regard for anyone else, and I felt it was dangerous to place

him in a position where he had such temptingly easy access to our money, or even a piece of it.

Still, I couldn't argue with Massha's logic in including him in the scheme, and at the time she approached him she had no idea he was going to end up reporting to us. Bunny assured me that she was personally auditing the financial reports for the casino that the Geek turned in along with our share of the take, but I found that in spite of that I tended to spend inordinate amounts of time studying the spreadsheets myself, half expecting to find some indication that he was somehow skimming a little off the top for his personal accounts.

That's what I was doing this particular afternoon, setting aside the countless letters and chores that were pressing on my time to take one more pass at auditing the Geek's financial reports. Bunny had told me once that a hefty percentage of accountants and financial analysts operated more out of spite than from any instinctive or learned insight. That is, rather than detecting that there's anything wrong from the figures they study, they single out some department that's been giving them grief or a manager who made snide comments about them at the company party, then go over their reports *very* carefully. She maintains that anyone's reports will come up flawed or suspicious if reviewed closely enough.

That may well be, if one is a skilled numbers cruncher. All I discovered was that prolonged periods of time spent staring at rows of little numbers are a pain . . . literally and figuratively. Specifically, after a few hours hunched over the reports, I was feeling cramps and stabbing pain in my eyes, my neck, my back, and regions lower.

Leaning back to ease the strain and stretching a bit, my eye fell on the pencil I had tossed down on my desk from disgust and frustration. With a smirk, I reached out with my mind, grabbed it, and flipped it into the air. What do magicians do when they get bored or depressed? Tinker around with magik, natch!

Remember once upon a time when I used to sweat and

groan to levitate a feather? Well, those days are long gone. Nothing like a few years of using the basics like levitation to save your skin to increase one's confidence . . . and, as Aahz always told me, confidence is the key to magik.

I took the pencil up to the ceiling, paused, then took it on a tour of the room, stopping cold at each corner to give it a right-angle turn. I realized I was humming a little tune under my breath as I put it through its paces, so I brought it down over the desk and started using it like a conductor's baton, cueing the drums and the horns as the tune built.

"Nice to see you're keeping your hand in."

I glanced over at the door, and discovered my old mentor leaning against the frame watching me work.

"Hi, Aahz," I said, keeping the pencil moving smoothly. "Well, things have been so busy I haven't had much time to practice, but I do still turn a spell now and then."

As offhand as I sounded, I was secretly very pleased that the pencil hadn't wavered when Aahz surprised me. Not breaking concentration on a spell, or, rather, maintaining a spell once concentration was broken, had been one of the harder lessons Aahz had taught me, and I thought I finally had it down pat. I only hoped he noticed.

"Got a few minutes for your old partner?"

"Sure, pull up a chair."

I decided it would be rude to keep playing with the pencil while I was talking to Aahz, so I brought it down to where I could pluck it smoothly from the air as I leaned forward. Aahz didn't seem to notice, though. He was craning his neck slightly to look at the papers scattered across my desk.

"What's all this?"

"Oh, just going over the financials from The Fun House. I still don't trust the Geek completely."

Aahz settled back in his chair and cocked his head at me.

"The Fun House, eh? Haven't really had a chance to

talk with you much about that one. That was quite a coup
you pulled off there."

I felt warmed and flattered by his comment. While we
were technically equals . . . had been for some time . . . he
was still my old teacher, and I couldn't help but react to
praise from him.

"It seemed like the best route out of a bad situation,"
I said offhandedly.

"That's right," he nodded. "It's always easier to solve
a problem by throwing money at it than by thinking your
way out."

Suddenly this no longer sounded particularly complimentary. I felt my pride turning to defensiveness with the
speed of a snuffed candle.

"I believe the financial returns to the company have
more than justified the wisdom of the investment."

It sounded a little stuffy, even to me. I had noticed that
more and more these days I was retreating into stuffiness
for defense in situations where I used to whine about my
inexperience or lack of working data.

"Well, I've never been one to complain about clearing
a profit," Aahz said, flashing one of his ear-to-ear displays
of teeth. "Even when it means acquiring a casino we neither want nor need."

This was definitely sounding like a lecture shaping up
instead of a testimonial as to what a fine job I had been
doing. While I could make time for a chat and would
always take time for "atta boys," I was in no mood to
have my shortcomings expounded upon.

"What's done is done, and hindsight is academic," I
said briskly, cutting short the casino conversation. "What
was it you wanted to see me about?"

I almost started fidgeting with the paper on my desk
to press the point home that I was busy, but remembered
in time that they were the casino financial reports . . . definitely *not* the way to draw conversation away from that
particular subject.

"Oh, nothing much," Aahz shrugged. "I was just head-

ing out on a little assignment and thought you might want
to tag along."

"An assignment? I haven't given you an assignment."

I regretted the words as soon as I said them. Not only
did they sound bureaucratic, they underscored the fact that
I hadn't been finding any work for Aahz, despite our
heavy work load.

My old mentor never batted an eye at the faux pas.

"It's not really an assignment. More a busman's holiday. I was going to do a little work on my own time. A
favor for a friend who can't afford our normal fees."

I should have been suspicious right then. If I'm at all
money-grubbing, it rubbed off from Aahz during our association. Anytime Aahz starts talking about giving something away that we could sell, like our time, I should
know there's something afoot.

"Gee, Aahz, I don't think I could take the time. I've
been really busy."

". . . Levitating pencils and checking for embezzlement
of funds that are all gravy anyway?"

His attempt at an innocent smile was short enough of
the mark to be a deliberate botch.

"C'mon, Aahz. That's not fair. I *have* been working
hard. I just need a break once in a while. That's all."

"My point precisely," my partner said, springing his
trap. "It's about time you got out of this office and out in
the field before you become a permanent part of that chair.
You don't want to get too far out of touch with the troops,
you know, and this little chore is just the thing to remind
you what it's like to be on assignment."

I could feel myself being outflanked the longer he
talked. In desperation, I held up a hand.

"All right, all right. Tell me about it. Who is this friend
of yours?"

"Actually, he's more of an acquaintance. You know
him too. Remember Quigley?"

"Quigley? Demon hunter turned magician? That Quigley?"

Aahz nodded vigorously.

"That's the one. It seems he's got a problem he's not up to handling himself . . . which isn't surprising, somehow. I thought you might be interested in lending a hand, since we were the ones who set him up for it."

Check and mate.

"Okay, Aahz," I said, looking mournfully at the unfinished work on my desk. "Just let me clear a few things with Bunny, and I'll be right with you."

Aahz's Tale

Jahk hadn't changed much from our last visit, but then these off-the-beaten-track dimensions seldom do. We were traveling in disguise, which we Pervects have gotten into the habit of doing when visiting a dimension we've been to before, and the Kid picked up the trick from me. You see, contrary to popular belief, Pervects don't like to fight *all* the time, and the second time through a dimension we usually end up in a fight with anyone who recognizes us and figures they're better prepared than the first meeting. This only confirms the belief we hold on Perv that the rest of the dimensions are antisocial and we'd best swing first to get the surprise advantage, not to mention doing our best to discourage off-dimension visitors whenever possible. Our dimension is unpleasant enough without having strange riffraff drifting through stirring up trouble.

Of course, being a Pervect wasn't the only reason certain citizens of Jahk might want to hang our scalps out to dry. The last time we passed through here, we stirred things up pretty well with our surprise entry into their Big Game. As old and cynical as I may be, I have to smile when I think of the havoc we wreaked then.

"How long do you think this problem of Quigley's is going to take, Aahz?" Skeeve said, breaking into my wandering thoughts.

"I really don't know," I shrugged. "I imagine we'll

have a better idea once he fills us in on exactly what the problem is."

The Kid stopped in his tracks and scowled at me.

"You mean you agreed to help without knowing what you were volunteering for? Then how did you know we set him up for it?"

Even though Skeeve's proved himself many times over to be a fast learner, there are still times when he can be dense to the point of being exasperating.

"What was Quigley doing when we first met him?"

"He was a demon hunter. Why?"

"And what's he doing now?"

"Last thing we heard, he was holding down a job as Court Magician for Ta-hoe."

"Now what do you suppose prompted him to take up magik for a living instead of sword-swinging?"

"Oh."

He looked a bit crestfallen for a few moments but rallied back gamely.

"I still think you should have found out what the problem was. Once we're in there, there's no telling how long it's going to take, and I can't be away from the office *too* long. I'm really busy these days."

"Well, then," I smiled, "we should probably be hooking up with him ASAP instead of standing here in the street arguing."

The Kid rolled his eyes melodramatically and set off marching down the road again.

Skeeve has changed a lot in the years I've worked with him. When we first met, he was a kid. Now, he's a young man . . . even though I still tend to think of him as "the Kid." Old habits die hard. He's grown from a gangly boy into a youth who has to shave . . . even though it's only necessary occasionally, so he tends to forget until Bunny reminds him. Even more astonishing is how much he's gained in confidence and poise to a point where he's acquired a certain amount of style. All in all, it's been interesting watching my young charge develop over the last few years. I just wish I felt better about the directions he's been developing in.

You see, Skeeve's most endearing trademark has always been that he cared for people . . . really cared. Whether it was his feeling for Garkin when his old teacher died, even though my colleague never really gave the Kid a fair shake as a student, or the lengths he went to to bolster Ajax's sagging ego when the old Archer was doubting his own value in a fight, Skeeve has always had an unerring ability to see the good in people and act accordingly. That's a lot of why I stuck around to work with him . . . as much to learn as to teach.

Lately, however, things seem to be changing. Ever since he has taken the slot as president of our corporation, Skeeve seems to be worrying more and more about business and less and less about people. The others may not have noticed it. Bunny and Tananda have been so busy trying to one-up each other they wouldn't notice if a brass band marched through the room, and Chumley's had his hands full just keeping them apart. Massha and the hoods are big on blind loyalty. They'd probably follow Skeeve right off a cliff without thinking twice or asking question one. Then again, they haven't known him as long or as well as I have and may simply think his current behavior is normal. To me, however, it represents a major change.

This whole casino purchase thing is just one example. The Skeeve I've known would have insisted that Hysterium know all the facts before signing the contract, or at least given him a more generous price for his efforts. Instead, we were treated to a display of opportunism that would make a hardened Deveel haggler envious.

Now, you all know that I have nothing against making a profit, especially a sinfully large one . . . but that's me. Skeeve is supposed to be the counterbalancing humanitarian. While I've been learning about people from him, I'm afraid he's been absorbing the wrong lessons from me . . . or the right one too well.

Anyway, that's why I didn't chuck Quigley's letter in

the wastebasket when it got forwarded to us at the Bazaar.
I figured it would give me some time alone with Skeeve to
find out whether I was just being a Nervous Nelly, or
if there was really something to worry about. So far, I
was leaning toward the latter.

Fortunately, Quigley hadn't moved. As impatient as
the Kid was being, I was afraid he'd back out of the whole
deal if we had to take extra time just to run him down.
Our knock was answered with a cautious eye appearing
at the crack of the door as it opened slightly.

"Oh! I was hoping . . . that is, I was expecting . . . Can
I help you gentlemen?"

We had seen the "old man" disguise before, so there
was no doubt that it was really Quigley peering out at us.

"It's us, Quigley," the Kid said briskly before I could
even say "Hi." "Will you let us in, or should we just go
home?"

"Skeeve? Oh, thank goodness. Certainly . . . come right
in."

I personally thought Skeeve was being a bit abrupt,
and Quigley's fawning over him wasn't going to improve
his manners at all.

"Sorry for the reception," the magician said, herding
us inside, "but I was afraid it might be one of my credi-
tors."

As he closed the door, Quigley let his disguise spell
drop . . . too much effort to maintain, I guess. Viewing his
true appearance, I was slightly shocked.

The years had not been kind to our old ally. There were
strain marks etched deeply into his face that hadn't been
there when we were here before. The place itself seemed
the worse for wear. The walls needed painting badly . . .
or at least washing, and the furnishings showed signs of
being repaired instead of replaced.

"This place is a dump!" Skeeve observed with his newfound lack of diplomacy. "Really, Quigley. If you won't
think of yourself, think of the profession. How are people

supposed to respect magicians if they see one of them living like this?"

"Ease up, partner," I said softly. "We can't all own casinos. Some of us have had to live in broken-down shacks in the forest . . . or even sleep under trees on the open road."

That earned me a sharp glance, but Quigley intervened.

"No, Skeeve's right. All I can say is that I've tried. That's part of what's gotten me into the mess I'm in. I've overextended my credit trying to keep up a good front, and now it's catching up with me."

"Gee, Quigley, if that's your only problem we can take care of it in no time at all. We can arrange a quick consolidation loan to get the wolves off your back . . . with a slight interest charge, of course. Right, Aahz?"

The possibility of a fast resolution of the problem seemed to brighten Skeeve's mood immensely. I was almost tempted to go along with it, but I had the feeling there was more to the situation than was meeting the eye.

"I dunno, Skeeve. I think I'd like to hear a little more about exactly what the problem is, if it's all right with you."

"C'mon, Aahz. Let's just settle his accounts and split. If we hurry, we can be back at the office by lunch."

While I had tried to be patient, even promised myself to be, his wheedling tones finally got to me.

"Look, *Kid*," I said, using the phrase deliberately. "If you're so all-fired eager to get back, then go! I'm going to give a shot at trying to solve the *real* problem here, if I can ever find out what it is, maybe even without just throwing money at it. Okay?"

It was a cheap shot, but Skeeve had been asking for it. For a minute I thought he was going to take me up on my suggestion and leave, but instead he sank onto a sofa and sulked. Terrific. I turned my back on him and switched my attention to Quigley.

It seemed funny after all these years to take the lead in what was essentially a "people" situation. Usually I handled the tactics . . . okay, and occasionally the money . . . and left the people-handling to Skeeve. It was his part of the partnership to keep my abrasive personality from alienating too many people, particularly our friends. With him off in a blue funk, however, the task fell to me, and I was badly out of practice. Heck, I'll be honest, I was never *in* practice for this sort of thing. Ironically, I found myself trying to think of what Skeeve would say and do at a time like this.

"So, Quigley," I said, trying to smile warmly, "what exactly seems to be the problem?"

He fidgeted uncomfortably.

"Well, it's a long story. I . . . I'm not sure where to begin."

I suddenly remembered that non-Pervects tend to get nervous at the sight of Pervect teeth and dumped the smile.

"Why don't you start at the beginning? How come you're having money problems? You seemed to be doing all right the last time we were here."

"That's when it started," he sighed, "the last time you were here. Remember how they used to settle who was going to be the government around here? With the Big Game?"

Actually I hadn't thought about it for years, but it was starting to come back to me as he talked.

"Uh-huh. The Big Game between Ta-hoe and Vey-gus each year would decide who would get the Trophy *and* be the capital for the next year."

Quigley nodded vaguely.

"Right. Well, that's all changed now. When you guys won the game and took off with the Trophy, it stood the whole five-hundred-year-old system on its ear. For a while there was a faction that maintained that since you had the Trophy in Possiltum, that's where the capital should be for a year. Fortunately, wiser heads won out."

It was nice to know that there were *some* hassles that passed us by. I noticed that in spite of himself, Skeeve had perked up and was listening as Quigley continued.

"What they finally decided was that a Common Council should run the government. The plan was put into action with equal representation from both city-states, and for the first time in five hundred years the government of the dimension stabilized."

It actually sounded like some good had come out of our madcap caper. That made me feel kind of good. Still . . .

"I don't get it, Quigley. How is that a problem?"

The magician gave a wry smirk.

"Think about it, Aahz. With the feud over between the two city-states, there was no reason to maintain two magicians. It was decided that one would do just fine."

"Whoops," I said.

" 'Whoops' is right. Massha was their first choice. She had served as magician for both city-states at one time or another, and, frankly, they were more impressed with her than with me . . . especially after I let their hostage demon escape at the Big Game. When they went to tell her, though, she had disappeared. That left them with me."

I found myself wondering if Massha had signed on as Skeeve's apprentice before or after she knew about the organizational change and Quigley getting the boot.

"She's working with us over on Deva," Skeeve commented, finally getting drawn into the conversation.

"Really? Well, I suppose it makes sense. After you've gone as far as you can go on the local level, it's only natural to graduate into the big time."

"I still don't see how you ended up behind the eight ball financially," I said, trying to steer the conversation back on course.

Quigley made a face.

"It's my contract. I ended up having to take a substantial pay cut under the new situation. My salary before was adequate, but nothing to cheer about. Now . . ."

His voice trailed off.

"I don't get it," Skeeve said. "How can you be making

less money for serving two city-states than you made working for one?"

"Like I said, it's my contract. There are clauses in there I didn't even know about until the council hit me with them."

"What kind of clauses?" I frowned.

"Well, that the employer has the right to set my pay scale is the biggest one I remember. ' . . . According to the need of the community,' and they pointed out that with no feud, my workload, and therefore my pay, should be reduced accordingly. Then there's the 'No Quit' clause . . ."

"The what?"

"The 'No Quit' clause. In short, it says that they can fire me, but I can't quit for the duration of my contract. If I leave, I have to pay my replacement, 'sub-contractor' I think they call it, myself . . . even if they pay him more than they were paying me. That's why I'm stuck here. I can't afford to quit. By the time I got done deducting someone else's wages out of whatever I was earning on my new job, I'd be making even less than I am now. I can't believe I could land a position making more than double what I'm currently earning. Not with my track record."

For a moment I thought Skeeve was going to offer him a position with our company, but instead he groaned and hid his face in his hands.

"Quig-ley! How could you sign a contract with those kind of terms in it? Heck, how could you sign *any* contract without knowing for sure what was in it?"

"Frankly, I was so happy to find work at all I didn't think to ask many questions."

" . . . There's also the minor fact," I put in, "that when he was getting started in this game, he was all alone. He didn't have a teacher or a bunch of friends to look over his contracts or warn him off bad deals."

It was getting harder and harder to keep the Kid from getting too intolerant of other people's mistakes. Even that not-too-subtle admonishment only had partial success.

"Well, he could have asked me," he grumbled. "I could have at least spotted the major gaffes."

"As I recall," I tried again, staring at the ceiling, "at the time you were working as the Court Magician at Possiltum . . . without any kind of written agreement at all. Would *you* have come to you for contract advice?"

"All right, all right. I hear you, Aahz. So what is it you want me to do, Quigley?"

I caught the use of "me" instead of "us," but let it go for the time being.

"Well, it's a little late, but I'd like to take you up on your offer. I was hoping you could look over the contract and see if there's a way out of it. My time is almost up, but I'm afraid they're going to exercise their renewal option and I'll be stuck here for another three years."

"Don't tell me, let me guess," I winced. "It's their option whether or not to renew your contract. You have no say in the matter. Right?"

"Right. How did you know?"

"Lucky guess. I figured it went nicely with the 'No Quit' clause. And I thought slavery had been outlawed. . . ."

"Just exactly what are your duties these days, Quigley?"

Skeeve had been maintaining a thoughtful silence on the sofa until he interrupted me with his question.

"Not much, really," Quigley admitted. "More entertainment than anything else. As a matter of fact, I'm going to have to be leaving soon. I'm due to put on an appearance at the game this afternoon."

"The game?" I said. "They're still playing that?"

"Oh, certainly. It's still the major activity for entertainment and betting around here. They just don't play it for the Trophy, is all. It's been a much less emotional game since you guys trounced the locals, but they still get pretty worked up over it. I'll be putting on the after-game entertainment. Nothing much, just a few . . ."

I glanced at him when he failed to finish his sentence, only to discover he was snoring quietly in his c' air, sound asleep. Puzzled, I shifted my gaze to Skeeve.

"Sleep spell," he said with a wink. "I figured it was only appropriate. After all, I learned that spell on our last trip here after our friend here used it on Tananda."

"Don't you want to hear more about the contract we're supposed to be breaking for him, or at least take a look at it?"

"Don't need to. I've already heard enough to rough out a plan."

". . . And that is . . . ?"

His smile broadened.

"I'll give you a hint."

His features seemed to melt and shift . . . and I was looking at the "old man" disguise Quigley favored for his work.

"We don't want two Quigleys attending the game, do we? The way I see it, the best way to get him out of the contract is to take his place this afternoon."

I didn't like the sound of that.

"You're going to get him fired? Isn't that a bit drastic? I mean, how's it going to look on his resume?"

"Look, Aahz," he snarled. "I was the one who wanted to take the easy out and buy him out of his troubles. Remember? *You're* the one who said there had to be another way. Well, I've got another way. Now are you coming, or do you just want me to tell you how it went after it's over?"

The stadium was impressive no matter how you looked at it. Of course, any time you get nearly 100,000 people together all screaming for blood, it's bound to be impressive. I was just glad that this time they weren't screaming for *our* blood.

There was one bad moment, though. It seems that Quigley/Skeeve as a City-State Official got in free, whereas I, in disguise as an ordinary Joe, had to get a ticket to get past the fences. This was well and good, except that it meant we were separated for a bit. During that time, it suddenly dawned on me that if Skeeve got a little lax or wandered out of range, my disguise spell would disappear, revealing my true identity. As one of the team that trounced the locals and made off with their beloved Trophy, it occurred to me that there could be healthier pastimes than being suddenly exposed in the middle of thousands of hopped-up Game fans. Fortunately, I never had to find out for sure. Skeeve loitered about until I gained admission, and we pushed on together. It did give me pause, however, to realize how much I had grown to depend on the Kid's skills since losing my own powers.

Quigley/Skeeve was apparently well known, and many of the fans called to him as we entered the stadium proper. The salutations, however, were less than complimentary.

"Quigley! How's it going, you old fart?"

"Hey, Quigley! Are you going to do the same trick again?"

"Yeah! Maybe you can get it right this time!"

Each of these catcalls was, of course, accompanied by the proper "Haw, haw, haw!" brays, as can only be managed by fans who have started drinking days before in preparation for *their* role in the game. Maybe Quigley was used to this treatment, but it had been a long time since anyone had spoken to the Great Skeeve like that, and I noticed a dangerous glint developing in his eye that boded ill for whoever he finally decided to focus his demonstration on.

The game itself was actually rather enjoyable. It was a lot more fun to watch when we weren't the ones getting our brains beaten out on the field. I found myself cheering for the occasional outstanding play and hooting the rare intervention of the officials, along with the rest of the crazed mob.

Quigley/Skeeve, on the other hand, maintained an ominous silence. I found this to be increasingly unnerving as the afternoon wore on. I knew him well enough to tell he was planning something. What I didn't know were the specifics of "what" and "when." Finally, as the end of the game loomed close, I could contain myself no longer.

"Say, uh, Skeeve," I said, leaning close so he could hear me over the din of the crowd. "Have you got your plan worked out?"

He nodded without taking his eyes off the field.

"Mind telling me about it?"

"Well, remember how I got fired from Possiltum?" he said, glancing around to see if anyone was eavesdropping.

"Yeah. You told the King off. So?"

". . . So I don't see any reason why the same thing shouldn't work here. I don't imagine that City-State Officials are any less pompous or impressed with themselves than the monarch of a broken-down kingdom was."

That made sense. It was nice to see the Kid hadn't completely lost his feel for people.

"So what are you going to chew them out over? Their treatment of Quigley?"

He shook his head.

"Out of character," he said. "Quigley isn't the type to make a fuss over himself. No, I figured to make the fight the key issue."

"Fight? What fight?"

"The one that's about to break out on the field," Quigley/Skeeve grinned. "The way I see it, these two teams have been rivals for over five hundred years. I can't believe *all* their old grudges have been forgotten just because the government's changed."

"I dunno, partner. It's been a pretty clean game so far. Besides, it's already a rough contact sport. What's going to start a fight?"

"Most of the contact is around the ball . . . or cube, or whatever they call it. Never did get that straight. This late in the game, all the players are hyped up but not thinking too clearly from butting heads all afternoon. Now watch close."

He leaned forward to hide his hands, as one finger stretched out and pointed at the field.

There were two particularly burly individuals who had been notably at each other's throats all day, to the delight of the crowd. At the moment, they were jogging slowly side by side along the edge of the main action of the field, watching for the ball/cube to bounce free. Suddenly, one player's arm lashed out in a vicious backhand that smashed into his rival's face, knocking his helmet off and sending him sprawling onto the turf. The move was so totally unexpected and unnecessary that the crowd was stunned into silence and immobility. Even the player who had thrown the punch looked surprised . . . which he undoubtedly was. Nothing like a little tightly focused levitation to make someone's limbs act unpredictably, unless they're expecting it and braced against the interference.

The only one who didn't seem immobilized by the move was the player who had been decked. Like I said, the actual players of the game, unlike their out-of-shape fans, are built like brick walls—with roughly the same sense of humor. The felled player was on his feet with a bounce and launched himself at his supposed attacker. While that party was unsure about the magik that had momentarily seized his arm, he knew what to do about being pummeled, and in no time at all the two rivals were going at it hammer and tongs.

It might have worked, but apparently the teams took whatever truce had been called seriously. Amid the angry shouts from the stands and the referee's whistle, they piled on their respective teammates and pried them apart.

"Too bad, Skeeve," I said. "I thought you had them there."

When there was no response, I glanced at him. Brow furrowed slightly now, he was still working.

The player who had been attacked was free of his teammates. Though obviously still mad, he was under control as he bent to pick up his helmet. At his touch, however, the helmet took off through the air like a cannonball and slammed into the rival team member who had supposedly thrown the first punch. Now helmets in this game are equipped with either horns or points, and this one was no exception. The targeted player went down like a marionette with its strings cut, but not before losing a visible splatter of blood.

That did it.

At the sight of this new attack on their teammate, this time when the ball wasn't even in play, the fallen player's whole team went wild and headed for the now unhelmeted attacker . . . whose teammates in turn rallied to his defense.

Both benches emptied as the reserves came off the sidelines to join the fray . . . or started to. Before they had a chance to build up any speed, both sets of reserves were imprisoned by the glowing blue cages of magikal wards, an application I'll admit I had never thought of. Instead of the fresh teams from the benches, Quigley/Skeeve took the field.

I hadn't realized he had moved from my side until I saw him vault the low railing that separated the spectators from access to the playing field. The move was a bit spry for the "old man" guise he was using, but no one else seemed to notice.

It was a real pleasure to watch the Kid work . . . especially considering the fact that I taught him most of what he knows. I had to admit he had gotten pretty good over the years.

"STOP IT!! THAT'S ENOUGH!!" he roared. "I SAID, STOP IT!!!"

Still shouting, he waded into the players on the field who were locked in mortal combat. The ones who were standing he crumpled in their tracks with a gesture . . . a gesture which I realized as a simple sleep spell. The others he easily forced apart with judicious use of his levitational abilities. Two players who were grappling with each other he not only separated, but held aloft some twenty feet off the ground. As swiftly as it had started, the fight was stopped, and right handily, too.

As could have been predicted, no sooner had the dust settled than a troop of officious-looking individuals came storming out onto the field, making a beeline for Quigley/ Skeeve. While I may have lost my powers, there's nothing wrong with my hearing, and I was easily able to listen in on the following exchange, unlike the restless fans in the stands around me.

"Quigley, you . . . How dare you interrupt the game this way?"

"Game?" Quigley/Skeeve said coolly, folding his arms. "That wasn't a game, that was a fight . . . even though I can see how you could easily confuse the two."

"You have no right to . . . Put them down!"

This last was accompanied by a gesture at the suspended players. Skeeve didn't gesture, but the two players suddenly dropped to the turf with bone-jarring thuds that drew the same "Ooooo's" from the crowd as you get from a really good hit during actual play.

". . . As to my rights," Quigley/Skeeve intoned, not looking around, "I'm under contract to use my magikal powers to help keep the peace in Vey-gus and Ta-Hoe. The way I see it, that includes stopping brawls when I happen across them . . . which I've just done. To that end, I'm declaring the game over. The current score stands as final."

With that, the cage/wards began migrating toward their respective tunnels, herding the players within along with them. Needless to say, the crowd did not approve.

"You . . . you can't do that!" the official's spokesman screamed over the rising tide of boos from the stands. "The most exciting plays happen in the last few minutes!"

As a final flourish, Quigley/Skeeve levitated the fallen players on the field down the tunnels after their teammates.

"I've done it," he said. "What's more, I intend to do it at every scheduling of this barbaric game when things get out of hand. My contract is up for renewal soon, and I realized I've been a bit lax in my duties. Consequently, I thought I'd remind you of exactly what it is you're keeping on the payroll. If you don't like it, you can always fire me."

I smiled and shook my head in appreciation. I had to hand it to the Kid. If attacking the dimension's favorite pastime didn't get Quigley canned, I didn't know what would.

"**Y**ou shut down the game?"

That was Quigley expressing his appreciation for Skeeve's help.

We were back at his place with our disguises off and the magician revived. Apparently our assistance wasn't quite what he had been expecting.

"It seemed like the surest way to get you out of your contract," Skeeve shrugged. "The locals seem rather attached to the game."

"Attached to . . . I'm dead!" the magician cried with a groan. "I won't just get fired, I'll be lynched!"

The Kid was unmoved.

"Not to worry," he said. "You can always use a disguise spell to get away, or if it'll make you feel better, we'll give you an escort to . . ."

There was a knock on the door.

"Ah. Unless I miss my guess, that should be the Council now. Get the door, Quigley."

The magician hesitated and glanced around the room as if looking for a way to escape. Finally he sighed and trudged toward the door.

"Speaking of disguises, Skeeve . . ." I said.

"Oh, right. Sorry, Aahz."

With an absent-minded wave of his hand we were disguised again, this time in the appearances we used when we first arrived.

"Oh! Lord Magician. May we come in? There are certain matters we must . . . oh! I didn't realize you had guests."

It was indeed the Council. Right on schedule. I snuck a wink at Skeeve, who nodded in encouragement.

"These are . . . friends of mine," Quigley said lamely, as if he didn't quite believe it himself. "What was it you wanted to see me about?"

Several sets of uneasy eyes swept us.

"We . . . um . . . hoped to speak with you in private."

"We'll wait outside, Quigley," Skeeve said, getting to his feet. "Just holler if you need us."

"Well, that's that," I sighed after the door closed behind us. "I wonder what Quigley's going to do for his next job?"

Skeeve leaned casually against the wall.

"I figure that's his problem," he said. "After all, he's the one who asked us to spring him from his contract. I assume he has something else lined up."

". . . And if he doesn't? Quigley's never been big in the planning-ahead department. It won't be easy for him to find work with a termination on his record."

"Like I said, that's his problem," Skeeve shrugged. "He can always . . ."

The door opened, and the Council trooped silently out. Quigley waited until they were clear, then beckoned us inside frantically.

"You'll never guess what happened," he said excitedly.

"You were fired, right?" Skeeve replied. "C'mon, Quigley, snap out of it. Remember us? We're the ones who set it up."

"No, I wasn't fired. Once they got over being mad, they were impressed by the show of magik I put on at the game. They renewed my contract."

I found myself looking at Skeeve, who was in turn looking back at me. We held that pose for a few moments. Finally Skeeve heaved a sigh.

"Well," he said, "we'll just have to think of something else. Don't worry, Quigley. I haven't seen a contract yet that couldn't be broken."

"Ummm . . . actually, I'd rather you didn't."

That shook me a bit.

"Excuse me, Quigley. For a moment there I thought you said . . ."

"That's right. You see, the Council was impressed enough that they've given me a raise . . . a substantial raise. I don't think I'll be able to do better anywhere else, especially if they ask for a demonstration of my skills. There have been some changes in the contract, though, and I'd really appreciate it if you two could look it over and let me know what I'm in for."

"I'm sorry about that, Skeeve," I said as we trudged along. "All that work for nothing."

We had finally finished going over the contract with Quigley and were looking for a quiet spot to head back to Deva unobserved.

"Not really. We solved Quigley's problem for him, and that new contract is a definite improvement over the old one."

I had meant that he had done a lot of work for no pay, but decided not to push my luck by clarifying my statement.

"You kind of surprised me when we were talking outside," I admitted. "I half expected you to be figuring on recruiting Quigley for our crew, once he got free of his contract."

The Kid gave a harsh bark of laughter.

"Throw money at it again? Don't worry, Aahz. I'm not that crazy. I might have been willing to spot him a loan, but hire him? A no-talent, do-nothing like that? I run a tight ship at M.Y.T.H. Inc, and there's no room for dead-wood . . . even if they are old friends. Speaking of the company, I wonder if there's any word about . . ."

He rambled on, talking about the work he was getting back to. I didn't listen too closely, though. Instead, I kept replaying something he had said in my mind.

"A no-talent do-nothing . . . no room for deadwood, even if they are old friends . . ."

A bit harsh, perhaps, but definitely food for thought.

V:

"What fools these mortals be."

—SMAUG

I never really realized how easy it was to buy something until I tried my hand at selling. I'm not talking about small, casual purchases here. I'm talking about something of size . . . like, say, a casino/hotel. Of course buying it had been simplified by the fact that the developer . . . what was his name? No matter . . . was desperate. Trying to off-load it, however, was an entirely different matter.

Leaning back in my chair, I stared at the sea of paper on my desk, trying to mentally sort out the various offers, only to discover they were starting to run together in my head. I've noticed that happening more and more after midnight. With a muttered curse, I cast about for my notes.

"Working late, Skeeve?"

"What?" I said, glancing up. "Oh. Hi, Bunny. What are you doing here at this hour?"

"I could say I was worried about you, which I am, but truthfully I didn't even know you were still here till I saw the light on and poked my head in to check. No, I was just fetching a few things I had stored in my desk. Now, I can return the same question: what are *you* doing here?"

I stretched a bit as I answered, grateful for the break.

"Just trying to organize my thoughts on selling The Fun House. I'm going to have to make my recommendations to the Board as to which of these offers to accept when we discuss it at our monthly meeting."

She came around the desk and stood behind me, massaging the knots out of my shoulders. It felt wonderful.

"I don't see why you have to make a presentation to the Board at all," she said. "Why don't you just go ahead and make the decision unilaterally? You made the decision to sell without clearing it with anyone else."

Something in what she said had a ominous ring to it, but I was enjoying the backrub too much to pin it down just then.

"I made the decision unilaterally to open our door to offers . . . not to sell. The actual final call as to whether or not to sell, and, and, which, if any, of the offers to accept, is up to the Board."

"Then if it's up to them, why are you killing yourself getting ready to make a pitch?"

I knew where she was coming from then. It was the old "you're working too hard" bit. It seemed like I was hearing that from everybody these days, or often enough that I could sing it from memory.

"Because I *really* want this motion to carry," I said, pulling away from her. "If there's going to be any opposition, I want to be sure I have my reasons and arguments down pat."

Bunny wandered back around the desk, hesitated, then plopped down into a chair.

"All right, then rehearse. Tell *me* why you want to sell, if you don't mind giving a preview."

I rose and began to pace, rubbing my lower lip as I organized my thoughts.

"Officially, I think it's necessary for two reasons. First,

pretty soon now the novelty of the place is going to wear off, and when it does the crowds . . . and therefore our revenues . . . will decline. That will make it harder to sell than right now, when it's a hot spot. Second, the place is so successful it's going to generate imitators. From what I've been hearing at my 'businessman's lunches,' there are already several plans under way to construct or convert several of the nearby hotels into casinos. Again, it will dilute the market and lower our price if we wait too long."

Bunny listened attentively. When I was done, she nodded her head.

". . . And unofficially?"

"I beg your pardon?"

"You said, 'Officially, etc., etc.' That implies there are reasons you haven't mentioned."

That's when I realized how tired I was getting. A verbal slip like that could be costly in the wrong company. Still, Bunny was my confidential secretary. If I couldn't confide in her, I was in trouble.

"Unofficially, I'm doing it for Aahz."

"Aahz?"

"That's right. Remember him? My old partner? Well, when we were taking care of that little favor for Quigley, he kept needling me about The Fun House. There was a fairly constant stream of digs about 'throwing money at a problem' and how 'we never planned to run a casino' . . . stuff like that. I don't know why, but it's clear to me that the casino is a burr under his saddle, and if it will make him happy, I've got no problems dumping it. It just doesn't mean that much to me."

Bunny arched an eyebrow.

"So you're selling off the casino because you think it will make your old partner happy?"

"It's the best reason I can think of," I shrugged. "Bunny, he's been a combination father, teacher, coach, and Dutch uncle to me since Garkin was killed. I've lost track of the number of times he's saved my skin, usually by putting his own between me and whatever was incoming. With all I owe him, disposing of something that's bothering him seems a pretty small payback, but one I'll deliver without batting an eye."

"You might try to give him an assignment or two," she said, pursing her lips. "Maybe if he were a bit busier, he wouldn't have the time to brood and fault-find over the stuff you're doing without him."

I waited a heartbeat too long before laughing.

"Aahz is above petty jealousy, really," I said, wishing I was more sure of it myself. "Besides, I *am* trying to find an assignment for him. It's just that Perverts . . . excuse me, Pervects . . . aren't noted for their diplomacy in dealing with clients."

Not wishing to pursue the subject further, I gathered up a handful of proposals.

"Right now, I've got to go through these proposals a couple more times until I've got them straight in my mind."

"What's the problem? Just pick the best one and go with it."

I grimaced bitterly.

"It's not that easy. With some of these proposals, it's like comparing apples and oranges. One offers an ongoing percentage of profits . . . another is quoting a high purchase price, but wants to pay in installments . . . there are a handful that are offering stock in other businesses in addition to cash . . . it's just not that easy to decide which is actually the best offer."

"Maybe I can help," Bunny said, reaching for the stack of proposals. "I've had a fair amount of experience assessing offers."

I put my hand on the stack, intercepting her.

"Thanks for the offer, Bunny, but I'd rather do it myself. If I'm going to be president, I've got to learn to quit relying on others. The only way I'll learn to be self-reliant is to not indulge in depending on my staff."

She slowly withdrew her hand, her eyes searching mine as if she weren't sure she recognized me. I realized she was upset, but, reviewing what I had said, couldn't find anything wrong with my position. Too tired to sort it out just then, I decided to change the subject.

"While you're here, though, could you give me a quick briefing of what's on the dockets for tomorrow? I'd like to clear the decks to work on this stuff if I can."

Whatever was bothering her vanished as she became the efficient secretary again.

"The only thing that's pressing is assigning a team to a watchdog job. The client has a valuable shipment we're supposed to be guarding tomorrow night."

"Guard duty?" I frowned. "Isn't that a little low-class for our operation?"

"*I* thought so," she smiled sweetly, "but apparently you didn't when you committed us to it two weeks ago. A favor to one of your lunch buddies. Remember?"

"Oh. Right. Well, I think we can cover that one with Gleep. Send him over . . . and have Nunzio go along to keep an eye on him."

"All right."

She started to leave, but hesitated in the door.

"What about Aahz?"

I had already started to plunge into the proposals again and had to wrench my attention back to the conversation.

"What about him?"

"Nothing. Forget I asked."

There was no doubt about it. The staff was definitely starting to get a bit strange. Shaking my head, I addressed the proposals once more.

Gleep's Tale

Inevitably, when conversing with my colleagues of the dragon set, and the subject of pets was raised, an argument would ensue as to the relative advantages and disadvantages of humans as pets. Traditionally, I have maintained a respectful silence during such sessions, being the youngest member in attendance and therefore obligated to learn from my elders. This should not, however, be taken as an indication that I lack opinions on the subject. I have numerous well-developed theories, which is the main reason I welcomed the chance to test them by acquiring a subject as young and yet as well-traveled as Skeeve was when I first encountered him. As my oration unfolds, you will note . . . but I'm getting ahead of myself. First things first is the order of business for organized and well-mannered organisms. I am the entity you have come to know in these volumes as . . . "Gleep! C'mere, fella."

That is Nunzio. He is neither organized nor well-mannered. Consequently, as is so often the case when dealing with Skeeve and his rather dubious collection of associates, I chose to ignore him. Still, an interesting point has been raised, so I had probably best address it now before proceeding.

As was so rudely pointed out, I am known to this particular batch of humans, as well as to the readers of these volumes, simply as Gleep. For the sake of convenience, I will continue to identify myself to you by that name, thereby eliminating the frustrating task of attempting to instruct you in the pronunciation of my *real* name. Not only am I unsure you are physically able to reproduce the necessary sounds, but there is the fact that I have limited patience when it comes to dealing with humans. Then, too, it is customary for dragons to adopt aliases for these cross-phylum escapades. It saves embarrassment when the human chroniclers distort the facts when recording the incidents . . . which they invariably do.

If I seem noticeably more coherent than you would expect from my reputed one-word vocabulary, the reason is both simple and logical. First, I am still quite young for a dragon, and the vocal cords are one of the last things to develop in regard to our bodies. While I am quite able to converse and communicate with others of my species, I have another two hundred years before my voice is ready to attempt the particular combination of sounds and pitches necessary to converse extensively with humans in their own tongue.

As to my mental development, one must take into consideration the vast differences in our expected lifespan. A human is considered exceptional to survive for a hundred years, whereas dragons can live for thousands of years without being regarded as old by their friends and relations. The implications of this are too numerous to count, but the one which concerns us here is that, while I am perhaps young for a dragon, I am easily the oldest of those who affiliate themselves with Skeeve. Of course, humans tend to lack the breeding and upbringing of my kind, so they are far less inclined to heed the older and wiser heads in their midst, much less learn from them.

"Hey, Gleep! Can you hear me? Over here, boy."

I made a big show of nibbling on my foot as if troubled by an itch. Humans as a whole seem unable to grasp the subtleties of communication which would allow them to ascertain when they are being deliberately ignored, much less what it implies. Consequently, I have devised the technique of visibly demonstrating I am preoccupied when confronted with a particularly rude or ignorant statement or request. This not only serves to silence their yammerings, it slows the steady erosion of my nerves. To date, the technique yields about a twenty percent success ratio, which is significantly better than most tactics I have attempted. Unfortunately, this did not prove to be one of those twenty percenters.

"I'm talkin' ta *you*, Gleep. Now are ya gonna go where I tell ya or not?"

While I am waiting for my physical development to enable me to attempt the language of another species, I have serious doubts that Nunzio or Guido will master their *native* tongue, no matter how much time they are allowed. Somehow it reminds me of a tale one of my aunts used to tell about how she encountered a human in a faraway land and inquired if he were a native. "I ain't no native!" she was told. "I was born right here!" I quite agree with her that the only proper response when confronted by such logic was to eat him.

Nunzio was still carrying on in that squeaky little-boy voice of his which is so surprising when one first hears it, except now he had circled around behind me and was trying to push me in the direction he had indicated earlier. While he is impressively strong for a human, I outweighed him sufficiently that I was confident that there was no chance he could move me until I decided to cooperate. Still, his antics were annoying, and I briefly debated whether it was worth trying to improve his manners by belting him with my tail. I decided against it, of course. Even the strongest humans are dangerously frail and vulnerable, and I did not wish to distress Skeeve by damaging one of his playmates. A trauma like that could set my pet's training program back years.

Right about then I observed that Nunzio's breathing had become labored. Since he had already demonstrated his mental inflexibility, I grew concerned that he might suffer a heart attack before giving up his impossible task. Having just reminded myself of the undesirability of his untimely demise, I decided I would have to humor him.

Delaying just long enough for a leisurely yawn, I rose and ambled in the indicated direction . . . first sliding sideways a bit so that he fell on his face the next time he threw his weight against me. I reasoned that if he wasn't sturdy enough to survive a simple fall, then my pet was better off without his company.

Fortunately or un-, depending on your point of view, he scrambled rapidly to his feet and fell in step beside me as I walked.

"I want youse to familiarize yourself with the shipment which we are to be protectin'," he said, still breathing hard, "then wander around the place a little so's yer familiar with the layout."

This struck me as a particularly silly thing to do. I had sized up the shipment and the layout within moments of our arrival, and I had assumed that Nunzio had done the same. There simply wasn't all that much to analyze.

The warehouse was nothing more than a large room . . . four walls and a ceiling with rafters from which a scattered collection of lights poured down sufficiently inadequate light as to leave large pockets of shadows through the place. There was a small doorway in one wall, and a large sliding door in another, presumably leading to a loading dock. Except for the shipment piled in the center of the room, the place was empty.

The shipment itself consisted of a couple dozen boxes stacked on a wooden skid. From what my nose could ascertain, whatever was inside the boxes consisted of paper and ink. Why paper and ink should be valuable enough to warrant a guard I neither knew nor cared. Dragons do not have much use for paper . . . particularly paper money. Flammable currency is not our idea of a sound investment for a society. Still, someone must have felt the shipment to be of some worth, if not the human who had commissioned our services, then definitely the one dressed head to foot in black who was creeping around in the rafters.

All of this had become apparent to me as soon as we had entered the warehouse, so there was no reason to busy oneself with make-work additional checks. Nunzio, however, seemed bound and determined to prod me into rediscovering what I already knew. Even allowing for the fact that the human senses of sight, hearing, taste, touch, and smell are far below those of dragons, I was nonetheless appalled at how little he was able to detect on his own. Perhaps if he focused less of his attention on me and more on what was going on around us, he would have fared better. As it was, he was hopeless. If Skeeve was hoping that Nunzio would learn something from me, which was the only reason I could imagine for including him on the assignment, my pet was going to be sorely disappointed. Other than the fact that he seemed to try harder than most humans to interact positively with dragons, however crude and ignorant his attempts might be, I couldn't imagine why I was as tolerant of him as I was.

Whoever it was in the rafters was moving closer now. He might have been stealthy for a human, but my ears tracked him as easily as if he were banging two pots together as he came. While I was aware of his presence two steps through the door, I had been uncertain as to his intentions and therefore had been willing to be patient until sure whether he were simply an innocent bystander, or if he indeed entertained thoughts of larceny. His attempts to sneak up on us confirmed to me he was of the latter ilk, however incompetent he might be at it.

Trying to let Nunzio benefit from my abilities, I swiveled my head around and pointed at the intruder with my nose.

"Pay attention, Gleep!" my idiot charge said, jerking my muzzle down toward the boxes again. "This is what we're suppose to be guardin'. Understand?"

I understood that either humans were even slower to learn than the most critical dragons gave them credit for, which I was beginning to believe, or this particular specimen was brain-damaged, which was also a possibility. Rolling my eyes, I checked on the intruder again.

He was nearly above us now, his legs spread wide supporting his weight on two of the rafters. With careful deliberation, he removed something from within his sleeve, raised it to his mouth, and pointed it at us.

Part of the early training of any dragon is a series of lessons designed to impart a detailed knowledge of human weapons. This may sound strange for what is basically a peace-loving folk, but we consider it to be simple survival . . . such as humans instructing their young that bees sting or fire is hot. Regardless of our motivations, let it suffice to say that I was as cognizant of human weapons as any human, and considerably more so than any not in the military or other heroic vocations, and, as such, had no difficulty at all identifying the implement being directed at us as a blowgun.

Now, in addition to having better sense, dragons have armor which provides substantially more protection than humans enjoy from their skin. Consequently, I was relatively certain that whatever was set to emerge from the business end of the blowgun would not pose a threat to my well-being. It occurred to me, however, that the same could not be said for Nunzio, and, as I have said before, I have qualms about going to some lengths to ensure my pet's peace of mind by protecting his associates.

Jerking my head free from Nunzio's grasp, I took quick aim and loosed a burst of #6 flame. Oh, yes. Dragons have various degrees of flame at their disposal, ranging from "toast a marshmallow" to "make a hole in rock." You might keep that in mind the next time you consider arguing with a dragon.

Within seconds of my extinguishing the pyrotechnics, a brief shower of black powder drifted down on us.

"Darn it, Gleep!" Nunzio said, brushing the powder from his clothes. "Don't do that again, hear me? Next time you might do more than knock some dust loose . . . and look at my clothes! Bad dragon!"

I had been around humans enough not to expect any thanks, but I found it annoying to be scolded for saving his life. With as much dignity as I could muster, which is considerable, I turned and sat with my back to him.

"GLEEP! UP, BOY! GOOD DRAGON! GOOD DRAGON!"

That was more like it. I turned to face him again, only to find him hopping around holding his foot. Not lacking in mental faculties, I was able to deduce that, in making my indignant gesture, I had succeeded in sitting on his lower extremities. It was unintentional, I assure you, as human feet are rather small and my excellent sense of touch does not extend to my posterior, but it did occur to me in hindsight (no pun intended) that it served him right.

"Look, you just sit there and I'll sit over here and we'll get along fine. Okay?"

He limped over to one of the cartons and sat down, alternately rubbing his foot and brushing his clothes off.

The powder was, of course, the remains of the late

intruder/assassin. #6 flame has a tendency to have that effect on humans, which is why I used it. While human burial rights have always been a source of curiosity and puzzlement to me, I was fairly certain that they did not include having one's cremated remains brushed onto the floor or removed by a laundry service. Still, considering my difficulty in communicating a simple "look out" to Nunzio, I decided it would be too much effort to convey to him exactly what he was doing.

If my attitude toward killing a human seems a bit shocking in its casualness, remember that to dragons humans are an inferior species. You do not flinch from killing fleas to ensure the comfort of your dog or cat, regardless of what surviving fleas might think of your callous actions, and I do not hesitate to remove a bothersome human who might cause my pet distress by his actions. At least we dragons generally focus on individuals as opposed to the wholesale slaughter of species humans seem to accept as part of their daily life.

"You know, Gleep," Nunzio said, regarding me carefully, "after a while in your company, even Guido's braggin' sounds good . . . but don't tell him I said that."

"Gleep?"

That last sort of slipped out. As you may have noticed, I am sufficiently selfconscious about my one-word human vocabulary that I try to rely on it as little as possible. The concept of my telling Guido anything, however, startled me into the utterance.

"Now, don't take it so hard," Nunzio scowled, as always interpreting my word wrong. "I didn't mean it. I'm just a little sore, is all."

I assumed he was referring to his foot. The human was feeling chatty, however, and I soon learned otherwise.

"I just don't know what's goin' on lately, Gleep. Know what I mean? On the paperwork things couldn't be goin' better, except lately everybody's been actin' crazy. First the Boss buys a casino we built for somebody else, then overnight he wants to sell it. Bunny and Tananda are goin' at each other for a while, then all of a sudden Bunny's actin' quiet and depressed and Tananda . . . did you know she wanted to borrow money from me the other day? Right after she gets done with that collection job? I don't know what she did with her commission or why she doesn't ask the Boss for an advance or even what she needs the money for. Just 'Can you spot me some cash, Nunzio? No questions asked?', and when I try to offer my services as a confidential type, she sez 'In that case, forget it. I'll ask someone else!' and leaves all huffy-like. I'll tell ya, Gleep, there's sumpin' afoot, and I'm not sure I like it."

He was raising some fascinating points, points which I'll freely admit had escaped my notice. While I had devoted a certain portion of my intellect to deciphering the intricacies of human conduct, there was much in the subtleties of their intraspecies relationships which eluded me . . . particularly when it came to individuals other than Skeeve. Reflecting on Nunzio's words, I realized that my pet had not been to see me much lately, which was in itself a break in pattern. Usually he would make time to visit, talking to me about the problems he had been facing and the self-doubts he felt. I wondered if his increased absences were an offshoot of the phenomenon Nunzio was describing. It was food for thought, and something I promised myself I would consider carefully at a later point. Right now, there were more immediate matters demanding my attention . . . like the people burrowing in under the floor.

It seemed that, in the final analysis, Nunzio was as inept as most humans when it came to guard duty. They make a big show of alertness and caution when they come on duty, but within a matter of hours they are working harder at dealing with their boredom than in watching whatever it is they're supposed to be guarding. To be honest, the fact that dragons have longer lives may explain part of why we are so much better at staving off boredom. After a few hundred years, days, even weeks shrink to where they have no real time value at all. Even our very young have an attention span that lasts for months . . . sometimes years.

Whatever the reason, Nunzio continued to ramble on about his concerns with the status quo, apparently oblivious to the scratching and digging sounds that were making their way closer to our position. This time it wasn't simply my better hearing, for the noise was easily within the human range, though admittedly soft. By using *my* hearing, I could listen in on the conversations of the diggers.

"How much farther?"

"Sshhh! About ten feet more."

"Don't 'sshhh' me! Nobody can hear us."

"*I* can hear you! This tunnel isn't that big, ya know."

"What are you going to do with your share of the money after we steal the stuff?"

"First we gotta steal it. *Then* I'll worry about what to do with my share."

That was the part I had been waiting to hear. There had always been the chance they were simply sewer diggers or escaping convicts or something equally nonthreatening to our situation. As it was, though, they were fair game.

Rising from where I had been sitting, I moved quietly to where they were digging.

". . . unless Don Bruce wants to . . . Hey! Where are you goin'? Get back here!"

I ignored Nunzio's shouting and listened again. On target. I estimated about four feet down. With a mental smirk, I began jumping up and down, landing as heavily as I could.

"What are you doin'? Stop that! Hey, Gleep!"

The noise Nunzio was making was trivial compared to what was being said four feet down. When I mentioned earlier that I was too heavy for Nunzio to move unassisted, I was not meaning to imply that he was weak. The simple poundage of a dragon is a factor to be reckoned

with even if it's dead, and if it's alive and thinking, you
have real problems. I felt the floor giving way and hopped
clear, relishing the sounds of muffled screams below.

"Jeez. Now look what you've done! You broke the
floor!"

Again I had expected no thanks and received none.
This did not concern me, as at the moment I was more
interested in assessing the damage, or lack of damage, I
had inflicted on this latest round of potential thieves.

The floor, or a portion of it, now sagged about a foot
lower, leading me to conclude that either the tunnel below
had not been very high, or that it had only partially collapsed. Either way, there were no more sounds emanating
from that direction, which meant the thieves were either
dead or had retreated emptyhanded. Having accomplished
my objective of removing yet another threat to the shipment, I set my mind once again on more important things.
Turning a deaf ear to Nunzio's ravings, I flopped down
and pretended to sleep while I indulged in a bit of leisurely analysis.

Perhaps Nunzio was right. It was possible that my pet
was reacting adversely to the change in his status from
free-lance operator to the head of a corporation, much the
same as tropical fish will suffer if the pH of the water in
their aquarium is changed too suddenly. I was very much
aware that an organism's environment consisted of much
more than their physical surroundings ... social atmo-
sphere, for example, often influenced a human's well-
being. If that were the case, then it behooved me to do
something about it.

Exactly how I was to make the necessary adjustments
would be a problem. Whenever possible, I tried to allow
my pet free will. That is, I liked to give him the illusion
of choosing his own course and associates without interference from me. Occasionally I would stray from this
stance, such as when they brought that horrible Markie
creature into our home, but for the most part it was an
unshakeable policy. This meant that if I indeed decided

that it was time to winnow out or remove any or all of Skeeve's current associates for his own good, it would have to be done in a manner which could not be traced to me. This would not only preserve the illusion that I was not interfering in his life, but also save him the angst which would be generated if he realized I was responsible for the elimination of one or more of his friends. Yes, this would require considerable thought and consideration.

"Here, fella. Want a treat?"

This last was uttered by a sleazy-looking Deveel as he held out a hand with a lump of some unidentifiable substance in it.

I realized with a guilty start that I had overindulged, sinking too far into my thoughts to maintain awareness of my surroundings. After the unkind thoughts I had entertained about Nunzio's attention span, this was an inexcusable lapse on my part. Ignoring the offered gift, I raised my head and cast about desperately to reassess the situation.

There were three of them: the one currently addressing me, and two others who were talking to Nunzio.

"I dunno," the latter was saying. "I didn't get any instructions about anyone pickin' up the shipment early."

Something was definitely amiss. From his words and manner, even Nunzio was suspicious . . . which meant the plot had to be pretty transparent.

"C'mon boy. Take the treat."

The Deveel facing me was starting to sound a little desperate, but I continued ignoring him and his offering. It was drugged, of course. Just because humans can't smell a wide range of chemicals, they assume that no one else can either. This one was no problem. I was more concerned as to whether or not Nunzio would require assistance.

"I can't help it if your paperwork is fouled up," the smaller Deveel with Nunzio snarled, with a good imitation of impatience. "I've got a schedule to keep. Look. Here's a copy of my authorization."

As Nunzio bent to look at the paper the Deveel was holding, the one standing behind him produced a club and swung it at his head. There was a sharp "CRACK" . . . but it was from the club breaking, not from Nunzio's head, that latter being, as I have noted, exceptionally dense.

"I'm sorry, I can't let you have the shipment," Nunzio said, handing the paper back to the short Deveel who took it without losing the astounded expression from his face. "This authorization is nothin' but a blank piece of paper."

He glanced over his shoulder at the larger Deveel who was standing there staring at his broken club.

"Be with you in a second, fella. Just as soon as we get this authorization thing cleared up."

I decided that he would be able to handle things in his own peculiar way and turned my attention to the Deveel with the drugged treat.

He was looking at the conversation across the room, his mouth hanging open in amazement. I noticed, however, that he had neglected to withdraw his hand.

There are those who hypothesize that dragons do not have a sense of humor. To prove that that is not the case, I offer this as a counterexample.

Unhinging my jaw slightly, I stretched out my neck and took the treat in my mouth. Actually, I took his hand in my mouth . . . all the way to the shoulder. This was not as hazardous as it sounds. I simply took care not to swallow and therefore avoided any dangerous effects which might be generated by the drugged treat.

The Deveel glanced back when he heard my jaws crash together, and we looked into each others' eyes from a considerably closer range than he had anticipated. For effect, I waggled my eyebrows at him. The eyebrows did it, and his eyes rolled up into his head as he slumped to the floor in a dead faint.

Funny, huh? So much for not having a sense of humor. Relaxing my jaws, I withdrew my head leaving the treat and his arm intact, and checked Nunzio's situation again.

The larger Deveel was stretched out on the floor unconscious while Nunzio was holding the other by the lapels with one hand, leisurely slapping him forehand and backhand as he spoke.

"I oughtta turn youse over to da authorities! A clumsy hijack like this could give our profession a bad name. Know what I mean? Are you listenin' ta me? Now take your buddies and get outta here before I change my mind! And don't come back until you find some decent help!"

I had to admit that Nunzio had a certain degree of style . . . for a human. If he had been fortunate enough to be born with a brain, he might have been a dragon.

While he was busy throwing the latest batch of attackers out the door, I decided to do a little investigating. After three attempts to relieve us of our prize, though Nunzio was only aware of one of them, I was beginning to grow a bit suspicious. Even for as crime-prone a lot as humans tend to be, three attempts in that close succession was unusual, and I wanted to know more about what it was we were guarding.

The cases still smelled of paper and ink, but that seemed an inadequate reason for the attention they had been drawing. As casually as I could, I swatted one of the cases with my tail, caving it in. Apparently I had not been casual enough, for the sound brought Nunzio sprinting to my side.

"Now what are you doin'? Look! You ruined . . . Hey! Wait a minute!"

He stooped and picked up one of the objects that had spilled from the case and examined it closely. I snaked my head around so I could look over his shoulder.

"Do you know what dis is, Gleep?"

As a matter of fact, I didn't. From what I could see, all it was was some kind of picture book . . . and a shoddily made one at that. What it *didn't* look like was anything valuable. Certainly nothing that would warrant the kind of attention we had been getting.

Nunzio tossed the book back onto the floor and glanced around nervously.

"This is over my head," he murmured. "I can't . . . Gleep, you keep an eye on this stuff. I'll be right back. I've gotta get the Boss . . . and Guido! Yea. He knows about this stuff."

Admittedly perplexed, I watched him go, then studied the book again.

Very strange. There was clearly something in this situation that was escaping my scrutiny.

I rubbed my nose a few times in a vain effort to clear it of the smell of ink, then hunkered down to await my pet's arrival.

"**C**omic books?"

Skeeve was clearly as perplexed as I had been.

"The 'valuable shipment' we're guarding is comic books?"

"That's what I thought, Boss," Nunzio said. "Screwy, huh? What do you think, Guido?"

Guido was busy prying open another case. He scanned the books on top, then dug a few out from the bottom to confirm they were the same. Studying two of them intently, he gave out with a low whistle.

"You know what these are worth, Boss?"

Skeeve shrugged.

"I don't know how many of them are here, but I've seen them on sale around the Bazaar at three or four for a silver, so they can't be worth much."

"Excuse me for interruptin'," Guido said, "but I am not referrin' to yer everyday, run-of-the-mill comic. I am lookin' at these, which are a horse from a different stable."

"They are?" my pet frowned. "I mean . . . it is? I

mean . . . these all look the same to me. What makes them special?"

"It is not easy to explain, but if you will lend me your ears I will attempt to further your education, Boss. You too, Nunzio."

Guido gathered up a handful of the books and sat on one of the cases.

"If you will examine the evidence before you, you will note that while all these comics are the same, which is to say they are copies of the same issue, they each have the number 'one' in a box on their cover. This indicates that it is the first issue of this particular title."

I refrained from peering at one of the books. If Guido said the indicator was there, it was probably there, and looking at it wouldn't change anything.

"Immediately that 'one' makes the comic more valu-able, both to someone who is tryin' to obtain a complete set, and especially to a collector. Now, certain titles is more popular than others, which makes them particularly valuable, but more important are titles which have indeed grown in popularity since they made their first debutante. In that situational, there are more readers of the title cur-rently than there were when it began, and the laws of supply and demand drive the price of a first-issue copy through the roof."

He gestured dramatically with one of the books.

"This particular title premiered several years ago and is currently hotter than the guy what swiped the crown jewels. What is more, the print run on the first issue was very small, makin' a first-issue copy exceedingly valu-able . . . with the accent on 'exceedingly.' I have with my own eyes seen a beat-up copy of the comic you are cur-rently holding on a dealer's table with an askin' price of a hundert-fifty gold on it. Mind you, I'm not sayin' he got it, but that's what he was askin'."

Now it was Skeeve's turn to whistle. I might have been tempted myself, but whistling is difficult with a forked tongue.

"If that's true, this shipment is worth a fortune. He's got enough of them here."

"That is indeed the puzzlement, Boss," Guido said, looking at the cases. "If my memory is not seriously in error, there were only two thousand copies of this issue printed . . . yet if all these cases are full of the same merchandise, there are considerably more copies than that in this shipment to which we are referrin'. How this could be I am uncertain, but the explanation which occurs to me is less than favorable to the owner."

"Forgeries!" Nunzio squeaked. "The guy's a multicolored paper hanger!"

"A multi . . . never mind!" Skeeve waved. "What good would forged comics be?"

"The same as any other forgery," Guido shrugged. "You pass 'em off as originals and split with the money before anyone's the wiser. In some ways it's better'n phony money, since it isn't as hard to duplicate comics and, as youse can see, they're worth more per pound. The paper's cheaper, too."

My pet surveyed the shipment.

"So we've been made unwitting accomplices to a comic-forging deal, eh?"

". . . And without even gettin' a piece of the action," Nunzio snarled.

"That wasn't what I was thinking about," Skeeve said, shaking his head. "I was thinking of all the collectors who are going to plunk down their money to get a genuine collector's item, only to have the bottom drop out of the market when it's discovered that it's been flooded with forgeries."

He rubbed his lower lip thoughtfully.

"I wonder how much my lunch buddy has insured this shipment for?"

"Probably not much, if at all," Guido supplied. "To do so would necessitate the fillin' out of documents declarin' the contents of said shipment, and any insurance type knowledgeable enough to give him full value would also know the discrepancy between the shipment count and what was originally printed. You see, Boss, the trouble with runnin' a fraud is that it requires runnin' additional frauds to cover for it, and eventually someone is bound to catch on."

Skeeve wasn't even listening by the time Guido finished his oration. He was busy rubbing the spot between my ears, a strange smile on his face.

"Well, I guess nobody wins all the time."

"What was that, Boss?"

My pet turned to face them.

"I said that M.Y.T.H. Inc. fumbled the ball this time. Sorry, Nunzio, but this one is going into the records as a botched assignment. I can only assure you that it will *not* be reflected on your next performance review."

"I don't get it," Nunzio frowned. "What went wrong?"

"Why, the fire of course. You know, the fire that destroyed the entire shipment due to our inattentiveness and neglect? Terribly careless of us, wasn't it?"

"Fire? What fire?"

Skeeve stepped to one side and bowed to me, sweeping one hand toward the cases.

"Gleep? I believe this is your specialty?"

I waffled briefly between using a #4 or a #6, then said "to heck with it" and cut loose with a #9. It was a bit show-offy, I'll admit, but with Guido and Nunzio watching, not to mention my pet, it was pointless to spare the firepower.

They were impressed, which was not surprising, as #9 is quite impressive. There wasn't even any afterburn to put out, since by the time I shut down the old flamethrower, there was nothing left to burn.

For several moments we all stood staring at the charred spot on the warehouse floor.

"Wow!" Guido breathed at last.

"You can say that double for me," Nunzio nodded, slipping an arm around my neck. "Good dragon, Gleep. Good dragon."

"Well, gentlemen," Skeeve said, rubbing his hands together, "now that that's over I guess we can head . . . What's that?"

He pointed to the collapsed portion of the floor, noticing it for the first time.

"That?" Nunzio squeaked innocently. "Beats me, Boss. It was like that when we got here."

I didn't bother to return his wink, for I was already starting to retreat into heavy thought. I only hoped that in the final analysis I wouldn't decide that either Guido or Nunzio was an unsettling influence on my pet. Time would tell.

VI:

"Not everything in life is funny."

—R. L. ASPRIN

The crew seemed to be in high spirits as they gathered in my office for our monthly board meeting. Congratulations and jibes were exchanged in equal portions, as was the norm, and they began to settle in for what promised to be a marathon session.

I was glad *they* were in a good mood. It might make what I had to say a little easier, though I doubted it. I was still reeling from the one-two punch I had just received, and now it was my job to pass it on to them.

My own view of the pending session was a mixture of dread and impatience. Impatience finally dominated, and I called the meeting to order.

"I know you all came prepared to discuss the sale of The Fun House," I said, looking around at the team members sprawled hither and yon, "but something has come up that I think takes priority over that. If no one objects, I'll temporarily table the casino discussion in favor of new business."

That caused a bit of a stir and an exchange of puzzled glances and shrugs. Not wanting to be sidetracked by a round of questions or comments, I hurried on.

"There's an assignment . . . no, I can't call it that. There's no payment involved and no client. It's just something I think M.Y.T.H. should get involved in. I don't feel I can order anyone to take part . . . in fact, I don't even see putting it to a vote. It's got to be on an individual volunteer basis."

Tananda raised her hand. I nodded at her.

"Do we get to hear what it is? Or are we supposed to volunteer blind?"

I searched for the words for a moment, then gave up. Instead of speaking, I pushed the little oblong box that was on my desk toward her. She frowned at it, glanced at me, then picked it up and raised the lid.

One look inside was all it took for her to get the message. Sinking back in her seat, we locked eyes for a moment; then she shook her head and gave a low whistle.

"I say, is this a private horror, or can any number play?" Chumley grumbled from across the office.

In response, Tananda held up the box, tilting it so everyone could see the contents. Inside was a severed finger, a woman's finger, to be exact. It was wearing a particularly gaudy ring.

There was a long silence as the assemblage stared at the missive. Then Massha cleared her throat.

"How much for just the ring?" she quipped, but from the tone of her voice she wasn't expecting anyone to laugh.

Nobody did.

"I don't get it, Boss," Guido scowled. "Is this supposed to be a joke or sumpin'?"

"You and Nunzio weren't around for the big finale, Guido," I said. "Remember Queen Hemlock? Back on my home dimension of Klah?"

"Sure," he nodded. "She was an okay skirt . . . a little creepy, though."

"I guess it depended on which side of her favor you were on," Tananda commented wryly, tossing the box back onto the table.

I ignored her.

"Bunny, you weren't around for any of this, so . . ."

"I've picked up some of it talking to Chumley," she waved.

"Well, Queen Hemlock had an interesting plan she wanted to put into effect after she married Rodrick: to combine Possiltum's military strength with the wealth of her own kingdom of Impasse and fulfill her lifelong dream of conquering the world. Of course, she also planned to kill Rodrick if he opposed the idea."

I picked up the box and toyed with it idly.

"I thought I had stopped her by giving Rodrick wedding rings that they thought linked their lives, rings that wouldn't come off. The one in the box here is hers . . . of course, she had to cut off her finger to get rid of it. I hadn't anticipated that."

"I rather suspect she wanted her dream more than her finger," Chumley said with a grimace.

"So it would seem," I nodded. "Now she's on the loose, with an army we inadvertently supplied her with back when I was Court Magician of Possiltum. I'm not the greatest military appraiser around, but I don't think there's anything on Klah that can stop her . . . unless M.Y.T.H. Inc. takes a hand in the game."

"What I don't understand," Chumley said, "is why she informed us of the situation via that missive. Wouldn't she be better off unopposed?"

"Don't you know a challenge when you see one, big brother?" Tananda sighed. "Gauntlets are out of style, so she's giving us the finger."

"You all seem ta have a higher opinion of Queenie than I do," Massha spoke up. "Ta me, it looks more like an invitation to a trap. As I recall, old Hemlock wasn't too well disposed toward us when we split. For all we know, her plan may have already run its course . . . in which case

we get to be the featured entertainment at the victory cele-
bration."

That hadn't occurred to me. I seemed to be missing a
lot lately.

"You may be right, Massha," I said. "Under the best
of circumstances, I'm not sure there's anything that can
be done. That's why I'm putting it up for discussion. It's
my home dimension, and I was the one who contributed
to the problem, so my judgment is biased. In many ways,
it's a personal problem. I can't expect anyone else to . . ."

"You're talking it to death, Hot Stuff," Massha interrupted. "You're our peerless leader, for better or worse.
Just go for it. We'll be right behind you."

I shook my head and held up a restraining hand.

"It's not that simple. First of all, I don't want this to
be a group commitment where a dissenting individual has
to be an exception or go along with something they don't
agree with. That's why I was calling for individual volunteers . . . with no stigma attached to anyone who
doesn't want to sign up. Second . . ."

This was the hard part. Taking a deep breath, I plunged
into it.

"Second, I won't be along for this one. Something else
has come up that takes priority over Queen Hemlock.
Now, if she's not that important to me . . ."

"Whoa. Stop the music!" Tananda exclaimed. "I want
to hear what this hot deal is you've got going on the side.
What's more important to you than defending your own
home dimension?"

I avoided her eyes.

"It's not a deal or a job, really. It . . . It's personal.
Something I can't delegate. I've got to handle it myself."

"So tell us," she demanded, crossing her arms. "We're
family. If nothing else, don't you think we have a right
to know what the head man is going to be doing while
we're off fighting a war for him?"

I had had a feeling I wouldn't be able to slip this by
unnoticed. With a sigh, I dropped the other shoe.

"Look around the room," I said. "Notice anything missing?"

There was a pause as everyone complied. It took a distressingly long time for them to figure it out.

"Aahz!" Chumley said at last. "Aahz isn't here."

"Say, that's right," Massha blinked. "I thought the meeting was a little quiet. Where is old Green and Scaly?"

"Gone."

It took a moment for it to sink in. Then the team stared at each other in shocked silence.

"The note was on my desk this morning," I continued. "It's his letter of resignation from M.Y.T.H. Inc. Apparently he feels that without his powers he's deadwood . . . taking up space without earning his pay. He's packed up and gone, headed back to Perv."

I dropped the paper back on my desk.

"That's why I'm not going after Queen Hemlock myself. I'm going to Perv . . . after Aahz."

The room exploded.

"To Perv?"

"You've got to be kidding, Hot Stuff."

"But, Boss . . ."

"Skeeve, you can't . . ."

"I say, Skeeve. What if he won't come back?"

I homed in on that last comment. As usual, Chumley managed to hit the heart of the matter.

"If he won't come back . . . well, I'll have tried. I've got to at least talk to him. We've been together too long to let it go with a letter. I'm going to Perv to talk with him face to face . . . and I'm going alone."

A new wave of protest rose in the room, but I cut it off.

"When you go after Queen Hemlock . . . excuse me . . . *if* you go after Queen Hemlock, you're going to need all the manpower you can muster. It's bad enough that I can't be there; don't divide your strength more than it already is. Besides . . ."

My voice faltered a little here.

"This is my problem . . . I mean *really* my problem. I've been doing a lot of thinking since I read this note, and the problem is bigger than Aahz."

I swept the assemblage slowly with my eyes.

"I've gotten pretty wrapped up with being president lately. It's been hard to . . . I've been trying to justify the faith you all have in me by making the business go. In the process, it's gotten so I'm pretty sparse with my 'thank yous' and 'atta boys,' and I've all but lost contact with all of you outside of a business context. Aahz has been my best friend for years, and if he . . . Let's just say I'll be looking for myself as much as for Aahz."

There was dead silence as my oration ground to a halt. If I had been hoping for any protests over my analysis, I was playing to the wrong audience. Suddenly, I wanted the meeting to be over with.

I cleared my throat.

"I'm taking a leave of absence to find Aahz. No discussion is required or allowed. Now, the subject at hand is whether or not M.Y.T.H. Inc. is going to attempt to stop Queen Hemlock's assumed attempt to take over Klah. Are there any volunteers?"

MYTH-NOMERS
AND IM-PERVECTIONS

I:

"Nobody's seen it all!"

—MARCO POLO

Those of you who have been following my mishaps know me as Skeeve (sometimes Skeeve the Great) and that I grew up in the dimension Klah, which is not the center of culture or progress for our age no matter how generously you look at it. Of course, you also know that since I started chronicling my adventures, I've knocked around a bit and seen a lot of dimensions, so I'm not quite the easily impressed bumpkin I was when I first got into the magik biz. Well, let me tell you, no matter how sophisticated and jaded I thought I had become, nothing I had experienced to date prepared me for the sights that greeted me when I dropped in on the dimension Perv.

The place was huge. Not that it stretched farther than any other place I had been. I mean, a horizon is a horizon. Right? Where it *did* go that other places I had visited hadn't, was up!

None of the tents or stalls I was used to seeing at the Bazaar at Deva were in evidence here. Instead, massive

buildings stretched up into the air almost out of sight.
Actually, the buildings themselves were plainly in sight.
What was almost lost was the sky! Unless one looked
straight up, it wasn't visible at all, and even then it was
difficult to believe that little strip of brightness so far overhead was really the sky. Perhaps this might have been
more impressive if the buildings themselves were pleas-
anter to look at. Unfortunately, for the most part they had
the style and grace of an oversized outhouse ... and
roughly the same degree of cleanliness. I wouldn't have
believed that buildings so high could give the impression
of being squat, but these did. After a few moments' reflection, I decided it was the dirt.

It looked as if soot and grime had been accumulating
in layers on every available surface for generations, give
or take a century. I had a flash impression that if the dirt
were hosed from the buildings, they would collapse from
the loss of support. The image was fascinating and I
amused myself with it for a few moments before turning
my attention to the other noteworthy feature of the dimension: The People.

Now there are those who would contest whether the
denizens of Perv qualified as "people" or not, but as a
resident of the Bazaar I had gotten into the habit of referring to all intelligent beings as "people," no matter
what they looked like or how they used their intelligence.
Anyway, whether they were acknowledged as people or
not, and whether they were referred to as "Per-vects" or
"Per-verts," there was no denying there were a lot of
them!

Everywhere you looked there were mobs of citizens,
all jostling and snarling at each other as they rushed here
and there. I had seen crowds at the Big Game that I
thought were rowdy and rude, but these teeming throngs
won the prize hands down when it came to size *and* rude-
ness.

The combined effect of the buildings and the crowds
created a mixed impression of the dimension. I couldn't

tell if I was attracted or repelled, but overall I felt an almost hypnotic, horrified fascination. I couldn't think of anything I had seen or experienced that was anything like it.

"It looks like Manhattan . . . only more so!"

That came from Massha. She's supposed to be my apprentice . . . though you'd never know it. Not only is she older than me, she's toured the dimensions more than I have. Even though I've never claimed to be a know-it-all, it irritates me when my apprentice knows more than I do.

"I see what you mean," I said, bluffing a little. "At least, as much as we can see from here."

It seemed like a safe statement. We were currently standing in an alley which severely limited our view. Basically, it was something to say without really saying anything.

"Aren't you forgetting something, though, Hot Stuff?" Massha frowned, craning her neck to peer down the street.

So much for bluffing. Now that I had admitted noticing the similarities between Perv and Man-hat-tin . . . wherever *that* was, I was expected to comment on the differences. Well, if there's one thing I learned during my brief stint as a dragon poker player, it's that you don't back out of a bluff halfway through it.

"Give me a minute," I said, making a big show of looking in the same direction Massha was. "I'll get it."

What I was counting on was my apprentice's impatience. I figured she would spill the beans before I had to admit I didn't know what she was talking about. I was right.

"Long word . . . sounds like disguise spell?"

She broke off her examination of the street to shoot me a speculative glance.

"Oh! Yeah. Right."

My residency at the Bazaar had spoiled me. Living at the trading and merchandising hub of the dimensions had gotten me used to seeing beings from numerous dimensions shopping side by side without batting an eye. One tended to forget that in other dimensions, off-world beings were not only an oddity, occasionally they were downright unwelcome.

Of course, Perv was one of those dimensions. What Massha had noticed while I was gawking at the landscape was that we were drawing more than a few hostile glares as passersby noticed us at the mouth of the alley. I had attributed that to two things: the well-known Pervish temperament (which is notoriously foul), and Massha.

While my apprentice is a wonderful person, her appearance is less than pin-up-girl caliber . . . unless you get calendars from the local zoo. To say Massha would look more natural with a few tick-birds walking back and forth on her would be an injustice . . . she's never *tried* to look natural. This goes beyond her stringy orange hair and larger-than-large stature. I mean, anyone who wears green lipstick and turquoise nail polish, not to mention a couple of tattoos of dubious taste, is not trying for the Miss Natural look.

There was a time when I would get upset at people for staring at Massha. She really *is* a wonderful person, even if her taste in clothes and makeup would gag a goat. I finally reached peace with it, however, after she pointed out that she *expected* people to look at her and dressed accordingly.

All of this is simply to explain why it didn't strike me as unusual that people were staring at us. Similarly, Pervish citizens are noted for not liking anyone, and offworlders in particular, so the lack of warmth in the looks directed at us did not seem noteworthy.

What Massha had reminded me of, though it shouldn't have been necessary, is that we were now on Perv, their home dimension, and instead of an occasional encounter we would be dealing with them almost exclusively. As I said I should have realized it, but after years of hearing about Perv, it was taking a while for it to sink in that I was actually there.

Of course, there was no way we could be mistaken for

natives. The locals here had green scales, yellow eyes, and pointed teeth, while Massha and I looked . . . well, normal. In some way, I think it goes to show how unsettling the Pervects look when I say that, by comparison, Massha looks normal.

However, Massha was correct in pointing out that if I hoped to get any degree of cooperation from the locals, I was going to have to utilize a disguise spell to blend with them. Closing my eyes, I got to work.

The disguise spell was one of the first spells I learned, and I've always had complete confidence in it . . . after the first few times I used it, that is. For those who are interested in technical details, it's sort of a blend of illusion and mind control. Simply put, if you can convince yourself that you look different, others will see it as well. That may sound complicated, but it's really very simple and easy to learn. Actors have been using it for centuries. Anyway, it's quite easy, and in no time at all my disguise was in place and I was ready to face Perv as a native.

"Nice work, Spell-slinger," Massha drawled with deceptive casualness. "But there's one minor detail you've overlooked."

This time I knew exactly what she was referring to, but decided to play it dumb. In case you're wondering, yes, this is my normal modus operandi . . . to act dumb when I know what's going on, and knowledgeable when I'm totally in the dark.

"What's that, Massha?" I said, innocently.

"Where's mine?"

There was a lot loaded into those two words, everything from threats to a plea. This time, however, I wasn't going to be moved. I had given the matter a lot of thought and firmly resolved to stand by my decision.

"You aren't going to need a disguise, Massha. You aren't staying."

"But, Skeeve . . ."

"No!"

"But . . ."

"Look, Massha," I said, facing her directly, "I appreciate your wanting to help, but this is my problem. Aahz is *my* partner, not to mention my mentor and best friend. What's more, it was my thoughtlessness that got him so upset he resigned from the firm and ran away. No matter how you cut it, it's my job to find him and bring him back."

My apprentice regarded me with folded arms and tight lips.

"Agreed," she said.

". . . So there's no point in your trying to . . . what did you say?"

"I said agreed," she repeated. ". . . As in, I agree it's your job to bring Aahz back!"

That took me by surprise. I had somehow expected more of an argument. Even now, it didn't look to me like she had really given up the fight.

"Well, then . . ."

". . . And it's my job as your apprentice to tag along and back your moves. By your own logic, Chief, I'm obligated to you the same way you're obligated to Aahz."

It was a good argument, and for a moment I was tempted to let her stay.

"Sorry, Massha," I said finally with real regret, "I can't let you do it."

"But . . ."

". . . Because you're going to be my stand-in when the rest of the team takes on Queen Hemlock."

That stopped her, as I thought it would, and she bit her lip and stared into the distance as I continued.

"It's bad enough that the rest of the crew is going to fight my battle for me, but to have both of us sit it out is unthinkable. They're going to need all the help they can get. Besides, part of the reason for having an apprentice is so that I can be two places at once . . . isn't it?"

I figured that would end the discussion, but I underestimated Massha's determination.

"Okay, then *you* lead the fight against Hemlock and *I'll* fetch the Scaly Wonder."

I shook my head.

"C'mon, Massha. You know better than that. It was my thoughtlessness that made him leave in the first place. If anyone should, if anyone *can* make him come back it's got to be me."

She muttered something under her breath that it's probably just as well I didn't hear, but I was pretty sure it wasn't wholehearted agreement. With one problem already at hand from my lack of attentiveness to my associates' moods, I thought it ill-advised to ignore the fact my apprentice was upset.

"Look, can we take a few minutes and discuss what it is that's really bothering you?" I said. "I'd just as soon we didn't part company on an off note."

Massha pursed her lips for a few moments, then heaved a great sigh.

"I just don't like the idea of your taking on this chore alone, Skeeve. I know you know more magik than I do, but this is one of the meanest of the known dimensions. I'd feel better if you had a backup is all . . . Even if it's just a mechanic like me. These little toys of mine have helped us out more than once in the past."

What she was referring to, of course, was her jewelry. Nearly all the magik Massha used was of the gimmick variety . . . magik rings, magik pendants, magik nose studs . . . hence the nickname within the trade of "mechanic." She was, however, polite enough to not stress too hard the fact that her toys were often more effective and reliable than my own "natural" form.

"You're right, Massha, and I'd love to have you along . . . but you're needed more against Hemlock. Before you get too worried, though, just remember I've handled some pretty tough situations in the past."

"Those weren't on Perv and you usually had your partner along to handle the rough stuff," she said bluntly. "You don't even have a D-hopper along."

"I'll get it back from Aahz when I find him. If I'm successful, we'll be along together. If not, I figure he'll give me the D-hopper and set it for Klah just to be rid of me."

". . . And if you can't find him at all?" Massha gestured pointedly at the crowds on the street. "In case you haven't noticed, this isn't going to be the easiest place to locate someone."

For a change, I was confident when I answered.

"Don't worry about that. I'll find him. I've got a few tricks up my sleeve for that chore. The trick is going to be getting him to change his mind."

"Well, can you at least do one thing? As a favor to your tired old apprentice?"

She tugged a ring off her left pinkie and handed it to me.

"Wear this," she said. "If you haven't shown up by the end of the week, I'll come looking for you. This'll help me locate you if you're still in this dimension . . . or do you want to run the risk of being stranded here?"

The ring fit loosely on my right thumb. Any larger, and I would have had to wear it like a bracelet. Staring at it, a sudden suspicion flitted through my mind.

"What else does it do?"

"Beg pardon?" Massha replied with such innocence I knew I was right.

"You heard me, *apprentice*. What does it do besides provide a beacon?"

"Wellll . . . it *does* monitor your heartbeat and alert me if there's a sudden change in your physical condition, like say if you were injured. If that happens, I might just drop in a little early to see what's wrong."

I wasn't sure I liked that.

"But what if my heartbeat changed for normal reasons . . . like because I met a beautiful girl close up?"

That earned me a bawdy wink.

"In that case, High Roller, I'd want to be here to meet

her. Can't have you running around with just *anybody*, can we?"

Before I could think of a suitable reply, she swept me into a bone-crushing hug.

"Take care of yourself, Skeeve," she whispered with sudden ferocity. "Things wouldn't be the same without you."

There was a soft pop in the air, and she was gone. I was alone in Perv, the nastiest of the known dimensions.

II:

"They don't make 'em like they used to!"

—H. FORD

Actually, I wasn't as worried as you might think I'd be from the situation. Like I'd told Massha, I had an ace up my sleeve . . . and it was a beaut!

A while back, I was part . . . heck, I was the instigator of a plan to force the Mob out of the Bazaar at Deva. I felt it was only fair, since I was the one who had given them access to the Bazaar in the first place, and besides, the Devan Merchants' Association had paid me well to get the Mob off their backs. Of course that was before the Mob hired me to run their interests at the Bazaar, and the Bazaar agreed to give me a house and pay me a percentage of the profits to keep the Mob at bay. Sound confusing? It was . . . a little. Fortunately, Aahz had shown me how the two assignments weren't mutually exclusive and that it *was* ethically possible to collect money from both sides . . . well, possible, anyway. Is it any wonder that I prize his counsel so highly? However, I digress.

During the initial skirmishes of that campaign, I had

acquired a litle souvenir that I had almost forgotten about until I was getting ready for this quest. It wasn't much to look at, just a small vial with its stopper held in place by a wax seal, but I figured it just might mean the difference between success and failure.

I probably could have mentioned it to Massha, but frankly I was looking forward to taking the credit for having pulled off this chore by myself. Smirking confidently, I glared around to be sure I was unobserved, then broke the seal and removed the stopper.

Now to really appreciate the full impact of this next bit, you have to realize what I was expecting. Living at the Bazaar, I had gotten used to some really showy stuff . . . lightning bolts, balls of fire . . . you know, special effects like that. It's a tight market, and glitz sells. Anyway, I was braced for nearly anything, but I was expecting a billowing cloud of smoke and maybe a thunderclap or a gong for emphasis.

What I got was a soft pop, the same as you get pulling a cork out of a bottle of flat soda, and a small puff of vapor that didn't have enough body to it to make a decent smoke ring. End of show. Period. *Das ist alles.*

To say I was a little disappointed would be like saying Deveels dabbled in trade. Understatement to the max. I was seriously considering whether to throw the bottle away in disgust or actually try to get a refund out of the Deveel who sold it to me, when I noticed there was something floating in the air in front of me.

Actually, I should say it was *someone* floating in the air, since it was clearly a figure . . . or to be accurate, half a figure. He was bare to the waist, and possibly beyond. I couldn't tell because the image faded to invisibility below his navel. He was wearing a fez low on his forehead so it hid his eyes, and had his arms folded across his chest. His arms and torso were pretty muscular, and he might have been impressive . . . if he weren't so small! I had been expecting something between my height and that of a three-story building. What I got would have been maybe six to eight inches high if all of him was visible. As it was, head and torso only measured about three inches. Needless to say, I was underwhelmed. Still, he was all I had and if nothing else, over my various trials and adventures, I had learned to make do with what was available.

"Kalvin?" I said, unsure of the proper form of address.

"Like, man, that's my name. Don't wear it out," the figure replied without emerging from under his hat.

Now, I wasn't sure what our exact relationship was supposed to be, but I was pretty sure this wasn't it, so I tried again.

"Ummm . . . do I have to point out that I am your Master and therefore Ruler of your Destiny?"

"Oh, yeah?"

The figure extended one long finger and used it to push the fez back to a point where he could look at me directly. His eyes were a glowing blood red.

"Do you know what I am?"

The question surprised me, but I rallied gamely.

"Ah, I believe you're a Djin. Specifically a Djin named Kalvin. The Deveel I bought you from said you were the latest thing in Djins."

The little man shook his head.

"Wrong."

"But . . ."

"What I am is drunk as a skunk!"

This last was accompanied by a conspiratorial wink.

"Drunk?!" I echoed.

Kalvin shrugged.

"What do you expect? I crawled into the bottle years ago. I guess you could say I'm a Djin Rummy."

Whether my mouth was open from astonishment or to say something, I'm not sure but I finally caught the twinkle in his eye.

"Djin rummy. Cute. This is a gag, right?"

"Right as rain!" the Djin acknowledged, beaming at

me with a disarming smile. "Had you going for a minute, didn't I?"

I started to nod, but he was still going strong.

"Thought we might as well get started on the right foot. I figure anyone who owns me has got to have a sense of humor. Might as well find out first thing, ya know? Say, what's yer name, anyway?"

He was talking so fast I almost missed the opening. In fact, I would have if he hadn't paused and looked expectantly at me.

"What? Oh! I'm Skeeve. I . . ."

"Skeeve, huh? Funny name for a Pervert."

My response was reflexive.

"That's Per-*vect*. And I'm not. I mean, I'm not one."

The Djin cocked his head and squinted at me.

"Really? You sure look like one. Besides, I've never met anyone who wasn't a Perver . . . excuse me, Pervect . . . who would argue the difference."

It was sort of a compliment. Anyway, I took it as one. It's always nice to know when your spells are working.

"It's a disguise," I said. "I figured it was the only way to operate on Perv without getting hassled by the natives."

"Perv!"

Kalvin seemed genuinely upset.

"By the gods, Affendi, what are we doing here?"

"Affendi?"

"Sure. You're the Affendi, I'm the Offender. It's tradition among Djins. But that's beside the point. You haven't answered my question. How did an intelligent lad such as yourself end up in this godforsaken dimension?"

"Do you know Perv? Have you been here before?" I said, my hopes rising for the first time since I opened the bottle.

"No, but I've heard of it. Most Djins I know avoid it like the plague."

So much for getting my hopes up. Still, at least I had Kalvin talking seriously for a change.

"Well, to answer your question, I'm here looking for

a friend of mine. He . . . well, you might say he ran away from home, and I want to find him and bring him back. The trouble is, he's . . . a bit upset at the moment."

"A bit upset?" The Djin grimaced. "Sahib, he sounds positively suicidal. Nobody in their right mind comes to Perv voluntarily . . . present company excepted, of course. Do you have any idea why he headed this way?"

I shrugged carelessly.

"It's not that hard to understand. He's a Pervect, so it's only natural that when things go wrong, he'd head for . . ."

"A Pervect?"

Kalvin was looking at me as if I'd just grown another head.

"You have one of these goons for a friend? And you admit it? And when he leaves you try to get him back?"

Now, I couldn't speak for any of the other citizens of Perv, but I knew Aahz was no goon. That's fact, not idle speculation. I knew the difference because I had two goons, Guido and Nunzio, working for me. I was about to point this out when it occurred to me that I wasn't required to give Kalvin any kind of explanation. I was the owner, and he was my servant.

"I rather think that's between my friend and me," I said stiffly. "As I understand it, your concern is to assist me in any way you can."

"Right-o," the Djin nodded, not seeming to take offense at my curtness. "Business it is. So what chore brings you to summon one of my ilk?"

"Simple enough. I'd like you to take me to my friend."

"Good for you. I'd like a pony and a red wagon, myself."

It was said so smoothly it took a moment for me to register what he had said.

"I beg your pardon?"

Kalvin shrugged.

"I said, 'I'd like a pony and . . .' "

"I know. I mean, I heard what you said," I interrupted.

"I just don't understand. Are you saying you won't help me?"

"Not won't . . . can't. First of all, you've never even gotten around to telling me who your friend is."

"Oh, that's easy. His name is Aahz, and he's . . ."

". . . And second of all, it's not within my powers. Sorry."

That stopped me. I had never paused to consider the extent of a Djin's power.

"It's not? But when I summoned you, I thought you were supposed to help me."

". . . Any way I can," Kalvin finished. "Unfortunately for you, that doesn't cover a whole lot. How much did you pay for me, anyway?"

"A silver . . . but that was a while ago."

"A silver? Not bad. You must be pretty good at bargaining to get a Deveel to part with a registered Djin for that price."

I inclined my head at the compliment, but felt obliged to explain.

"He was in a state of shock at the time. The rest of his stock had been wiped out."

"Well, don't feel too proud," the Djin continued. "You were still overcharged. I wouldn't pay a silver for my services."

This was sounding less and less assuring. My easy solution to the problem seemed to be disappearing faster than a snowball on Deva.

"I don't get it," I said "I always thought Djins were supposed to be heavy hitters in the magik department."

Kalvin shook his head sadly.

"That's mostly sales hype," he admitted regretfully. "Oh, some of the big boys can move mountains . . . literally. But those are top-of-the-line Djins and usually cost more than it would take to do the same things non-magikally. Small fry like me come cheaper, but we can't do whole bunches, either."

"I'm sorry, Kalvin. None of this makes any sense. If

Djins actually have less power than, say, your average
magician for hire, why would anybody buy them at all?"

The Djin gestured grandly.

"The mystique . . . the status . . . do you know anything
at all about Djinger?"

"Ginger? As in ginger beer?"

"No, *Djin*-ger . . . with a 'D' . . . As in the dimension
where Djins and Djeanees come from."

"I guess, not."

"Well, once upon a time, as the story goes, Djinger
had a sudden disastrous drop in its money supply."

This sounded a little familiar.

"An economic collapse? Like on Deva?"

The Djin shook his head.

"Embezzlement," he said. "The entire Controller's office for the dimension disappeared, and when we finally
found someone who could do an audit, it turned out most
of the treasury was gone too.

"There was a great hue and cry, and several attempts
to track the culprits, but the immediate problem was what
to do for money. Manufacturing more wouldn't work,
since it would simply devalue what we did have. What
we really needed was a quick influx of funds from outside
the dimension.

"That's when some marketing genius hit on the 'Djin
In A Bottle' concept. Nearly everyone in the dimension
who had the least skill or potential for magik was recruited for service. There was resistance, of course, but
the promoters insisted it called for temporary contracts
only, so the plan went into effect. In fact, the limited
contract thing became a mainstay of the sales pitch . . . the
mystique I was mentioning. That's why most Djins have
conditions attached . . . three wishes only or whatever,
though some are more ethical than others about how the
wishes are fulfilled."

A thought suddenly occurred to me.

"Um, Kalvin? How many wishes do I get from you?

Like I said, the Deveel was a bit shell-shocked and never said anything about limitations."

". . . On wishes *or* powers, eh?" the Djin winked. "Not surprising. Shell-shocked or not, Deveels still know how to sell. In their own way they're truly amazing."

"How many?"

"What? Oh. I'm afraid my contract only calls for one wish, Skeeve. But don't worry, I'll play it clean. No tricks, no word traps. If you're only going to get one for your money, it's only fair that it's legit."

"I see," I said. "So what *can* you do?"

"Not much, actually. What I'm best at is bad jokes."

"Bad jokes?"

"You know, like 'How do you make a djin fizz?"

"I don't think . . ."

"Drop him in acid. How do you . . ."

"I get the picture. That's it? You tell bad jokes?"

"Well, I give pretty good advice."

"That's good. I think I'm going to need some."

"I'll say. Well, the first piece of advice I've got for you is to forget about this and head for home before it's too late."

For a moment the thought was almost tempting, but I shook it off.

"Not a chance," I said firmly. "Let's go back to my original request. Can you advise me on how to find Aahz?"

"I might have a few ideas on the subject," the Djin admitted.

"Good."

"Have you tried a phone book?"

By now suspicion had grown into full-blown certainty. My hidden ace had turned out to be a deuce . . . no, a joker. If I was counting on Kalvin for the difference between success and failure, I was in a lot of trouble.

Until now I had taken finding Aahz for granted, and

had only been worrying about what to say once we were face-to-face. Now, looking at the streets and skyscrapers of Perv, I was painfully aware that just *finding* Aahz was going to be harder than I thought . . . a *lot* harder!

III:

"It's not even a nice place to visit!"

—FODOR'S *GUIDE TO PERV*

Even after getting used to the madness that was the Bazaar at Deva, the streets of Perv were something to behold. For one thing, the Bazaar was primarily geared for pedestrian traffic, the Merchants' Guild being strong enough to push through ordinances that favor modes and speed of travel that almost forced people to look at every shop and display they passed. My home dimension of Klah was a pretty backward place, and I had rarely seen a vehicle more advanced or faster than an oxcart.

Perv, on the other hand, had thoroughfares split between foot and vehicle traffic, and, for an unsophisticated guy like me, the vehicle traffic in particular was staggering. Literally hundreds of contraptions of as many descriptions jostled and snarled at each other at every intersection as they clawed for a better position in the seemingly senseless tangle of streets through which the torrent surged. Almost as incredible as the variety of vehicles was the collection of beasts which provided the locomotive power, pushing or pulling their respective burdens while adding their voices to the cacophony which threatened to drown out all other sounds or conversation. Of course, they also added their contribution to the filth in the streets and smells in the air. It might be the metropolitan home of millions of beings, but Perv had the charm and aroma of a swamp.

What concerned me most at the moment, however, was the traffic. Walking down the street on Perv was a little like trying to swim upstream through a logjam. I was constantly having to dodge and slide around citizens who seemed intent on walking through the space I was already occupying. Not that they seemed to be trying to hit me deliberately, mind you. It's just that nobody except me seemed to be looking where they were going. In fact, just making eye contact was apparently a rare occurence.

"This friend of yours must really be something for you to put up with this," Kalvin commented drily.

He was hovering in the vicinity of my shoulder, so I had no difficulty hearing him over the din. I had worried about how it would look having a Djin tagging along with me, but it seems that while they're under control Djins can only be seen and heard by their owner. It occurred to me that this was fairly magikal and therefore in direct contrast to the line Kalvin was selling me about how powerless he was. He in turn assured me that it was really nothing, simply part of a Djin's working tools that would be no help to me at all. I wasn't assured. Somehow I had the feeling he wasn't telling me everything about his abilities or lack thereof, but having no way to force additional information out of him, I magnanimously decided to let it ride.

"He's more than a friend," I said, not realizing I was slipping into the explanation I had decided earlier not to give. "He was my teacher, and then my business partner as well. I probably owe him more than any other person in my life."

". . . But not enough to respect his wishes," the Djin supplied carelessly.

That brought me to a dead stop, ignoring the crush and jostling of the other pedestrians.

"What's that supposed to mean?"

"Well, it's true, isn't it? This guy Aahz obviously wants to be left alone or he wouldn't have walked out on you, but you're determined to drag him back. To me that doesn't sound like you really care much about what's important to *him*."

That hit uncomfortably close to home. As near as I could tell Aahz had left because I had been rather inconsiderate in my dealings with him. Still, I wasn't going to turn back now. At the very least I wanted a face-to-face talk before I let him disappear from my life.

"He was a bit upset and throwing a snit-fit at the time," I muttered, avoiding the question of my motives completely. "I just want him to know that he's welcome if he wants to come back."

With that I resumed my progress down the street. Half a dozen steps later, however, I realized the Djin was laughing ruefully.

"Now what?"

"Skeeve, you're really something, you know?" Kalvin said, shaking his head. "Perverts . . . excuse me, Pervects . . . are feared throughout the dimension for their terrible, violent tempers. But you, you not only describe it as a snit-fit, you're willing to show up on Perv itself just to make a point. You're either very good or an endangered species."

It suddenly occurred to me that I wasn't making as much use of my Djin as I might. I mean, he *had* said that one of the things he was good at was advice, hadn't he?

"I don't know, Kalvin. I've never had much trouble with them. In fact, one of the things Aahz told me was that Pervects manufacture and spread a lot of the bad rumors about themselves just to discourage visitors."

"Oh, yeah?"

The Djin seemed unconvinced.

"Well, let's see then. Could you share some of the things you've heard about this dimension with me?"

Kalvin shrugged.

"If you want. I remember hearing about how one of your buddy's fellow citizens ripped off some guy's head and spit down his throat . . . literally!"

I ducked around a heavyset couple who were bearing down on me.

"Uh-huh. I heard the same rumor, but the one doing the ripping was a Troll, not a Pervect. Nobody actually *saw* that one, either. Besides, right now I'm more interested in information about the dimension than hearing tales of individual exploits."

I thought I lost Kalvin for a moment when I flattened against a wall to avoid a particularly muscular individual and the Djin didn't make the move with me, but when I stepped out again he was back in his now-accustomed place.

"Well, why didn't you say so, if that's what you wanted to hear?" he said as if there had been no interruption. "About Perv itself. Let me think. There's not that much information floating around, but what there is . . . Ah! Got it!"

He plucked a thick book out of thin air and started leafing through it. I was so eager to hear what he had to say that I didn't comment on that little stunt at the moment, but I also vowed anew to inquire further into Kalvin's "meager powers" when the opportunity presented itself.

"Let's see . . . Parts . . . P'boscus . . . Perv! You want the statistics or should I skip to the good part?"

"Just give me the meat for now."

"Okay. It says here, and I quote, 'Perv: One of the few dimensions where magik and technology have advanced equally through the ages. This blend has produced a culture and lifestyle virtually unique in the known dimensions. *Perverts* are noted for their arrogance, since they strongly believe that their dimension possesses the best of everything, and they are extremely vocal in that belief wherever they go. This is despite ample proof that other dimensions which have specialized in magik or technology exclusively have clearly surpassed Perv in both fields. Unfortunately, Pervects are also disproportionately strong and are *notorious for their bad tempers and ferocity*, so few care to argue the point with them.' End quote."

Coming from Klah; a dimension which excelled at neither magik nor technology, I found the writeup to be pretty impressive. Kalvin, on the other hand, seemed to find endless amusement in it.

". . . 'Despite ample proof . . .' I love it!" he chortled. "Wait'll the next time I see that blowhard."

For some reason, I found this vaguely annoying.

"Say, Kalvin," I said, "what does your book say about Djinger?"

"What book?"

"The one you . . ."

I took my eyes off the foot traffic and glanced at him. He was dusting his hands innocently. The book was nowhere in sight.

I was opening my mouth to call him on his little disappearing act when something piled into me and sent me careening into a wall hard enough to make me see stars.

"Where do you think you're goin', Runt?"

This last came from the pudgy individual I had just collided with. He had stopped to confront me and stood with his fists clenched, leaning slightly forward as if being held back by invisible companions. Fat or not, he looked tough enough to walk through walls.

"Excuse me . . . I'm sorry," I mumbled, shaking my head slightly to try to clear the spots that still danced in front of my eyes.

"Well . . . watch it next time," he growled. He seemed almost reluctant to break off our encounter, but finally spun on his heel and marched on down the sidewalk.

"You shouldn't let that fat lug bluff you like that," Kalvin advised. "Stand up to him."

"What makes you think he was bluffing?" I said, resuming my journey, taking care to swerve around the other Pervects crowding the path. "Besides, there's also the minor detail that he was big enough to squash me like a bug."

"He raised a good point, though," the Djin continued as if I hadn't spoken. "Just where *are* we going, anyway?"

"Down the street."

"I meant, 'what's our destination?' I thought you said the phone book was no help."

Despite its millions of inhabitants, the Pervish phone book we found had turned out to have less than a dozen pages. Apparently unlisted phone numbers were *very* big in this dimension, just one more indication of the social nature of the citizens. Of course, leafing vainly through it, it had occurred to me that Aahz had been with me off-dimension for so long that it was doubtful he would have been in the book even if it contained a full listing.

"I repeat, we're going down the street," I repeated. "Beyond that, I don't know where we're going. Is that what you wanted to hear?"

"Then why are we moving at all?" the Djin pressed. "Wouldn't it be better to wait until we decided on a course of action before we started moving?"

I dodged around a slow-moving couple.

"I think better when I'm walking. Besides, I don't want to draw unnecessary attention to us by lurking suspiciously in alleys while I come up with a plan."

"Hey, you! Hold it a minute!"

This last was blasted with such volume that it momentarily dominated the street noise. Glancing behind me, I saw a uniformed Pervect who looked like a giant bulldog with scales bearing down on me with a purposeful stride.

"What's that?" I said, almost to myself.

Of course, unlike the direct questions I had put to him, Kalvin decided to answer this one.

"I believe it's what you referred to as 'unnecessary attention' ... also known in some dimensions as a cop."

"I can see that. I just can't understand what he wants with me."

"What did you say?" the cop demanded, heaving to a halt in front of me.

"Me? Nothing," I replied, barely remembering in time that he couldn't see or hear Kalvin. "What's the trouble, officer?"

"Maybe you are. We'll see. What's your name?"

"Don't tell him!" Kalvin whispered in my ear.

"Why?" I said, the words slipping out before I had a chance to think.

"Because it's my job to keep track of suspicious characters," the cop growled, taking my question as being directed at him.

"Me? What have I done that's suspicious?"

"I've been following you for a couple of blocks now, and I've seen how you keep swervin' around folks. I even saw you apologize to someone and ... say, I'll ask the questions here. Now, what's your name?"

"Tell him to bag it!" Kalvin advised. "He doesn't have a warrant or anything."

"Skeeve, sir," I supplied, desperately trying to ignore the Djin. All I needed now was to get in trouble with the local authorities. "Sorry if I'm acting strange, but I'm ... not from around here and I'm a little disoriented."

I decided at the last moment to try to keep my off-dimension origins a secret. The policeman seemed to be fooled by my disguise spell, and I saw no point in enlightening him unless asked directly.

"You're being too polite!" the Djin whispered insistantly. "That's what made him suspicious in the first place, remember?"

"Not from around here, eh?" the cop snarled. "So tell me, Mr. Can't-Walk-Like-Normal-Folks-Skeeve, just where is it you're from ... *exactly*?"

So much for keeping my origins a secret.

"Well, I was born on Klah, but lately I've been living at the Bazaar at Deva where I . . ."

"From off-dimension! I might have known. I suppose comin' from Deva that you're going to try to tell me you're here on business."

"Well, sort of. I'm here looking for my business partner."

"Another one from off-dimension! Any more and we'll have to fumigate the whole place."

The cop's mouth was starting to get on my nerves, but I thought it wise to keep a rein on my temper, despite the warning from Kalvin.

"Actually, he's from here. That is, he's a Pervect."

"A Pervect? Now I've heard everything. A fellow from off-dimension who claims to have a Pervect for a business partner!"

That did it.

"That's right!" I barked. "What's more, he happens to be my best friend. We had a fight and I'm trying to find him and get him to rejoin the company. What's it to you, anyway?"

The cop gave ground a little, then scowled at me.

"Well, I guess you're tellin' the truth. Even someone from off-dimension could come up with a better lie than that. Just watch your step, fella. We don't like outsiders much on Perv."

He gave me one last hard glare, then wandered off, glancing back at me from time to time. Still a little hot under the collar, I matched him glare for glare.

"That's better," Kalvin chortled, reminding me of his presence. "A Klahd, huh? That explains a few things."

"Oh, yeah? Like what?"

Like I said, I was still a little miffed.

"Like why we've been wandering around without a plan. You aren't used to metropolises this size, are you?"

Mad as I was, I couldn't argue with that.

"Well . . ."

"If you don't mind, could I offer you a little advice without your asking for it?"

I shrugged non-committally.

"It's obvious to me this little search of yours could take some time. It might be a good idea if we hunted up a hotel to use for a base camp. If that cop had asked where you were staying on Perv, things might have gotten a little awkward."

That made sense. It also brought home to me just how much of a stranger in a strange land I was. On most of my adventures I had either slept under the stars or had housing provided by friends or business associates. Consequently, I had remarkably little experience with hotels . . . like none.

"Thanks, Kalvin," I said, regaining a bit of my normal composure. "So how do you recommend we find a hotel?"

"We could hail a cab and ask the driver."

Terrific. The Djin was being his normal, helpful self. I was beginning to feel some things weren't going to change.

IV:

"Taxis are water soluble."

—G. KELLY

"I'll tell ya, this would be a pretty nice place, if it weren't for all the Perverts."

The taxi driver said this the same way he had made all his comments since picking us up: over his shoulder while carelessly steering his vehicle full tilt through the melee of traffic.

I had ignored most of his chatter, which didn't seem to bother him. He apparently didn't expect a response, but this last comment caught my interest.

"Excuse me, but aren't you a Pervert . . . I mean, a Pervect?"

The driver nodded vigorously and half turned in his seat to face me.

"There. See what I mean?"

Frankly, I didn't. If there was logic in his statement, it escaped my comprehension. What I did see, however, was that we were still plunging forward without slacking our speed. There was a tangle of stopped vehicles ahead which the driver seemed oblivious to as he tried to make his conversational point. A collision seemed inescapable.

"Look out!" I shouted, pointing frantically at the obstructions.

Without losing eye contact, the driver's hand lashed out and smashed down on the toy stuffed goose that was taped down in front of him. The thing let out a harsh, tremendous "HONK!!" that would have gotten it named king of the geese if they ever held an election.

"Anyway, that's what I'm talkin' about." The driver finished and turned his attention forward again.

The traffic jam had miraculously melted away before he had finished speaking, and we sailed through the intersection unscathed.

"Relax, Skeeve," Kalvin laughed. "This guy's a professional."

"A professional what?" I muttered.

"How's that?" the driver said, starting to turn again.

"NOTHING! I . . . nothing."

I had been unimpressed with the taxi since it had picked us up. Actually, 'picked us up' is much too mild a phrase and doesn't begin to convey what had actually happened.

Following Kalvin's instructions, I had stepped to the curb and raised my hand.

"Like this?" I said, making the mistake of turning my head to ask him directly.

Facing away from the street, I missed what happened next, which is probably just as well. The normal traffic din suddenly erupted with shrieks and crashes. Startled, I jerked my hand back and jumped sideways to a spot a safer distance from the street. By the time I focused on the scene, most of the noise and the action had ceased.

Traffic was backed up behind the vehicle crouched at the curb beside us, and blocked drivers were leaning out to shout and/or shake their fists threateningly. There may have been a few collisions, but the condition of most of the vehicles on the street was such that I couldn't be certain which damages were new and which were scars from earlier skirmishes.

"That's right," Kalvin said, apparently unruffled by the mayhem which had just transpired. "Get in."

"You're kidding!"

The vehicle which had stopped for us was not one to inspire confidence. It was sort of a box-like contraption hanging between two low-slung, tailless lizards. The reptiles had blindfolds wrapped around their head obscuring their eyes, but they kept casting from side to side while their tongues lashed in and out questing for data on their surroundings. Simply put, they looked powerful and hungry enough for me to want to keep my distance.

"Maybe we should wait for another one," I suggested hopefully.

"Get in," the Djin ordered. "If we block traffic too long the cop will be back."

That was sufficient incentive for me, and I bravely entered the box and took a seat behind the driver, Kalvin never leaving my shoulder. The interior of the box seemed safe enough. There were two seats in the rear where I was sitting, and another beside the driver, although the latter seemed filled to overflowing with papers and boxes that would occasionally spill to the floor when we took a corner too fast . . . which was always. There were notes and pictures pinned and taped to the walls and ceiling in a halo around the driver, and a confusing array of dials and switches on the panel in front of him. Basically, one had the suspicion the driver lived in his vehicle, which was vaguely reassuring. I mean, the man wouldn't do anything to endanger his own home, would he?

"Where to?" the driver said, casually forcing his vehicle back into the flow of traffic.

"Um, just take me to a hotel."

"Expensive . . . cheap . . . what?"

"Oh, something moderate, maybe a bit on the inexpensive side."

"Right."

I was actually pretty well set financially. A money belt around my waist had over two thousand in gold I had brought along to cover expenses on my search. Still, there was no sense throwing it away needlessly, and I figured since I didn't plan to spend much time in my room, I wouldn't need anything particularly grand.

Within the first few blocks, however, I had pause to reconsider the wisdom of my choice of vehicles. As far as I could tell, the lizards were blindfolded to prevent their animal survival instinct from interfering with the driver's orders. I couldn't figure out how he was controlling them, but he seemed determined to maintain a breakneck pace regardless of minor considerations like safety and common sense.

"So, have you two been on Perv long?"

The driver's voice dragged me back to the present my mind had been trying so desperately to ignore.

"Just got here today. In fact."

Suddenly, I zeroed in on what he had said.

"Excuse me, did you say 'you *two*'?"

The driver bobbed his head in acknowledgment.

"That's right. It isn't often I get a Klahd or a Djin, much less one of each in the same fare."

He not only knew how many we were, he had spotted *what* we were! Needless to say, the news was not welcome.

"What the . . ." Kalvin started, but I silenced him with a gesture.

"Before I answer, do you mind my asking how you knew?" I said, casually glancing around to see if there was a way we could exit rapidly if necessary.

"Scanned you when you got in," the driver said, pointing briefly to a small screen amidst the clutter of his other devices. "A cabbie can't be too careful these days . . . not with the crime rate the way it is. We're moving targets for every amateur stick-up artist or hijacker who needs a quick bankroll. I had that baby installed so I'd know in advance what was sittin' down behind me."

He shot me a quick wink over his shoulder.

"Don't worry, though. I won't charge you extra for the Djin. He don't take up much space. So far as I can tell, you two are harmless enough."

That reassured me, at least to a point where I no longer considered jumping from the moving vehicle.

"I take it you don't share the general low opinion of folks from off-dimension?"

"Don't make no never mind to me, as long as you pay your way," the driver waved. "As far as I can tell, you got enough money on ya that I don't think you'll try to welch on anything as piddling as a cab fare. Keep up the disguise, though. Some of the merchants around here will raise their prices at the sight of someone from off-dimension just to make you feel unwelcome . . . and things are already priced sky-high."

"Thanks for the warning."

". . . And you might be careful carrying so much cash. Everything you've heard about crime on the streets in this place is true. In fact, you'd probably be best off hiring yourself a bodyguard while you're here. If you want, I can recommend a couple good ones."

"You know, that might not be a bad idea," Kalvin said. "In case I hadn't mentioned it, Djinger is a pretty peaceful dimension. I won't be much help to you in a fight."

I ignored him as the cabbie continued, apparently unable to hear the Djin despite his various devices. Remembering some of the dangers I had faced in my adventures, the idea of hiring someone to guard me just to walk down the street seemed a little ludicrous.

"I appreciate your concern, but I'm pretty good at looking out for myself."

"Suit yourself, it was just a suggestion. Say, you want something to eat? I sell snack packs."

He used one hand to pick up a box from the seat beside him and shove it in my direction. It was filled with small bags with stuff oozing through the sides.

"Uh . . . not just now, thanks," I said, trying to fight down the sudden queasiness I felt.

The driver was not to be daunted. He tossed the box back onto the seat and snatched up a booklet.

"How about a guidebook, then? I write and print 'em myself. It's better'n anything you'll find on the stands . . . and cheaper, too."

That might have come in handy, but glancing at it I could see the print was a series of squiggles and hieroglyphics that were meaningless to me. I always travel with a translator pendant to get around the language barrier, but unfortunately its powers don't extend to the written word.

"I don't suppose you have a Klahdish translation, do you?"

"Sorry," he said, tossing the booklet in the same general direction the box had gone. "I'm takin' a few courses to try to learn some other languages, but Klahdish isn't one of them. Not enough demand, ya know?"

Despite my continuing concern over his attention to his driving, the cabbie was beginning to interest me.

"I must say you're enterprising enough. Cab driver, publisher, cook, translator . . . is there anything else you do?"

"Oh, I'm into a lot of things. Photography, tour guide . . . I even draw a little. Some of these drawings I did. I'd be willing to part with them for the right price."

He gestured at some of the sheets adorning the interior, and the cab veered dangerously to the right.

"Ah . . . actually, I was interested in something else you said just now."

"Yeah? What's that?"

"Tour guide."

"Oh, that. Sure. I love to when I get the chance. It's sweet money. Beats the heck out of fighting the other hacks for fares all day long."

I glanced at Kalvin and raised a questioning eyebrow.

"Go ahead," he said. "We could use a guide, and you

seem to be getting along with this guy pretty well. You know what they say, 'Better the Deveel you know.' "

Obviously the Djin's knowledge did not extend to Deveels, but this wasn't the time or place to instruct him. I turned my attention back to the driver.

"I was thinking of hiring you more as a guide than a tour guide. How much do you make a day with this cab?"

"Well, on a good day I can turn better than a hundred."

"Uh-huh," I said. "How about on an average day?"

That earned me another over-the-shoulder glance.

"I gotta say, fella, you sure don't talk like a Klahd."

"I live at the Bazaar at Deva," I smiled. "It does wonders for your bargaining skills. How much?"

We haggled back and forth for a few minutes, but eventually settled on a figure. It seemed fair, and I wasn't exactly in a position to be choosy. If the device the cabbie had used was widespread in his profession, my disguise would be blown the second I stepped into a cab, and there was no guarantee the next driver would be as well disposed toward off-dimensioners as our current junior entrepreneur.

"Okay, you've got yourself a guide," the driver said at last. "Now, who am I working for?"

"I'm Skeeve, and the Djin with me is Kalvin."

"Don't know about the Djin," the cabbie shrugged. "Either he don't talk much or I can't hear him. Pleased to meetcha, though, Mr. Skeeve. I'm Edvik."

He extended a hand into the back seat, which I shook cautiously. I had encountered Pervish handshakes before and could still feel them in my joints in wet weather.

"So, where do you want to go first?"

That seemed like a strange question to me, but I answered it anyway.

"To a hotel, same as before."

"Uh-uh."

"Excuse me?" I said, puzzled.

"Hey, you hired a guide, you're going to get one. You're about to check into a hotel, right?"

"That's right."

"Well, you try to check into a Pervish hotel the way you are, without luggage, and they're going to give you a rough time whether they figure you're from off-dimension or not. They'll be afraid that you're trying to get access to a room to steal the furniture or maybe to try to break into other rooms on the same floor."

That was a new concept to me. While I had a fairly extensive wardrobe at home, I usually traveled light when I was working . . . like with the clothes I was wearing and money. It had never occurred to me that a lack of luggage would cause people to be suspicious of my intentions.

"What do you think, Kalvin?"

"Beats me," the Djin shrugged. "I've never run into the problem. Of course, I travel in a bottle and people can't see me anyway."

"Well, what do you recommend, Edvik?"

"Let me take you by a department store. You can pick up a small bag there and maybe some stuff to put in it. Believe me, it'll pay in the long run in dealing with a hotel."

I pondered the point for a moment, then decided it was senseless to hire a guide, then not listen to his advice.

"All right," I said at last. "How far is it to this store you were talking about?"

"Oh, not far at all. Hang on!"

This last warning was a bit late, as he had already thrown the cab into a tight U-turn which scrambled the traffic around us and sent me tumbling across the seat. Before I could recover my balance we were well on our way back in the direction we had come from.

As accustomed as I was to madcap excursions, it occurred to me that this one was quickly becoming more complex than anything I had previously experienced. I hoped the education would prove to be more enjoyable and beneficial than it had been so far.

V:

"I just need to pick up a few things."

—I. Marcos

I've made numerous references to the Bazaar at Deva, where I make my home. For the benefit of those who do not travel the dimensions or read these books, it's the largest market center in the known dimensions. Anything you can imagine, as well as many an item you can't, is for sale there. Competition is stiff, and the Deveel merchants will turn themselves or their customers inside out before they'll let a sale get away.

I mention this so that everyone following this adventure will realize what a shock shopping on Perv was to me. The differences were so many, it was almost hard to accept that the same activity was under way in both instances.

For openers, there was the basic layout. The Bazaar is an endless series of stalls and shops that stretch over the horizon in all directions. There are various concentrations of specialty shops, to be sure, but no real pattern and, more important, no way of finding anything without looking. In direct contrast, Pervish shopping is dominated by what Edvik referred to as "department stores." One store could take up an entire city block with as many as six stories crammed full of merchandise. The goods are organized into sections or "departments" and carefully controlled so as not to be in competition with each other. Signs are prominently displayed to tell shoppers where everything is, though it is still relatively easy to get lost in the maze of aisles and counters. Of course, it also helps if you can read Pervish.

Perhaps the biggest difference, however, is in the general attitude toward customers. This was apparent when I made my first stop in the luggage department.

There was a good selection of bags and cases there, and the displays were laid out well enough so that I could distinguish between the magikal and non-magikal bags without being able to read the signs. It wasn't even that hard to make my selection. There was a small canvas suitcase roughly the size of a thick attache case which caught my eye both from the simplicity of the design and the fact that it was magikally endowed. That is, it had a permanent spell on it which made it about three times as large on the inside as it showed on the exterior. It occurred to me it might be a handy item to have, and if I was going to buy something to check into a hotel with, it might as well be something I could actually get some use out of later. The difficulties started when I was ready to make my purchase.

Up to this point, I had been pleasantly surprised that the sales help had left me alone. On Deva, I would have been approached by the proprietor or one of his assistants as soon as I set foot in the display area, and it was kind of nice for a change to browse leisurely without being pressured or having whatever overstock was on sale that day touted to the heavens. Once I had made my selection, however, I found that getting the attention of one of the salesmen was astoundingly difficult.

Standing by the display which featured the bag I

wanted, I looked toward the cash register where two salesmen were engrossed in conversation. On Deva, this would
have been all that was necessary to have the proprietor
swoop down on me, assuming he had given me any room
to start with. Here, they didn't seem to notice. Slightly
puzzled, I waited a few moments, then cleared my throat
noisily. It didn't even earn me a glance.

"Are you coming down with something, Skeeve?" Kalvin said anxiously. "Anything contagious, I mean?"

"No, I'm just trying to signal for one of the salesmen."

"Oh."

The Djin floated a few feet higher to peer toward the
cash register.

"It doesn't seem to be working."

"I can see that, Kalvin. The question is, what will?"

We waited a few more moments and watched the salesmen in their discussion.

"Maybe you should go over there," the Djin suggested
at last.

It seemed strange to pursue a salesman to get him to
take my money, but lacking a better idea I wandered over
to the sales counter.

. . . And stood there.

The salesmen finished their discussion of sports and
started on dirty jokes.

. . . And stood there.

Then the subject was the relative merits of the women
they were dating. It might have been interesting, not to
mention instructional, if I hadn't been getting so annoyed.

"Do you get the feeling I'm not the only one who's
invisible?" Kalvin muttered sarcastically.

When a Djin who's used to sitting in a bottle for years
starts getting impatient, I figure I'm justified in taking
action.

"Excuse me," I said firmly, breaking into the conversation. "I'd like to look at that bag over there? The small
magik one in green canvas?"

"Go ahead," one of the salesmen shrugged and returned to his conversation.

I stood there for a few more moments in sheer disbelief, then turned and marched back over to the bag.

"Now you're starting to move like a Pervect," the Djin observed.

"I don't care," I snarled. "And that's *Pervert!* I've tried to be nice . . . didn't want to mess up their display . . . *but*, if they insist . . ."

For the next several minutes I took my anger out on the bag, which was probably the safest object to vent my spleen on. I hefted it, swung it over my head, slammed it against the floor a couple times, and did everything else to it I could think of short of climbing inside. I've got to admit the thing was sturdily made. Then again, I was starting to see why goods on Perv had to be tough. The salesmen never favored me with so much as a glance.

"Check me on this, Kalvin," I panted, my exertions finally starting to wear on my endurance. "The price tag on this bag *does* say 125 gold, doesn't it?"

I may not be able to read many written languages, but numbers and prices have never given me any trouble. I guess it comes from hanging around with Aahz as long as I have . . . not to mention Tananda and Bunny.

"That's the way I read it."

"I mean, that's not exactly cheap. I've seen clerks treat 10-copper items with more concern and respect than these guys are showing. Don't they care?"

"Not so's you'd notice," the Djin agreed.

"Do you think they'd notice if I tried to just tuck it under my arm and walk out without paying? It would be nice to know *something* can get to these guys."

The Djin glanced around nervously.

"I really don't know, but I don't think you should try."

That cooled me down a bit. I was still in strange territory on a mission, and it was no time to start testing security systems.

"Okay," I growled. "Let's try this again."

This time, when I approached the sales counter, I figured I had learned my lesson. No more Mr. Nice Guy. No more waiting around for them to end their discussion.

"I'd like to buy that green magik bag, the small canvas one," I said, bursting into their conversation in mid-sentence.

"All right."

The salesman I had first spoken with was halfway to the display before I realized what he was doing. Now that I had his attention, my normal shopping instincts cut in.

"Excuse me. I'd like a new case rather than the floor display . . . and is there any chance you have it in black?"

The salesman gave me a long martyred look.

"Just a moment, I'll have to check."

He went slouching off while his partner began wandering aimlessly through the section straightening displays.

"If you don't mind my saying so, Skeeve, I think you're pushing your luck," Kalvin observed.

"Hey, it's worth asking," I shrugged. "Besides, however inconsiderate the help is, this is still a store. There's got to be some interest in giving the customer what he wants."

Fifteen minutes later, the salesman still hadn't reappeared and I found my temper was starting to simmer again.

"Um . . . is it time to say 'I told you so' yet?" the Djin smirked.

Ignoring him, I intercepted the second salesman.

"Excuse me, how far is it to the storeroom?"

"Why do you ask?" he blinked.

"Well, your partner was checking on something for me, and it's been a while."

The salesman grimaced.

"Who? Him? He's gone on break. He should be back in an hour or so if you'd like to wait."

"What??"

"I suppose I could go look for you, if you'd like. What was it you wanted?"

As I've said before, I may be slow, but I *do* learn. This was the last salesman in the section and I wasn't about to let him out of my sight.

"Forget it. I'll take the small green magik bag over there. The one in canvas."

"Okay. That'll be 125 in gold. Do you want to carry it or shall I give you a sack?"

Before I could think, my Bazaar reflexes cut in.

"Just a second. That's 125 for a new bag. How much will you knock off the price for one that's been used for a floor display?"

Kalvin groaned and covered his eyes with one hand.

"I don't set the prices," the salesman said, starting to turn away. "If you don't like it, shop somewhere else."

The thought of starting this fiasco all over again defeated me.

"Wait a minute," I called, fumbling with my money belt. "I'll take it. But can I at least get a receipt?"

Shopping for clothes turned out to be a trial of a different sort. There were magik lifts that carried me up two floors to the clothing section, which fortunately gave me time to think things through.

The trouble was that I was disguised as a Pervect. Because of their build, this made me appear much more heavyset than I really was. If I bought clothes to fit my disguised form, they'd hang on the real me like a tent. If I went for my real size, however, it would be a dead giveaway when I asked to try them on.

What I finally decided to do was to shop in the kids' section, which would be the best bet for finding my real size anyway, and say I was buying them for my son. I had gotten pretty good at eyeballing clothes for size, so the fit probably wouldn't be too bad.

I needn't have worried.

It seems a lot more people shop for clothes than shop for luggage. A *lot* more.

Not being able to read the signs, I couldn't tell if there was a sale on or if this was the normal volume of customers the section got. Whatever the case, the place was a madhouse. Throngs of shoppers, male and female, jostled and clawed at each other over tables heaped with various items of apparel. To say angry voices were raised fails to capture the shrieks and curses which assaulted my ears as I approached the area, but I could make out the occasional sounds of cloth tearing. Whether this was from items on sale being ripped asunder by rival shoppers, or the rival shoppers themselves being ripped asunder I could never tell for sure. It was like watching a pileup at the Big Game, but without teams and without breaks between plays.

"Don't tell me you're going into that!" Kalvin gasped. "Without armor or artillery?"

It seemed a strange question for someone from a supposedly peaceful dimension to ask, but I was busy concentrating on the task ahead.

"This shopping thing is already taking too long," I said grimly. "I'm *not* going to lose any more time by having Edvik hunt us up another store . . . especially since there's no guarantee it will be any better than this one. I'm going to wade in there, grab a couple of outfits, and be done with it once and for all."

Good taste and a queasy stomach at the memory prevent me from going into detail on how the next half hour went. Suffice it to say that Kalvin abandoned me and hovered near the ceiling to watch and wait until I was done. Now I've knocked around a bit, and *been* knocked around more times than I care to recall, but if there's any memory that compares to holding my own against a mob of Pervish shoppers, my mind has successfully suppressed it. I elbowed and shoved, used more than a little magik when no one was looking and called on most of the dirty tricks I learned in the Big Game, and in the end I had two outfits I wasn't wild about but was willing to settle for rather than enter the fracas anew in search of something better.

I also had a lingering fondness for the fat Pervish lady I hid behind from time to time to catch my breath.

Having sat out the battle, Kalvin was in good shape to guide me back to the exit. That was fortunate, since the adrenalin drop after emerging from the brawl was such that I could barely see straight, let alone walk steadily.

I don't know where Edvik was waiting, but his cab materialized out of the traffic as soon as we emerged from the store and in no time we were back in the safety of the back seat. It wasn't until later that I realized what a commentary it was on department stores that the cab now seemed safe to me.

"Can we go to the hotel now?" I said, sinking back in the seat and shutting my eyes.

"Like that? Don't you want to change first?"

"Change?" Somehow I didn't like the sound of that.

"You know, into a conservative suit. Business types always get the best service at hotels."

Kalvin groaned, but he needn't have worried. If there was one thing I knew for sure, it's that I wasn't heading back to that store.

"Tell you what, Edvik. Describe a suit to me."

The cabbie rubbed his chin as he plotted his way through the traffic.

"Well, let's see. They're usually dark grey or black . . . three piece with a vest . . . thin white pinstripes closely spaced . . . and, you know, the usual accessories like a white shirt and a striped tie."

Just as I thought. The same as was worn on Deva . . . and every other dimension I've met businessmen on. I closed my eyes again and made a few adjustments to my disguise spell.

"Like this?"

The cabbie glanced over his shoulder, then swiveled around to gape openly.

"Say! That's neat!" he exclaimed.

"Thank you," I said smugly. "It's nothing really. Just a disguise spell I use."

"So why didn't you use that to fake the new outfits and the luggage instead of hassling with the stores?"

"I was about to ask the same thing," Kalvin murmured.

For the life of me, I couldn't think of a good answer.

VI:

"There's no place like home!"

—H. Johnson

Once we finally arrived at the hotel Edvik had chosen to recommend, I was a bit put off by the sight. It had a sign that declared it to be The New Inn, but it looked like most of the other buildings we had seen so far, which is to say it was old, dilapidated, and covered with soot. Then again, even if its appearance had been better, the neighborhood it was in would have given me pause. Between the garbage in the streets and the metal shutters on the store windows, it wasn't an area in which I would normally be inclined to get out of the cab, much less rent a room. I was about to comment on this to my driver/guide, when I noticed the uniformed doorman and decided to make my inquiry a bit more gentle.

"Ah . . . this is the low-price hotel you've been figuring on?"

"It's about as low as you can go without ending up in a real dive," the cabbie shrugged. "Actually, it's a little nicer than most in the same price range. They've had to lower their prices because of the trouble they've been having."

"Trouble?"

"Yeah. There's an ax murderer loose around here that the police haven't been able to catch. He's been killing about one a week . . . last week he got one right in the lobby."

"Ax murderer??!"

"That's right. You don't have to worry about it, though."

"How do you figure that?"

"Well, it's been going on for a month now, and since you're just checking in, and you've never been here before, there's not much chance they'll try to blame you for it."

Actually, *that* hadn't been my worry. I had been more concerned with my odds on being the next victim. Before I could clarify this to Edvik, however, the doorman had jerked open the door of the cab and snatched up my bag.

"You'd better follow your bag and keep an eye on it," the driver advised. "I'll be by in the morning to pick you up. Oh, and be sure to tip the baggage handler. Otherwise it may not be recognizable by the time you get it back."

The lizards were already starting to move as he imparted this last piece of wisdom, so I dove for the door before the vehicle gathered too much momentum and I ended up permanently separated from my luggage. Needless or not, I had gone through far too much to get it to lose it now. Before I had pause to think that I was losing touch with my guide and advisor for this dimension, the cab had turned a corner and disappeared.

"I think this guy wants a tip," Kalvin said, gesturing toward the doorman. At least I still had the Djin with me.

I had to acknowledge his point. The uniformed Pervect was standing stuffily, with his palm up and a vague sneer on his face that would probably pass for a smile locally. I only hesitated a second before slipping him some loose change. Normally, I would expect someone to wait until *after* he had performed a service before hinting for a tip, but obviously things differed from dimension to dimension. This was probably what Edvik had been warning me about . . . that the doorman would want money *before* moving my bag, and that if the juice wasn't big enough, it was "Goodbye luggage!" In a way, it made sense.

My speculation on this philosophy was cut short when I noticed another person, a bellhop this time, picking up my bag and heading inside with it, leaving the doorman outside weighing the tip I had just given him in his hand. I began to smell a rat.

"Where is he going?" I said to the smug doorman, as casually as I could manage.

"To the front desk, sir."

"But he has my bag."

"Yes. I suggest you follow him closely. He's not to be trusted, you know."

"But . . . Ohhh . . . !"

I knew when I had been outmaneuvered. Apparently, all the doorman did was open cab doors and off-load the baggage . . . *not* carry the bags inside. Of course, the fact that I had tipped him assuming he would perform that service was my fault, not his. Defeated, I trailed after the bellhop, who was waiting inside with his hand out in the now all-too-familiar gesture that means "Pay or you'll never see the end of me." This time, however, I was more than happy to pay him off. Whatever Edvik had said, I had decided I would be better off handling my own luggage from here on out.

Kalvin muttered something in my ear about not paying the help until they had finished their work, but the bellhop seemed to understand what it was all about, since he disappeared as soon as I paid him. Ignoring Kalvin's grumbles, I turned my attention to the hotel interior.

The reception area wasn't much larger than the space we used for similar purposes back at M.Y.T.H. Inc., except the furnishings were dominated by a huge counter which I assumed was what the doorman had referred to as the front desk. Of course, to my mind this made the lobby rather small since, as a hotel, this place was supposed to get more public traffic than our consulting offices did. Personally, I felt it boded ill for the size of the rooms. Then again, I had told Edvik to take us somewhere inexpensive. I supposed I couldn't expect low rates *and* stylish accomodations, and given a choice . . .

"May I help you?"

This last came from the Pervect behind the front desk. It might read polite, but the tone of his voice was that of one addressing someone who just walked through the front door with a box of garbage.

"Yes," I said, deciding to give pleasant one last try. "I'd like a room, please. A single."

The desk clerk looked as if I had just spat on the floor.

"Do you have reservations?"

The question surprised me a little, but I decided to stick with honesty.

"Well, I'm not wild about the neighborhood . . . and then there's the rumor about the ax murderer . . ."

"Skeeve . . . SKEEVE!!" Kalvin hissed desperately. "He means, 'Do you have a reservation for a room?'"

So much for honesty. I shot a look at the desk clerk, who was staring at me as if I had asked him to sell his first-born into slavery.

". . . But, um, if you're asking if I reserved a room in advance, the answer is no," I finished lamely.

The clerk stared at me for a few more moments, then ran a practiced finger down a list on the desk in front of him.

"I'm afraid that all we have available at this time is one of our Economy Rooms. You really should reserve in advance for the best selection."

"An Economy Room will be fine," I assured him. "I'll need it for about a week."

"Very well," the clerk nodded, pushing a form at me across the desk, "If you'll just fill this out, the rate will be a hundred in gold."

I was glad I had been warned about prices on Perv. A hundred in gold seemed a bit steep to me, but having been forewarned I managed to hide my surprise as I reached for the form.

". . . A day. Payable in advance, of course."

My hand stopped just short of the form.

"A hundred in gold a day?" I said as carefully as I could.

"Skeeve!" Kalvin yipped in my ear. "Remember, you were warned things were expensive here! This is a low-priced hotel, remember?"

"Payable in advance," the clerk confirmed.

I withdrew my hands from the desk.

"How much time do you want to spend looking for a room, Skeeve?" the Djin continued desperately. "The cab won't be back until morning and it's getting dark out. Do you really want to walk these streets at night?"

I took a hundred in gold from my money belt and dropped it on the desk, then started filling out the form.

"I assumed that *each day* is payable in advance, considering the interest rates," I said calmly. "Oh, yes, I'd like a receipt for that, as well."

The desk clerk whisked the form from under my pen and glanced at it almost before I had finished signing it.

"Quite right, Mr . . . Skeeve. I'll have a receipt for you in a moment."

It was nice to know some Pervects were efficient, once you had met their price. The hundred in gold had already disappeared.

The desk clerk slipped the receipt across the desk, a key held daintily in his other hand. I claimed the receipt and was starting to go for the key when he casually moved it back out of my reach, slapping his palm down on a small bell that was on the desk.

"Front!"

Before I could ask what this little declaration was supposed to mean, a bellhop had materialized at my side . . . a different one than before.

"Room 242," the desk clerk declared, handing the bell-hop my key.

"Yessir. Is this your luggage?"

"Well, yes. It's . . ."

Without waiting for me to finish, the bellhop snatched up my bag and started for the stairs, beckoning me to follow. I trailed along in his wake. At this point, I had had it with Pervects and hotels and tips. If this clown thought I was . . .

"Going to tip him?" Kalvin asked, floating around to hang in the air in front of me. Fortunately, he was trans-lucent enough for me to see through him.

I gave him my toothiest smile.

"If that means 'No' like I think it does, you'd better reconsider."

Whether I needed to hear this or not, I definitely didn't want to. I deliberately let my gaze wander to the ceiling and promptly tripped over a step.

"Remember what Edvik said," the Djin continued in-sistently. "You need all the allies you can get. You can't afford to get vindictive with this guy."

Slowly, my irritation began to give way to common sense. Kalvin was right. If nothing else, I had heard that bellhops were prime sources of local information, and if being nice to this character would speed my search for Aahz, thereby shortening my stay on Perv, then it would definitely be worth at least a decent tip. Taking a deep breath, I caught the Djin's eye and gave a curt nod, whereupon he subsided. It occurred to me it was nice to deal with someone who would let an argument drop once he'd won it.

The bellhop unlocked a door and ushered me into my room with a flourish. The first view of my temporary headquarters almost reversed my mind all over again.

The room was what could only be politely referred to as a hole . . . and I wasn't in a particularly polite mood. For openers, it was small . . . smaller than most of the closets in my place back at the Bazaar. There was barely enough space to walk around the bed without scooting sideways, and what little room there was was cramped further by a small bureau which was missing the knob on one of the two drawers, and a chair which looked about as comfortable as a bed of nails. The shade of the bedside lamp was askew, and the wallpaper was torn with one large flap hanging loose except where it was secured by cobwebs. I couldn't tell if the texture of the carpet was dust or mildew, though from the smell I suspected the latter. The ceiling had large waterstains on it, but you couldn't tell without looking hard because the light in the place was dim enough to make a vampire feel claustrophobic. All this for a mere hundred in gold a night.

"Great view, isn't it?" the bellhop said, pulling the shades aside to reveal a window that hadn't been washed since the discovery of fire. At first I thought the curtain rod was sagging, but closer examination showed it had actually been nailed in place crooked.

"This is what you call a great view?"

That comment kind of slipped out despite my resolve. I had just figured out that it wasn't that the window was so dirty I couldn't see out of it. Rather, the view consisted of a blank stone wall maybe an arm's length away.

The bellhop didn't seem the least put out by my rhetorical question.

"You should see the view from the first floor," he shrugged. "All the rooms there look out onto the courtyard, which includes the garbage dump. At least this view doesn't have maggots."

My stomach tilted to the left and sank. Swallowing hard, I resolved not to ask any more questions about the room.

"Could you lay off about the view?" Kalvin whined desperately.

"Way ahead of you," I replied.

"How's that again?" the bellhop said, turning to face me.

"I said, 'I'll settle for this view,' " I amended hastily.

"Thought you would. No, sir, you don't see many rooms this good at these prices."

I realized he was looking at me expectantly for confirmation.

"I . . . I've never seen anything like it."

He kept looking at me. I cast about in my mind for something vaguely complimentary to say about the room.

"The tip, Skeeve! He's waiting for a tip!"

"Oh! Yes, of course."

I fumbled a few more coins out of my money belt.

"Thank you, sir," the bellhop nodded, accepting my offering. "And if you have any more questions, the name's Burgt."

He was heading for the door when it occurred to me I might make further use of his knowledge.

"Say . . . um, Burgt."

"Yes, sir?"

"Is there someplace around here I can get a bite to eat? Maybe someplace that specializes in off-dimension food?"

"Sure. There's a little place about half a block to your left as you come out of the main entrance. It's called Bandi's. You can't miss it."

That was worth a few extra coins to me. It also gave me an idea.

"Say, Burgt, I've heard you bellhops have a bit of an information network. Is that true?"

The bellhop eyed the coins I was pouring back and forth from hand to hand.

"Sort of," he admitted. "It depends on what kind of information you're looking for."

"Well, I'm looking for a guy, name of Aahz. Would have hit town in the last couple of days. If you or any of your friends should find out where he is and let me know, I'd be *real* appreciative. Get me?"

I let the coins pour into his uniform pocket.

"Yes, *sir*. Aahz, was it? I'll spread the word and see what we can turn up."

He departed hastily, shutting the door firmly but quietly behind him.

"You did that very well, Skeeve," Kalvin said.

"What? Oh. Thanks, Kalvin."

"Really. You looked just like a gangster paying off an informant."

I guess my work with the Mob had influenced me more than I had realized. It wasn't a line of conversation I wanted to pursue too far, though.

"Just something I picked up," I said casually, pocketing the room key. "Come on. Let's try to find something eatable in this dimension."

VII:

". . . On the street where you live."

—QUOTE FROM AN ANONYMOUS
EXTORTION NOTE

I had thought the streets of Perv were intimidating walking or riding through them by day. At night, they were a whole new world. I didn't know if I should be frightened or depressed, but one thing I knew I wasn't was comfortable.

It wasn't that I was alone. There were a lot of Pervects on the street, and of course Kalvin was still with me. It's just that there is some company to which being alone is preferable. Kalvin's company was, of course, welcome . . . which should narrow it down for even the most casual reader as to exactly what the source of my discomfort was.

The Pervects. (Very good! Move to the head of the class.) Now, saying one felt uncomfortable around Pervects may sound redundant. As has been noted, the entire dimension is not renowned for its sociability, much less its hospitality. What I learned on the streets that night, however, is that there are Pervects and there are Pervects.

Most of the natives I had dealt with up to this point had been just plain folk . . . only nasty. In general, they seemed to have jobs and were primarily concerned with making a living and looking out for themselves (not necessarily in that order). The ones populating the terrain after sunset, however, were of a different sort entirely.

Most noticeable were the ones sleeping in the doorways and gutters. At first, this struck me as a way to avoid paying a hundred a night for a room, and I said as much to Kalvin. He, in turn, suggested that I look a little closer at the Pervects who were sprawled about. I did, and consequently decided that *five* hundred in gold a night would not be too much to spend, to avoid joining their ranks.

For openers, they were dirty . . . which probably isn't surprising if one sleeps in the gutter. While I've never claimed to have much of an eye for color, even in the poor light of the nighttime streets I could see that the green of their scales was an unhealthy hue. Frankly, they looked like something that was dead . . . only they weren't dead. I was to find out later, when I mentioned them to Edvik, that these were simply Pervects whose income had fallen below the dimensional standard of living. For whatever reason, they had gotten behind in the game, and now couldn't afford the lodgings and wardrobe to reestablish themselves.

Whatever financial problem the sleepers had encountered, they didn't have it in common with the Pervects who shared the night streets with them. Since they were primarily engaged in selling things, I'll refer to this second group as hustlers . . . even though doing so gives a negative connotation to that name I've never encountered before. While the daytime Pervects I had met might be described as "enterprising," the hustlers struck me more as "predatory."

They were as brightly dressed as any Imp, though they tended to hang back in the shadows, easing out to make muttered offers to passersby. What they were selling I was never sure, since none of them approached me directly.

This is not to say they didn't notice my passing, for they watched me with flat reptilian eyes, but something in what they saw apparently convinced them to leave me alone. I can't say I was heartbroken by the omission.

I was so intent on watching the watchers I almost missed our restaurant. Kalvin spotted it, though, and after he'd brought it to my attention, we went in.

Way back when I first met Aahz, I had been exposed to a Pervish restaurant. Of course, that was at the Bazaar where there was an ordinance that Pervish restaurants had to have spells on them so they would keep moving around instead of lowering the property values by staying in one place, but it had still prepared me to a certain extent for what to expect.

Kalvin, on the other hand, had had no experience with Pervish eateries before. I almost lost him two steps into the place just from the smell. To be honest, I almost lost me, too. While I had been *exposed* to, I had never actually set foot *inside* one before. If there are those out there in a similar position to where I was experience-wise at this point, let me warn you: The smell loses a lot by the time it gets to the street.

"What died!?"

The Djin was holding his nose as he glanced disdainfully around the restaurant's interior.

"Come, come now, Kalvin," I said, trying to make light of the matter. "Haven't you ever smelled a good home-cooked meal before? You know, like mother used to burn?"

If the reader deduces from the foregoing that Pervish cooking is less than fragrant . . . that, perhaps, it stinks to high heaven, I can only say that my skill as a writer has finally reached the level of my readership. That is, indeed, what I have been attempting to say. Fortunately for the dimensions at large, however, mere words cannot convey the near-tangible texture of the stench.

"If my mother cooked like that, we would have gotten

rid of her ... even earlier than we did," Kalvin declared bluntly.

Curious comment, that.

"You can't tell me you *like* this," he insisted. "I mean, you may be a little strange, but you're still a sentient being."

"So are the Pervects."

"I'm willing to debate that ... more than ever, now that I'm getting a feel for what they eat. You're avoiding the question, though. Are you really going to eat any of this stuff?"

I decided the joke had gone far enough.

"Not on a bet!" I admitted in a whisper. "If you watch closely, you'll see that some of the food actually crawls out of the bowl."

"I'd rather not!" Kalvin said, averting his eyes. "Seriously, Skeeve, if you aren't going to eat anything, why are we here?"

"Oh, I'm going to try to get something to eat. Just nothing they would prepare for the natives. That's why I was hunting for a place that served food from—and therefore, hopefully, stomachable by—off-world and off-worlders."

The Djin was unimpressed.

"I don't care *where* the recipe comes from. You're telling me you're going to take something that's been prepared in this kitchen and been in proximity with other dishes that stink the way these do, and then put it in your mouth? Maybe we should debate *your* qualifications as an intelligent being."

Looking at it that way, he had a point. Suddenly I didn't feel as clever as I had a few moments before.

"Cahn I help you, *sir*?"

The Pervect who materialized at my elbow was as stiffly formal as anything I'd seen that wasn't perched on a wedding cake. He had somehow mastered the technique of being subservient while still looking down on you. And they say that waiters can't be trained!

"Well, we . . . that is, I . . ."

"Ah! A Tah-bul for *one*!"

Actually, I had been preparing to beat a retreat, but this guy wasn't about to leave me that choice.

Chairs and tables seemed to part in his path as he swept off through the diners like a sailing ship through algae, drawing me along in his wake. Heads turned and murmurs started as we passed. If they were trying to figure out where they had seen me before, it could take a lot of talking.

"I wish I had thought to dress," I murmured to Kalvin. "This is a pretty classy place. I'm surprised they let me in without a tie."

The Djin shot me a look.

"I don't know how to say this, Skeeve, but you *are* dressed, and you *are* wearing a tie."

"Oh! Right."

I had forgotten I had altered my disguise spell in the taxi. One of the problems with the disguise spell is that I can't see the results myself. While I've gotten to a point where I can maintain the illusion without giving it a lot of conscious thought, it also means I occasionally forget what the appearance I'm maintaining really is.

I plopped down in the chair being held for me, but waved off the offered menu.

"I understand you serve dishes from off-dimension?"

The Pervect gave a little half-bow.

"Yas. Ve haff a wide selection for the most discriminating taste."

I nodded knowingly.

"Then just have the waiter bring me something Klah-dish . . . and a decent wine to go with it."

"Very good, Sir."

He faded discreetly from view, leaving me to study our fellow diners. It was too much to hope that coincidence would lead Aahz to the same dining room, but it didn't hurt to look.

"You handled that pretty smoothly."

"What's that, Kalvin? Oh. The ordering. Thank you."

"Are you really that confident?"

I glanced around at the nearby tables for eavesdroppers before answering.

"I'm confident that I couldn't even read the menu," I said quietly. "Trying to fake it would only have made me look like a bigger fool. I just followed the general rule of 'When in doubt, rely on the waiter's judgment.' It usually works."

"True enough," Kalvin conceded. "But the waiter's not usually Pervish. It's still braver than I'd feel comfortable with, personally."

The Djin had a positive talent for making me feel uneasy about decisions that had already been made.

Fortunately, the wine arrived just then. I fidgeted through the tasting ritual, then started in drinking with a vengeance. A combination of nerves and thirst moved me rapidly through the first three glasses with barely a pause for breath.

"You might go a little easy on that stuff until you get some food in you," Kalvin advised pointedly.

"Not to worry," I waved. "One thing Aahz always told me: If you aren't sure of the food on a dimension, you can always drink your meals."

"He told you that, huh? What a buddy. Tell me, did it ever work?"

"Howzat?"

"Drinking your meals. Did it ever do you any good, or just land you in a lot of trouble?"

"Oh, we've had lots of trouble. Sometime lemme tell you about the time we decided to steal the trophy from the Big Game.

"You and Aahz?"

"No. Me and . . . um . . . it was . . ."

For some reason, I was having trouble remembering exactly who had been with me on that particular caper. I decided it might be wisest to get the subject of conversation off me until my meal arrived.

"Whoever. Speaking of bottles, though, how long had you been waiting before I pulled the cork on that one of yours?"

"Oh, not long for a Djin. In fact, I'd say it hadn't been more than . . ."

"Tananda!"

"Excuse me?"

"It was Tananda who was with me when we tried for the trophy . . . the first time, anyway."

"Oh."

"Glad that's off my back. Now, what was it you were saying, Kalvin?"

"Nothing important," the Djin shrugged.

He seemed a little distracted, but I thought I knew why.

"Kalvin, I'd like to apologize."

He seemed to relax a little.

"Oh, that's okay, Skeeve. It's just that . . ."

"No, I insist. It was rude of me to order without asking if you wanted something to eat, too. It's just that it would have been awkward trying to order food for someone no one else could see. Understand what I'm trying to say?"

"Of course."

I seemed to be losing him again.

"It wasn't that I had forgotten about you, really," I pressed. "I just thought that as small as you are, you wouldn't eat much and we could probably share my order. Now I can see that that's rather demeaning to you, so if you'd like your own order . . ."

"Sharing your meal will be fine. Okay? Can we drop the subject now?"

Whatever was bothering the Djin, my efforts to change his mood were proving woefully inadequate. I debated letting it go for the moment, but decided against it. Letting things go until later was how the situation with Aahz had gotten into its current state.

"Say . . . um . . . Kalvin?"

"Now what?"

"It's obvious that I've gotten you upset, and my trying

to make amends is only making things worse. Now, it wasn't my intent to slight you in any way, but it seems to have happened anyway. If I can't make things better, can you at least tell me what it was I did so that I don't fall into the same trap again?"

"The wine doesn't help."

I nodded at Kalvin's terse response. He was right. The wine was hitting me harder than I had expected, making it difficult to focus on him and what he was saying.

"It doesn't help . . . but that's not the whole problem," I said. "All alcohol does is amplify what's there already. It may make my irritating habits more irritating, but it isn't causing them."

"True enough," he admitted grudgingly.

"So lay it on me," I urged. "What is it about me that's so irritating? I try to be a nice guy, but lately it hasn't been working so well. First with Aahz, and now with you."

The Djin hesitated before answering.

"I haven't really known you all that long, Skeeve. Anything I could say would be a snap judgment."

"So give me a snap judgment. I really want to . . ."

"Your dinner, Sir!"

The Pervect who had first seated me was hovering over my table again, this time with the waiter in tow. That latter notable was staggering under a huge covered platter which had steam rising from it enticingly.

I was desperately interested in hearing what Kalvin had to say, but the sight of the platter reminded me that I was desperately hungry as well. Apparently the Djin sensed my dilemma.

"Go ahead and eat, Skeeve," he said. "I can hold until you're done."

Nodding my thanks, I turned my attention to the waiting Pervect.

"It smells delicious," I managed, honestly surprised. "What is it?"

"Wan uf ze House Specialties," he beamed, reaching for the tray cover. "From Klah!"

The tray cover disappeared with a flourish, and I found myself face-to-face with someone else from my home dimension of Klah. Unfortunately, he wasn't serving the meal . . . he *was* the meal! Roasted, with a dead rat in his mouth as a garnish.

I did the only sane thing that occurred to me.

I fainted.

VIII:

"There's never a cop around when you need one!"

—A. CAPONE

"**S**keeve!"

The voice seemed to come from far away.

"C'mon, Skeeve! Snap out of it! We've got trouble!"

That caught my attention. I couldn't seem to get oriented, but if there was one thing I didn't need it was more trouble. *More* trouble? What . . . later! First, deal with whatever's going on now!

I forced my eyes open.

The scene which greeted me brought a lot of the situation back with a rush. I was in a restaurant . . . on the floor, to be specific . . . a Pervish waiter was hovering over me . . . and so was a policeman!

At first I thought it was the same one we had encountered earlier, but it wasn't. The similarities were enough that they could have come out of the same litter . . . or hatching. They both had the same square jaw, broad shoulders and potbelly, not to mention a very hard glint in their otherwise bored-looking eyes.

I struggled to sit upright, but wobbled as a wave of dizziness washed over me.

"Steady, Skeeve! You're going to need your wits about you for this one!"

Kalvin was hovering, his face lined with concern.

"W . . . what happened?" I said.

Too late I remembered that I was the only one who could see or hear the Djin. Ready or not, I had just opened the conversation with the others.

"It seems you fainted, boyo," the policeman supplied.

"I theenk he just does not vant to pay for zee food he ordered."

That was from the Pervect who had seated me, but his words brought it all back to me. The special dish from Klah!

"He served me a roast Klahd on a platter!" I said, leveling a shaky but accusing finger at the Pervect.

"Is that a fact now?"

The policeman cocked an eye at the Pervect, who became quite agitated.

"Non-sense! Eet is against the law to serve sentient beings without a li-cense. See for yourself, Offi-sair! Thees is a replica on-ley."

Sure enough, he was right! The figure on the platter was actually constructed on pieces of unidentifiable cuts of meat with what looked like baked goods filling in the gaps. The rat seemed to be authentic, but I'll admit I didn't look close. The overall effect was, as I can testify, horrifyingly real.

The policeman studied the dish closely before turning his attention to the waiter once more.

"Don't ya think it was a trifle harsh, servin' the lad with what seemed to be one of his own?"

"But he deed not look like thees when he came in! I on-ley served heem what he asked for . . . sometheeng from Klah!"

That's when I became aware of the fact that my disguise spell was no longer on. I must have lost control of it when I fainted. When it disappeared, however, was not as important as the fact that it was gone! I was now seen by one and all as what I really was . . . a Klahd!

The policeman had now turned his gaze on me and was studying me with what I felt was unhealthy interest.

"Really, now," he said. "Perhaps you could be tellin' how it is you come to be wearin' a disguise in such a fine place? It couldn't be that you were plannin' to skip out without payin' fer yer meal, could it?"

"No. It's just that . . ." I paused as a wave of dizziness passed. "Well, I've heard you can get better service and prices on Perv if folks don't know you're from off-dimension."

"Bad answer, Skeeve," Kalvin hissed, but I had already figured that out.

The policeman had gone several shades darker, and his head almost disappeared into his neck. Though his tone was still cordial, he seemed to be picking his words very carefully.

"Are ya tryin' to tell me you think our whole dimension is full of clip joints and thieves? Is that what yer sayin'?"

Too late I saw my error. Aahz had always seemed to be proud of the fact that Pervects were particularly good at turning a profit. It had never occurred to me that to some, this might sound like an insult.

"Not at all," I said hastily. "I assumed it was like any other place . . . that the best prices and services were reserved for locals and visitors got what was left. I was just trying to take advantage of normal priorities, that's all."

I thought it was a pretty good apology. The policeman, however, seemed unimpressed. Unsmiling, he produced a notepad and pencil.

"Name?"

His voice was almost flat and impersonal, but managed to still convey a degree of annoyance.

"Look. I'll pay for the meal, if that's what the problem is."

"I didn't ask if you were payin' for the meal. I asked you what your name is. Now are you going to tell me here, or should we be talkin' down at the precinct station?"

Kalvin was suddenly hovering in front of me again.

"Better tell him, Skeeve," he said, his tone matching his worried expression. "This cop seems to have an Eath up his Yongie."

That one threw me.

"A what up his what?"

The policeman looked up from his notepad.

"And how are ya spellin' that, now?"

"Umm . . . forget it. Just put down 'Skeeve.' That's my name."

His pencil moved briskly, and for a moment I thought I had gotten away with my gaffe. No such luck.

". . . And what was that you were sayin' before?"

"Oh, nothing. Just a nickname."

Even to me, the explanation sounded weak. Kalvin groaned as the policeman gave me a hard look before scribbling a few more notes on his pad.

"An alias, is it?" he murmured under his breath.

This was sounding worse all the time.

"But . . ."

"Residence?"

"The New Inn."

My protests seemed to be only making things worse, so I resolved to answer any other questions he might have as simply and honestly as possible.

"A hotel, eh?" The pencil was moving faster now. "And where would your regular residence be?"

"The Bazaar at Deva."

The policeman stopped writing. Raising his hand, he peered at me carefully.

"Now I thought we had gotten this matter of disguises settled," he said, a bit too casually. "So tell me, Mr. Skeeve, are you a Klahd . . . or a Deveel masquerading as one?"

"I'm a Klahd . . . really!"

". . . Who lives on Deva," the policeman finished

grimly. "That's a pretty expensive place to be callin' home, boyo. Just what is it you do for a livin' that you can afford such an extravagant address . . . or to pay for expensive meals you aren't going to eat, for that matter?"

"I uh, work for a corporation . . . M.Y.T.H. Inc. . . . It's a co-op of magik consultants."

"Is that a fact?" The policeman's skepticism was open. "Tell me, boyo, what is it you do for them that they had to hire a Klahd instead of one of their local lads?"

Maybe I was recovering from passing out, or maybe his sarcasm was getting to me, but I started to get a bit annoyed with the questions.

"I'm the president *and* founder," I snapped, "and since I personally recruited the staff, they didn't have whole bunches to say about my qualifications."

Actually, they had had a lot to say. Specifically, they were the ones who railroaded me into my current lofty position. Somehow, though, this didn't seem to be the time to try to point that out.

"Really?" The policeman was still pushing, but he seemed a lot more respectful now. "It's clear that there's more to you than meets the eye, *Mister* Skeeve."

"Steady, Skeeve," the Djin said quietly. "Let's not get too aggressive with the representatives of the local law."

It was good advice, and I tried to get a handle on my temper.

"You can check it out if you like," I said stiffly.

"Oh, I intend to. Would you mind tellin' me what the president of a corporation from Deva is doin' in our fair dimension? Are you here on business?"

"Well . . . I guess you could say that."

"Good. Then I'm sure you won't mind givin' me the names of our citizens you're dealin' with."

Too late I saw the trap. As a businessman, I should have local references. This may seem like a silly oversight to you, but you'll have to remember my background up to this point. Most of my ventures into the various dimensions have been more of the raider or rescue mission

variety, so it never occurred to me there was another way
of doing business. Of course, admitting this would probably do little toward improving the impression I was making on this stalwart of the law.

I considered my alternatives. I considered trying to lie
my way out of the predicament. Finally, I decided to give
the truth one last try.

"There isn't anyone specifically that I'm dealing with,"
I said carefully. "The fact of the matter is that I'm looking
for someone."

"Oh? Then you're hirin' for your corporation? Out to
raid some of our local talent?"

That didn't sound too good either.

"It's not a recruiting mission, I assure you. I'm trying
to find my . . . one of our employees."

The policeman straightened a bit, looking up from his
notebook once more.

"Now, that's a different matter entirely," he said.
"Have you been by a station to fill out a missing person
report?"

I tried to imagine Aahz's reaction if I had the police
pick him up. Mercifully, my mind blocked the image.

"Are you kidding? I mean . . . no, I haven't."

". . . Or do you think you're better at locatin' folks than
the police are?"

I was getting desperate. It seemed that no matter what
I said, it was getting twisted into the worst possible in-
terpretation.

"He's not really missing. Look, officer, I had a falling
out with my old partner, who happens to also be the co-
founder of the corporation *and* a Pervect. He left in a huff,
presumably to return here to Perv. All I want to do is
locate him and try to convince him to come back to the
company, or at least make amends so we can part on more
agreeable terms. In short, while it's business related, it's
more of a personal matter."

The policeman listened intently until I had finished.

"Well, why didn't you say so in the first place, lad?"

he scowled, flipping his notebook shut. "I'll have you know my time's too valuable to be wastin' chattin' with everybody who wants to tell me his life story."

"Nice going, Skeeve!" Kalvin winked, flashing me a high sign. "I think we're off the hook."

I ignored him. The policeman's comment about wasting his time had reignited my irritation. After all, he had been the one who had prolonged the interrogation.

"Just a moment," I said, as he started to turn away. "Does this mean you won't be running that check on me?"

"Skeeve!" the Djin warned, but it was too late.

"Is there any reason I shouldn't?" the policeman said, turning back to me again.

"It's just that you've taken up so much of your valuable time asking questions about a simple fainting, I'd hate to see you waste any more."

"Now don't go tryin' to tell me how to do my job, *Mister* Skeeve," he snarled, pushing his face close to mine. "Fer yer information, I'm not so sure this is as simple as you try to cut it out to be."

"It isn't?"

That last snappy response of mine was sort of squeaked out. I was suddenly aware that I was not as far out of the woods as I had believed.

"No, it isn't. We have what seems to be a minor disturbance in a public restaurant, only the person at the center of it turns out to be travelin' in disguise. What's more, he's from off-dimension and used to usin' aliases, and even though he claims to be an honest businessman, there doesn't seem to be anyone locally who can vouch for him, or any immediate way of confirmin' his story. Now doesn't that strike you as bein' a little suspicious?"

"Well, if you put it that way . . ."

"I do! However, as I was sayin', we're pretty busy down at the station, and for all yer jabberin' you *seem* harmless enough, so I don't see much point to pursuin' this further. Just remember, I've got you down in my book, boyo, and if there's any trouble you'll find I'm not so understandin' next time!"

With that, he turned on his heel and marched out of the restaurant.

"That was close," Kalvin whistled. "You shouldn't have mouthed off that last time."

I had arrived at much the same conclusion, but nodded my agreement anyway.

The waiter was still hovering about, so I signaled him for our check. The last thing I needed to do now would be to forget and try to walk out without paying.

"So where do we go from here?" the Djin asked.

"I think we'll settle up here and head back to the hotel for some sleep. Two run-ins with the police in one day is about all the excitement I can handle."

"But you haven't eaten anything."

"I'll do it tomorrow. Like I said, I don't relish the thought of risking another brush with the law . . . even accidentally."

Despite his advice to go easy with the police, the Djin seemed unconcerned.

"Don't worry. So far it's been just talk. I mean, what can they do to you? There's no law against being polite on the sidewalk or fainting in a restaurant."

"They could run that check on me. I'm not wild about having the police poking around in my affairs."

The Djin gave me a funny look.

"So what if they do? I mean, it's annoying, but nothing to worry about. It's not like you have a criminal record or have connections with organized crime or anything."

I thought about Don Bruce and the Mob. Suddenly, my work with them didn't seem as harmless as it had when I first agreed to take the position as the Mob's representative on Deva. Fortunately, no one on Deva except my own crew was aware of it, and they weren't likely to talk. Still, with the way my luck had been running lately, there was no point in risking a police check. Also, I could see no point in worrying Kalvin by letting him know what kind of a powder keg I might be sitting on.

IX:

". . . You gotta start somewhere."

—S. McDuck

I had planned to sleep late the next morning. I mean, I was eager to locate Aahz and all that, but it was rare that I had the opportunity to lounge in bed a couple extra hours. Business had been brisk enough that I usually headed into the offices early to try to get some work done before the daily parade of questions and problems started. Even when I did decide to try to sleep in, the others would be up and about, so I felt pressured to rise and join in for fear I might be excluded from an important or interesting conversation. Consequently, now that I had a chance to laze about I fully intended to take advantage of it. Besides, between the restaurant and the police it had been a rough night.

Unfortunately, it seemed the rest of the world had different ideas about my sleeping habits.

I had had trouble dozing off anyway, what with the unaccustomed traffic noise and all. When I did finally manage to get to sleep, it seemed I had barely closed my eyes when there was a brisk knocking at the door of my room.

"Wazzit?" I called, struggling to get my eyes open far enough to navigate.

In response, the door opened and the bellhop who had brought my luggage up the day before came bustling into the room.

"Sorry to bother you so early, Mr. Skeeve, but there's . . ."

He stopped abruptly and peered around the room. I was still trying to figure out what he was looking for when he returned his attention to me once more.

"Mr. Skeeve?" he said again, his voice as hesitant as his manner.

"Yes?" I responded, trying to hold my annoyance in check. "You had something to tell me? Something I assume couldn't wait until a decent hour?"

If I had hoped to rebuff him, I failed dismally. At the sound of my voice his face brightened and he relaxed visibly.

"So it *is* you. You had me going there for a minute. You've changed since you checked in."

It took me a second to realize what he was talking about. Then I remembered I hadn't renewed my disguise spell since I had my run-in with the law the night before. I suppose it could be a little jarring to expect to find a Pervect and end up talking to a Klahd instead. I considered casting the spell again, then made a snap decision to leave things the way they were. The Pervect disguise seemed to be causing me more trouble than it was averting. I'd try it for a day as a Klahd and see how things went.

"Disguise," I said loftily. "What is it?"

"Well, there's . . . Is *this* the disguise or was the other?"

"This is the real me, if it matters. Now what is it?"

"Oh, it doesn't matter to me. We get folks from all sorts of strange dimensions here at the hotel. I always say, it doesn't matter where they're from, as long as their gold is . . ."

"WHAT IS IT??"

I have found that my tolerance for small talk moves in a direct ratio to how long I've been awake, and today was proving to be no exception.

"Oh, sorry. There's a cabbie downstairs in the loading zone who says he's waiting for you. I thought you'd like to know."

I felt the operative word there was "waiting," but it seemed to have escaped the bellhop entirely. Still, I was awake now, and my search wasn't going to get any shorter if I just sat around my room.

"Okay. Tell him I'll be down in a few minutes."

"Sure thing. Oh . . . the other thing I wanted to ask you . . . Is it okay if this guy Aahz finds out you're looking for him?"

I had to think about that for a few moments. Aahz had left without talking to me, but I didn't think he was avoiding me to a point where he'd go into hiding if he knew I was on Perv.

"That shouldn't be a problem. Why?"

"I was thinking of running an ad in the personal section of the newspaper, but then it occurred to me that he might owe you money or something, so I thought I'd better check first."

"The personal section?"

"It's a daily bulletin board the paper prints," Kalvin supplied as he joined us in mid-yawn. "Notes from people to people . . . birthday greetings, messages from wives to wayward husbands, that sort of thing. A lot of people read them faithfully."

Somehow that didn't sound like Aahz's cup of tea, but there was always a chance that someone who knew him would see it and pass on the information. In any case, it couldn't hurt.

"Oh, right. The personal ads. Sorry, I'm still waking up. Sounds like a good idea," I said, rummaging around for some loose change. "How much does it cost?"

To my surprise, the bellhop held up a restraining hand.

"I'll go the cost on my own if you don't mind, Mr. Skeeve."

"Oh?"

"Sure. That way, if it works, there won't be any doubt who gets that reward you mentioned."

With that, he flashed me a quick grin and left. It occurred to me that I should start watching my spending to be sure I'd have enough to actually pay a reward if the bellhop or one of his friends managed to locate Aahz for me.

"So what's the plan for today, Skeeve?"

Kalvin followed me into the bathroom and asked his question as I was peering at my face in the mirror. Things were getting to a point where I had to shave, but only occasionally . . . and I decided today wasn't one of those occasions. It's funny, when I was younger I used to look forward to shaving, but now that it was fast upon me I tended to see it as the nuisance it was. I began to understand why some men grew beards.

"Well, I don't think we should just sit around here waiting for Aahz to answer the bellhop's personal ad," I said. "Besides, it won't produce any results today, anyway. I figure we should do a little looking on our own."

As soon as I said it, I realized how simplistic that sounded. Of course we were going to go looking for Aahz. That's what we would have done if the bellhop hadn't come up with his "personal ad" idea. If Kalvin noticed, however, he let me get away with it.

"Sounds good to me. Where do we start?"

I had been giving that some thought. Unfortunately, the end result was that I was embarrassed to realize how little I knew about Aahz's background . . . or the background of any of my other colleagues, for that matter.

"The main things Aahz seems to specialize in are magik and finances. I thought we'd poke around those circles a while and see if anyone can give us a lead."

As it turned out, however, there was one small episode which delayed the start of our quest.

We had just stepped out of the doors of the hotel and were looking around for Edvik when I noticed the street vendors. They had been there the day before when we checked in, but I had failed to really notice or comment on them. Today, however, they caught my attention, if for no other reason than their contrast to the hustlers who populated the same area at night.

The night hustlers were an intense, predatory lot who seemed willing to trade for *some* of your money only if they felt like they couldn't simply knock you down and take it *all* directly. The day people, on the other hand, seemed to be more like low-budget retailers who stood quietly behind their makeshift briefcase stands or blankets and smiled or made their pitches to any passersby who chanced to pause to look at their displays. If anything, their manner was furtive rather than sinister, and they kept glancing up and down the street as if they were afraid of being observed at their trade.

"I wonder what they're watching for?" I said, almost to myself. I say almost because I forgot for the moment that Kalvin was hovering within easy hearing.

"Who? Them? They're probably watching for the police."

"The police? Why?"

"For the usual reason . . . what they're doing is illegal."

"It is?"

I had no desire to have another run-in with the police, but I was genuinely puzzled. Maybe I was missing something, but I couldn't see anything untoward about the street vendors' activities.

"I keep forgetting. You're from the Bazaar at Deva," the Djin laughed. "You see, Skeeve, unlike the Bazaar, most places require a license to be a street vendor. From the look of them, these poor souls can't afford one. If they could, they'd probably open a storefront instead of working the street."

"You mean this is it for them? They aren't distributing for a larger concern?"

On Deva, most of the street vendors were employees of larger businesses who picked up their wares in the morning and returned what was unsold at the end of their shift. Their specific strategy was to look like a small operation so that tourists who were afraid of dickering at a storefront or tent would buy, assuming they knew more and could get better prices from a lowly street peddler. It never occurred to me that the street vendors I had been seeing really were small, one-person operations.

"That's right," Kalvin was saying. "What you see is what you get. Most of those people have their life savings tied up in . . . Hey! Where are you going?"

I ignored him, stepping boldly up to one of the vendors I *had* noticed the day before. He was in the same spot as yesterday, squatting behind a blanket full of sunglasses and cheap bracelets. What had caught my eye yesterday was that he was young, even younger than I was. Considering the longevity of Pervects, that made him very young indeed.

"See anything you like?" he said, flashing an expanse of pointed teeth I would have found unnerving if I hadn't gotten used to Aahz's grins.

"Actually, I was hoping you could answer a few questions for me."

The smile disappeared.

"What are you? A reporter or something?"

"No. Just curious."

He scowled and glanced around.

"I suppose it's all right, as long as it doesn't interfere with any paying customers. Time's money, ya know."

In response, I tossed a gold coin into his blanket.

"So call me a customer who's buying some of your time. Let me know when that's used up."

He made a quick pass with his hand and the coin disappeared as his smile emerged from hiding.

"Mister, you just got my attention. Ask your questions."

"Why do you do this?"

The smile faded into a grimace.

"Because I'm independently wealthy and get my kicks sitting in the rain and running from the cops . . . why do you think? I do it for the money, same as everybody else."

"No. I meant why do you do *this* for money instead of getting a job?"

He studied me for a moment with his Pervish yellow eyes, then gave a small shrug.

"All right," he said. "I'll give you a straight answer. You don't get rich working for someone else . . . especially not at the kind of jobs I'd been qualified for. You see, I don't come from money. All my folks gave me was my name. After that I was pretty much on my own. I don't have much school to my credit, and, like I say, my family isn't connected. I can't get a good job from an old pal of my dad's. That means I'd start at the bottom . . . and probably end there, too. Anyway, I gave it a good long think, and decided I wanted more out of life."

I tried to think of a tactful way of saying that this still looked pretty bottom of the barrel to me.

". . . So you think this is better than working at an entry-level job for someone else?"

His head came up proudly.

"I didn't say that. I don't figure to be doing this forever. This is just a way to raise the capital to start a bigger business. I'm risking it all on my own abilities. If it works, I get all the profits instead of a wage and I can move on to better things. What's more, if it works well enough, I've got more to pass on to my kids than my parents did. If it doesn't . . . well, I'm no worse off than when I started."

"You've got kids?"

"Who, me? No . . . at least, not yet. Maybe someday. Right now, the way things are going, I can't even afford a steady girlfriend, if you know what I mean."

Actually, I didn't. I had plenty of money personally, but no girlfriend. Therefore, I didn't have the vaguest idea what the upkeep on one would be.

"Well, I'd say it's a noble cause you have there . . . wanting to build something to leave for your kids."

At that he laughed, flashing those teeth again.

"Don't try to make me sound too good," he said. "I won't kid you. I'd like a few of the nicer things in life myself . . . like staying at fancy hotels and driving around in cabs. I'd use up some of the profits before I passed them on to my kids."

I was suddenly aware of the differences in our economic standing . . . that what he was dreaming about I tended to take for granted. The awareness made me uncomfortable.

"Yeah . . . well, I've got to be going now. Oh! What was it, anyway?"

"What was what?"

"The name your parents gave you."

"It wasn't that hot, really," he said, making a face. "My friends just call me J. R."

With that, I beat a hasty retreat to my waiting cab.

"What was that all about?" Edvik said as I sank back into my seat.

"Oh, I was just curious about what made the street vendors tick."

"Them? Why bother? They're just a bunch of low-life hustlers scrabbling for small change. They're never going to get anywhere."

I was surprised at the sudden vehemence in his voice. There was clearly no love lost there.

It occurred to me that Edvik's appraisal of the street vendors pretty much summed up my initial reaction to his own enterprising efforts with his cab and self-publishing company.

It also occurred to me, as I reflected on my conversation with J. R., that I had been even more lucky than I had realized when I had taken to studying magik . . . first with Garkin and then with Aahz. It didn't take the wildest stretching of the imagination to picture myself in the street vendor's place . . . assuming I had that much initiative to begin with.

All in all, it wasn't a particularly comforting thought.

X:

"All financiers are not created equal!"

—R. CORMAN

"So where are we off to today, Mr. Skeeve?"

Edvik's words interrupted my thoughts, and I fought to focus my attention on the problem at hand.

"Either to talk with the magicians or some financial types," I said. "I was hoping that as our trusty native guide you'd have some ideas as to which to hit first . . . and it's just 'Skeeve,' not 'Mr. Skeeve.' "

The "Mr. Skeeve" thing had been starting to get to me with the bellhop, but it hadn't seemed worth trying to correct. If I was going to be spending the next few days traveling with Edvik, however, I thought I'd try to set him straight before he got on my nerves.

"All right. Skeeve it is," the cabbie agreed easily. "Just offhand, I'd say it would probably be easier to start with the financial folks."

That hadn't been what I had hoped he'd say, but as I've noted before, there's no point in paying for guidance and then not following it.

"Okay. I'll go along with that. Any particular reason, though?"

"Sure. First of all, there are a lot of people in the magik business around here. We got schools, consultants, co-ops, entertainers, weather control and home defense outfits . . . all sorts. What's more, they're spread out all over. We could spend the next year trying to check them out and still have barely scratched the surface. There aren't nearly as many financiers, on the other hand, so if they're on your list I figured we could start with them. Maybe we'll get lucky and not have to deal with the magik types."

I was a little staggered by his casual recitation. The enormity of what I was trying to do was just starting to sink in. I had only allowed a week to find Aahz and convince him to come back. At the moment, it seemed next to impossible to accomplish that in so short a time, yet I couldn't take any longer with the rest of the crew taking on Queen Hemlock without me. With an effort, I tried to put my doubts out of my mind. At the very least, I had to try. I'd face up to what to do next at the end of the week . . . not before.

"What's the other reason?"

"Excuse me?"

"You said 'First of all. . . .' That usually implies there's more than one reason."

The cabbie shot me a glance over his shoulder.

"That's right. Well, if you must know, I'm a little uncomfortable around magicians . . . current company excepted, of course. Never had much call to deal with 'em and just as happy to keep it that way. I've got a buddy, though, who's a financier. He just might be able to help you out. Most of these finance types know each other, you know. Leastwise, I can probably get you in to see him without an appointment."

Kalvin was waving a hand at me, trying to get my attention.

"I probably don't have to remind you of this," he said, "but your time *is* rather limited. I didn't say anything

about your chatting with that scruffy street vendor, but
are you really going to blow off part of a day talking to
a supposed financier who hangs out with cab drivers?"

"How did you meet this guy?" I queried, trying desperately to ignore the Djin's words . . . or, to be exact,
how closely they echoed my own thoughts.

"Oh, we sort of ran into each other at an art auction."

"An art auction?"

I didn't mean to let my incredulity show in my voice,
but it kind of slipped out. In response, Edvik twisted
around in his seat to face me directly.

"Yeah. An auction. What's the matter? Don't you think
I can appreciate art?"

Left to their own devices, the lizards powering our vehicle began veering toward the curb.

"Well . . . no. I mean, I've never met an art collector
before. I don't know much about art, so it surprised me,
that's all. No offense," I said hurriedly, trying not to tense
as the cab wandered back and forth in our lane.

"You asked. That's where we met."

The cabbie returned his attention to the road once
more, casually bringing us back on course.

"Were you both bidding on the same painting?"

"No. He offered to back half my bid so I could stay
in the running . . . only it wasn't a painting. It was more
what you would call literary."

Now I was getting confused.

"Literary? But I thought you said it was an art auction."

"It was, but there was an author there who offered to
auction off an appearance in his next book. Well, I knew
the author . . . I had done an interview with him in one of
the 'zines I publish . . . so I thought it would be kind of
neat to see how he would do me in print. Anyway, it came
down to two of us, and the bidding got pretty stiff. I
thought I was going to have to drop out."

"That's when the financier offered to back your bid?"

"Actually, he made the offer to the other guy first.
Lucky for me the other bidder wanted the appearance for

his wife, so he wouldn't go along with the deal. That's when the Butterfly turned to me."

"Wait a minute. The Butterfly?"

"That's what he calls himself. It's even on his business cards. Anyway, if he hadn't come in on the bid, you'd be spending a couple chapters talking to some guy's winsome but sexy wife instead of . . ."

At that point I was listening with only half an ear as Edvik prattled on. A financier named Butterfly who backs cabbies' bids at auctions. I didn't have to look at Kalvin to tell the Djin was rolling his eyes in an anguished "I told you so." Still, the more I thought about it, the more hopeful I became. This Butterfly just might be offbeat enough to know something about Aahz. I figured it was at least worth a try.

Strange as it may sound, I was as nervous about meeting the Butterfly as Edvik claimed to be about dealing with magicians. Magicians I had been dealing with for several years and knew what to expect . . . or if my experiences were an accurate sample, what *not* to expect. Financiers, on the other hand, were a whole different kettle of fish. I had no idea what I was getting into or how to act. I tried to reassure myself by remembering that this particular financier had dealt with Edvik in the past, and so could not be *too* stuffy. Still, I found myself straightening my disguise spell nervously as the cabbie called up to the Butterfly from the lobby. I was still traveling as a Klahd, but had used my disguise spell to upgrade my wardrobe a bit so that I at least *looked* like I was comfortable in monied circles.

I needn't have worried.

The Butterfly did not live up to any of my preconceived notions or fears about what a financier was like. First of all, instead of an imposing office lined with shelves full of leatherbound books and incomprehensible charts, it seemed he worked out of his apartment, which

proved to be smaller than my own office, though much
more tastefully furnished. Secondly, he was dressed quite
casually in a pair of slacks and a pastel-colored sweater,
that actually made me feel uncomfortably overdressed in
my disguise-spell generated suit. Fortunately, his manner
itself was warm and friendly enough to put me at my ease
almost immediately.

"Pleased to meet you . . . Skeeve, isn't it?" he said, extending a hand for a handshake.

"Yes. I . . . I'm sorry to impose on your schedule like
this . . ."

"Nonsense. Glad to help. That's why I'm self-
employed . . . so I can control my own schedule. Please.
Have a seat and make yourself at home."

Once we were seated, however, I found myself at a
loss as to how I should begin the conversation. But, with
the Butterfly watching me with attentive expectation, I felt
I had to say something.

"Um . . . Edvik tells me you met at an art auction?"

"That's right . . . though I'll admit that for me it was
more of a whim than anything else. Edvik is really much
more the collector and connoisseur than I am."

The cabbie preened visibly under the implied praise.

"No. I just dropped by out of curiosity. I had heard
that this particular auction had a reputation for being a lot
of fun, so I pulled a couple thousand out of the bank and
wandered in to see for myself. The auctioneers were
amusing, and the bidding was lively, but most of the art
being offered didn't go with my current decor. So when
that one particular item came up . . ."

I tried to keep an interested face on, but my mind
wasn't on his oration. Instead, I kept pondering the easy
way he had said ". . . so I pulled a couple thousand . . ."
Clearly this was a different kind of Pervect than Aahz
was. My old partner would have been more willing to
casually part with a couple pints of his blood than with
gold.

". . . But in the long run it worked out fine."

The Butterfly was finishing his tale, and I laughed dutifully along with him.

"Tell him about your friend, Skeeve."

"That's right. Here I've been rattling on and we haven't even started to address your problem," the financier nodded, shifting forward on his chair. "Edvik said you were trying to locate someone who might have been active in our financial circles."

"I'm not sure you'll be able to help," I began, grateful for not having to raise the subject myself. "He's been off-dimension for several years now. His name is Aahz."

The Butterfly pursed his lips thoughtfully.

"The name doesn't ring any bells. Of course, in these days of nesting corporations and holding companies, names don't really mean much. Can you tell me anything about his style?"

"His style?"

"How would you describe his approach to money? Is he a plunger? A dabbler?"

I had to laugh at that.

"Well, the words 'tight-fisted' and 'penny-pinching' are the first that come to mind."

"There's 'tight-fisted' and there's 'cautious,'" the Butterfly smiled. "Perhaps you'd better tell me a little about him, and let me try to extract and analyze the pertinent parts."

So I told him. Once I had gotten started, the words seemed to come rushing out in a torrent.

I told him about meeting Aahz when he got stranded on my home dimension of Klah after a practical joke gone awry robbed him of his magikal powers, and how he took me on as an apprentice after we stymied Isstvan's plan to take over the dimensions. I told him about how Aahz had convinced me to try out for the position of Court Magician for the kingdom of Possiltum, and how that had led to our confrontation with Big Julie's army as well as introducing me to the joys of bureaucratic in-fighting. He clucked sympathetically when I told him about how Tananda and I had tried to steal the trophy from the Big Game as a birthday present for Aahz, and how we had had to put together a team to challenge the two existing teams after Tananda got caught. He was amused by my rendition of how I got stuck masquerading as Roderick, the king, and how I got Massha as an apprentice, though he seemed most interested in the part about how we broke up the Mob's efforts to move into the Bazaar at Deva and ended up working for both sides of the same brawl. I even told him about our brief sortie into Limbo when Aahz got framed for murdering a vampire, and my even briefer career into the arena of professional Dragon Poker which pitted my friends and me against the Sen-Sen Ante Kid and the Ax. Finally, I tried to explain how we expanded our operation into a corporation, ending with how Aahz had walked out, leaving a note behind stating that, without his powers, he felt he was needless baggage to the group.

The Butterfly listened to it all, and, when I finally ground to a halt, he remained motionless for many long minutes, apparently digesting what he had heard.

"Well, one thing I can tell you," he said at last. "Your friend isn't a financier . . . here on Perv, or anywhere else, for that matter."

"He isn't? But he's always talking about money."

"Oh, there's more to being a financier than talking about money," the Butterfly laughed. "The whole idea is to put one's money to work through investments. If anything, this Aahz's hoarding techniques would indicate that he's pretty much an amateur when it comes to money. You, on the other hand, by incorporating and diversifying through holdings in other businesses, show marked entrepreneurial tendencies. Perhaps sometime we might talk a bit about mutual investment opportunities."

I suppose it was all quite flattering, and under other circumstances I might have been happy to chat at length with the Butterfly about money management. Unfortunately, I couldn't escape the disappointment of the bottom line . . . that he wouldn't be able to give me any information that would help me locate Aahz.

"Thanks, but right now I think I'd better focus on one thing at a time, and my current priority is finding my old partner."

"Well, sorry I couldn't have been of more assistance," the financier said, rising to his feet. "One thing, though, Skeeve, if you don't mind a little advice?"

"What's that?"

"You might try to take a bit more of an active role in your own life. You know . . . instead of reactive?"

That one stopped me short as I was reaching for the door.

"Excuse me?"

"Nothing. It was just a thought."

"Well, could you elaborate a little? C'mon, Butterfly! Don't drop a line like that on me without some kind of an explanation to go with it."

"It's really none of my business," he shrugged, "but I couldn't help but notice during your story that you seemed to be living your life reacting to crisis rather than having any real control over things. Your old partner and mentor got dropped in your lap and the two of you teamed up to stop someone who might try to assassinate either of you next. It was Aahz who forced you to try for the job as court magician, and ever since then you've been yielding to pressure, real or perceived, from almost everybody in your life: Tananda, Massha, the Mob, the Devan Chamber of Commerce . . . even whatzisname, Grimble and that Badaxe have leaned on you. It just seems to me that for someone as successful as you obviously are, you really haven't shown much gumption or initiative."

His words hit me like a bucket of cold water. I had been shouted out by experts, but somehow Butterfly's calm criticism cut me deeper than any tonguelashing I had ever received from Aahz.

"Things have been kind of scrambled . . ." I started, but the financier cut me off.

"I can see that, and I don't mean to tell you how to run your life. You've had some strong-willed, dominating people who have been doing just that, though, and I'd have to say the main offender has been this fellow, Aahz. Now, I know you're concerned about your friendship, but if I were you, I'd think long and hard about inviting him back into my life until I had gotten my own act together."

XI:

"How come I get all the hard questions?"

—O. NORTH

"Skeeve! Hey, Skeeve! Can ya ease up for a bit?"

The words finally penetrated my self-imposed fog and I slackened my pace, letting Kalvin catch up with me.

"Whew! Thanks," the Djin said, hovering in his now-accustomed place. "I told you before I'm not real strong. Even hovering takes energy, ya know. You were really moving there."

"Sorry," I responded curtly, more out of habit than anything else.

In all honesty, the Djin's comfort was not a high priority item in my mind just then. I had had Edvik drive us back to the hotel after we left the Butterfly's place. Instead of going on up to my room, however, I had headed off down the sidewalk. The street vendor I had spoken to earlier waved a friendly greeting, but I barely acknowledged it with a curt nod of my head. The Butterfly's observations on my life had loosed an explosion of thoughts in my mind, and I figured maybe a brisk walk would help me sort things out.

I don't know how long I walked before Kalvin's plea snapped me out of my mental wheel-spinning. I had only vague recollections of shouldering my way past slower-moving pedestrians and snarling at those who were quick enough to get out of my path on their own. The police would have been pleased to witness it . . . only on Perv two days and already I could walk down the street like a native.

"Look, do you want to talk about this? Maybe some place sitting down?"

I looked closer at the Djin. He really did look tired, his face streaked with sweat and his little chest heaving as he tried to catch his breath. Strange, I didn't feel like I had been exerting myself at all.

"Talk about what?" I said, realizing as I spoke that the words were coming out forced and tense.

"Come on, Skeeve. It's obvious that what the Butterfly said back there has you upset. I don't know why, it sounded like pretty good advice to me, but maybe talking it out would help a bit."

"Why should I be upset?" I snapped. "He only challenged all the priorities I've been living by and suggested that my best friend is probably the worst thing in my life. Why should that bother me?"

"It shouldn't," Kalvin responded innocently, "unless, of course, he's right. Then I could see why it *would* bother you."

I opened my mouth for an angry retort, then shut it again. I really couldn't think of anything to say. The Djin had just verbalized my worst fears, ones I didn't have any answers for.

". . . And running away from it won't help! You're going to have to face up to it before you're any good to yourself . . . or anyone else, for that matter."

Kalvin's voice came from behind me, and I realized I had picked up my pace again. At the same moment, I saw that he was right, I was trying to run away from the issues, both figuratively and literally. With that knowledge, the fatigue of my mental and physical efforts hit me all at once and I sagged, slowing to a stop on the sidewalk.

"That's better. Can we talk now?"

"Sure. Why not? I feel like getting something in my stomach, anyway."

The Djin gave a theatrical wince.

"Ootch! You mean we're going to try to find a restaurant again? Remember what happened the last time?"

In spite of myself I had to smile at his antics.

"As a matter of fact, I was thinking more on the order of getting something to drink."

While I spoke, I was casting about for a bar. One thing about Perv I had noticed, you never seemed to be out of sight of at least one establishment that served alcoholic beverages. This spot proved to be no exception, and now that I was more attuned to my environment, I discovered just such a place right next to where we were standing.

"This looks like as good a spot as any," I said, reaching for the door. "C'mon, Kalvin, I'll buy the first round."

It was meant as a joke, because I hadn't seen the Djin eat or drink anything since I released him from the bottle. He seemed quite agitated at the thought, however, hanging back instead of moving with me.

"Wait, Skeeve, I don't think we should . . ."

I didn't dally to hear the rest. What the heck, this *had* been his idea . . . sort of. Fighting a sudden wave of irritation, I pushed on into the bar's interior.

At first glance, the place looked a little seedy. Also the second and third glances, though it took a moment for my eyes to adjust to the dim light. It was small, barely big enough to hold the half-dozen tiny tables that crowded the floor. Sagging pictures and clippings adorned the walls, though what they were about specifically I couldn't tell through the grime obscuring their faces. There was a small bar with stools along one wall, where three tough-looking patrons crouched hunched forward in conversation with the bartender. They ceased talking and regarded me briefly with cold, unfriendly stares as I surveyed the place, though whether their hostility was because I was a stranger or because I was from off-dimension I wasn't sure. It did occur to me that I was still wearing my disguise spell business suit which definitely set me apart from the dark, weather-beaten outfits the other patrons wore almost like a uniform. It also occurred to me that this might not be the wisest place to have a quiet drink.

"I think we should get out of here, Skeeve."

I don't know when Kalvin rejoined me, but he was there hovering at my side again. His words echoed my own thoughts, but sheer snorkiness made me take the opposite stance.

"Don't be a snob, Kalvin," I muttered. "Besides, sitting down for a while was *your* idea, wasn't it?"

Before he could answer, I strode to one of the tables and plopped down in a seat, raising one hand to signal the bartender. He ignored it and returned to his conversation with the other drinkers.

"C'mon, Skeeve. Let's catch a cab back to the hotel and have our conversation there," Kalvin said, joining me. "You're in no frame of mind to start drinking. It'll only make things worse."

He made a lot of sense. Unfortunately, for the mood I was in, he made too much sense.

"You heard the Butterfly, Kalvin. I've been letting too many other people run my life by listening to their well-meaning advice. I'm supposed to start doing what I want to do more often . . . and what I want to do right now is have a drink . . . here."

For a moment I thought he was going to argue with me, but then he gave a sigh and floated down to sit on the table itself.

"Suit yourself," he said. "I suppose everyone's entitled to make a jackass out of themselves once in a while."

"What'll it be?"

The bartender was looming over my table, saving me from having to think of a devastating comeback for Kalvin's jibe. Apparently, now that he had established that he wouldn't come when summoned, he wanted to take my order.

"I'll have . . ."

Suddenly, a glass of wine didn't feel right. Unfortunately, my experience with drinks was almost as limited as my experience with members of the opposite sex.

". . . Oh, just give me a round of whatever they're drinking at the bar there."

The bartender gave a grunt that was neither approving nor disapproving and left, only to return a few moments later with a small glass of liquid which he slammed down on the table hard enough for some of the contents to slop over the edge. I couldn't see it too clearly, but it seemed to be filled with an amber fluid with bubbles in it that gathered in a froth at the top.

"Ya gotta pay by the round," he sneered, as if it were an insult.

I fished a handful of small change out of my pocket and tossed it on the table, reaching for the glass with the other hand.

Now, some of you might be wondering why I was so willing to experiment with a strange drink after everything I've been saying about food on Perv. Well, truth to tell, I was sort of hoping this venture would end in disaster. You see, by this time I had cooled off enough to acknowledge that Kalvin was probably right about going back to the hotel, but I had made such a big thing out of making an independent decision that changing my mind now would be awkward. Somewhere in that train of thought, it occurred to me that if this new drink made me sick, I would have an unimpeachable reason for reversing my earlier decision. With that in mind, I raised the glass to my lips and took a sip.

The icy burst that hit my throat was such a surprise that I involuntarily took another swallow . . . and another. I hadn't realized how thirsty I was after my brisk walk until I hit the bottom of the glass without setting it down or taking a breath. Whatever this stuff was, it was absolutely marvelous, and the vaguely bitter aftertaste only served to remind me I wanted more.

"Bring me another of these," I ordered the bartender, who was still sorting through my coins. "And can you bring it in a larger container?"

"I could bring you a pitcher," he grumbled.

"Perfect . . . and pull a little extra there for your trouble."

"Say . . . thanks."

The bartender's mood and opinion of me seemed to have improved as he made his way to the bar. I congratulated myself for remembering what Edvik had said about tipping.

"I suppose it would be pushy to try to point out that you're drinking on an empty stomach," the Djin said drily.

"Not at all," I grinned.

For once I was ahead of him and raised my voice to call the bartender.

"Say! Could you bring me some of that popcorn while you're at it?"

Most of the bar snacks that were laid out seemed to be in mesh-covered containers to keep them from crawling or hopping away. Amidst these horrors, however, I had spotted a bin of popcorn when I came in, and had made special note of it; thinking that at least some forms of junk food appeared to be the same from dimension to dimension.

"Happy now?"

"I'd be happier if you picked something that was a little less salty," Kalvin grimaced, "but I suppose it's better than nothing."

The bartender delivered my pitcher along with a basket of popcorn, then wandered off to greet some new patrons who had just wandered in. I tossed a handful of the popcorn into my mouth and chewed it while I refilled my glass from the pitcher. It was actually more spicy than salty, which made me revise some of my earlier thoughts about the universality of junk food, but I decided not to mention this discovery to Kalvin. He was fussing at me enough already.

"So, what do you want to talk about?" I said, forcing myself not to immediately wash down the popcorn with a long drink from the glass.

The Djin leaned back and cocked an eyebrow at me.

"Well, your mood seems to have improved, but I was under the impression *you* might want to talk about the Butterfly's advice this afternoon."

As soon as he spoke, my current bubble of levity popped and my earlier depression slammed into me like a fist. Without thinking I drained half the contents of my glass.

"I don't know, Kalvin. I've got a lot of respect for the Butterfly, and I'm sure he meant well, but what he said has raised a lot of questions in my mind . . . questions I've never really asked myself before."

I topped off my glass casually, hoping the Djin wouldn't notice how fast I was drinking the stuff.

"Questions like . . . ?"

"Well, like . . . What are friends . . . really? On the rare occasions the subject comes up, all people seem to talk about is the need to be needed. All of a sudden I'm not sure I know what that means."

Somehow, my glass had gotten empty again. I refilled it as I continued.

"The more I look at it, the more I think that if you *really* need your friends, it's either a sign of weakness or laziness. You either need or want people to do your thinking for you, or your fighting for you, or whatever. Things that by rights you should be able to do for yourself. By rights, that makes you a parasite, existing by leeching off other people's strength and generosity."

I started to take a drink and realized I was empty. I suspected there was a leak in the glass, but set it aside, resolving to let it sit there for a while before I tried refilling it again.

"On the other hand, if you *don't* need your friends,

what good are they? Friends take up a big hunk of your time and cause a lot of heartache, so if you don't really need them, why should you bother? In a sense, if they need you, then you're encouraging them into being parasites instead of developing strength on their own. I don't know. What do you think, Kalvin?"

I gestured at him with my glass, and realized it was full again. So much for my resolve. I also realized the pitcher was almost empty.

"That's a rough one, Skeeve," the Djin was saying, and I tried to focus on his words. "I think everybody has to reach their own answer, though it's a rare person who even thinks to ask the question. I will say it's an oversimplification to try to equate caring about someone with weakness, just as I think it's wrong to assume that if we can learn from our friends, they're actually controlling our thinking."

He stopped and stared at my hand. I followed his gaze and realized I was trying to fill my empty glass from an empty pitcher.

"I also think," he sighed, "that we should *definitely* head back to the hotel now. Have you paid the tab? Are we square here?"

"Thass another thing," I said, fighting to get the words out past my tongue, which suddenly seemed to have a mind of its own. "What he said about money. I haven't been using my money right."

"For cryin' out loud, Skeeve! Lower your voice!"

"No, really! I've got all thissh money . . ."

I fumbled my moneybelt out and emptied the gold onto the table.

". . . And has it made ME happy? Has it made ANYBODY happy?"

When no answer came, I blinked my eyes, trying to get Kalvin back into focus. When he finally spoke, he seemed to be very tense, though his voice was very quiet.

"I think you may have just made someone happy, but I don't think it'll be you."

That's when I noticed the whole bar was silent. Looking around, I was surprised to see how many people had come in while we were talking. It was an ugly-looking crowd, but no one seemed to be talking to each other or doing anything. They just stood there looking at me . . . or to be more exact, looking at the table covered with my money.

XII:

*"HOLY BATSHIT, FATMAN! I
mean . . ."*

—ROBIN

"I . . . think I've made a tactic . . . tacl . . . an error," I
whispered with as much dignity as I could muster.

"You can say that again," Kalvin shot back merci-
lessly. "You forgot the first rule of survival: Don't tease
the animals. Look, Skeeve, do you want to get out of here,
or do you want to get out with your money?"

"Want . . . my money." I wasn't *that* drunk . . . or
maybe I was.

The Djin rolled his eyes in exasperation.

"I was afraid of that. That's going to be a little rougher.
Okay, the first thing you do is get that gold out of sight.
I don't think they'll try anything in here. There are too
many witnesses, which means too many ways to split the
loot."

I obediently began to pick up the coins. My hands
seemed to lack the dexterity necessary to lead them back
into my moneybelt, so I settled for shoving them into my
pockets as best I could.

The bar was no longer silent. There was a low murmur going around that sounded ominous even in my condition as various knots of patrons put their heads together. Even without the dark looks they kept shooting in my direction it wasn't hard to guess what the subject of their conversation was.

"The way I see it, if there's going to be trouble, it will hit when we leave. That means the trick is to leave without their knowing it. Order another pitcher."

That's when I realized how much I'd already had to drink. For a moment there, I thought the Djin had said . . .

"You want me to . . ."

". . . Order another pitcher, but whatever you do, don't drink any of it."

That made even less sense, but I followed his instructions and gestured at the bartender who delivered another pitcher with impressive speed.

I paid him from my pocket.

"I don't get it," I said. "Why should I order a pitcher when you say I shouldn't . . ."

"Shut up and listen," Kalvin hissed. "That was so everybody watching you will think you're planning to stick around for a while. In the meantime, we move."

That made even less sense than having some more to drink.

"But, Kalvin . . . most of them are between us and the door! They'll see me . . ."

"Not out the front door, stupid! You see that little hallway in back? That leads to the restrooms. There's also an exit back there which probably opens into an alley. That's the route we're taking."

"How do you know there's an exit back there?" I said suspiciously.

"Because one of the things I do when I come into a new bar is count the exits," the Djin retorted. "It's a habit I suggest you develop if you're going to keep drinking."

"Don't want any more to drink," I managed, my stomach suddenly rebelling at the thought.

"Good boy. Easy now. Nice and casual. Head for the restrooms."

I took a deep breath in a vain effort to clear my head, then stood up . . . or at least I tried to. Somewhere in the process, my foot got tangled in my chair and I nearly lost my balance. I managed not to fall, but the chair went over on its side noisily, drawing more than a few snickers from the roughnecks at the bar.

"That's all right," Kalvin soothed, his voice seeming to come from a great distance. "Now just head down the hallway."

I seemed to be very tall all of a sudden. Moving very carefully, I drew a bead on the opening to the hallway and headed in. I made it without touching the walls on either side and felt a small surge of confidence. Maybe this scheme of Kalvin's would work after all! As he had said, there was an exit door in the wall just short of the restrooms. Without being told, I changed course and pushed out into the alley, easing the door shut behind me. I was out!

"Oops."

I frowned at the Djin.

"What do you mean, 'Oops!'? Didn't you say I should . . ."

"Nice of you to drop by, mister!"

That last was said by a burly Pervect, one of six actually who were blocking our path down the alley. Apparently our little act hadn't fooled everybody.

"Skeeve, I . . ."

"Never mind, Kalvin. I just figured out for myself what 'Oops' means."

"Of course, you know this here's what you'd call a toll-alley. You got to pay to use it."

That was the same individual talking. If he noticed me talking to Kalvin, which to him would look like talking to thin air, he didn't seem to mind or care.

"That's right," one of his cronies chimed in. "We figure

what you got in your pockets ought to just about cover it."

"Quick! Back inside!" Kalvin hissed.

"Way ahead of you," I murmured, feeling behind myself for the door.

I found it . . . sort of. The door was there, but there was no handle on this side. Apparently the bar owners wanted it used for exits only. Terrific.

". . . The only question is: Are you gonna give it to us quietly, or are we gonna have to take it?"

I've faced lynch mobs, soldiers, and sports fans before, but a half-dozen Pervish plug-uglies was the most frightening force I've ever been confronted with. I decided, all by myself, that this would be an excellent time to delegate a problem.

"C'mon, Kalvin! Do something!

"Like what? I told you I'm no good in a fight."

"Well, do SOMETHING! You're supposed to be the Djin!"

I guess I knew deep inside that carping at Kalvin wouldn't help matters. To my surprise, however, he responded.

"Oh, all right!" he grimaced. "Maybe this will help."

With that, he made a few passes with his hands and . . .

. . . And I was sober! Stone-cold sober!

I looked at him.

"That's all I can do for you," he shrugged. "From here, you're on your own. At least now you won't have to fight 'em drunk."

The thugs were starting to pick up boards and pieces of brick from the alley.

"Time's up!" their leader declared, starting for me.

I smiled at Kalvin.

"I think your analysis of friendship was only a little short of brilliant," I said, "There are a couple of points I'd like to go over, though."

"NOW?" the Djin shrieked. "This is hardly the time to . . . Look out!"

The leader of the pack was cocking his arms to take a double-handed swing at me with a piece of lumber he had acquired somewhere along the way. As the wood whistled toward its target, which is to say, my head, I made a circular gesture in the air between us with my hand . . . and the board rebounded as if it had struck an invisible wall!

"Magikal ward," I informed the gape-mouthed Djin. "It's like a force field, only different. I *did* mention I was a magician, didn't I!"

The gang stopped dead in their tracks at this display; a few had even retreated a few steps.

"Oh, before I forget, thanks for the sobering-up job, Kalvin. You're right. It does make it a lot easier to focus the mind. Anyway, as I was saying, I've gotten a lot of mileage out of wards. They can be used like I just did, as a shield, or . . ."

I made a few quick adjustments to the spell.

". . . You can widen them out into a wall or a bubble. Coming?"

I had expanded the ward and was now starting to push the gang back down the alley ahead of us. It was a minor variant of the trick I used to break up a fight at the Big Game a while back, so I had reason to have confidence in it. I figured we would just walk out of the alley keeping the thugs at a respectful distance, then hail a cab to get us the heck out of there.

The gang leader had turned and trotted out ahead of the others a few paces.

"Cute. Real cute," he called, turning to face me again. "Hadn't figured you for magik. Well, let's see how you handle *this*, wise guy!"

With that, he pulled what looked like a couple of blackboard erasers from the pocket of his jacket. At first, I thought he was going to try to throw them at me, but instead he clapped them together over his head, showering himself with what appeared to be white chalk dust. It would have been funny . . . if he hadn't looked so grim as he started for me again.

Just to be on the safe side, I doubled up on the ward in front of him . . . and he walked right through it!

"That's what I thought!" he called to his cronies, pausing once he had penetrated my defenses. "Real low-level stuff. Go to Class Two or heavier, guys . . . in fact, the heavier the better!"

I should have seen it coming . . . maybe would have if I had more time to think. In a dimension that used both magik and technology, there were bound to be counter-magik spells and weapons available. Unfortunately, it seemed I was about to learn about them first hand!

The other gang members were all reaching into their pockets and producing charms or spray cans. I had a bad feeling that my magikal ward wasn't going to protect me much longer. Apparently Kalvin was of the same opinion.

"Quick, Skeeve! Have you got any other tricks up your sleeve?"

"I've always figured that, in times of crisis, it's best to play through your strongest suit. Still hoping to avoid any actual violence, I pulled my energy out of the wards and threw it into a new disguise: an over-muscled Pervect easily half again as tall as I really was.

"Do you boys *really* want me to get rough?" I shouted, trying as best as I could to make my voice a threatening bass.

I had thought of making myself look like a policeman, but had discarded the idea. With my luck they probably would have surrendered, and then what would I have done with them? I wanted them to run . . . as far out of my life as possible!

It didn't work.

I had barely gotten the words out when a large chunk of brick ripped through the air just over my head . . . passing through what would have been the chest of the disguised me.

"Disguise spell!" the thrower called. "Go for him like we saw him before!"

To say the least, I figured it was time for the better part of valor. Trying to keep my mind under control, which is harder to do than it sounds with half a dozen bully-boys charging down on you, I slapped on a levitation spell and took to the skies.

. . . At least, I tried to.

I was barely airborne when a vise-like grip closed on my ankle.

"I've got him!"

The grip hurt, which made it difficult to concentrate on my spell. Then, too, it seemed the day had taken a lot more out of me than I had realized. Normally, I can, and have, levitated as many as two people besides myself . . . count that as three since one of them was Massha. In the scramble of the moment, however, I was hard pressed to lift myself and the guy who was holding my ankle. I struggled to get him into the air, then something bounced off my head and . . .

The ground slammed into me at an improbable angle, and for a moment, I saw stars. The pressure seemed to be gone from my ankle, but when I opened my eyes, the leader was standing over me with his trusty board in his hands.

"Nice try, wise guy!" he sneered. "But not good enough. Now give me the . . ."

Suddenly he went sprawling as someone piled into him from behind.

"Quick, Mr. Skeeve! Get up!"

It took me a moment to realize it was the street vendor I had spoken to that morning. He crouched over me, facing down the circling gang.

"Hurry up! I can't hold these guys off by myself!"

I wasn't sure I could get up if I wanted to, but at this point I was willing to abandon any hopes of a non-violent solution to our problems. Propping myself up on one elbow, I reached out with my mind, grabbed a garbage can, and sent it sailing through the gang's formation.

"What the . . ."

"Look out!"

If they wanted physical, I'd give it to them. I mentally grabbed two more trash cans and sent them into the fray, keeping all three flying back and forth in the narrow confines of the alley.

"Cripes! I'm on your side! Remember?" the street vendor cried, ducking under one of my missiles.

I summoned up a little more energy and threw a ward over the two of us. Somehow, I didn't think anyone had thought to use their anti-magik stuff on a garbage can.

A few more swings with the old trash cans, and it was all over.

Heaving a ragged breath, I dropped the ward and brought my makeshift weapons to a halt. Four of my attackers lay sprawled on the ground, and the other two had apparently taken to their heels.

"Nice work, Skeeve," Kalvin crowed, appearing from wherever it was he had taken cover when the fracas started.

"Are you all right, Mr. Skeeve?" the street vendor asked, extending a hand to help me to my feet.

"I think so . . . yes . . . thanks to you . . . J.R., isn't it?"

"That's right. I was walkin' home when I saw these jokers pilin' into you. It looked a little uneven, so I thought I'd lend a hand. Cheez! I didn't know you wuz a magician!"

"A mighty grateful magician right now," I said, digging into my pocket. "Here, take this. Consider it my way of saying thank you."

"Excuse me," the Djin drawled, "but didn't we just get into this whole brawl so you could *keep* your money?"

He needn't have worried. J.R. recoiled from the gold as if I had offered him poison.

"I didn't help you for money!" he said through tight lips. "I know you don't mean . . . Cripes! All you rich guys are the same. You think your money . . . Look! I work for my money, see! I ain't no bum lookin' for a handout!"

With that he spun on his heel and marched away, leaving me with an outstretched hand full of gold.

It would have been a beautiful exit, if the alley hadn't suddenly been blocked by a vehicle pulling in . . . a vehicle with blue and red flashing lights on top.

XIII:

"Who? Me, Officer?"

—J. DILLINGER

"I still don't see why we should be detained."

It seemed like hours that we had been at the police station, we being myself, J.R., and, of course, Kalvin, though the police seemed unaware of the latter's existence and I, in turn, was disinclined to tell them. Despite our protests, we had been transported here shortly after the police had arrived. The thugs had been revived and placed in a separate vehicle, though I noticed they were handled far less gently than we were. Still, it was small consolation to being held against our will.

"You don't? Well, then we'll have to go over it all again slowly and see if you can get a hint."

This was spoken by the individual who had been conducting our interrogation since we arrived. From the deferential way the other policemen treated him, I assumed he was a ranking officer of some sort. He possessed bad breath, a foul disposition, and what seemed to be an endless tolerance for repetition. As he launched into his oration, I fought an impulse to chant along with the now-familiar words.

"We could charge you with Being Drunk in Public."

"I'm stone cold sober," I interrupted, thanking my lucky stars for Kalvin's assistance. "If you don't believe it, test me."

"There are a lot of witnesses who said you were falling down drunk in the bar."

"I tripped over a chair."

"Then there's the minor matter of Assault . . ."

"I keep telling you, they attacked me! It was self-defense!"

". . . And Destruction of Private Property . . ."

"For cryin' out loud, it was a garbage can! I'll pay for a new one if that's . . ."

". . . And, of course, there's Resisting Arrest."

"I asked them where we were going. That's all."

"That's not the way the arresting officers tell it."

Realizing I was getting nowhere in this argument, I did the next most logical thing: I took out my frustration on an innocent bystander. In this case, the nearest available target happened to be J.R., who seemed to be dozing off in his chair.

"Aren't you going to say anything?" I demanded. "You're in this too, you know."

"There's no need," the street vendor shrugged. "It's not like we were in trouble or anything."

"That's funny. I thought we were in a police station."

"So what? They aren't really serious. Are you, Captain?"

The Pervect who had been arguing with me shot him a dark look, but I noticed he didn't contradict what had been said.

"I'll bite J.R.," I said, still watching the captain. "What are you seeing that I'm not in this situation?"

"It's what *isn't* happening that's the tip-off," he winked. "What isn't happening is we aren't being booked.

We've been here a long time and they haven't charged us with any crimes."

"But the Captain here said . . ."

"He said they *could* charge us with etc., etc. You notice he hasn't actually done it. Believe me, Mr. Skeeve, if they were going to jail us, we'd have been behind bars an hour ago. They're just playing games to stall for a while."

What he said seemed incredible considering the amount of grief we were being put through, yet I couldn't find a hole in his logic. I turned to the captain and raised an eyebrow.

"Is that true?" I said.

The policeman ignored me, leaning back in his chair to stare at J.R. through half-closed eyes.

"You seem to know a lot about police procedure, son. Almost as if you've been rousted before."

A sneer spread across the street vendor's face as he met the challenge head on.

"Anyone who works the streets gets hassled," he said. "It's how you police protect the upstanding citizens from merchants like me who are too poor to afford a storefront. I suppose it *is* a lot safer than taking on the real criminals who might shoot back. We should be grateful to our defenders of the law. If it wasn't for them, the dimension would probably be overrun with street vendors and parking violators."

I should have been grateful for the diversion after being on the hot seat myself for so long. Unfortunately, I had also logged in a fair amount of time as the Great Skeeve, and as such was much more accustomed to being hassled than I was to being overlooked.

"I believe the question was 'Are we or are we not being charged with any crimes?' " I said pointedly. "I'm still waiting for an answer."

The captain glowered at me for a few moments, but when I didn't drop my return gaze, he heaved a sigh.

"No. We won't be bringing any charges against you at this time."

"Then we're free to go?"

"Well, there are a few more questions you'll have to answer first. After that, you're free to . . ."

"That's 'more' as in new questions, not the same ones all over again. Right?"

The policeman glared at me, but now that I knew we were in the clear, I was starting to have fun with this.

"That's right," he said through gritted teeth.

"Okay. Shoot."

I suddenly realized that was an unfortunate use of words in a room full of armed policemen, but it escaped unnoticed.

The captain cleared his throat noisily before continuing.

"Mister Skeeve," he began formally, "do you wish to press charges against the alleged attackers we currently have in custody?"

"What kind of a silly question is that? Of course I want to."

Kalvin was waving frantically at me and pointing to J.R. The street vendor was shaking his head in a slow, but firm, negative.

". . . Um . . . before I make up my mind on that, Captain," I hedged, trying to figure out what J.R. was thinking, "could you tell me what happens if I don't press charges?"

"We can probably hold onto them until tomorrow morning for questioning, but then we'll let them go."

That didn't sound like particularly satisfying treatment for a gang that had tried to rob me. Still, J.R. seemed to know what he was doing so far, and I was disinclined to go against his signaled advice.

". . . And if I DO press charges?" I pressed, trying to sort it out.

"I'm not a judge," the captain shrugged, "so I can't say for sure . . . but I can give you my best guess."

"Please."

"We'll charge them with Attempted Robbery and Assault with Intent To Do Great Bodily Harm . . . I don't think we could make Attempted Murder stick."

That sounded pretty good to me, but the policeman wasn't finished.

". . . Then the court will appoint a lawyer—if they don't already have one—who will arrange for bail to be set. They'll probably raise the money from a bondsman and be back on the streets before noon tomorrow."

"What? But they . . ."

"It'll take a couple of months for the trial to be scheduled, at which point it'll be your word against theirs . . . and they're not only locals, they have you outnumbered."

I was starting to see the light.

". . . That is, if it gets to trial. More than likely there'll be some plea bargaining, and they'll plead guilty to a lesser charge, which means a smaller sentence with an earlier parole—if the sentence isn't suspended as soon as it's handed down . . ."

"Whoa! Stop! I think I'll just pass on pressing charges."

"Thought you would," the captain nodded. "It's probably the easiest way for everybody. After all, you weren't hurt, and you've still got your money."

"Of course, the next person they jump may not be quite so lucky," I said drily.

"I didn't say it was the best way to handle it, just the easiest."

Before I could think of a witty answer to that one, a uniformed policeman rapped at the doorframe, entered the room, and passed a sheet of paper to the captain. Something about the way the latter's lips tightened as he scanned the sheet made me nervous.

"Well, well, *Mis*-ter Skeeve," he said at last, dropping the paper onto the desk in front of him. "It seems this isn't the first time you've dealt with the police since arriving in this dimension."

"Uh-oh," Kalvin exclaimed, rolling his eyes, "here it comes!"

"What makes you say that, Captain?"

I had a hunch it wouldn't do any good to act innocent. Unfortunately, I didn't have any other ideas about how to act.

"What makes me say that is the report I just received. I thought I should check with the other precincts to see if they had heard of you, and it seems they have."

"*That's* why they've been stalling," J.R. put in. "To wait until the reports came in. It's called police efficiency."

The captain ignored him.

"According to this, you've had two run-ins with the police already. First for acting suspicious on the public streets . . ."

"I was being polite instead of barreling into people!" I broke in, exasperated. "I'm sorry, I was new here and didn't know 'rude' was the operative word for this dimension. You should put up signs or something warning people that being polite is grounds for harassment on Perv!"

The captain continued as if I hadn't spoken.

". . . And later that same day, you tried to get out of paying for a pretty expensive meal."

"I fainted, for Pete's sake! As soon as I came to, I paid for the meal, even though I hadn't eaten a bite."

"Now that in itself sounds a little suspicious," the captain said, pursing his lips. "Why would you order a meal you couldn't, or wouldn't, eat?"

"Because I didn't know I couldn't eat it when I ordered it, obviously. I keep telling you . . . I'm new here!"

"Uh huh," the policeman leaned back and studied me through slitted eyes. "You've got a glib answer for everything . . . don't you, Mister Skeeve."

"That's because it's true! Would I be less suspicious if I *didn't* have answers for your questions? Tell me, Captain, I really want to know! I know I'm not a criminal, what does it take to convince *you?*"

The captain shook his head slowly.

"Frankly, I don't know. I've been on the force for a long time, and I've learned to trust my instincts. Your story *sounds* good, but my instinct tells me you're trouble looking for a place to happen."

I could see I was playing into a stacked deck, so I abandoned the idea of impressing him with my innocence.

"I guess the bottom line is the same as before that sheet came in, then. Are you going to press charges against me . . . or am I free to go?"

He studied me for a few more moments, then waved his hand.

"Go on. Get out of here . . . and take your little street buddy with you. Just take my advice and don't carry so much cash in the future. There's no profit in teasing the animals."

If I had been thinking, I would have let it go at that. Unfortunately, it had been a long day and I was both tired and annoyed . . . a dangerous combination.

"I'll remember that, Captain," I said, rising to my feet. "I had been under the impression that the police were around to protect innocent citizens like me . . . not to waste everybody's time harassing them. Believe me, I've learned my lesson."

Every policeman in the room suddenly tensed, and I realized too late that there was also no profit in critiquing the police.

". . . And if we don't check on suspicious characters *before* they make trouble, then all we're good for is filling out reports AFTER a crime had been committed," the captain spat bitterly. "Either way, 'innocent citizens' like you can find something to gripe about!"

"I'm sorry, Captain. I shouldn't have . . ."

I don't know if he even heard my attempted apology. If he did, it didn't make a difference.

"You see, I've learned my lesson, too. When I first joined the force, I thought there was nothing better I could do with my life than to spend it protecting innocent citizens . . . and I still believe that. Even then I knew this

would be a thankless occupation. What I *hadn't* realized
was that 'innocent citizens' like you are not only ungrate-
ful, the tendency is to treat the police like they're enemies!"

I decided against trying to interrupt him. He was on a
roll, lecturing about what seemed to be his favorite subject. Opening my mouth now would probably be about as
safe as getting between my pet dragon, Gleep, and his
food dish.

"Everybody wants the crooks to be in jail, but nobody
wants a prison in their community . . . or to vote in the
taxes to build new jails. So the prisons we have are over-
crowded, and the 'innocent citizens' scream bloody murder every time a judge suspends a sentence or lets an
offender out on parole."

He was up and pacing back and forth now as he
warmed to his subject.

"Nobody sees the crimes that aren't committed. We
can reduce the crime rate 98%, and the 'innocent citizens'
blame US for that last 2% . . . as if we were the ones com-
mitting the crimes! Nobody wants to cooperate with the
police or approve the tax allocations necessary to keep up
with inflation, so we can't even keep abreast of where we
are, much less expand to keep up with the population
growth."

He paused and leveled an accusing finger at J.R.

"Then there are 'innocent citizens' like your buddy
here, who admits he's running an illegal, unlicensed business. What that means, incidentally, is that he doesn't
have to pay *any* taxes, even the existing ones, although
he expects the same protection from us as the storekeepers
who *do*, even though most of them cheat on their taxes
as well."

"So we're supposed to keep the peace and apprehend
criminals while we're understaffed and using equipment
that's outdated and falling apart. About all we *have* to
work with is our instincts . . . and then we get hassled for
using that!"

He came to a halt in front of me, and pushed his face close to mine, treating me to another blast of his breath. I didn't point it out to him.

"Well *this* time we're going to see just how good my instincts are. I'm letting you go for now, but it occurs to me it might be a good idea to run a check on you on other dimensions. If you're just an innocent businessman like you claim, we won't find anything . . . but if I'm right," he gave me a toothy grin, "you've probably tangled with the law before, and we'll find that too. I'm betting you've left a trail of trouble behind you, a trail that leads right to here. If so, we'll be talking again . . . real soon. I don't want you to switch hotels or try to leave the dimension without letting me know, understand? I want to be able to find you again, MISTER Skeeve!"

XIV:

"Parting is such sweet sorrow."

—FIGARO

The possibility of an extensive check on my off-dimension background worried me, but not so much that I forgot my manners. J.R. had saved my skin in the alley fight, and, throughout the police grilling, a part of my mind had been searching for a way to repay him. As we left the police station, I thought I had the answer.

"Say, J.R.," I said, turning to him on the steps, "about that business you want to start ... how much capital would you need to get started?"

I could see his neck stiffening as I spoke.

"I told you before, Mr. Skeeve, I won't take a reward for saving your life."

"Who said anything about a reward? I'm talking about investing in your operation and taking a share of the profits."

That one stopped him in his tracks.

"You'd do that?"

"Why not? I'm a businessman and always try to keep

an eye open for new ventures to back. The trickiest thing is finding trustworthy principals to manage the investments. In your case, you've already proved to me that you're trustworthy. So how much would you need for this plan of yours?"

The street vendor thought for a few moments.

"Even *with* backing I'd want to start small and build. Figuring that . . . yeah. I think about five thousand in gold would start things off right."

"Oh," I said, intelligently. I wasn't about to question his figures, but the start-up cost was higher than I had expected. I only had a couple thousand with me, and most of that was going to cover Edvick's services and the hotel bill. So much for a grand gesture!

"I'll . . . uh . . . have to think about it."

J.R.'s face fell.

"Yeah. Sure. Well, you know where to find me when you make up your mind."

He turned and strode off down the street without looking back. It was silly to feel bad about not fulfilling an offer I didn't have to make, but I did.

"Well, I guess it's time for us to head back to the hotel . . . right, Skeeve?" Kalvin chimed in.

I had botched the job with J.R., but I resolved that this one I was going to do right.

"No," I said.

"No?" the Djin echoed. "So where are we going instead?"

"That's the whole point, Kalvin. *We* aren't going anywhere. *I'm* going back to the hotel. *You're* going back to Djinger."

He floated up to eye level with me, frowning as he cocked his head to one side.

"I don't get it. Why should I go back to Djinger?"

"Because you've filled your contract. That means you're free to go, so I assume you're going."

"I did?"

"Sure. Back in the alley. You used a spell to sober me

up before I had to fight those goons. To my thinking, that fulfills your contract."

The Djin stroked his beard thoughtfully.

"I dunno," he said. "That wasn't much of a spell."

"You never promised much," I insisted. "As a matter of fact, you went to great lengths to impress me with how little you could do."

"Oh, that," Kalvin waved his hand deprecatingly. "That's just the standard line of banter we feed to the customers. It keeps them from expecting too much of a Djin. You'd be amazed at some of the things folks expect us to do. If we can keep their expectations low, then they're easier to impress when we strut our stuff."

"Well, it worked. I'm impressed. If you hadn't done your thing back there in the alley, my goose would have been cooked before J.R. hit the scene."

"Glad to help. It was less dangerous than trying to lend a hand in the fight."

"Maybe, but by my count it still squares things between us. You promised one round of minor help, and delivered it at a key moment. That's all your contract called for . . . and more."

The Djin folded his arms and stared, frowning into the distance for several moments.

"Check me on this, Skeeve," he said finally, "I've been helpful to you so far, right?"

"Right," I nodded, wondering what he was leading up to.

"And I've been pretty good company, haven't I? I mean, I do tend to run off at the mouth a bit, but overall you haven't seemed to mind having me around."

"Right again."

"So why are you trying to get rid of me?"

Suddenly, the whole day caught up with me. The well-meant advice from the Butterfly, the drinking, the fight, the head-butting with the police all swelled within me until my mind and temper burst from the pressure.

"I'M NOT. TRYING TO GET RID OF YOU!!" I

shrieked at the Djin, barely aware my voice had changed. "Don't you think I want to keep you around? Don't you think I know that my odds of finding Aahz on my own in this wacko dimension are next to zip? Dammit, Kalvin, I'M TRYING TO BE NICE TO YOU!!!"

"Um . . . maybe you could be a little less nice and quit shouting?"

I realized that I had backed him across the sidewalk and currently had him pinned against the wall with the force of my "niceness." I took a long, deep breath and tried to bring myself under control.

"Look," I said carefully, "I didn't mean to yell at you. It's just . . ."

Something trickled down my face and it dawned on me that I was on the verge of tears. On the verge, heck! I was starting to cry. I cleared my throat noisily, covertly wiping away the tear as I covered my mouth, hoping Kalvin wouldn't notice. If he did, he was too polite to say anything.

"Let me try this again from the top."

I drew a ragged breath.

"You've been a big help, Kalvin, more than I could have ever hoped for when I opened your vial. Your advice has been solid, and if I've been having trouble it's because I didn't listen to it enough."

I paused, trying to organize my thoughts.

"I'm not trying to get rid of you . . . really. I'd like nothing better than to have you stick around at least until I found Aahz. I just don't want to trade on our friendship. I got your services in a straightforward business deal . . . one you had no say in, if your account of how Djinger works is accurate. If I sounded a bit cold when I told you I thought our contract was complete, it's because I was fighting against begging you to stay. I was afraid that if I did, it would put you in a bad position . . . actually, it would put *me* in a bad position. If I made a big appeal to you and you said no, it would leave us both feeling pretty bad at the end of what otherwise has been a mutually beneficial association. The only thing I could think of that would be worse would be if you agreed to stay out of pity. Then I'd feel guilty as long as you were around, knowing all the while that you could and should be going about your own business, and would be if I weren't so weak that I can't handle a simple task by myself."

The tears were running freely now, but I didn't bother trying to hide them. I just didn't care anymore.

"Mostly what you've done," I continued, "is to keep me company. I've felt scared and alone ever since I hit this dimension . . . or would have if you hadn't been along. I'm so screaming afraid of making a mistake that I'd probably freeze up and do nothing unless I had some-body in tow to applaud when I did right and to carp at me when I did wrong . . . just so I'd know the difference. That's how insecure I am . . . I don't even trust my own judgment as to whether I'm right or not in what I do! The trouble is, I haven't been doing so well in the friendship department lately. Aahz walked out on me, the M.Y.T.H. team thinks I've deserted them . . . heck, I even managed to offend J.R. by trying to say thanks with my wallet instead of my mouth."

It occurred to me I was starting to ramble. Making a feeble pass at my tear-streaked face with my sleeve, I forced a smile.

"Anyway, I can't see imposing on you, either as a friend or a business associate, just to hold my hand in troubled times. That doesn't mean I'm not grateful for what you've done or that I'm trying to get rid of you. I'd appreciate it if you stuck around but I don't think I have any right to ask you to."

Having run out of things to say, I finished with a half-hearted shrug. Strangely enough, after baring my soul and clearing my mind of the things which had been troubling me, I felt worlds better.

"Are you through?"

Kalvin was still hovering patiently with his arms

folded. Perhaps it was my imagination, but there seemed
to be a terse edge to his voice.

"I guess so. Sorry for running on like that."

"No problem. Just as long as I get my innings."

"Innings?"

"A figure of speech," he waved. "In this case, it means
it's my turn to talk and your turn to listen. I've tried before,
but it seems like every time I start, we get interrupted . . . or
you get drunk."

I grimaced at the memory.

"I didn't mean to get drunk. It's just that I've
never . . ."

"Hey! Remember? It's my turn," the Djin broke in. "I
want to say . . . just a second."

He made a sweeping gesture with his hand and . . .
grew! Suddenly he was the same size I was.

"There, that's better!" he said, dusting his hands together. "It'll be a littler harder to overlook me now."

I was about to ask for a full accounting of his "meager"
powers, but his last comment had stung me.

"I'm sorry, Kalvin. I didn't mean to . . ."

"Save it!" he ordered, waving his hand. "Right now
it's my turn. There'll be lots of time later for you to wal-
low in guilt. If not, I'm sure you'll make the time."

That had a nasty sound to it, but I subsided and gestured for him to continue.

"Okay," he said, "first, last, and in between, you're
wrong, Skeeve. It's hard for me to believe such a right
guy can be so wrong."

It occurred to me that I had already admitted my confidence in my perception of right and wrong was at an
all-time low. I didn't verbalize it, though. Kalvin had said
he wanted a chance to have his say, and I was going to
do my best to not interrupt. I owed him that much.

"Ever since we met, you've been talking about right
and wrong as if they were absolutes. According to you,
things are either right or they're wrong . . . period. 'Was
Aahz right to leave?' . . . Are you wrong to try to bring

him back? . . . Well, my young friend, life isn't that simple. Not only are you old enough to know that, you'd better learn it before you drive yourself and everyone around you absolutely crazy!"

He began to float back and forth in the air in front of me with his hands clasped behind his back. I supposed it was his equivalent of pacing.

"It's possible for you, or anyone else to not be right and still not be wrong, just as you can be right from a business standpoint, but wrong from a humanitarian viewpoint. The worlds are complex, and people are a hopeless tangle of contradictions. Conditions change not only from situation to situation and person to person, but from moment to moment as well. Trying to kid yourself that there's some master key to what's right and wrong is ridiculous . . . worse than that, it's dangerous, because you'll always end up feeling incompetent and inadequate when it eludes you."

Even though I was having trouble grasping what he was saying, that last part rang a bell. It described with uncomfortable accuracy how I felt about myself more often than not! I tried to listen more closely.

"You've got to accept that life is complicated and often frustrating. What's right for you may not be right for Aahz. There are even times when there is no right answer . . . just the least objectionable of several bad choices. Recognize that, then don't waste time and energy wondering why it is or railing that it's unfair . . . accept it."

"I . . . I'll try," I said "but it's not easy."

"Of course it's not easy!" the Djin shot back. "Who ever said it was easy? Nothing's easy. Sometimes it's less difficult than at other times, but it's never easy. Part of your problem is that you keep thinking things should be easy, so you assume the easy way is the right way. Case in point: You knew it would be hard to ask me to stay on after I had fulfilled the contract, so you decided the right thing to do was not to ask . . . ignoring how hard it would be for you to keep hunting for Aahz without me."

"But if it would be easier for me if you stayed . . ."

"That's right. It's a contradiction," Kalvin grinned. "Confusing, isn't it? Forget right and wrong for a while. What do *you* want?"

That one *was* easy.

"I'd like you to stay and help me look for Aahz," I said firmly.

The Djin smiled and nodded.

"Not a chance," he replied.

"What?"

"Did I stutter? I said . . ."

"I know what you said!" I cut him off. "It's just that you said . . . I mean before you said . . ."

"Oh, there's no problem in your asking me . . . or in your terms. I'm just not going to stay."

By now my head was spinning with confusion, but I tried to maintain what little poise I had left.

". . . But I thought . . . Oh, well. I guess I was mistaken."

"No you weren't. If you had asked me in the first place, I would have stayed.

"Then why . . ." I began, but the Djin waved me into silence.

"I'm sorry, Skeeve. I shouldn't tease you with head games at a time like this. What changed my mind was something you said while you were explaining why you didn't ask. You said you were scared and insecure, which is only sane, all things considered. But then you added something about how you were afraid to trust your own judgment and therefore needed someone else along to tell you whether you were right or not."

He paused and shook his head.

"I can't go along with that. I realized then that if I stayed, I'd fall into the same trap all your other colleagues have . . . of inadvertently doing your thinking for you when we express our own opinions. The sad thing is that we aren't, really. You decide yourself what advice you do and don't listen to. The trouble is, you only remember when you go against advice and it goes wrong ... like when you got drunk tonight. Any correct judgment calls you assume were made by your 'advisors.' Well, you've convinced me that you're a right guy, Skeeve. Now all you have to do is convince yourself. That's why I'm going to head on back to Djinger and let you work this problem out on your own. Right or wrong, there'll be no one to take the credit or share the blame. It's all yours. I'm betting your solution will be right."

He held out his hand. I took it and carefully shook hands with this person who had been so much help to me.

"I ... well, thanks, Kalvin. You've given me a lot to think about."

"It's been a real pleasure, Skeeve ... really. Good luck in finding our friend. Oh, say ..."

He dug something out of his waistband and placed it in my hand. As he released it, it grew into a full-sized business card.

"That's my address on Djinger. Stay in touch ... even if it's just to let me know how this whole thing turns out."

"I will," I promised. "Take care of yourself, Kalvin ... and thanks again!"

"Oh, and one more thing ... about your having problems with your friends? Forget trying to be strong. Your real strength is in being a warm, caring person. When you *try* to be strong, it comes across as being cold and insensitive. Think about it."

He gave one last wave, folded his arms, and faded from view.

I stared at the empty space for a few moments, then started the walk back to my hotel alone. I knew where it was ... what I *didn't* know was where Djinger was.

XV:

"Easy credit terms available . . ."

—SATAN

"I hear you got jumped last night."

I paused in mid-move of easing myself into the cab's back seat to give the cabbie a long stare.

". . . And good morning to you, too, Edvick," I said drily. "Yes, thank you, I slept very well."

My sarcasm was not lost on the driver . . . a fact for which I was secretly grateful. Sometimes I have cause to wonder about my powers of communication.

"Hey! Nothing personal. It's just that people talk, ya know?"

"No, I don't . . . but I'm learning."

It seemed that however large and populated Perv appeared to be, there was a thriving network of gossip lurking just out of sight.

I had come down early, hoping to have a chance to talk with J.R., but between my room and the front door I had been stopped by two bellhops and the desk clerk, all of whom knew that I had been in a fight the night before.

Of course, they each expressed their sympathies . . . in varying degrees. As I recall, the desk clerk's sympathy went something like "You're welcome to use the hotel safe for your valuables, sir . . . but we can't accept responsibility for any losses."

Terrific!!

I had rapidly discovered that I wasn't wild about the idea of my escapade being discussed by the general populace. Especially not since it ended with a session with the police.

Even though he had noted my displeasure at discussing the prior night's incident, Edvick seemed determined not to let the subject die as we started on our way.

"I told you you should have gotten a bodyguard," he lectured. "Carrying that kind of cash around is just askin' for trouble."

"Funny, the police said the same thing . . . about the cash, I mean."

"Well, they're right . . . for a change. Things are dangerous enough around here without drawing unnecessary attention to yourself."

I leaned back in the seat and closed my eyes. I hadn't slept well, but the brief time I had spent in a horizontal position had allowed my muscles to tighten, and I ached all over.

"So I discovered," I said. "Oh well, it's over now. Besides, I didn't do such a bad job of taking care of myself."

"The way I heard it, someone showed up to help bail you out," Edvick pointed out bluntly, "and even then it was touch and go. Don't kid yourself about it being over, though. You'd just better hope your luck holds the next time."

Suddenly, my aching muscles were no longer the main claim to my attention.

"Next time?" I said, sitting up straight. "What next time?"

"I don't want to sound pessimistic," the cabbie shrugged, "but I figure it's a given. Those guys you messed up are going to be back on the street today, and will probably devote a certain amount of their time and energy trying to find you for a rematch."

"You think so?"

"Then again, even if I'm wrong, the word is out that you're carrying a good-sized wad around with you. That's going to make you fair game for every cheap hoodlum looking to pick up some quick cash."

I hadn't stopped to consider it, but what Edvick was saying made sense. All I needed to make my mission more difficult was to have to be watching my back constantly at the same time!

"I'm sorry, what was that again?" I said, trying to concentrate on what the driver was saying.

"Huh? Oh, I was just sayin' again that what you should really do is hire a bodyguard . . . same as I've been sayin' right along."

He *had* been saying that all along, and Kalvin had agreed with him. I had pooh-poohed the idea originally, but now I was forced to reexamine my stance on the matter.

"Nnnnno," I said, finally, talking to myself. "I can't do it."

"Why not?" Edvick chimed in, adding his two cents to the argument drawing to a close in my mind.

"Well, the most overpowering reason is that I can't afford one."

The cabbie snorted.

"You've got to be kidding me. With the money you've got?"

"It may seem like a lot, but nearly all of it is already committed to you and the hotel."

The cab swerved dangerously as Edvick turned in his seat to stare at me.

"You mean that's all the money you have? You're carrying your whole bankroll?"

As upset as I was, that thought made me laugh.

"Not hardly," I said. "The trouble is that most of my

money is back on Deva. I only brought some of it along
for pocket expenses. Unfortunately I badly underestimated
what the prices would be like here, so I have to keep an
eye on my expenses."

"Oh, that's no problem," the cabbie retorted, turning
his attention to the road again. "Just open a line of credit
here."

"Do what?"

"Talk to a bank and borrow what you need against your
assets. That's how I came up with the money for this
cab . . . not to mention my other ventures. Sheese! If
everybody tried to operate on a cash basis, it would ruin
the dimension's economy!"

"I don't know," I hesitated. "Nobody on this dimension
really knows me. Do you really think a bank would be
willing to trust me with a loan?"

"There's only one way to find out," Edvick shrugged.
"Tell you what . . . there's a branch of my bank not far
from here. Why don't you pop in and talk to them. You
might be surprised."

The bank itself was not particularly imposing; a
medium-sized storefront with a row of teller windows and
a few scattered desks. Some doors in the back wall presumably led to offices and the vault, but they were painted
assorted bright colors and in themselves did not appear
particularly ominous. Still, I realized I felt no small degree
of nervousness as I surveyed the interior. There were
small clues here and there which bespoke a seriousness
which belied the studied casualness of the decor. Little
things, like the machines mounted high in the corners
which constantly swept the room as if monitoring the
movements of both tellers and customers. The tellers
themselves were secure behind high panes of innocent-
looking glass, doing business through an ingenious slot
and drawer arrangement at each station. An observant person such as myself, however, could not help but notice
that if the degree of distortion were any indication, the
glass was much thicker than it might first appear. There

were also armed guards scattered around the room draped
with an array of weapons which did not look at all cere-
monial or decorative. There was a great deal of money
here, and an equally great effort was being made to be
sure no one decided to simply help themselves to the sur-
plus.

I had a hunch the kind of business I had in mind would
not be handled over the counter by a teller, and, sure
enough when I inquired, I was ushered immediately
through one of the brightly painted doors into a private
office.

The individual facing me across the desk rose and extended a hand in greeting as I entered. He was impeccably
dressed in a business suit of what could only be called a
conservative cut . . . particularly for a Pervect, and he
oozed a sincere warmth that bordered on oily. Green
scales and yellow eyes notwithstanding, he reminded me
of Grimble, the Chancellor of the Exchequer I had feuded
with back at Possiltum. I wondered briefly if this was
common with professional money guardians, everywhere
. . . maybe it was something in a ledger paper. If so, it
boded ill for my dealing today . . . Grimble and I never
really got along.

"Come in, come in," the individual purred. "Please,
have a seat Mister . . . ?"

"Skeeve," I said, sinking into the indicated chair. "And
it's just 'Skeeve,' not Mr. Skeeve."

I had never been wild about the formality of "Mister"
title, and after having it hissed at me by the police the
night before, I was developing a positive aversion to it.

"Of course, of course," he nodded, reseating himself.
"My name is Malcolm."

Perhaps it was his similarity to Grimble, but I was finding his habit of repeating himself to be a growing annoyance. I reminded myself that I was trying to court his
favor and made an effort to shake the feeling off.

". . . And how can we be of service to you today?"

"Well, Malcolm, I'm a businessman visiting here on

Perv," I said, aware as I spoke that I was unconsciously falling into a formal speech pattern. "My expenses have been running a bit higher than I anticipated, and frankly my ready cash supply is lower than I find comfortable. Someone suggested that I might open a line of credit with your bank, so I stopped in to see if there was any possibility we might work something out."

"I see."

He ran his eyes over me, and much of the warmth went out of the room. I was suddenly acutely aware of how I was dressed.

After overdressing for my interview with the Butterfly, I had decided to stick with my normal, comfortable, informal appearance. I had anticipated that bankers would be more conservative than financiers, and that a bank would probably be equipped to detect disguise spells, so it would be wisest if I was as open and honest as possible. Courtesy of a crash course by Bunny, my administrative assistant, on how to dress, my wardrobe was nothing to be embarrassed about, but I probably didn't look like most of the businessmen Malcolm was used to dealing with. His visual assessment of me reminded me of the once-over I would get when encountering a policeman . . . only more so. I had a feeling the banker could tell me how much money I had in my pockets down to the loose change.

"What line of work did you say you were in, Mister Skeeve?"

I noted that the "Mister" had reappeared, but wasn't up to arguing over it.

"I'm a magician . . . Well, actually I'm the president of an association of magicians . . . a corporation."

I managed to stop there before I started babbling. I've noticed a tendency in myself to run on when I'm nervous.

". . . And the name of your corporation?"

"Um . . . M.Y.T.H. Inc."

He jotted the information down on a small notepad.

"Your home offices are on Klah?"

"No. We operate out of Deva . . . At the Bazaar."

He glanced up at me with his eyebrows raised, then caught himself and regained his composure.

"Would you happen to know what bank you deal with on Deva?"

"Bank? I mean, not really. Aahz and Bunny . . . our financial section usually handles that end of the business."

Any hope I had of a credit line went out the window. I didn't know for sure we *did* any banking. Aahz was a stickler for keeping our funds readily available. I couldn't imagine a bank wanting to deal with someone who didn't trust banks, or to take my word for what our cash holdings were . . . even if I *knew* what they were.

The banker was studying his notes.

"Of course you understand, we'll have to run a check on this."

I started to rise. At this point all I wanted was out of his office.

"Certainly," I said, trying to maintain a modicum of poise. "How long will that take, just so I'll know when to contact you again?"

Malcolm waved a casual hand at me as he turned to a keyboard at the side of his desk.

"Oh, it won't take any time at all. I'll just use the computer to take a quick peek. I should have an answer in a couple of seconds."

I couldn't make up my mind whether to be astonished or concerned. Astonished won out.

". . . But my office is on Deva," I said, repeating myself unnecessarily.

"Quite right," the banker responded absently as he hammered busily on the keys. "Fortunately, computers and cats can see and work right through dimensional barriers. The trick is to get them to do it when you want them to instead of when they feel like it."

Of the assorted thoughts which whirled in my mind at this news, only one stood out.

"Do the police have computers?"

"Not of this quality or capacity." He favored me with a smug, tight-lipped smile. "Civil services don't have access to the same financial resources that banks do . . . Ah! Here we go."

He leaned forward and squinted at the computer's screen, which I couldn't see from where I sat. I wondered if it was coincidence that the view was blocked from the visitor's chair, then decided it was a silly question.

"Impressive. Very impressive indeed." He shot a glance at me. "Might I ask who handles your portfolio?"

"My portfolio? I'm not an artist. I'm a magician . . . like I told you."

"An artist. That's a good one, Skeeve . . . you don't mind if I call you Skeeve, do you?" The banker laughed as if we shared a mutual joke. "I meant your portfolio of stocks and investments."

His original warmth had returned . . . and then some. Whatever he had seen on the screen had definitely improved his opinion of me.

"Oh. That would be Bunny. She's my administrative assistant."

"I hope you pay her well. Otherwise some other outfit might be tempted to swoop down and hire her away from you."

From his tone, I could make a pretty good guess as to which outfit might be interested in doing just that.

"Among other things, she holds stock in our operation," I said pointedly.

"Of course, of course. Just a thought. Well Mis . . . Skeeve, I'm sure we can provide you with adequate financial support during your stay on Perv. What's more I hope you'll keep us in mind should you ever want to open an office here and need to open a local account."

Pervects have an exceptional number of teeth, and Malcolm seemed determined to show all of his to me without missing a syllable. I was starting to get impressed myself. I had known our operation was doing well, but had never stopped to assess exactly how well. If the banker's reaction was an accurate gauge, however, we must have been doing very well indeed!

"If you'll give me just a moment here, Skeeve," he said, lunging out of his seat and heading for the door, "I'll get the staff started while we fill out the necessary paperwork. We should be able to have some imprinted checks and one of our special, solid gold credit cards ready for you before you leave."

"Hold it, Malcolm!"

Things were suddenly starting to move uncomfortably fast, and I wanted a bit of clarification before they went much further.

The banker stopped as if he had hit the end of an invisible leash.

"Yes?"

"As you can probably tell, I'm not as at home with financial terms as I should be. Would you mind defining 'adequate financial support' to me . . . in layman's terms?"

The smile vanished as he licked his lips nervously.

"Well," he said, "we should be able to cover your day-to-day needs, but if you were to require substantial backing . . . say, over seven figures, we'd probably appreciate a day's warning."

Seven figures! He was saying the bank was ready to supply me with up to ten million . . . more if I gave them warning. I resolved that when I got back to the office, I was going to have to have Bunny go over our exact financial condition with me!

XVI:

*"You can judge the success of a man by
his bodyguards!"*

—PRINCE

E dvik was visibly impressed by my success with the
bank. That was all right. I was impressed, too.

"Gee! A solid gold card! I've heard about those, but
I've never really seen one before," he exclaimed as I
proudly displayed my prize. "Not bad for a guy who
didn't think the bankers would want to even talk to him."

"It's my first time to deal with a bank," I said loftily.
"To be honest with you, I didn't even know about credit
cards until Malcolm explained them to me."

A cloud passed over the cabbie's face.

"You've never had a credit card before? Well, watch
your step is all I can say. They can be a dangerous habit,
and if you get behind, bankers can be worse than Deveels
to deal with."

"Worse than Deveels?"

I didn't like the sound of that. Deveels were a devil I
knew . . . if you'll pardon the pun. Now I was starting to
wonder if I should have asked a few more questions before accepting the bank's services.

"Don't worry about it," Edvick said, giving my back a hearty slap. "With your money, you can't go wrong. Now then, let's see about finding you a bodyguard."

"Um . . . excuse me, but something just occurred to me."

"What's that?"

"Well, now that I have checks and a credit card, I don't have to carry a lot of cash around."

"Yeah. So?"

"So if I'm not carrying a lot of cash, what do I need a bodyguard for?" The cabbie rubbed his chin thoughtfully before answering.

"First of all, just because you and I and the bank know you aren't carrying a big wad anymore doesn't mean the muggers know it."

"Good point. I . . ."

"Then again, there's the gang that might still be after you for roughing them up last night . . ."

"Okay. Why don't we . . ."

". . . And there's still an ax murderer loose somewhere around your hotel . . ."

"Enough! I get the picture! Let's go find a bodyguard."

It occurred to me that if I listened to Edvick long enough, I'd either want more than one bodyguard or decide not to set foot outside my room at all.

"Good," my guide declared, rubbing his hands together as the cab commenced its now familiar swerving. "I think I know just the person."

Settling back in my seat, it occurred to me that Edvick would probably get a kickback from this bodyguard he was lining me up with. That would explain his enthusiasm to get us together. I banished the thought as a needless suspicion.

The alert reader may have noticed that with the exception of a vague reference to the fat lady in the department store, I have said absolutely nothing about female Pervects. There's a reason for that. Frankly, they intimidate me.

Now don't get me wrong, male Pervects are quite fear-some, as can be ascertained by my accounts of my friend and partner, Aahz. On the whole, they are big and mus-cular and would just as soon break you in two as look at you. Still, they possess a certain rough and tumble sense of humor, and are not above blustering a bit. All in all, they remind me of a certain type of lizard: the kind that puffs itself up and hisses when it's threatened ... it can give a nasty bite, but it would probably prefer you to back down.

Female Pervects seem to be cut from a whole different bolt of cloth. Their eyes are narrower and set further back on the head, making them look more ... well, reptilian. They never smile or laugh, and they don't *ever* bluff. In short, they look and act more dangerous than their male counterparts.

Some of you may wonder why I am choosing this point of the narrative to expound on the subject of female Per-vects. The rest of you have already figured it out. For the former, let it suffice to say that the bodyguard Edvick introduced me to was a female.

We found her in a bar, a lounge, actually, which the cabbie informed me she used as an office between jobs. She didn't move or blink as we approached her table, which I came to realize meant she had been watching us from the moment we walked through the door. Edvick slid into a vacant chair at her table without invitation and motioned me into another.

"This is Skeeve ... the Klahd I was telling you about," he announced, then turned to me. "Skeeve, this here's the bodyguard I'd recommend for you. There may be some better at doing what she does, but if so, I don't know 'em. For protection against physical or magikal attacks, she's top of the line."

With that, he leaned back in his chair, letting us size each other up like two predators meeting over a fresh kill.

Female Pervects seem to come in two body types. I'll tell you about the other type later, but the kind the bodyguard was was the lean, wiry variety. Even sitting down I could tell she was tall, taller than me, anyway. Where Pervish males, as typified by Aahz, were generally built like walls, she was as slender and supple as a whip . . . a rapier to their ax. I've mentioned that the men reminded me of lizards, well, she made me think of a poisonous snake . . . graceful and beautiful without being attractive. She was wearing a dark waist-length cape that was almost a poncho except it was open in front, revealing a form-fitting jumpsuit underneath. Even a violence know-nothing like me could tell the cape would be perfect for producing and vanishing weapons with unsettling ease. Overall, she impressed me as being the most deadly woman I had ever met . . . realizing I haven't met that many green, bald, scaly women.

"I hear you drink," she said bluntly, breaking the silence.

"Not well . . . and, after last night, not often," I returned. That earned me a curt nod.

"Good. A girl's got to watch her reputation."

It never even occurred to me that she might be referring to her way with me. She was stating quite simply that if anything happened to me while she was on guard, her professional status would suffer. What's more, she didn't want to risk that reputation on a fool. As one inclined to talk too much, I was impressed with how much she could communicate with so few words.

"Ever work with a bodyguard before?"

"Yes. I have two back on Deva. They were . . . busy elsewhere, so I came to Perv alone."

There was a flicker in her eye and a slight tightening of her lips, which was as close as she came to expressing her opinion of bodyguards who let their principal come to Perv unescorted, then she continued with the subject at hand.

"Good. That means you already know the basic drill. The way I work, I go where you go and sleep where you sleep. I go through any door ahead of you unless I'm covering your exit, and I taste everything before you put it in your mouth. Clear?"

"I don't think you have to worry about poison on this one," Edvick said, "just muggers and . . ."

She cut him off with a glance.

"If he pays for the full treatment, he gets the full treatment. Clear, Skeeve?"

"On covering my exit . . . how do we handle it if we don't know what's on the other side of the door?"

I was thinking of how I got mousetrapped sneaking out of the last bar I was in.

"I cover you as far as the door, then you stand beside me while I check the exit. If there's trouble, I'll tell you which way to move . . . in or out."

"Clear."

"Any other questions?"

"Just if you'll be available for anywhere from a few days to a week," I said. "If so, I'd like to retain your services."

"Don't you want to know what I charge?"

I shrugged. "Why? I'm impressed. I'm ready to pay whatever it costs." I paused, then smiled. "Besides, you don't strike me as the type to either up the cost for a well-heeled client or to haggle over prices."

That earned me a brief, flat stare.

"I'll take the job," she said finally. "And you're right. I don't haggle *or* pad the bill. Those are two of my more endearing traits."

I wasn't sure if that last was intended as a joke or not, but decided it was as close as she was apt to get, and chuckled appreciatively.

"One more thing . . . what's your name?"

"Pookanthimbusille."

"Excuse me?" I blinked.

She gave a small shrug.

"Just call me Pookie. It's easier."

"Pookie?"

At first it struck me as a ridiculously silly name for

her. Then I ran my eyes over her again, and allowed as how she could be called anything she wanted to be called. If anyone laughed, it wouldn't be me.

"Pookie it is then . . . just checking to be sure I had the pronunciation right. Shall we go?"

I had Edvick drive us back to the hotel. While I hadn't gotten a lot accomplished today toward finding Aahz, what I had done had left me feeling a little drained. Besides, there was another little matter I wanted to take care of.

For a change, luck seemed to be with me. As the cab pulled up in front of the hotel I could see J.R. at his usual place by the entrance. I figured that was fortunate since I wouldn't have known where to find him otherwise. I caught his eye through the window and waved him over. Unfortunately, Pookie *didn't* see me wave. All she saw was a street vendor moving to intercept us as we emerged from the cab.

"Pookie! NO!"

I was barely in time.

My bodyguard had a sinister-looking weapon out and was drawing a bead on J.R. almost before I could say anything. At the sound of my warning, however, all movement froze and she shot me a vaguely quizzical look.

"It's all right," I said hastily. "He's a friend of mine. He's coming over because I waved at him as we pulled up."

The weapon vanished as she gave the street vendor a hard, appraising look.

"Interesting friends you have."

"He was the one who saved my bacon in last night's encounter with the local wildlife. Hang on a few . . . I've got a little business to transact with him."

Pookie nodded and began scanning the immediate area with a watchful eye as I turned to J.R.

"Interesting friends you've got," he said, staring at my bodyguard.

"Funny, she was just saying the same thing about you.

She's my new bodyguard. After last night, it seemed like a good idea. Incidentally, sorry about that welcome. I forgot to warn her you were coming over."

"No problem. What's up?"

"I paid a little visit to the bank today," I explained, holding up my checkbook. "Now I've got the funding for that little venture of ours."

"Hey! That's terrific! That's all I need to start making us some *real* money."

"Not so fast," I cautioned. "Let's settle the details and paper this thing first."

"What for? You've already said you trust me and I sure trust you."

"It's cleaner this way. Contracts are the best way to be sure we're both hearing the same thing in this arrangement . . . not to mention it documents the split at the beginning instead of waiting until we're arguing over a pile of profits."

He was still a bit reluctant, but I managed to convince him and we scribbled down the details in duplicate on some pieces of paper he produced from one of his many pockets. I say 'we' because I couldn't read or write Pervish, and he was equally ignorant of Klahdish, so we each had to make two copies of the agreement in our own language. To say the least, I didn't drive a particularly hard bargain . . . 25% of the profits after expenses. I figured he would be doing all of the work, so he should get the bulk of the reward. All I was doing was funding him. I even put in a clause where he could buy out my share if things went well. When it was done, we each signed all the copies and shook hands.

"Thanks, Skeeve," the vendor beamed, stuffing one copy of each translation into a pocket. "Believe me, this is a sure money maker."

"Any idea yet where your storefront is going to be?"

"No. Remember I said I was going to start out small? Well, I figure to start by supplying the other street vendors, then using the profits from that to lease and stock the storefront. It'll probably be three weeks to a month before I'm ready for that move."

A month wasn't too bad for start-up time. I admired his industry and confidence.

"Well, good luck!" I said sincerely. "Be sure to leave word for me at the bank when you have a permanent address. I'll be in touch."

He gathered his wares and headed off down the street as I joined Pookie once more.

"I'd like to apologize for that mix-up," I said. "I should have let you know he was coming over."

"I figured he was okay," the bodyguard replied, still watching the street. "He didn't move like a mugger. It just seemed like a good time for a little demonstration, so I did my thing."

"You really didn't have to put on a demonstration for me. I don't have any doubts about your abilities."

Pookie glanced at me.

"Not for you," she corrected. "For them . . . the folks watching here on the street. It was my way of announcing that you're covered now and they should keep their distance."

That possibility had never occurred to me.

"Oh," I said. "Well, I guess I should stick with my business and let you handle yours."

"Agreed," she nodded, "though I'll admit the way you do business puzzles me a bit. Sorry, but I couldn't help but overhear your dealings there."

"What? You mean my insisting on a contract? The reason I pushed for it there and not for *our* deal is that it was a long-term investment as opposed to a straight-forward purchase of services."

"That isn't it."

"What is it then . . . the contract terms? Maybe I was a little more generous than I had to be, but the situation is . . ."

I broke off as I realized the bodyguard was staring hard at me.

"What I meant," she said flatly, "was that before I put money into a business, I'd want to know what it was."

"You heard him. It's a wholesale/dealer operation."

"Yes, but what's he selling?"

I didn't answer that one because I didn't *have* an answer. In my eagerness to do J.R. a good turn, I had completely forgotten to ask what kind of business he was starting!

XVII:

"Bibbity . . . bobbity . . ."

—S. STRANGE, M.D.

Bright and early the next morning, I launched into the next phase of my search for Aahz. The Butterfly had convinced me it was unlikely I'd find him traveling in financial circles. That left the magicians.

As Edvick had warned, the sheer volume of Pervects in the magik business made the task seem almost impossible. It was my last idea, though, so I had to give it a try and hope I got lucky. By the time I had visited half a dozen or so operations, however, I was nearly ready to admit I was licked.

The *real* problem facing me was that the market glut had made the magicians extremely competitive. No one was willing to talk about any other magicians, or even acknowledge their existence. What I got was high-powered sales pitches and lectures on "the layman's need for magikal assistance in his day-to-day life." Once I admitted I was in the business myself, I either got offered a partnership or was accused of spying and thrown out of the office. (Well, a couple of them threatened, but thanks to Pookie's presence I got to walk out with dignity.) What I *didn't* get was any leads or information about Aahz.

Despite my growing despair of succeeding with my quest, it was interesting to view magikal hype as an outsider. Kalvin had admonished me for being too insecure and down-playing my abilities. What I learned that day after sitting through several rounds of bragging in close succession, was that the louder someone blew his own horn, the less impressed the listener, in this case, me, was apt to be. I thought of the quiet confidence exuded by people such as the Butterfly and Pookie, and decided that, in general, that was a much wiser way to conduct oneself in business situations . . . or social ones for that matter. As far as I could tell, the goal was not to impress people, but rather to *be* impressive. In line with that, I resolved to not only discourage the "Mister Skeeve" title, but to also drop "The Great Skeeve" hype. I had never really believed it anyway. What I was was "Skeeve," and people could either be impressed or not by what I was, not by what I called myself.

If this seems like a sudden bolt from the blue to you, it isn't. The area of Perv I was covering was large enough that I was spending considerable time riding back and forth in Edvick's taxi, and it gave me lots of time to think and reflect on what I was seeing and hearing. What's more, the advice given me by the Butterfly and Kalvin, not to mention the questions I had to ask myself about trying to fetch Aahz, had given me cause to reexamine my own attitudes and priorities, so I had plenty to think about.

Dealing with what seemed to be an endless parade of people who had never heard of me before, much less met me, gave me a unique chance to observe how people interacted. More and more I found myself reflecting on how I reacted to them and they reacted to me.

Pervects had a reputation for being nasty and vicious, not to mention arrogant. There was also ample evidence that they could be more than slightly rude. Still, I had also encountered individuals who had been helpful and gentle, such as the Butterfly, and even those like J.R. who would risk themselves physically for a near stranger who was in trouble. Clearly there was danger in stereotyping people, though it was interesting to observe the behavior patterns which had developed to deal with a crowded, competitive environment. Even more interesting was noting those who seemed immune to the environmental pressure that ruled the others about them.

The more I thought about it, the more I began to see pieces of myself reflected in the Pervish behavior. Kalvin had commented on my actively trying to be strong . . . of being cold and ruthless in an effort to hide my own feared weaknesses. Was it all that different with the blustering Pervects who would rather shout than admit they might be wrong? Were my own feelings of insecurity and inadequacy making me insensitive and closed to the very people who could help me?

The thought was enough to inspire me to voice my frustrations to Edvick and ask if he had any thoughts as to alternate methods of searching the magikal community.

"I was just thinking about that, Skeeve," he said over his shoulder, "but I didn't figure it was my place to say anything unless you asked."

"Well, I'm asking. After all, there's no shame in admitting you know this dimension better than I do."

That last was said as much to myself as to Edvick, but the cabbie accepted it in stride.

"Too true. Well, what I was thinking was that instead of working to get magicians to talk about potential competitors, maybe you should try checking the schools."

"The schools?"

"Sure. You know, the places that teach these spellslingers their trade. They should have some kind of records showing who's learned what. What's more, they should be willing to share them since you're not a competitor."

That made sense, but it seemed almost too easy.

"Even if that's true, do you think they would bother to keep current addresses on their old students?"

"Are you kidding?" the cabbie laughed. "How else could the old Alma Mater be able to solicit donations from their alumni? This may not be Deva, but do you think a Pervect would lose track of a revenue source?"

I felt my hope being renewed as he spoke.

"That's a great idea, Edvick! How many magik schools are there, anyway?"

"Not more than a dozen or so of any note. Nowhere near the number of businesses. If I were you, I'd start with the biggest and work your way down."

"Then that's what we'll do. Take me to the top of the list and don't spare the lizards . . . and Edvick? Thanks."

The grounds of the Magikal Institute of Perv (MIP) occupied an entire city block. I say grounds because much of it was well-trimmed lawns and bushes, a marked contrast to the closely packed buildings and alleys that seemed to compose the majority of Perv. Stately old buildings of brick or stone were scattered here and there, apparently oblivious to the bustling metropolis that screeched and honked scant yards from their tranquility. Looking at them, one could almost read their stoic thoughts: that if they ignored it long enough, maybe the rest of the world would go away.

There was an iron fence surrounding the school in token protection from intrusion, but the gate stood wide open. I peered out the windows of the cab in curiosity as we drove up to what Edvick said was the administration building, hoping to catch a glimpse of the students practicing their lessons, but was disappointed. The people I saw were much more interested in being young—skylarking and flirting with each other—than in demonstrating their learning to a casual visitor. I did, however, notice there were more than a few students from off-dimension in their number. Either the school was much more tolerant of off-worlders than the rest of the dimension, or they simply weren't as picky about who they accepted money from. I never did get a chance to find out which it really was.

After a few inquiries, I was shown into the office of the head record keeper. That individual listened carefully to my story, though he was so still and outwardly calm that I found myself fighting a temptation to make a face at him in midsentence just to see if he was really paying attention. I have a hunch I would not do well in a formal educational environment.

"I see," he said, once I had ground to a halt. "Well, your request seems reasonable. Aahz . . . Aahz . . . I don't recall the name off-hand, but it does ring some sort of a bell. Oh well, we can check it easily enough. GRETTA!?"

In response to his call, a young female Pervect appeared in the office door. She glanced quickly at Pookie who was leaning against the wall behind me, but except for that ignored my bodyguard as completely as the record keeper had.

"Yes sir?"

"Gretta, this is Mr. Skeeve. He's trying to locate someone who might have been a student here. I'd like you to help him locate the appropriate file in the archives . . . if it exists. Mr. Skeeve, this is Gretta. She's one of the apprentices here who helps us . . . is something wrong?"

I had suddenly drawn back the hand I had been extending to shake hands with Gretta, and the record keeper had noted the move.

"Oh, nothing . . . really," I said embarrassed. I quickly reached out and shook the offered hand. "It's a . . . bad habit I learned from Aahz. I really should break it. You were saying?"

The record keeper ignored my efforts to cover the social gaffe.

"What bad habit is that?"

"It's silly, but . . . Well, Aahz, back when he was my teacher, wouldn't shake hands with me once I became his apprentice. When we first met and after we became partners it was okay, but not while I was his student. I don't

shake hands with apprentices, he used to say . . . only
louder. I hadn't realized I had picked it up until just now.
Sorry, Gretta. Nothing personal."

"Of course . . . Aahzmandius!"

The record keeper seemed suddenly excited.

"Excuse me?" I said, puzzled.

"Gretta, this won't require a file search after all. Bring
me the file on Aahzmandius . . . it will be in the dropout
file . . . three or four centuries back if I recall correctly."

Once the apprentice had scampered off, the record
keeper returned his attention to me once more.

"I'm sorry, Mr. Skeeve. I just managed to recall the
individual you're looking for. Refusing to shake hands
with apprentices was the tipoff. It was one of his least
objectionable quirks. Aahzmandius! After all these years
I can still remember him."

After searching so long I was reluctant to believe my
luck.

"Are you sure we're talking about the same person?
Aahz?"

"Oh my, yes. That's why the name rang a bell. Aahz
was the nickname Aahzmandius would use when he was
exercising his dubious love of practical jokes . . . or doing
anything else he didn't want reflected on his permanent
record, for that matter. There was a time when that name
would strike terror into the hearts of any under-classman
on campus."

"I take it he wasn't a particularly good student?" I said,
trying to hide my grin.

"Oh, on the contrary, he was one of the brightest students we've ever had here. That's much of why the faculty and administration were willing to overlook the . . .
um, less social aspects of his character. He was at the
head of his class while he was here, and everyone assumed a bright future for him. I'm not sure he was aware
of it, but long before he was slated to graduate, there was
a raging debate going on about him among the faculty.
One side felt that every effort should be made to secure

him a position with the institute as an instructor after he graduated. The other felt that with his arrogant distaste for inferiors, placing him in constant contact with students would . . . well, let's just say they felt his temperament would be better suited to private practice, and the school could benefit best by simply accepting his financial contributions as an alumni . . . preferably mailed from far away."

I was enthralled by this new insight into Aahz's background. However, I could not help but note there was something that didn't seem to fit with the record keeper's oration.

"Excuse me," I said, "but didn't I hear you tell Gretta to look in the dropout file for Aahz's records? If he was doing so well, why didn't he graduate?"

The Pervect heaved a great sigh, a look of genuine pain on his face.

"His family lost their money in a series of bad investments. With his financial support cut off, he dropped out of school . . . left quietly in the middle of a semester even though his tuition had been paid in full for the entire term. We offered him a scholarship so that he could complete his education . . . there was even a special meeting held specifically to get the necessary approvals so he wouldn't be kept dangling until the scholarship board would normally convene. He wouldn't accept it, though. It's a shame, really. He had such potential."

"That doesn't sound like the Aahz I know," I frowned. "I've never known him to refuse money. Usually, he wouldn't even wait for it to be offered . . . not nailing it down would be considered enough of an invitation for him to help himself. Did he give any reason for not accepting the scholarship?"

"No, but it was easy enough to understand at the time. His family had been quite well off, you see, and he had lorded his wealth over the less fortunate as much or more than he had harassed them with his superior abilities. I think he left school because he couldn't bear to face his old cronies, much less his old victims, in his new cash-poor condition. Basically, he was too proud to be a scholarship student after having established himself as a campus aristocrat. Aahzmandius may not refuse money, but I think you'll find he has an aversion to charity . . . or anything that might be construed as such."

It all made sense. The portrait he was painting of Aahz, or as he was known here, Aahzmandius, seemed to confirm the Butterfly's analysis of my old mentor's financial habits. If he had suffered from embarrassment and seen his plans for the future ruined because of careless money management, it stood to reason that he would respond by becoming ultraconservative if not flat out miserly when it came to accumulating and protecting our cache of hard cash.

"Ah! Here we are."

I was pulled out of my musings by the record keeper's exclamation at Gretta's return. I felt my anticipation rise as he took the offered folder and began perusing its contents. For the first time since arriving on Perv, I was going to have a solid lead on how to find Aahz. Then I noticed he was frowning.

"What's wrong?"

"I'm sorry, Mr. Skeeve," the record keeper said, glancing up from the folder. "It seems we don't have a current address for your associate. The note here says 'Traveling.' I guess that, realizing his financial situation, we haven't been as diligent about keeping track of him as we've been with our other alumni."

I fought against a wave of disappointment, unwilling to believe that after everything I had been through, this was going to turn out to be another dead end.

"Didn't he have a school or business or something? I met one of his apprentices once."

The Pervect shook his head.

"No. That we would have known about. He may have been willing to instruct a few close friends or relatives . . . that's not uncommon for someone who's studied here. But

I think I can say for sure that he hasn't been doing any formal teaching here or on any other dimension. We would have heard, if for no other reason than his students would have contacted us to confirm his credentials."

Now that he mentioned it, I did recall that Rupert, the apprentice I had met, had specifically been introduced as Aahz's nephew. Overcome with a feeling of hopelessness, I almost missed what the record keeper said next.

"Speaking of relatives. We *do* have an address for his next of kin . . . in this case, his mother. Perhaps if you spoke to her, you might find out his current whereabouts."

XVIII:

*" 'M' is for the many things she taught
me . . ."*

—OEDIPUS

The search for the address the record keeper had given
me led us onto some of the dimension's side streets
which made up the residential areas. Though at first Perv
seems to be composed entirely of businesses, there is also
a thriving neighborhood community just a few steps off
the main business and transportation drags.

I'll admit to not being thrilled by the neighborhood
Aahz's mother lived in once we found it. Not that it
looked particularly rough or dirty . . . at least no dirtier
than the rest of the dimension. It's just that it was . . . well,
shabby. The buildings and streets were so run-down that
I found it depressing to think anyone, much less the
mother of a friend of mine, would live there.

"I'll wait for you here on the street," Pookie announced
as I emerged from the taxi.

I looked at her, surprised.

"Aren't you coming in?"

"I figure it's more important to guard your escape

route," she said. "I don't think there's any danger inside, unless the place falls down when you knock on the door . . . and I couldn't help there anyway. Why? Are you expecting more trouble than you can handle from one old lady?"

Since I didn't have a snappy retort for that, I proceeded up the porch steps to the door. There was a list of names with a row of buttons beside them. I found the name of Aahz's mother with no difficulty, and pressed the button next to it.

A few moments later, a voice suddenly rasped from the wall next to my elbow.

"Who is it?"

It only took a few seconds for me to figure out that it was some kind of speaker system.

"It's . . . I'm a friend of your son, Aahz . . . Aahzmandius, that is. I was wondering if I might talk to you for a few moments?"

There was a long pause before the reply came back.

"I suppose if you're already here I might as well talk to you. Come right up."

There was a sudden raucous buzzing at the door. I waited patiently, and in a few moments it stopped. I continued waiting.

"Are you still down there?"

"Yes, Ma'am."

"Why?"

"Excuse me?"

"Why didn't you open the door and come in when I buzzed you through?"

"Oh, is that what that was? I'm sorry, I didn't know. Could you . . . buzz me through again?"

"What's the matter, haven't you ever seen a remote lock before?"

I suppose it was meant as a rhetorical question, but my annoyance at being embarrassed prompted me to answer.

"As a matter of fact, I haven't. I'm just visiting this dimension. We don't have anything like it back on Klah."

There was a long silence, long enough for me to wonder if it had been a mistake to admit I was from off-dimension. The buzzer went off, somehow catching me unaware again even though I had been expecting it.

This time, I managed to get the door open before the buzzing stopped, and stepped through into the vestibule. The lighting was dim, and got downright dark after I let the door shut. I started to open it again to get my bearings, but pulled my hand back at the last minute. It might set off an alarm somewhere, and if there was one thing I didn't need right now it was more trouble.

Slowly my eyes adjusted to the shadowy dimness, and I could make out a narrow hall with an even narrower flight of stairs which vanished into the gloom above. "Come right up" she had said, so I took her literally and started up the stairs . . . hoping all the while I was right.

After ascending several flights, this hope was becoming fervent. There was no sign of habitation on any of the halls I passed, and the way the stairs creaked and groaned under me, I wasn't at all sure I wasn't heading into a condemned area of the building.

Just when I was about to yield to my fears and retreat to the ground floor, the stairs ended. The apartment I was looking for was right across the hall from where I stood, so I had little choice but to proceed. Raising my hand, I knocked gently, afraid that anything more violent might trigger a catastrophic chain reaction.

"Come in! It's open!"

Summoning my courage, I let myself in.

The place was both tiny and jammed with clutter. I had the impression one could reach out one's arms and touch the opposing walls simultaneously. In fact, I had to fight against the impulse to do exactly that, as the walls and their contents appeared to be on the brink of caving in. I think it was then I discovered that I was mildly claustrophobic.

"So you're a friend of that no-account Aahzmandius. I knew he'd come to no good, but I never dreamed he'd sink so low as to hang around with a Klahd."

This last was uttered by what had to be Aahz's mother . . . it had to be because she was the only person in the room besides myself! My eye had passed over her at first, she was so much a part of the apartment, but once she drew my attention, she seemed to dominate the entire environ . . . if not the whole dimension.

Remember when I said that Pookie was one of two types of females I had noted on Perv? Well, Aahz's mother was the other type. While Pookie was sleek and muscular in an almost serpentine way, the figure before me resembled nothing so much as a huge toad . . . a green, scaly, reptilian toad. (I have since had it pointed out to me that toads are amphibians and not reptiles, but at the time that's what she made me think of.)

She was dressed in a baggy housecoat which made her seem even more bloated than she really was. The low, stuffed chair she was sitting in was almost obscured from view by her bulk, which seemed to swell over the sides of the chair and flow onto the mottled carpet. There was a tangle of white string on her lap which she jabbed at viciously with a small, barbed stick she was holding. At first, it gave the illusion she was torturing string, but then I noticed there were similar masses draped over nearly every available flat surface in the apartment, and concluded that she was involved in some kind of craft project, the nature of which was beyond my knowledge or appreciation.

"Good afternoon, Mrs. . . ."

"Call me Duchess," she snapped. "Everyone does. Don't know why, though . . . haven't had royalty on this dimension for generations. Beheaded them all and divvied up their property . . . those were the days!"

She smacked her lips at the memory, though of royalty or beheadings I wasn't sure, and pointed vaguely at the far wall. I looked, half expecting to see a head mounted on a plaque, then realized she was pointing at a faded picture hanging there. I also realized I couldn't make it out through the dust and grime on its surface.

"It's the maid's day off," the Duchess said sharply, noting my expression. "Can't get decent work out of domestics since they outlawed flogging!"

I have seldom heard such an obvious lie . . . about the maid, I mean, not the flogging. The cobwebs, dust, and litter which were prevalent everywhere could not have accumulated in a day . . . or in a year for that matter. The shelves and cases throughout the room were jammed with the tackiest collection of bric-a-brac and dustcatchers it had ever been my misfortune to behold, and every dust-catcher had caught its capacity and more. I had no idea why the Duchess felt it necessary to imply she had servants when she obviously had little regard for me, but there was no point in letting her know I didn't believe her.

"Yes. Well . . . Duchess, I've been trying to locate your son, Aahz . . . mandius, and was hoping you might have some information as to his whereabouts."

"Aahzmandius? That wastrel?" Her narrow yellow eyes seemed to glow angrily. "If I had any idea where he was, do you think I'd be sitting here?"

"Wastrel?"

I was starting to wonder if we were talking about the same Aahz.

"What would you call it?" she snapped. "He hasn't sent me a cent since he left school. That means he's spending so much on himself there's nothing left to share with the family that nurtured him and raised him and made him what he is today. How does he expect me to maintain the lifestyle expected of our family, much less keep up my investing, if he doesn't send me any money?"

"Investing?" I said, the light starting to dawn.

"Of course. I've been doing all the investing for our family since my husband passed on. I was just starting to get the hang of it when Aahzmandius quit school and disappeared without a cent . . . I mean a trace. I'm sure that if I just had a few million more to work with I'd get it right this time."

"I see."

"Say, you wouldn't by any chance have access to some venture capital, would you? I could invest it for you and we could split the profits . . . except it's best to put your money to work by reinvesting it as soon as you get it."

I was suddenly very aware of the weight of the checkbook in my pocket. The conversation was taking a decidedly uncomfortable turn.

"Um . . . actually I'm a little short right now," I hedged. "In fact, I was looking for . . . Aahzmandius because he owes me money."

"Well, don't you have any friends you could borrow a million or two from?"

"Not really. They're all as poor as I am. In fact, I've got to go now, Duchess. I've got a cab waiting downstairs and every minute I'm here is costing more than you'd imagine."

I suppose I should have been despairing as Edvick drove Pookie and me back to the hotel. My last hope for finding Aahz was gone. Now that tracking him down through the magicians had proved to be futile, I had no idea how to locate him other than knocking on every door in the dimension . . . and I just didn't have the energy to attempt that even if I had the time. The mission was a bust, and there was nothing to do but pay off Edvick and Pookie, check out of the hotel, and figure out how to signal Massha to pick me up and take me to Klah. I hoped that simply removing the ring she had given me would bring her running, but I wasn't sure. Maybe I would be more effective at stopping Queen Hemlock than I had been in finding Aahz. I *should* have been despairing as I wrote out the checks for my driver and bodyguard in preparation for our parting, but I wasn't. Instead, I found myself thinking about the Duchess.

My first reaction to her was that she was a crazy old lady trying to live in the past by maintaining an illusion

of wealth that nobody believed except her. Ideally, someone who cared should give her a stern talking-to and try
to bring her back into contact with reality so she could
start adjusting to what *was* instead of what *had been* or
should be. I guess, on reflection, I found her situation to
be more sad than irritating or contemptible.

Then, somehow, my thoughts began wandering from
her case to my own. Was I as guilty as she was of trying
to run my life on *was* and *should be* instead of accepting
and dealing with reality? I *had been* an untraveled, un-
trained youth, and that self-image still haunted me in
everything I said and did. I felt I *should be* a flawless
businessman and manager, and treated both myself and
others rather harshly pursuing that goal. What was my
reality?

Even before coming to Perv, many of my associates,
including Aahz, had tried to convince me I was something
more than I felt I was. Time and time again, I had dis-
counted their words, assuming they were either trying to
be nice to 'the Kid', or, in some cases, trying to badger
me into growing up faster than I was ready to.

Well, maybe it was time I decided I *was* ready to grow
up, mentally at least. The physical part would take care
of itself. One by one, I started knocking down the excuses
that had been my protective wall for so long.

Okay, I was young and inexperienced. So what? "Inexperienced" wasn't the same as "stupid." There was no
reason to expect myself to be adept or even familiar with
situations and concepts I had never encountered before. It
was crucial not to dwell on my shortcomings. What *was*
important was that I was learning, and learning fast . . .
Fast enough that even my critics and enemies showed a
certain degree of grudging admiration for what I was.
They, like the Pervects I had encountered on this mission,
didn't care what I didn't know last year or what I still had
to learn, they reacted to what I was now. Shouldn't I be
doing the same thing?

Speaking of learning, I had always been self-conscious

about what I didn't know, yet I planned to keep on learning my whole life. I always figured that if I ever stopped learning, it would either mean that I had closed my mind, or that I was dead. Putting those two thoughts together, it occurred to me that in being ashamed of what I didn't know, I was effectively apologizing for being alive! Of course there were things I didn't know! So what? That didn't make me an outsider or a freak, it gave me something in common with everyone else who was alive. Instead of wasting my energy bemoaning what I didn't know, I should be using what I *did* know to expand my own horizons.

The phrase "Today is the first day of the rest of your life" was almost a cliché across the dimensions. It occurred to me that a better phrasing would be "Your whole life to date has been training for right now!" The question wasn't what I had or didn't have so much as what I was going to do with it!

I was still examining this concept when we pulled up to the curb in front of the hotel.

"Here we are, Skeeve," Edvick said, swiveling around in his seat. "Are you sure you aren't going to need me anymore?"

"There's no point," I sighed, passing him his check. "I've run out of ideas and time. I'd like to thank you for your help, though. You've been much more than a driver and guide to me during my stay here. I've added a little extra onto the check as a bit more tangible expression of my gratitude."

Actually I had added a *lot* more onto it. The cabbie glanced at the figure and beamed happily.

"Hey, thanks, Skeeve. I'm sorry you couldn't find your friend."

"That's the way it goes sometimes," I shrugged. "Take care of yourself, Edvick. If you ever make it to Deva, look me up and I'll show you around *my* dimension for a change."

"I just might take you up on that," the cabbie waved as I let myself out onto the street.

Pookie had popped out of the taxi as soon as we stopped, so it seemed I was going to have to settle accounts with her out in the open.

"Pookie, I . . ."

"Heads up, Skeeve," she murmured, not looking at me. "I think we've got problems."

I followed her gaze with my eyes. Two uniformed policemen were bracketing the door to my hotel. At the sight of me, they started forward with expressions of grim determination on their faces.

XIX:

"I am not a crook!"

—ANY CROOK

"**Z**at ees heem! Ze third from ze right!"

Even with the floodlights full in my face, I had no difficulty recognizing the voice which floated up to me from the unseen area in the room beyond the lights. It was the waiter I had clashed with the first night I was on Perv. The one who claimed I had tried to avoid paying for my meal by fainting.

I wasn't surprised by his ability to identify me in the lineup. First of all, I had no reason to suspect his powers of observation and recall were lacking. More important, of all the individuals in the lineup, I was the only one who wasn't a Pervect. What's more, all the others were uniformed policemen! Nothing like a nice, impartial setup, and this was just that ... nothing like a nice, impartial setup.

What *did* surprise me was that I didn't seem to be the least bit upset by the situation. Usually, in a crisis like this, I would either be extremely upset or too angry to care. This time, however, I simply felt a bit bemused. In fact, I felt so relaxed and in control of myself and the situation, I decided to have a bit of fun with it . . . just to break the monotony.

"Look again, sir. Are you absolutely sure?"

I knew that voice, too. It was the captain who had given J.R. and me so much grief the last time I had the pleasure of enjoying police hospitality. Before the waiter could respond, I used my disguise spell and switched places with the policeman standing next to me.

"I am sure. He ees the third . . . no, the second from the right!"

"What?"

Resisting the urge to grin, I went to work again, this time changing everyone in the lineup so they were identical images of me.

"But . . . but thees ees imposs-ible!"

"MISTER Skeeve. If you don't mind?"

"Excuse me, captain?" I said innocently.

"We'd appreciate it a lot if you'd quit playing games with the witnesses!"

"That makes us even," I smiled. "I'd appreciate it if you quit playing games with me! However, I think I've made my point."

I let the disguise spell drop, leaving the policemen in the lineup to glare suspiciously at each other as well as at me.

"What point is that?"

"That this whole lineup thing is silly. We'll ignore the bit with putting all of your colleagues up here with me for the moment and assume you were playing it straight. My point is that I'm not the only one who knows how to use a disguise spell. Anyone who's laid eyes on me or seen a picture of me could use a disguise spell well enough to fool the average witness. That invalidates the lineup identification as evidence. All you've established is that someone with access to my image has been seen by the witness . . . not that I personally, was anywhere near him."

There was a long silence beyond the lights.

"You're denying having had any contact with the witness? I take it you recognize his voice."

"That's a rather transparent catch question, Captain," I laughed. "If I admit to recognizing his voice, then at the same time I'm admitting to having had contact with him. Right?"

I was starting to actually enjoy myself.

"As a matter of fact, I'm willing to admit I've had dealings with your witness there. Also with the doorman and bellhop, as well as the other people you've dragged in to identify me. I was just questioning the validity of your procedure. It seems to me that you're putting yourself and everyone else through a lot of trouble that, by itself, won't yield any usable results. If you want information about me and my movements, why don't you just ask me directly instead of going through all this foolishness?"

The floodlights went out suddenly, leaving me even more blinded than when they had been on.

"All right, *Mister* Skeeve. We'll try it your way. If you'll be so good as to follow me down to one of our 'interview' rooms?"

Even "trying it my way" was more hassle than I expected or liked. True, I was out from in front of the floodlights, but there were enough people crowded into the small "interview room" to make me feel like I was still on exhibition.

"Really, Captain," I said, sweeping the small crowd with my eyes. "Is all this really necessary?"

"As a matter of fact, it is," he retorted. "I want to have witnesses to everything you say as well as a transcript of our little conversation. I suppose I should inform you that anything you say can and may be used against you in court. What's more, you're entitled to an attorney for advice during this questioning, either one of your choice or one of those on call to the court. Now, do we continue or shall we wait for a legal advisor?"

My feeling of control dimmed a bit. Somehow, this seemed much more serious than my last visit.

"Am I being charged with anything?"

"Not yet," the captain said. "We'll see how the questioning goes."

I had been thinking of trying to get in touch with Shai-ster, one of the Mob's lawyers. It occurred to me, however, that just having access to him might damage the image I was attempting to project of an innocent, injured citizen.

"Then I'll give the questioning a shot on my own," I said. "I may holler for legal help if it get's too rough, though."

"Suit yourself," the policeman shrugged, picking up the sheaf of papers he had brought in with him.

Something in his manner made me think I had just made the wrong choice in not insisting on having a lawyer. Nervously, I began to chatter, fishing for reassurance that things really weren't as bad as they were starting to seem.

"Actually, Captain, I'm a little surprised that I'm here. I thought we had covered everything pretty well my last visit."

The police who had picked me up in front of my hotel and delivered me to the station had been extremely tight-lipped. Beyond the simple statement that "The captain wants to see you," they hadn't given the slightest indication of why I was being pulled in.

"Oh, the IDs were just to confirm we were dealing with the right person," the captain smiled. "A point you have very generously conceded. As to why you're here, it seems there are one or two minor things we didn't cover the last time we chatted."

He picked up one of the sheets, holding it by his fingertips as if it were extremely fragile or precious.

"You see, just as I promised, we've run a check on

you through some of the other dimensions."

My confidence sank right along with my heart . . . deep into the pit of my stomach.

"For the record," the captain was saying, "you are Skeeve, sometimes known as 'the Great Skeeve' . . . originally from Klah with offices on Deva?"

"That's right."

"Now it seems you were somehow involved in a war a while back . . . somewhere around Possiltum?"

There was nothing for me to duck there.

"I was at that time employed as Court Magician of Possiltum. Helping to stop an invading army was simply a part of my duties."

"Really? I also have a report from Jahk that says you were part of a group that stole the Trophy from the Great Game. Was that part of your duties, too?"

"We won that fair and square in a challenge match," I flared. "The Jahks agreed to it in advance . . . and darn near beat our brains out before we won."

". . . Which you did with much the same team as you used to stop the aforementioned invading army," the captain commented drily.

"They're friends of mine," I protested. "We work together from time to time, and help each other out when one of us gets in a jam."

"Uh-huh. Would you describe your relationship with the Mob the same way? You know, friends who work together and help each other out of jams from time to time?"

Whoops! There it was. Well, now that the subject was on the table, it was probably best to deal with it openly and honestly.

"That's different," I dodged.

"I'll say it is!" the captain snarled. "In fact, I don't think different begins to describe it! In all my years on the force I've never heard of anything like it!"

He scooped up a handful of paper and held it up dramatically.

"From Klah, we have conflicting reports. One source says that you were instrumental in keeping the Mob from moving in on Possiltum. Another has you down as being a sub-chieftan in the Mob itself!"

He grabbed another handful.

"That's particularly interesting, seeing as how Deva reports that you stopped the Mob from moving into *that* dimension. What's more, you're being paid a fat retainer to maintain the defenses against the Mob, even though it seems that much of that retainer is going toward paying off your staff . . . which includes two bodyguards from the Mob and the niece of the current head of the Mob! All of which, of course, has nothing to do with the fact that you own and operate a combination hotel and casino and are known to associate with gamblers and assassins. Just what kind of game are you playing, MISTER Skeeve? I'm dying to hear just how *you* define 'different!' "

I considered trying my best to explain the rather tangled set of relationships and circumstances that define my life just now. Then I considered saving my breath.

"First, let me check something here, Captain. Does your jurisdiction extend to other dimensions? To put it another way, is it any of your business what I do or don't do away from Perv, or did you just pull me in here to satisfy your curiosity?"

Pursing his lips, the Pervect set the papers he was holding back on the table and squared them very carefully.

"Oh, I'm *very* curious about you, *Mister* Skeeve," he said softly, "But that's not the reason I sent for you."

"Well then, can we get down to what the problem *really* is? As much as I'd like to entertain you with my life story, there are other rather pressing demands on my time."

The policeman stared at me stonily.

"All right. We'll stick to cases. Do you know a street vendor named J.R.?"

The sudden change of subject threw me off-stride.

"J.R.? Sure I know him. Don't you remember? The last time I was here he was sitting . . ."

"How would you describe your relationship with the individual in question?" the captain interrupted.

"I guess you'd say we're friends," I shrugged. "I've been chatting with him off and on since I arrived on Perv, and, as you know, he helped me out that time I got into a fight."

"Anything else?"

"No . . . except we're going into business together. That is, I've put up the money for a venture of his."

The captain seemed taken aback.

"You mean you admit it?" he said.

A little alarm started to ring in the back of my head.

"Sure. I mean, what's so unusual about a businessman investing in a new enterprise?"

"Wait a minute. What kind of an enterprise did you think you were buying into?"

"He said he was going to open a retail storefront," I said uneasily. "But he did say something about supplying the other street vendors for a while to build up his operating capital. Exactly *what* he was supplying I was never really sure."

"You weren't sure?"

"Well, the truth is I was in a hurry and forgot to ask. Why? What was he . . ."

"We just picked him up for smuggling! It seems your buddy and business partner was using your funds to buy and sell contraband!"

Needless to say, the news upset me. It had occurred to me that, in his enthusiasm, J.R. would go outside the law for the sake of quick profits.

"How serious is it, Captain? Can I post bail for him . . . or arrange for a lawyer?"

"Don't worry about him," the Pervect advised. "It turns out he has some information on the ax murderer we've been looking for and is willing to share it with us if we drop the smuggling charges. No, you should be more worried about yourself."

"ME?"

"That's right. You've admitted you're his partner in this, which makes you just as guilty as he is."

"But I didn't know what he was going to do! Honest!"

Now I *was* worried. The whole thing was absurd, but I was starting to think I should have insisted on having a lawyer after all.

"That's what you say," the captain said grimly. "Would you like to see what he was smuggling?"

He gestured at one of the other policemen in the room who held up several plastic bags with small items in them. I recognized them at a glance, a fact which did nothing for my peace of mind.

"Those are all products of the Acme Joke and Novelty Company," the captain intoned. "A company I believe you've worked with in the recent past?"

"A team of my employees did some work there on a pilferage case," I mumbled, not able to take my eyes off the items in the bags. "Are those things really illegal on Perv?"

"We have a lot of ordinances that try to keep the quality of life on Perv high. We haven't been able to stop porn, but we have managed to outlaw trashy, practical joke items like Rubber Doggie Doodle with Realistic Life-Like Aroma that Actually Sticks to Your Hand."

It seemed like a very minor achievement to me, considering the crime on the streets I had already been exposed to. I didn't think that it was wise to point this out just now, though.

"Okay, Captain, let me rephrase my question," I said, looking at the floor. "How much trouble am *I* in? I mean, what's really involved here . . . a fine, a jail term, what?"

The Pervect was so silent I finally raised my head to meet his gaze directly. He was looking at me with a flat, appraising stare.

"No charges. I'm letting you go," he sighed, finally, shaking his head.

"But I thought . . ."

"I *said* it depended on how the questioning went! Well, I just can't believe you'd be stupid enough to get involved in this smuggling thing knowingly. If you had, you'd have protected yourself better than you did. What you did was dumb . . . but just dumb enough to ring true."

"Gee, thanks, Captain. I . . ."

"No thanks necessary. Just doing my job. Now get outta here . . . and Mister Skeeve?"

"I know," I smiled, "don't change hotels or leave the dimension without . . ."

"Actually," the captain said drily without a trace of warmth in his voice. "I was going to suggest the exact opposite . . . that you leave the dimension . . . say, by to-morrow morning?"

"What?"

"I still think you smell of trouble, and these reports confirm it. The smuggling thing just seems like too much small potatoes for you to bother with. I'd rather see you gone than put you in jail on a piddling charge like that . . . but it's going to be one or the other, get me?"

I couldn't believe it! Perv was the nastiest, roughest dimension around and *I* was being thrown off as an un-desirable!!

XX:

"Were you looking for me?"

—Dr. Livingstone

I was surprised to find Pookie waiting for me when I got back to the hotel. The police had been nice enough to wait until I had given her her check before hauling me off, so I had thought I'd never see her again.

"Hello, Pookie. What brings you here?"

"I wanted to talk a little business with you," she said. "It didn't seem the right time before, so I waited."

"I see."

After my last experience, I wasn't wild about the idea of doing business with Pervects . . . especially ones who didn't want to talk in front of the police. Still, Pookie had given me no reason to distrust her.

"Okay. Come on upstairs and say what's on your mind. It seems I'm leaving . . . on request."

If my statement seemed at all strange to her, she never let on. Instead, she fell in step with me as I entered the hotel.

"Actually, what I have to say shouldn't take too long.

If I understand correctly, you're on your way off-dimension to rejoin your regular crew in a campaign against someone named Queen Hemlock. Right?"

"That's a fair summation," I nodded. "Why?"

"I thought I'd offer my services to you for the upcoming brawl. I can give you a special discount for work away from Perv because off-dimension prices are lower. That keeps my overhead down."

She flashed me a smile that was gone almost as soon as it appeared.

For some reason, it had never occurred to me to hire her for the Hemlock campaign. Still, the idea had merit.

"I don't know, Pookie," I said, trying to weigh the pluses and minuses without taking too much time. "I've already got a couple of bodyguards waiting for me."

"I know," she nodded. "I can do more than bodyguard, and from the sound of the odds you can probably use a little extra help."

"I can use a *lot* of help!" I admitted.

"Well, even though you couldn't find your friend, it does show that you and yours don't mind working with Pervects. Besides, I can travel the dimensions well enough to get us to Klah directly."

That settled it. I had been unsure that my plan to simply remove my monitor ring would be an effective way to signal Massha for a pickup, and Pookie had just come up with a good way to get there. Whatever Massha was doing right now, I wasn't wild about her dropping everything just to provide me with transport.

"All right. You've got yourself a job," I announced. "Just give me a minute to get things together and we'll be off."

That was my original plan, but as I opened the door to my room, I realized I had a visitor.

"Well, don't just stand there with your mouth open. Are you coming or going?"

If there was any doubt in my mind as to who my visitor was, that greeting banished it.

"AAHZ!"

After all my searching—and soul-searching—I couldn't believe my mentor, friend, and partner was finally in front of my eyes, but there he was!

"That's right. I heard you wanted to talk to me . . . so talk."

"I suppose it's reassuring to know that some things never change, Aahzmandius . . . like you."

That last came from Pookie as she slipped past me into the room.

"Pookie!? Is that you?"

For the moment, Aahz seemed to be as dumbstruck as I was.

"You two know each other?"

Surprised and off-stride, I returned to familiar patterns and asked a redundant question.

"Know each other?" Aahz laughed. "Are you kidding? We're cousins!"

"Distant cousins," Pookie corrected without enthusiasm.

"Really? Why didn't you say anything, Pookie?"

"You never asked."

"But . . . you knew I was looking for him!"

"Actually, it took me a while to put it together, and when I did, I didn't know where he was either. Besides, to tell you the truth, from what I recall, I figured you'd be better off without him."

"Well, well. Little Pookie! Still have the razor tongue, I see."

"Not so little any more, Aahzmandius," the bodyguard said, a dangerous note creeping into her voice. "Try me sometime and you'll see."

It was clear the two of them weren't on the best of terms. I felt it best to intercede before things got ugly.

"How did you get into my room?"

"Bribed the bellhop," my old partner said, returning his attention to me. "Those guys would sell the key to their mother's store if there was a big enough tip in it for them."

An awkward silence followed. Desperately, I cast about for something to say.

"So how have you been, Aahz?" I ventured, realizing how lame it sounded. "You look great."

"Oh, I've been swell . . . just swell," he spat. "As a matter of fact, it's a good thing I saw your ad in the personals when I did. I was about to head off-dimension. I had forgotten how high the prices are around here."

I made a mental note to pay off the bellhop. It looked like his idea of placing an ad had paid off better than all my running around.

"You can say that again," I agreed. "I sure got ambushed by the cost. Of course, I've never been here before, so I couldn't know . . ."

I broke off, realizing he was staring at me.

"Which brings us back to my original question, Skeeve. What are you doing here and why do you want to talk to me?"

My moment had come, and if Aahz's mood was any indication, I had better make my first pitch good. I probably wouldn't get a second chance. Everything I had considered saying to him the next time we met face to face whirled through my head like a kaleidoscope, mixing randomly with my recent thoughts regarding myself.

My search had given me new insight into Aahz. Seeing the dimension that spawned and shaped him, having learned about his schooldays, and having met his mother, I had a much clearer picture of what made my old partner tick. While I was ready to use that information, I resolved never to let him know how much I had learned. Someday, when he was ready, he might share some of it with me voluntarily, but until then I felt it was best to let him think his privacy was still unbroached. Of course, that still left me groping for what to say here and now. Should I beg him to come back with me? Should I play on our friend-

ship . . . or use the campaign against Queen Hemlock to
lure him back for just one more job?

Suddenly, Kalvin's advice came back to me. There was
no right or wrong thing to say. All I could do was try,
and hope that it was good enough to reach my alienated
friend. If not . . .

Taking a deep breath, I gave it my best shot.

"Mostly, I came to apologize, Aahz."

"Apologize?"

My words seemed to startle him.

"That's right. I treated you rather shabbily . . . back before you left. I've got no right to ask you to come back,
but I did want to find you to offer my apology and an
explanation, for what it's worth. You see . . ."

Now that I had started, my words poured out in a rush,
popping out without conscious thought on my part.

"I was so afraid in my new position as head of
M.Y.T.H. Inc. that I went overboard trying to live up to
what I thought everybody expected of me. I tried to cover
up my own weaknesses . . . to appear strong, by doing
everything without any help from anybody. I wouldn't
even accept the same help that had been given to me before I accepted the position, and either ignored or snapped
at any offers of advice or assistance because I saw them
as admissions of my own shortcomings."

I looked at him steadily.

"It was a dumb, immature, jackass way to act, but
worst of all it hurt my friends because it made them feel
useless and unwanted. That was bad enough for Tananda
and Chumley and the others, and I'll be apologizing to
them, too, but it was an unforgivable way to treat you."

Licking my lips, I went for it.

"I've never been all that good with words, Aahz, and
I doubt I'll ever be able to tell you how much you mean
to me. I said I couldn't ask you to come back, and I won't,
but I will say that if you do come back, you'll be more
than welcome. I'd like a chance to show you what I can't
find the words to say . . . that I admire you and value the

wisdom and guidance you've always given me. I can't promise that I'll be able to change completely or immediately, but I'm going to try . . . whether you come back or not. I *do* know it'll be easier if you're there to box my ears when I start to slip. I wish . . . well, that's all. It doesn't start to even things out, but you've got my apology."

I lapsed into silence, waiting for his response.

"You know, Skeeve, you're growing up. I think we both forget that more often than we should."

Aahz's voice was so soft I barely recognized it as his.

"Does this mean you'll come back?"

"I . . . I'll have to think about it," he said, looking away. "Let me get back to you in a couple of days. Okay?"

"I'd like to, but I can't," I grimaced. "I've got to leave tonight."

"I see," Aahz's head snapped around. "You could only allow so much time for this little jaunt, huh? Work piling up back at the office?"

An angry, indignant protest rose to my lips, but I fought back. From what he knew, Aahz's assumption wasn't only not out of line, it was a logical error.

"That's not it at all," I said quietly. "If you must know, the local police have told me to be off-dimension by morning."

"What!!?? You've been tossed off Perv?"

My old partner's eyes fixed on Pookie with cold fury.

"What have you two been up to that could get you tossed off a dimension like this?"

"Don't look at me, cousin! This is the first I've heard of it. The last thing I knew he was heading off-dimension because he couldn't find you."

"That was before my last interview with the police," I supplied. "Really, Aahz, Pookie had nothing to do with it. It's a little mess I got into on my own over . . . the details aren't really important right now. The bottom line is that I can't hang around while you make up your mind."

"Well someday I want to hear those 'unimportant details,' " Aahz growled. "In the meantime, I suppose you can go on ahead and I'll catch up with you after I've thought things out."

"Um . . . actually, if you decide to come, I'll be over on Klah, not Deva."

I tried to make it sound casual, but Aahz caught it in a flash.

"Klah? What would take you back to that backwater dimension?"

There was no way around the direct question. Besides, my old mentor's tone of voice called for a no-nonsense answer.

"Well, there's a problem I've got to deal with there. Remember Queen Hemlock? It seems she's on the move again."

"Hemlock?" Aahz frowned. "I thought you cooled her jets with a ring that wouldn't come off."

I decided it wasn't the time to ask what a jet was.

"I did," I acknowledged. "She sent it back to me . . . finger and all. It looked like a pretty clear announcement and a warning that she was all set to launch her world conquest plans again . . . and wasn't about to put up with any interference."

". . . And you're about to go up against her alone? Without even mentioning it to me?"

"I . . . I didn't think it would be fair to try to pressure you with it, Aahz. Face it, the way things seem to go there will always be some kind of trouble cropping up. You can't be expected to spend your life covering my tail every time I get in a scrape. Besides, I'm not going to try to take her on myself. In fact, the rest of the team is already there. I sent them on ahead while I came back to look for you."

I was expecting an explosion and a lecture. Instead, Aahz seemed to be studying my face.

"Let me see if I've got this right," he said, finally. "Your home dimension is under attack . . . and instead of leading the team in the campaign, you put it all on hold to come looking for me?"

When he put it that way, it *did* sound more than a little irresponsible.

"Well . . . yes," I stammered. "But I told Massha to come pick me up at the end of a week. I figured that I'd have to go and pitch in at that point, whether I had found you or not."

Aahz started to say something, then shook his head. Heaving a great sigh, he tried again.

"Skeeve . . . don't worry about not being able to find the right words. I think you've given me a pretty good idea of what I really mean to you."

"I did?"

He nodded.

"Enough that I've decided I don't need any more time to make up my mind. Grab your stuff, partner. Let's get going. Are you square with the hotel, or do you still have to settle accounts?"

"I'm all set on that front," I said. "There's no balance . . . since they made me pay in advance."

"That figures," Aahz grumbled. "Unless you're a VIP or something, everybody gets the same treatment."

It was just too good an opening to pass up, and I yielded to the temptation.

"Of course, it'll probably be easier for me next time around . . . now that I have a line of credit and a credit card."

"What next time around? I thought you said the police . . ."

His train of thought stopped abruptly as he turned to loom over me.

"CREDIT CARD? What credit card? Who's been teaching you about credit cards?"

That wasn't exactly the reaction I had been expecting.

"The bank suggested it, actually," I explained. "They said . . ."

"What bank? How did you know what to look for in a bank?"

"Well, it was recommended to me by Edvick, he's the cabbie I hired while I was here, and . . ."

"That you hired? Why didn't you . . ." He paused and seemed to regain a bit of control. "It sounds like you've got quite a bit to discuss with me . . . when we have the time. Right, *partner*?"

"Right, Aahz," I said, glad to be off the hook for the moment.

"Is there anything that has to be done *before* we leave?"

"Well, I've got to get some money to the bellhop. I promised him . . ."

"Spare me the details . . . for the moment anyway. Anything else?"

"No, Aahz."

"All right. Finish packing while I hunt up this bellhop for you. Then, we're off for Klah . . . if I can find the settings on the D-hopper, that is. It's been a while, and . . ."

"Save the batteries, cousin," Pookie said. "I think I can handle getting us all there without help."

"You? Since when were you coming along?" Aahz gaped.

"Since I hired on with Skeeve here," the bodyguard countered, "While we're on the subject, since when did you need a D-hopper to travel through the dimensions?"

"Um . . . if the two of you don't mind," I said, stuffing my dirty clothes into my new bag, "could we save all that until later? Right now, we've got a war to catch!"

About the Author

Robert (Lynn) Asprin was born in 1946. While he has written some stand-alone novels such as *Cold Cash War*, *Tambu*, *The Bug Wars*, and also the *Duncan and Mallory* illustrated stories, Bob is best known for his series: *The Myth Adventures of Aabz and Skeeve*; the *Phule* novels; and, more recently, the *Time Scout* novels written with Linda Evans. He also edited the groundbreaking *Thieves World* anthologies with Lynn Abbey. His most recent collaboration is *License Invoked*, written with Jody Lynn Nye. It is set in the French Quarter, New Orleans, where he currently lives.